D1391743

PENGUIN BOOKS

THE BLADE ITSELF

The Blade Itself

MARCUS SAKEY

PENGUIN BOOKS

PENGUIN BOOKS

Published by the Penguin Group

Penguin Books Ltd, 80 Strand, London WC2R ORL, England

Penguin Group (USA) Inc., 375 Hudson Street, New York, New York 10014, USA

Penguin Group (Canada), 90 Eglinton Avenue East, Suite 700, Toronto, Ontario, Canada M4P 2Y3
(a division of Pearson Penguin Canada Inc.)

Penguin Ireland, 25 St Stephen's Green, Dublin 2, Ireland (a division of Penguin Books Ltd)

Penguin Group (Australia), 250 Camberwell Road,
Camberwell, Victoria 3124, Australia (a division of Pearson Australia Group Pty Ltd)

Penguin Books India Pvt Ltd, 11 Community Centre, Panchsheel Park, New Delhi – 110 017, India

Penguin Group (NZ), 67 Apollo Drive, Rosedale, North Shore 0632, New Zealand
(a division of Pearson New Zealand Ltd)

Penguin Books (South Africa) (Pty) Ltd, 24 Sturdee Avenue,
Rosebank, Johannesburg 2196, South Africa

Penguin Books Ltd, Registered Offices: 80 Strand, London WC2R ORL, England

www.penguin.com

Published in the United States of America by Minotaur Books 2007
First published in Great Britain by Michael Joseph 2007
Published in Penguin Books 2007

1

Typeset by Rowland Phototypesetting Ltd, Bury St Edmunds, Suffolk
Printed in Great Britain by Clays Ltd, St Ives plc

978-0-141-03445-4

For Mom and Dad, who said the stars were in reach;
and for g.g., who wished on one as it fell

Acknowledgments

No book belongs to just one person. My deepest thanks to:

Scott Miller, my extraordinary agent, who believed in the novel from first reading – and who promptly told me how to make it better. Here's to a long partnership, my friend.

My remarkable editor, Ben Sevier, who asked questions that were so good that I had to make the answers live up to them, who tirelessly shepherded the story from manuscript to book, and who is a hell of a guy to boot.

All the amazing folks at St Martin's, especially Sally Richardson, Matthew Shear, George Witte, Matt Baldacci, Christina Harcar, Kerry Nordling, Dori Weintraub, Rachel Ekstrom, and Jenness Crawford. Thanks also to the art and production teams, who turned a stack of scrubby pages into a beautiful book.

This novel would not have been written were it not for the generous nudging of Patricia Pinianski and Joe Konrath, two of the most giving folks in the biz. Thank you both.

Authors need experts. For questions about dead people, I turned to Dr Vince Tranchida, New York City Medical Examiner, who eagerly provided wonderfully gruesome details. I also owe a special thanks to the Chicago Police Department, who are good people doing a hard job. Assistant Director Patrick Camden and Detective Kenneth Wiggins put up with many stupid questions, and I'm grateful for it. Any errors are mine, not theirs.

Books grow just like people, and I'm fortunate to have friends who were willing to deal with this one during its pimply adolescence. Big thanks to Jenny Carney, Brad Boivin, and Michael Cook for their early feedback.

Thanks to the members of my writing group, whose suggestions were never short of stellar, and whose names you'll soon be seeing on bestseller charts.

To my friends, who kept me going with a steady diet of beer and laughter. You know who you are.

To my loving and supportive family, Mom, Dad, and Matthew, who read the manuscript more times than anyone should and who propped me up more times than I ever thought I'd need. Authors are supposed to have miserable family lives, guys. Get with the program.

And lastly, to g.g., my wife and my smile. Living with a novelist can't be easy, but you always manage to slip a pillow between my head and the walls I tend to hit with it. Thank you, baby.

The blade itself incites to violence.

– Homer

1. But for the Grace

The alley wasn't as dark as Danny would've liked, and Evan was driving him crazy, spinning the snub-nose like a cowboy in some Sunday matinee. 'Would you put that away?'

'Keeps me cool.' Evan smiled the bar-fight grin that showed his chipped tooth.

'I don't care if it makes you feel like Rick James. You shouldn't have brought it.' Danny stared until his partner sighed and tucked the pistol into the back of his belt. Evan had always lived for the thrill of the job, all the way back to when they had stolen forties of Mickeys from the 7-Eleven. But the addition of the gun made Danny uneasy. Made him wonder if Karen was right to suggest he start thinking long-term. Reconsider his options.

He shook his head and stared out the window. Earlier, munching greasy chips in a taco bar across the street, they'd watched the owner of the pawnshop lock up. The dashboard clock now read just after eleven, and the alley was stone quiet. Chicago life centered on the neighborhoods; once night fell, the downtown area died. Twenty minutes ago they'd cut the phone lines without a show from the cops, which meant no cellular alarm. Everything looked good.

Until something moved.

Fifteen yards away, in a pocket of black. There, then gone again. Like someone stepping carefully. Like someone hiding. Danny leaned forward, one hand covering the glowing radio to sharpen his night vision. Shadows painted dingy brick walls with a black brush. A breeze sent a newspaper tumbling by the passenger side window. Maybe he'd just seen blowing trash and his mind had filled in the rest of the picture. The tension could get to you.

Then he saw it again. A slight motion. Someone getting closer to the wall, deeper in the shadow. His pulse banged in his throat.

Beat cops didn't sneak around that way. They just rolled up with their lights spinning. Unless the police hoped to catch them actually robbing the place. Danny pictured Terry, that weasel mustache, the moist stink of a habitual farter. He'd told them about the job – had he sold them out?

Out of the darkness stumbled a stooped man with greasy hair. He ran one hand along the wall to steady his cautious shuffle. A pint bottle nosed out of a frayed pocket. Reaching the trash bin, he glanced in either direction and unzipped his fly. Took a piss with one hand in his pocket like he was in the men's room of his country club.

Danny breathed again, then chuckled at his nerves. When the bum finished, he crossed to the other side of the alley and leaned against the wall. He slid down to a squat and closed his eyes. Danny said, 'He's camping.'

Evan nodded, rubbed one hand across his chin, the stubble making a grating sound. 'Now what?'

'Guess we could give him a minute.'

'He looks pretty tucked in.' Evan paused, then looked over. 'Should I shoot him?'

Danny shrugged. 'Sure.'

Evan drew the gun, sighted through the windshield. He closed one eye. 'Bang.' He spun the gun to his lips and blew imaginary smoke.

Danny laughed, then turned back to the problem at hand. The drunk sat directly across from the pawnshop door. With his head resting on his knees, he looked almost peaceful.

'Chase him off?'

'No. He might yell,' Danny said. 'Might run into a cop, who knows.'

'So I'll knock him down.' Evan smiled. 'You know they don't get up after I knock 'em down.'

The idea wasn't totally without merit, but lacked elegance. Too much noise, and it wasn't like the bum had done anything to deserve a beating. Besides, Evan was Golden Gloves. Probably end up killing the poor bastard. Danny squinted, trying to think of a way to get rid of the guy without complicating the job. Then smiled. 'I'll take care of it.' He reached for the door handle.

'He looks dangerous. Don't forget the pistola.' Evan held it out, a mocking smile on his lips.

'Fuck you.' Danny stepped out of the car.

At the sound of the door, the bum scrambled to his feet, holding his hands in front of him. The sleeves of his suit jacket were three inches too short. Beneath it he wore several sweatshirts. 'I got nothing.' Drink rounded the edges of his words, and he reeked of urine and panic. 'Don't hurt me.'

Danny shook his head. But for the grace. 'Relax, old man.'

The man peered at him suspiciously, ready to run. 'You got a cigarette?'

'Don't smoke. My friend,' jerking a thumb toward the car, 'he smokes. But he *will* hurt you.'

The man stiffened, yellowed eyes darting. 'Listen, mister –'

'Shut up.' Danny reached in his pocket, took out his wallet. 'See this? Twenty bucks.'

The bum froze, eyes locked on the bill. 'I – I don't do that stuff, the faggot stuff . . .'

Danny couldn't help chuckling. The guy clearly had no idea what he smelled like. 'Take this money and go up to Grand and LaSalle. There's a liquor store there. Buy a bottle, take a seat in the parking lot.' Danny stepped closer, his voice conspiratorial. 'In about half an hour, a friend of mine will come by. I need to tell him something, but I don't want to say it on the phone, know what I mean? My friend, he'll be wearing a tan raincoat. You tell him – you listening? – you tell him the birds have flown the cage. You do that, he'll give you another twenty.'

'That's it?'

'Easiest money you ever made.' He proffered the bill, trying to keep the laugh from his eyes. The bum reached, hesitated, took it. 'Good man. Don't let me down.'

The guy turned, started east down the alley, the wrong direction. Danny almost called him back, figured what the hell, stood in the shadows until he was out of sight. The car door opened. 'How much you give him?'

'Ten.'

Evan snorted, shook his head. 'Let's work.' He popped the trunk, light flooding across his black T-shirt, dug around and came up with a fistful of thick chain. Danny took one end and walked to the door, playing it out slow, the rattle loud in the close confines of the alley. The bum had gotten his blood up, and he let the rush take him, everything clear and sharp, his movements precise. A heavy steel cage sealed the rear door of the pawnshop, the metal discolored with age. Danny hooked the chain to the bars, thinking of the movies, the way thieves always tunneled up through the streets with plastic explosives or cracked safes with diamond-tipped drills. Eight bucks at Home Depot had bought them all the supplies they needed.

Robbing pawnshops was generally a dicey proposition. Because they kept cash on hand, security could be a hassle. According to Terry, this guy sold more than old TVs and secondhand bling. He also dealt weed in weight. That meant extra cash – more than enough to make up for the trouble.

4

Sure. Easy money. Same line you just sold the bum.

No time. Danny double-checked the chain, then turned and nodded. Evan inched the Mustang forward, headlights off, the car a black shark. As the links grew taut, Danny stepped behind the shelter of the rust-stained Dumpster. He cocked his head to listen, one hand up.

A long minute passed before he heard it. Slow at first, just a distant rattle, but it swiftly grew to a full clattering roar. From the elevated tracks, sparks blew sideways into the night, heralding the passing of the Orange Line El.

Danny dropped his hand. Evan gunned the engine quick and hard. With a screech – tortured, but barely audible over the train – the metal latch gave. The gate ripped open, chain still attached, hinges straining from the pull of the car. For a second Danny thought Evan might tear it right off the wall. But brake lights washed red across him, then the white of reverse, and finally the engine fell to silence.

The chain felt warm as Danny detached it and crouched to check the revealed door. Twin Schlages. He slid the Crown Royal bag from his inside pocket. Some guys cut down hacksaw blades, some liked the professional kits. Personally, he'd always found the bristles of a street sweeper made the best lock picks, hard but flexible. He'd popped both deadbolts by the time Evan had stowed the chain.

The rattle of the El faded as they stepped into the cramped pawnshop office. Danny generally liked to take a moment inside to listen to the darkness, but Evan already had the flashlight out. As it glared to life, Danny caught a glint off the gun in Evan's other hand. Showboating, chasing the thrill. He thought about saying something, decided against it.

'There.' A battered metal desk winked in the flashlight beam, below a calendar with a swimsuit model cozying up to a carburetor. He could make out a rumpled mattress on the floor beside it. 'Terry said the bag would be in the manager's desk.'

'Not in a safe?'

'Owner's a gun nut, apparently. Figures no one will mess with him.'

Evan nodded, moving over to test the drawer. 'Locked.'

Danny smiled, pulled out the Crown Royal bag again.

'I'm going to look around.' Evan had the door half open already.

'What?'

'It'll take you a minute, I'm going to check the front room. See if there's anything in the register.'

'The flashlight –'

'Relax, Danny-boy. I'll be right back.' Not waiting for an answer, he slid into the pawnshop.

Shaking his head, Danny fumbled in the dark to find his own flashlight and set to work. He ran a pick down the inside of the lock, counting clicks. Four. Factory-issue. He eased in the tension wrench and started with the farthest pin.

Twenty seconds later, the lock twisted open. He pulled the top drawer, rifled around, his gloves inky in the flashlight's warm glow. Papers, pushpins, day-job junk. The second was crammed with *Hustler* magazines from the seventies. In the third drawer lay a sleek black automatic pistol, big, with an extra-long clip jutting out the bottom. It looked like it could punch through an engine block, and something about its cold, machined intent sent shivers down the backs of his thighs. Next to the pistol sat a nylon bank bag with a brass lock. The bag was two, maybe three inches thick.

Jackpot. He stood up and slid through the door, his soft-soled gym shoes silent on the concrete. The pawnshop was a forest of dim shapes, electric guitars strung above what looked like power tools, a couple of racks of looming TVs. Danny couldn't see Evan, but a glow behind the counter marked his spot. The cabinet doors on one wall stood open, and there was a thumping sound.

'Come on, man.' Danny pitched it low but urgent. 'I found the money.'

'Give me a hand.' Evan's voice was muffled.

'With what? Let's go.'

'I was thinking.' Evan rose behind the counter, stretching, vertebrae popping as he flexed his broad shoulders. 'Man sold weight, right? So there's gotta be a pound of dope here, maybe two. That's another couple grand easy.'

'That wasn't the plan.'

'Ah, fuck the plan. It'll take two minutes. Help me out, check those cabinets over there.' Evan squatted, facing the counter, and started feeling around beneath. From his belt the gun handle gleamed like a lethal comma.

Danny felt a trickle of sweat run down his side, the drop cold against his muscles. Half the cons he knew – the smart ones, even – had landed inside because they got reckless, decided to push their luck. Anything could give you up. A stray flashlight beam. A pedestrian who heard voices. A beat cop on a random patrol.

Still, he knew Evan well enough to know he'd have to drag the guy out of here. It'd be faster to just try and find the dope. 'All right, damn you. Two minutes.' He moved to the far side of the pawnshop and opened the first cabinet, his flashlight playing across stacks of neatly bundled cables, a box of computer paper. He tapped the inside, wondering if he'd be able to hear a false bottom. Wondering how a false bottom sounded different from a regular one.

As Danny moved to the second cabinet, he heard Evan stand up. 'Nothing here. I'll check the office.' Danny nodded, sorting through a selection of cheap porcelain figurines. A crystal unicorn winked in the flashlight. His mind drifted as he worked, thinking of Karen's apartment. Candles on the nightstand, traffic noises through the open window. Waiting in the sleigh bed for her to get home after her shift. Her soft smile to find him awake. He saw it all, and wondered why he was here instead of there.

And then he heard the sound.

A metal rattle, like –

'Evan!'

– a security gate. The front door swung open, the night street glowing outside. A silhouette, big, stepped in, saying, 'Come on, little darlin', a couple puffs before we do it won't make you lose control. I won't do nothing you don't want me to.' The lights flickered on as Danny scrambled to his feet, recognizing the owner they'd watched earlier. A bearded guy in an orange hunting vest, leading a skinny chick with bad skin. Everything went slow motion as the guy spotted him, a hand already sliding inside his vest, a practiced move that produced a shiny automatic. The man racking the gun as he raised it, the snap echoing. Spreading his legs for better footing. Danny thinking this was it, the owner was going to shoot his ass. Mind telling body to leap aside, but his muscles not moving. The man with both eyes open and the gun in both hands, a target shooter's stance that put the barrel square at Danny's chest.

An explosion. Somehow the owner's stomach bloomed red. He collapsed like he'd been dropped from a great height. His gun clattered on the floor beside him. In the doorway to the office, Evan stood with one arm extended, the pistol in his hand.

Everything stopped.

The hum of fluorescent lights and the wet sounds of breathing. Danny's head throbbed, but in his chest, deep, he felt a cold sensation. Cold and deep and knotted. He knew

8

that no matter how hard he squinted, he wouldn't be able to see Karen's bedroom now.

Then adrenaline hit, and he lunged. The girl was frozen, eyes and mouth wide, and he shoved her aside to slam the door. He jumped back to avoid the slow spread of something red, Jesus, blood, a crimson pool of it, creeping from where the owner moved in a sort of crab-writhing, fingers clutched over his stomach.

'No.' The word slipped feathery soft from his mouth.

'He alive?' Evan asked, voice distant after the roar of the gun.

The man rocked back and forth. His hands were scarlet. A stain crept up his chest. There was a lot of blood. A kid from the South Side grew up knowing what blood looked like, broken noses and teeth knocked out, but to see it pouring from someone's stomach . . .

'Danny.' Evan's voice jerked his head up. 'Is he alive?'

'Yeah.'

'Ask him where the weed is. You,' gesturing with the pistol, 'Little Darlin'. Over here.' White-faced and shaking, the woman moved next to a shelf of beat-up VCRs.

Danny stared at Evan, the gun still in his hand, fingers loose on the grip. He couldn't decipher the energy playing across his old friend's face. Nerves? Excitement? He seemed calm. Potent. It was like pulling the trigger had freed something inside him. He almost swaggered as he walked over.

It scared hell out of Danny. 'Let's go.'

Evan kicked the owner's gun across the floor, then stared down at his prone form. 'Look at that shit.' He popped his head to either side. 'You ever see anything like that?'

'We have to go.'

'In a minute.' Evan nudged the guy with his boot. 'Where's your stash, old man?'

The owner groaned, a strange, raspy sound. Danny's heart roared so loud it seemed to muffle the world, and his gut turned in knots. They'd shot someone. Jesus. They'd shot someone, and they had to go.

'Where is it?' This time Evan kicked the owner, steel-toed boot driving into the man's stomach near where his hands clenched the wound. The guy gasped for air, an agonized keening.

'Evan!'

'What?' Evan spun, eyes narrowed and arm half raised. The air-conditioning chilled the place cold as January. For a long moment, they stared at each other, Danny wondering how he'd ended up here, calculating ways to get out. Then he saw motion, turned to look.

'Fuck!' Evan yelled after the girl as she sprinted to the back room. 'Stop!' For a moment she seemed to hesitate, then leapt a pile of junk from one of the cabinets and sailed into the dark office, slamming the heavy door behind her. Danny heard the click of a lock.

Evan roared with frustration, his face burning bright red, that angry color he got in a fight. Turning, he kicked the owner again, the guy trying to cover his head with one hand and his bleeding stomach with the other, a whimpering sound coming now, fast and hard, a sound Danny had never heard a human make and never wanted to again.

He stepped in front of Evan, hands to shoulders, and shoved him back. His partner stumbled, almost went down, came up mad. Eyes narrowed, he looked like he was about to bull rush Danny. The gun shook in his hand.

'Stop.' Danny kept his voice cool and his hands out, no threat. 'Stay cool. Brothers.'

For a moment, he wasn't sure it was going to work. But then Evan straightened, slowly. He exhaled loudly, then nodded. 'All right, forget the weed. We've got the money.'

Danny's guts tumbled to his knees. His mouth opened, but he didn't know what to say.

Evan looked at him, then at the office door, closed and locked. 'Where is it?'

Danny spoke softly. 'It's in the drawer.'

'Jesus, Danny.'

'Well, I wasn't planning on shooting anybody. If we'd left earlier we'd be halfway home.'

'Don't start.' Evan's eyes blazed. 'I don't want to hear that shit.'

'Fine.' Danny kept his hands out. 'But look, now there's no choice. Let's go.'

Evan stared at him, shook his head. 'No.'

'The cops will be here any second,' Danny said.

'I'm not leaving empty-handed.' He started for the office door.

Danny knew this mood. It was Evan at his most volatile, ten drinks in and more than willing to go three rounds with God Almighty.

Standing outside the office, Evan spoke loud and precise. 'Lady, open the door or I will break it fucking down.' Silence. Maybe the woman had spotted the back exit, been smart enough to leave.

'Have it your way.' Evan lashed out with his boot. The door shivered in its frame, but held. As he stepped back to wind up again, a sharp roar tore a chunk of wood out of the door, spraying splinters in all directions. As the second bullet punched through, Danny remembered the gun in the open drawer.

For a hesitant second nothing happened.

Then Evan exploded. Whatever demons shooting the pawnshop owner had freed took control of him again. He raised his pistol and pulled the trigger, aiming in a triangle of quick blasts. Not pointing at the lock but trying to hit

11

her, trying to kill. At Danny's feet, the man groaned. Evan frothed and raged, kicking the door again. The frame was cracking, and Danny thought he could hear a whimper behind it. Everything had gone crazy, he was standing beside a pool of blood, Evan making enough noise to pull people for blocks, the lights on, for Christ's sake, the fucking *lights* on.

Danny had taken two falls, one county and one state, done the time like a man, but for this they'd get years.

No. No more.

He opened the front door and slipped out into the night. His body screamed to run, just go, but he made himself walk. Not draw attention. Just a guy headed for the El, nothing noteworthy about that.

When he was two blocks away, he heard the sirens.

2. Young Lions

It started different ways, but always ended the same.

This time he'd been in a church. It wasn't the Nativity, but he'd known that he was in the old neighborhood. A deep voice intoned alien words. Stained glass spilled bloody light across polished pews. Karen held a hymnal, terror squirming in her eyes. He'd tried to read the book, knowing the key to her fear lay on the page, but the words twisted and blurred. Sliding metal rattled behind him. In the half awareness of an ending dream, he knew he wouldn't make it, that he couldn't impose sense onto this world in time. He looked up to find that Karen had turned into Evan, and that the hymnal had become a pistol aimed at Danny's chest.

The furious orange of the soundless gun blast yanked him from sleep, as it always did.

Beside him, Karen murmured something soft and rolled away, pulling the blankets with her. The draft cooled his sweat-soaked body. Danny sighed and rubbed his eyes, glanced at the clock. Ten minutes. He should probably just get up. Instead he wormed closer to Karen, let her soft skin and brown-sugar smell fill him. Why did she always feel best when it was nearly time to leave her?

He let himself drift until the alarm rang. Karen fumbled for the snooze button; she'd hit it two, three times before getting up. He rolled out of bed, careful not to disturb her, popped his head to either side and stretched his arms. Thirty-two years old, and it was already harder to get out of bed than it used to be.

In the shower, the water diamond sharp against his back, he replayed the dream. Probably two months since the last one. For a while they'd been weekly. It had been a hairy time, seven years ago.

Waiting for the train had been maybe the toughest ten minutes of his life. He'd wanted to take a cab, even just to sprint, but he needed the anonymity of the El. Mouth dry, sirens in his ears, a quarter mile from the pawnshop, and he'd stood waiting for the train, certain every moment that this would be the one when they'd come for him.

But when the Brown Line had finally rattled in, the wind from it stale breath on his face, he'd boarded like any civilian. There'd been a kid with baggy pants hanging off his ass, and a fat woman with a Marshall Field's bag, and he'd stepped on between them as though he had nothing to fear. The train ran north, into the land of yuppies and condos and coffeehouses, and he made a fresh compact with God at every stop. Each one a step farther from where he'd come. A preview of things ahead. A series of geographically minor hops that took him from his old world into what would become his new one.

And good goddamn riddance.

Karen opened the bathroom door, rubbing at her eyes. She sat on the toilet, yawned.

'You have a nightmare, baby?'

'Yeah.'

'Bad?'

'The same.'

She flushed, and he almost jumped out from under the shower before remembering that wasn't a Lincoln Park problem. It was the little things that brought home the difference between his old world and new. Karen slid open the curtain and stepped into the shower, eyes half closed. He swapped places with her, watched her tip her head back, the water sluicing over her body, flattening her dark hair to her shoulders.

On second thought, thirty-two didn't look so bad. Not so bad at all.

'Christ, I hate mornings.' She fumbled for the shampoo. 'Aren't you late?'

'It's Wednesday.' Most days he spent the bulk of his time on-site. Wednesdays he spent in the office, reviewing paperwork, filing permits, trying to juggle the budgets of half a dozen construction projects so that each, barely working out, could finance the next. When he'd reached management, it'd struck him as funny to realize that life as a contractor wasn't much more stable than life as a thief.

'I'm off tonight.' Her eyes still closed. 'Let's go out.'

'I'm meeting Patrick.'

'Again?'

'He's like my brother, Kar.' He couldn't keep the tone out of his voice.

She opened her eyes then, her hands up in her hair. 'I'm sorry. It's just . . .'

'I understand, babe.' He put his hands on her waist, resting them on the thin ridge of her pelvic bone. 'Don't worry.'

He kissed her, her small breasts firm against his chest. She ran a hand down his back. Her fingertips sent electric shivers through his groin. Reluctantly, he pulled away, breaking the kiss. 'I still have to make it to the office. Rain check?'

She smiled. 'Any time.'

The Iron Crown was a copy of a replica of a pub, but not too bad for all that. Danny ordered a shot and a beer and settled at the bar. Patrick would be late. In twenty years, he hadn't been on time for anything that wasn't illegal.

Danny couldn't blame Karen for her love-hate with Patrick. He was Danny's last tie to the old neighborhood, the old life. Since walking out of the pawnshop he'd not so much as spit on the sidewalk. But in the swaggering flush of youth it had been different. His whole crew had wandered the city like young lions, thrilled and a little surprised by the ferocity of their own roar.

They just hadn't realized the world would roar back.

Evan had landed in Stateville Maximum Security. The Jimmy brothers were serving twenty in Glades, some Florida bank job gone wrong. Marty Frisk had walked into a liquor store with an empty pistol; both barrels of the owner's sawed-off turned out to be loaded. Those who hadn't been busted or killed mostly still lived the life, and Danny had no common ground with them.

Patrick was different. After his mother passed – cancer – his dad had concentrated on drinking himself to death. Most things in life he'd failed at, but at this he turned out to be a natural. Faced with seeing another Irish kid from the neighborhood end up bouncing through foster homes at sixteen, Danny's father had taken Patrick in. Tight as money was, that was the kind of thing you did in Bridgeport in those days.

And they'd thanked the old man by getting busted stealing a car two years later.

Danny shook his head, sipped his beer, and picked up the paper. He'd finished the Metro section when something hard poked his kidneys, coffee breath over his shoulder.

'Hands on the bar, son.'

'Patrick. That one never gets old.'

'You're already losing your instincts. Lose your sense of humor, too, you may as well take up golf with the rest of the North Side fairies.'

Danny picked up the whiskey and poured it down slow,

savoring the amber glow. In the smoked mirror above the bar he could see Patrick behind him, tall and angular, the smile cocky.

'You passed twice on your bike before you parked. Came in the side door, stopped to bullshit the girls at the corner table. Your wallet's in your back right pocket. And after everything I told you, you still carry a blade in your boot.'

Patrick's smile had faded. 'How?'

Danny raised his right hand, cocked it like a gun, and shot Patrick in the mirror. 'Losing instincts my ass.'

Patrick threw his head back and howled, then settled on the bar stool and finger-combed his black hair. Over a long-sleeve thermal he wore a threadbare T-shirt advertising a defunct bowling alley. The bartender poured Jameson's into their glasses without taking his eyes from the classifieds, then moved to the other end of the bar.

'I got a good one tonight.'

Patrick always had a story.

He'd been cruising in his low-loader, looking for just the right car. BMWs and Mercedes, they were too likely to have LoJack. Hondas were good, Explorers, your midrange Fords. And if you were smart, you'd pick one parked illegally. Two inches into a fire lane. Expired meter. Just a little cover.

'So I'm in the West Loop, where they're building all those fake warehouses for yuppies.'

'Lofts, Patrick. We call them lofts.'

'I bet you love them, folks paying four hundred grand for a house with no walls. Anyway, it's a good spot, decent cars, not too many people. And there's a GTO, you know the one with the V-8?'

Straight as he was these days, the thought still made Danny smile, Patrick backing up his tow truck, lighting a cigarette as he worked the hydraulics. Put on a pair of overalls, nobody questioned you stealing a car in broad daylight.

'So I've got it half loaded, the alarm has shut off now that it's hit the tow angle, and all of a sudden, running down the street is some guy looks like he just stepped out of a Banana Republic ad. Actually,' his eyes rolling up and down Danny's khakis and pressed shirt, 'you probably know him.'

'Fuck you.'

'I don't have the car locked down yet, and I don't want to just dump my truck. Worse, I see the guy's got a cell phone, he's talking into it as he runs.'

Danny winced. 'Ouch.'

'No shit. Maybe he's calling the cops, right? But I figure okay, stay cool. Pop the guy hard enough to drop him, lock down the car, drive away.' Patrick paused, reached for his shot.

'And?'

He laughed. 'Just as I'm about to hit him, he yells that his car's getting towed and hangs up. So I hold off and stand there staring at him. Guy barely looks at me, just asks what the problem is. I tell him he was sticking into the alley.' He laughed again, lifting the glass to his nose to smell the whiskey. 'And then this joe, type of asshole who thinks he knows all the angles, you know what he does?'

Danny smiled, shook his head, though he could see it coming.

'He takes out his wallet, asks can we settle it right here.'

'No kidding.' Laughing now.

'Man offers me fifty bucks to lower the car I was in the process of stealing from him.'

'What did you say?'

'I said a hundred.' Patrick grinned and tossed back the shot.

They had a couple of rounds and then went down the

street for a steak. It should have been a good night, but something was throwing Danny off, nagging at him. Had been all day. Maybe the nightmare this morning. But Patrick was in a good mood, all jokes and stories, and didn't seem to notice.

After they finished – Danny stuck with the check – they stepped out onto Halsted. Though it was only October, the air felt crisp, with the smell of winter sharp on it.

'How 'bout another round?' Patrick smiled. 'I gotta tell you about this girl I hooked up with last week.'

'Next time, Romeo. Which reminds me, Karen wants you to come over for dinner.'

Patrick groaned. 'And the friend she invites, social worker or librarian?'

'Both, probably.'

'With a face like a boot, but the sex drive of a jumped-up gerbil. The last one chased me to Lakeshore, waving her panties over her head and neighing.'

'All right, all right,' Danny said, laughing. 'No blind date this time, I promise.'

'I'm gonna hold you to that.' They reached Patrick's motorcycle, an old Triumph that had been taken apart and put back together enough times to render it unrecognizable. He brushed a speck of dirt off the leather seat, and then swung one leg over to straddle the bike. 'Oh, I almost forgot. I heard somebody was asking about you.'

Old instincts tightened Danny's skin. 'Who's that?'

Patrick looked up at him, the joking in his eyes replaced by something more serious, like he was watching for a reaction. 'Evan McGann.'

Danny's mouth went dry, and he felt that tingling in his chest, the sense of his heart beating hard enough to rattle his ribs. He scrambled for his game face, almost got it.

'Chief?' Patrick looked at him quizzically.

'Yeah.' He forced a smile. 'How is he?'

Patrick shrugged. 'Haven't seen him myself. Just heard he was around, asking questions.'

'I thought he was doing twelve years.'

'Good behavior, I guess.'

'Sure.' The dream came back to him, the sense of rushing danger, Evan with the gun pointed at his chest.

'You awright?'

'Yeah.' Danny shook his head. 'Fine. Just surprised me.'

His friend laughed, turned the key. The bike started with a throaty rumble. 'I told you.'

'What?' Shouting over the sound of the engine.

'You're losing your instincts, brother.' Patrick smiled, gunned the bike, and disappeared down Halsted.

3. No Luggage

On his last day, they gave him back his clothes. Traded state-issue Bob Barker slip-ons for size-twelve steel-toes, passed a bus voucher across the scuffed counter. Handed him his gold money clip and fifty dollars to put in it, a gift from the state of Illinois. Money to send him on his righteous way into life as an upstanding citizen.

He'd stood outside between two mean-eyed black women bitching about their bills and another newly released con he didn't know and had no interest in meeting. Thinning trees flanked the long asphalt driveway. The rusted water tower with STATEVILLE neatly lettered sat at a different angle than he was used to. Above it, the sky was very blue, and very wide, and the fall air seemed alive with possibility. He'd closed his eyes and smelled it, just smelled, taking it deep inside.

His watch had run down, and the irony amused him in a bitter sort of way. After all, he'd lived the exact same day over and over again for seven years, two months, and eleven days. Up at five thirty, cell count, shower, lunch, rec in the yard, day room, dinner, cell count, lights out. Repeat two thousand times.

But when the yellow-striped Pace bus pulled up, no one had to unlock the door before he could climb aboard. No chains rattled between his wrists. He took a seat near the front and stared out the windshield, let Stateville vanish behind him. Every faded billboard and dying tree looked fresh and clean.

He got off in Joliet and hiked half a mile to a chain steak

house. The hostess smiled as she led him to a back booth, past soft padded seats and the smell of cooking meat. Conversations were low and civil. The tinkly music in the background sounded like a piano player had popped a handful of quaaludes before working his way through the Eagles' back catalog. He ordered a twenty-dollar prime rib and three cold beers.

Every bite was bliss.

After he'd mopped up the last puddle of juice with the last piece of sourdough, he went to the bathroom. Fluorescent lights gleamed off white tile walls, and the bright sterility put him on edge. He turned on the water and began finger-combing his hair. There was no reason to hurry, and he took his time, smoothing the curls and sculpting the back. A couple of college kids in T-shirts came and went. An older gent in a dark suit strolled in, whistling to himself, and they exchanged a little nod in the mirror as the guy walked to the urinal. He let the man unzip, waited till his hands were busy with his dick, then he came up behind and bounced the old man's head off the tile wall.

One crack was all it took.

Unconscious, the guy was hard to maneuver, but he hauled the limp body into the far stall and hoisted him up on the toilet. Took his thick billfold and leaned him against one wall, pants around his ankles and blood trickling from his temple. He closed the stall door, locked it, then crawled under the divider to the one next door. Stepped out, washed his hands, and left.

The state's fifty dollars covered the bill and a tip with nine bucks to spare.

At a strip mall across the street he used the guy's Gold MasterCard for a pair of jeans and a cable-knit sweater, a suede jacket and a new watch. The prices were higher than he remembered. Two doors down he picked out half-carat diamond earrings and a necklace of cultured pearls. The salesgirl was a nice-looking blonde, maybe a little on the heavy side.

'Your girlfriend will love these,' she said as she wrapped them.

'Hope so. I'm kind of in the doghouse.' He passed her the American Express.

'Why's that?'

'I keep making eyes at blondes.' He winked to let her know he was easy, not to sweat it. 'Anybody tell you you've got a great smile?'

She blushed, and giggled, and forgot to ask for his ID.

At the Mobil station across the parking lot, a bored teenager lounging behind the counter sold him cigarettes and pointed toward the Metra. It was a beautiful day, and he took his time walking there, smoking and checking out the new models of cars as they whizzed by. They hadn't changed as much as he'd expected. Funny, only seven years, but he'd half thought they'd be hovercars.

The Metra looked exactly the same, grimy tracks and clean trains, the seating double-stacked to pack in rush-hour commuters neat as a matchbook. It was only about three, so the train was less than half full. Four dollars and ninety cents bought a ticket to Union Station. He took a window seat and propped his boots on the row in front of him. The speed made a blur of the scenery, reds and yellows and oranges melting like candle wax.

An hour later, he stepped into the graceful halls of Union Station. Rush hour was beginning, and a crowd of commuters already pushed through the marble corridors. Clothes were different, and hairstyles. From a bench he watched the crush of everyday people. Everyone had a mobile phone to one ear, tiny things like something out of *Star Trek*. As they flowed complacently along, they whined

23

into the phones about their little emergencies. Called home to say they were running late, not to wait for them. Glared at watches and sighed at the lost time.

Assholes.

At the Amtrak counter he used the old guy's Visa to buy a ticket to St Pete, Florida. No luggage. He smiled, walked around the corner, and threw the ticket in the trash, tossing all three credit cards in after it.

Then Evan McGann stepped out into a spectacular Chicago afternoon, two grand in jewelry in his pocket and a money clip filled with a righteous two hundred and twelve dollars – counting the remaining four the state had provided to bring him home.

4. A Man in Mind

Nothing clicked today, and it didn't help that Danny couldn't focus.

In front of him, five skeletal stories of structural steel rose to cut the sky in neat rectangles. A yard hand strode across a beam forty feet in the air, his orange jacket stark against swirling gray clouds. In one corner, a welder knelt over a torch, sparks cracking as flame kissed metal. The wind made plastic sheeting snap.

Evan was back in town.

Not the problem, he reminded himself. The problem was that on the schedule he'd prepared, this building had a roof and walls. In reality, it stood exposed. The materials they'd been waiting on hadn't shown, and winter was fast approaching.

Still. Evan was back.

'We get our shipment next week, we're fine.' The foreman, a burly guy named Jim McCloskey, moved a toothpick from one corner of his mouth to the other as he spoke. His son stood beside him, lips turned up in a permanent sneer. 'You know these things, Dan. Never on time. But it'll get here.'

Being called 'Dan' always set his teeth on edge, like he was back in school, the nuns preaching arithmetic and the Holy Trinity in the same breath. Father and Son making two he could deal with, but the mathematics of the Holy Spirit had never quite added up for him.

'Everybody in town is fighting to finish before the freeze,'

Danny said. 'There's what, four high-rises going up in the Loop? Plus office parks out by the airport, the new hospital. All we got is a midsized loft complex and a couple of restaurants.'

'Even if it's the week after, we'll be okay. Ruiz and my boys have already got the floors, some of the wall studding, a lot of the stuff we usually do later. Once the steel arrives, we'll get the exterior up pronto.'

Danny shook his head. 'It's getting cold already.'

'Just an early chill.'

'Sure. Seventy again before you know it. We'll be working in bathing suits.'

The younger McCloskey snorted. 'You mean *we'll* be working.'

Danny stiffened, then turned slowly, letting his gaze slide like he had all the time in the world. Gave the kid a street stare that mingled boredom and threat, like a predator who wasn't hungry but would consider a sport kill. The kid's eyes flicked to the building, back to Danny for a fraction of a second, then quick down to his feet. He muttered something vague. Danny held the stare as he spoke. 'Why don't we finish in the office?'

Neither McCloskey needed to be told whom he was talking to. Danny turned and walked to the trailer that served as the on-site office, a single-wide with cinder blocks stacked as a staircase. As he pushed open the thin door, dry air and the smell of burned coffee washed over him. Space heaters blew on either side of a cluttered desk, below cheap horizontal blinds. A tired green couch ran along one wall; Danny's boss, Richard, liked to joke that his son had been conceived on it, usually slapping backs and braying with laughter as he said it. The trailer, one of several owned by O'Donnell Construction, moved from job to job, a gypsy home for the men who built Chicago. Danny took off his hard hat – project-manager white, as opposed to McCloskey's blue – and walked to the Mr Coffee.

'I'm sorry about that, Dan. He's a good kid, a worker. He's just young.' McCloskey stood like a supplicant, hands folded and eyes down.

Danny laughed. 'You think I brought you in here to chew you out about the boy?'

McCloskey shrugged.

'Don't worry about it. I mouthed off to a few guys in my day. I imagine you did, too.'

'One or two.' The foreman smiled.

'It's forgotten. No, I wanted to talk privately is all. Jim, I'm sorry, but I'm going to recommend to Richard that we put this site on hold for the winter.'

'That's a mistake. We've got two months, maybe more. We can get it done.'

'Maybe.'

'I'm telling you, I think we can.'

Danny paused. McCloskey was a good man, a thirty-year veteran. No point pissing in his yard. Besides, the kid's jibe had touched a nerve, damn him. All those years of listening to Dad, dirty-nailed and half dead in the kitchen, giving his mother an earful about the goddamn management, how they came in and messed with a man's livelihood, then drove off in a shiny new truck. That was the way most managers worked – contracting was fiercely competitive, and the unspoken rule was that the less the grunts on the ground knew about the abstractions of economics, the better.

Screw that.

Danny gestured to the card table. 'Let me level with you.'

McCloskey looked surprised, then nodded, set down his hat and took a seat. Danny laid it out, the hard facts of the business. How if they split their resources trying to finish this site, they risked not getting the other two enclosed.

Once the walls were up, crews could work inside, hanging drywall, rigging electrical, and detailing.

'Dan, no disrespect, but I got yard boys out there know this stuff.'

'What they don't know is how high the stakes are now.'

'What do you mean?'

'Money's tight. The economy, the whole Internet thing, it hit us, too. We had two projects default on final payments this year. Not bad people, just ran out of money.' Danny sipped his coffee. 'You remember the office building over on Racine, our big score? That was one of them.'

'Jesus.'

'Exactly. Listen, I'd love to see this place humming over the winter. But it's a bad play. Something goes wrong, we can't get the other two ready . . .' He let it dangle, gave McCloskey time to make up his own mind.

After a pause, the man spoke. 'My crew?'

'I've talked Richard into moving them to the other two. We've thrown some big bids for next year. We may have to go to shifts, but nobody loses their job this winter.'

'Me?'

'We have work for you. And you'll get to finish here, Jim.'

McCloskey nodded slowly, the splintered toothpick in his mouth bobbing. 'All right. I'll tell the boys.'

He rose with quiet dignity, and for a moment Danny remembered his father mopping up the last egg scraps and straightening for work. He'd always taken a moment to glance around the kitchen, as though confirming everything was in the right place – wife washing dishes, son rubbing sleep from his eyes, sunbeams playing through the curtains. He'd nod, just barely, giving man-to-man respect to God for keeping an orderly world. Then he'd grab his hard hat and leave, his step marked by the shuffle from his bad knee.

McCloskey opened the door, paused. 'Dan. Thanks.'

'No worries. One thing, though.'

'Yeah?'

'Call me Danny, would you?'

The foreman smiled, nodded, and stepped out. The shutting door cut off the crackle of welding and the wind's whistle.

Danny took a sip of the godawful burned coffee and rocked the folding chair back on two legs. He felt good. He'd done what needed doing, protected the company and saved Richard's ass – again – but he'd done it right. For a moment, he imagined how his father would have felt being included in a conversation like that, treated like a man in mind as well as body.

He suspected the old man would have liked that quite a bit.

The thought made him grin. Then, unbidden, a stretch of the Eisenhower arose in his mind. Soft flakes of snow. A squeal of tires. His smile wilted.

A clatter from outside brought him back to the moment. Forget it. Square up the paperwork here, then head back to the office. Forward motion. Forget Dad, and forget Evan.

So he was back in town. So what?

Danny was done with him.

5. Little Boxes

Danny hadn't really been in the mood for a drink, and at first he'd told McCloskey he had to get home; then, seeing what it had cost the foreman to invite a manager out for a beer, he'd said what the hell, there was time for one or two. They'd ended up at Lee's, a workingman's bar on Division with press-paneled walls and a faded newspaper cutout of an American flag pinned above the bourbon. A shovel-faced bartender poured their shots while he yelled at his granddaughter to change the damn music before it attracted yuppies. The girl, a petite thing with Kool-Aid hair, smilingly ignored him, nodding to the mellow electronic textures she'd put on the boom box.

They'd been there half an hour, chatting about nothing in particular, before McCloskey got serious. 'Listen, Dan – Danny, sorry – about this afternoon. I want to thank you again.'

'Don't worry about it. Really.' As McCloskey extricated a toothpick from his vest pocket, Danny took the opportunity to change the subject. 'What's with those, anyway?'

'The picks?' McCloskey grimaced. 'Smoked two packs a day for twenty years. Quit a couple back. My youngest daughter. Chew one of these instead of lighting a straight.'

'It help?'

'Some. But anything you do that long, you never get all the way over it.'

Danny nodded, sipped his whiskey, enjoying the bite. 'How many kids you have?'

'Nine. You believe it?'

Danny laughed. 'I'm Irish.'

'So cheers, then.' They clinked glasses and threw down the whiskey. McCloskey gestured to the girl, and she came over with the bottle. Up close Danny saw a diamond stud in one side of her nose. She smiled as she poured copper into the heavy-bottomed glasses.

Danny said to her, 'Can I ask you something?' She narrowed her eyes, but nodded. 'This music.'

'Bugging you? I can put on that shit-kicker stuff we usually play.'

'Nah, it's fine. Just curious what it is.'

'It's trip-hop,' she said. 'With dub influences.'

Danny smiled over at McCloskey. 'Used to be it only took one word.'

'Tell me,' the foreman said. 'You should hear the stuff my kids listen to.'

'So now can I ask you something?' The girl set the bottle down, looking at Danny.

He shrugged. 'Sure.'

'You guys aren't planning any trouble, are you? Because if you are, you ought to know we keep a pistol under the bar.'

He squinted at her, surprised. 'No, no trouble. Just here for a couple of drinks.' A tingle ran up the backs of his hands. 'Why?'

'Because that big guy's been eye-fucking you since he came in.'

Tension locked his neck muscles. Over the stereo, a woman's voice whispered something about black flowers blossoming. Slowly, Danny spun on his stool.

He loomed near the back wall, feet apart like a boxer. His gaze smashed through the cigarette smoke and gruff laughter to hit Danny with physical force, and Danny's fingers slipped a little on the glass, splashing some of the whiskey on his shirt. They stared at each other for a long moment, and then with measured steps, Evan started over.

'Someone you know?' McCloskey spoke with the quiet of a man who could handle himself.

Danny's mind raced. What the hell was Evan doing here? And what was he supposed to do now? Introduce the foreman like they were all buddies? Spin the stool away and pretend Evan didn't exist? Who was this guy walking toward him, and what did he mean to Danny Carter, regular civilian?

'It's okay,' he said, not sure it was.

And then Evan was there. Prison had boiled him down, hardening the angles of his face and neck. Whip-cord muscles bulged against his sweater. His curly hair was neatly kept, the sides slicked back.

His dark eyes betrayed nothing at all.

'Long time.' Danny struggled to keep his game face, his heart thumping.

Evan flicked his gaze over to McCloskey, then back again. Danny turned. 'Jim, would you give us a minute? Evan's an old friend.'

The foreman drew himself up on the stool. 'You sure?'

'Yes.'

The man hesitated, then stood. 'You know, I should probably get gone anyway. The wife'll be expecting me.'

Danny nodded. 'Thanks for the drinks.' He kept his eyes locked on Evan's as the foreman stood, paused, and then walked toward the door. For a moment, Danny felt an urge to call the guy back, but instinct kicked in, and instinct had only one rule. So he played it cool. 'Buy you a beer?'

Evan smiled thinly. 'Same old Danny. Slick as shit.' He pulled the stool out of his way and leaned on the bar. He looked awesomely fit, his movements spare but powerful, like inside he was all coiled springs.

'So.'

'So.'

'Bad?'

Evan shrugged.

The granddaughter came over with beer and whiskey, her eyes framing questions Danny ignored. It was like that nightmare he had: One minute, he'd been in the life he knew, then without warning, here he was sitting beside his childhood friend and former partner. He didn't know what to feel. He wasn't scared exactly, but he had that knife's edge thinness he used to get on the job, the sense that things could go either way. There'd been moments standing in some stranger's living room, flashlight in hand, when it'd come on him, this sense that fate wasn't a guide written in a celestial book, but rather a tightrope, a narrow and shaking line above the abyss. One wrong breath could overbalance you.

'How about you, Danny? How you been keeping yourself?'

'I'm good. Better than ever.'

'Yeah?' Evan glanced over with a smile. 'You a million-aire, gonna remember your friends?'

Danny grinned, surprised. The conversation came easier than he'd expected. It was almost fun, trading snaps and sparring. 'Sure. I'll buy you a house next to the mayor.'

'Daley don't live in Bridgeport these days. Left 'bout the same time I did. Different places, of course.'

'I left, too,' Danny said. 'I'm on the North Side now.'

'No shit.'

'No shit.'

'And you're not in the game anymore?'

'No.'

'Too bad.' Evan took a long pull of beer.

It wasn't, but Danny didn't see any point in saying that.

So he reached for the whiskey, held it up to Evan. 'Cheers. To being out.'

They clinked glasses. Danny had always felt you could go too far trying to read someone's soul in his eyes, but still, something he saw in Evan's reminded him that they weren't exactly buddies anymore. After all, the guy hadn't turned up by accident. Danny thought about asking what he was doing here, decided he didn't want to haul the answer out in the open, where they would have to deal with it directly. Sometimes a mutual lie was easier for everybody.

'You still seeing that same woman, the one you were getting serious about?'

'Karen,' Danny said. 'Yeah.'

'Long time. Congratulations.'

'Thanks.'

'You know, I thought maybe I saw her.' Evan took out a pack of Winstons, tapped one free, lit it with a shiny silver Zippo. 'At the trial.'

Danny's heart went to his throat.

'I'd only met her the once, but I'm pretty sure it was Karen. Yeah?'

Danny had wanted to sneak in himself, one last gesture of solidarity, but couldn't have imagined a more boneheaded play. So he'd cooked dinner, opened wine, and asked Karen for the biggest favor of their relationship. Her older brothers had been rough guys that had landed in County more than once, so it wasn't a totally alien world. Still, he'd expected a refusal. Instead she'd just stared at the candles and asked, in voice so soft it was nearly a whisper, if he had quit for good.

Until that moment, he hadn't been sure. Not in his marrow. But when she'd asked him, this half-Italian bartendress with ambitions to manage the place, this woman who knew his past but still trusted in their future, that was it.

He'd promised, and she'd gone to the trial. Watched the pawnshop owner testify from a wheelchair. Looked at photographs of the woman's face, one eye swollen shut, nose broken, as the police described how they arrived just in time. And when it was all over, her cheeks white and a little tremble in her voice, Karen had made the only ultimatum of their relationship. If he ever slipped, she'd walk without a backward glance.

Now, seven years later, the man she'd gone to watch stared at him with an expression Danny couldn't read, and spoke her name.

'Yeah, it was her.' He paused. 'I asked her to go.'

'You had other plans.'

'They would have made me. The owner of the store, the woman, they would have made me.'

Evan blew a plume of gray smoke. 'So why send her?'

'I felt like I owed it to you.' Picking his words carefully. 'To have someone there.'

'Seeing as I was taking a solo fall, you mean.' Evan's eyes hard again. 'I thought maybe you just wanted to see if I'd drop your name.'

'I knew you wouldn't.' And he had, too, known that Evan would do the time cold, even though Danny had walked out, even though a word might have saved him years.

Evan nodded. 'Got that right.'

The music was repeating 'I've got to get away from here,' and part of Danny knew just what the singer meant. But he was surprised to realize that another part of him was enjoying this.

Thing was, some nights, lying in bed in his safe neighborhood, he pictured a round metal door a foot thick, like a bank vault. Inside waited a dim room with racks like safe deposit boxes. He'd step in, close the door behind him, slide open one of the little boxes and remember the electric-dicked thrill of drag racing stolen cars down the Dan Ryan at four in the morning. Or the soft, almost sexual yielding of a lock to his picks. His fist in the air in St Andrew's, lungs raw with howling as Evan fought in the finals of the Golden Gloves.

It was his little secret, and it didn't change anything. There was a reason he walled off those memories behind a foot of imaginary steel. But talking to Evan, the real guy, not the symbol from his dreams, it was like visiting that vault.

'So you got out early.'

Evan nodded. 'They needed to clear some bunks. It was my first fall for a violent crime. And inside I kept myself to myself.' He shrugged.

'Simple as that.'

'If you say so.' Their eyes met again, feeling each other out. Danny sipped his beer, more aware of the taste than usual. He didn't know what to say next, looked at Evan, looked back at his drink. A moment passed in silence.

Then Evan spoke. 'You hear about Terry?'

Danny could picture him, stringy hair and bad breath. The last time he'd seen Terry was when he'd tipped them off to the pawnshop. A lifetime ago. 'No.'

'I met one of his old dealers inside. Apparently Terry cleaned up, quit using. Managed to talk someone into letting him middleman product, God knows how, fucking track marks on his arm. He was doing well, selling to college kids wanna walk on the wild side. Then one day, he decides to take a little blast himself, for old times' sake.'

Danny shook his head.

'Soon he's cutting his stuff to skim for his own supply. Isn't long before he's selling milk sugar. Even the college kids can tell the difference. He has to hit the street. Only now his habit is back, and shorting is the only way he can supply himself.'

Something about this story felt familiar. Not the specifics, but the structure. The course of it. The illicit thrill of the conversation began to evaporate as Danny guessed how the story would end.

'One day he sells a couple of weak grams to a Mexican kid. The guy turns out to be a baby banger, a Latin King trying to earn his stripes.' Evan took a sip of beer. 'So Terry bled out in the basement of a tar house on South Corliss.'

A wave of rolling nausea washed through Danny. Of course the story had seemed familiar. He'd heard it before in a thousand variations. It was the story of what happened if you stuck with the life. Terry had been a junkie, but that wasn't what killed him. It wasn't even the gangbanger he'd cheated. What had killed him was the inexorable fact that there was only one ending to stories like his. He'd died because he was too weak to stop. To escape. Danny found himself remembering his earlier thought, the question of what Evan meant to him now. He realized he knew the answer.

Nothing.

It was time to go home.

'Listen, brother, it's good to see you, but I've got to head out.'

Evan's expression hardened, and he turned to the bar, one hand on his pint. 'Yeah?'

'Yeah, you know, I'm a civilian now. I've got work.' He stood up, reached for his jacket. 'Construction.'

'Just like your dad.'

'Sort of. I work in the office, though.' A voice inside him told him to shut up, not to go any further, but the words slipped out. 'I'm a project manager.'

Evan nodded, still not looking at Danny. 'Good for you. Beats shoveling shit.'

'Yeah. Hey, congratulations again.' He fumbled for his wallet, took out a couple of twenties.

'You don't need to buy my beer.'

'Shit, it's my pleasure. Least I can do.' What was he *saying*? Evan sat silent.

The voice inside whispered that this was all wrong, that the tightrope was swaying and he was off balance and the darkness was hungry, but between the booze and the music and the thought of junkie Terry bleeding to death on dingy concrete, he pushed it away. All he wanted was to get out.

Evan kept staring straight ahead as Danny took a half step toward the door. Danny knew he should say something, but had no idea what. Finally, he put a hand on Evan's shoulder, feeling the stone-carved muscles rigid beneath. 'Good luck.'

Evan only nodded.

6. Sky Burned Blue

A roar from Wrigley Field drifted up through the autumn air. The Cubs must have scored. In Bridgeport, they'd have been rooting for the White Sox. Danny, he didn't much care one way or the other, but he loved the way the sun fell on his fire escape, and he loved the tree-lined streets that spread out beneath it.

Come to think of it, he loved the whole damn place. Loved their condo, a second-story flat with hardwood floors and a working fireplace. He even loved weekend afternoons spent repairing crown molding or laying tile. Evan would have howled to see it, Danny on his knees, painting trim with the delicate care he'd once used to pick locks. The thought of his old partner gave him a momentary chill, but he pushed it aside. It didn't matter what Evan would think. He had no place in Danny's life anymore.

Laugh it up, buddy. Just don't expect me to care.

'What are you still doing here?' Karen stepped out, smiling as she pulled her hair back into a ponytail. 'Didn't you promise me a date?'

He grinned and drew her close, feeling the soft tension of her muscles, the way her body nestled just so. All those years, and still not tired of the way she felt in his arms. He slid his palm down the small of her back.

'Easy, Romeo.' She stepped away from him with a teasing smile. 'Isn't your boss expecting you?'

He groaned. 'Richard can wait.'

'Quit stalling. Go take care of business. Then take me to the zoo and buy me cotton candy.' She turned to go inside, stopped, and glanced over her shoulder with a flirty look. 'Who knows? You might get lucky.'

He laughed, and followed her in.

It took thirty minutes to make it out to the North Shore. In a neighborhood where half a million dollars bought two bedrooms, Danny's boss had five. Located a block from the lake, the house was an English manor with a sprawling lawn. In front stood a mailbox built as a miniature replica, down to the paintwork. The mailman would hook the bay window and pull open the house.

Danny parked on the street, hopped out, and found himself in the midst of a domestic explosion. Tommy, Richard's twelve-year-old son, burst through the front door, yelling and pointing. 'Why not? Everybody has one.'

His boss followed, meaty face red. 'I don't care. I'm not buying you a damn PlayStation so you can rot your brain.'

'What do you care?' Tommy glared at his father. 'You're never even *here*.'

'Don't you talk that way to me, young man. I'm still your father.'

'Barely.' The boy turned and stormed away.

'Get back here. Thomas Matthew O'Donnell, get your ass back here!'

The kid flipped the bird over his shoulder and kept walking. He was stomping away with such righteous adolescent fury that he almost bumped into Danny before noticing him standing beside his truck. Danny smiled bemusedly and rolled his eyes. Showed him a little camaraderie. He didn't really know why – he barely knew the boy. Maybe something to do with having caught plenty of Richard's yelling fits.

Tommy caught his look, nodded angrily. 'I hate him.'

'Ahh, don't say that.' Danny shut the truck door. 'Not over a PlayStation.'

The kid shook his head. 'It's not that. I don't care about that. He's just never . . .' He straightened, wiped at one eye with the back of his hand. 'I wish I lived with Mom.'

'Cut him a little slack. I'm sure he loves you.' He was, too. Richard was a loudmouth, but his office was plastered with photos of the boy, and company meetings routinely began with everyone giving their best impression of sincere interest while Richard regaled them with his son's minor accomplishments.

Tommy snorted. 'Whatever.' He stormed away, little fists pumping.

Danny shook his head and walked to the porch. The truck had blocked him from Richard's view, and his boss seemed suddenly embarrassed to see him, though he covered with a salesman's smile wide as it was fake.

'Kids. Can't live with them, can't chain 'em up in the basement.' Richard wore boat shoes without socks, and extended a hand that was softer than you'd expect from a guy in construction. 'Want a drink?'

He started inside without waiting for an answer. Danny followed, wiping his feet on the mat before stepping on the living room's soft carpeting. Shafts of sunlight splashed across professionally decorated rooms. Everything smelled faintly of lemon. Richard led the way to his private office at the end of the hall. A sumptuous leather couch rested beneath an abstract canvas of scarlet and black. On the walnut desk sat twin flat-screen monitors, both of them displaying graphs and stock quotes. Richard glanced over distastefully, then hurried to shut them off. 'And the goddamn market's more irritating than the kid.'

'Bad run?'

'I'm taking a bath. I got in on these sure-thing tech stocks? I may as well have just gone to Arlington, put Tommy's college fund on the ponies.' He stepped to an

41

antique bar and poured single-malt into Waterford glasses.

Danny had never seen much difference between the stock market and betting on a football game, except that in another one of those ironies legitimate life afforded, day traders were likelier than bookies to show up with a rifle and start shooting strangers. Richard passed him the scotch, dropped into a leather chair, put his feet on a custom ottoman, and continued ranting about his bad luck.

Richard considered himself a self-made man, claiming he'd turned 'a trailer, a toolbox, and a tower of bills' into a company employing nearly forty men. When he told the story – which was often – he always skimped on the details of how he'd accomplished it. The reason was simple: He hadn't. Richard had inherited the company, and before he adopted Danny as his lieutenant, he'd been busily running it into the ground.

It'd taken less than two years for Danny's strategic sense and hands-dirty experience to turn things around. He made it possible for Richard to earn a profit without troubling to learn anything about the business. It was an arrangement that suited Danny fine. He'd always preferred running things to carrying them, and as dense as Richard could be, he was smart enough to know that taking care of Danny was equivalent to taking care of himself.

Still, it involved a lot of stupid errands like this one. Saturday afternoon, and he had to endure twenty minutes of babble about the post-Internet market and the dangers of IPOs before Richard finally asked about the bids Danny had brought.

'Right here.' He took the documents from his satchel. 'I pulled them together last night.'

'Heya, you shouldn't be working Friday nights.'

Considering the opportunity had surprised them yesterday morning and that the deadline was this afternoon,

Danny wasn't sure when else Richard had thought it would get done, but he told him it was no trouble. 'Just sign the last page. I'll drop them off.'

Richard smiled. 'Attaboy. Full service.' He glanced at the documents, nodded, and scribbled his name with a gold pen he took from his pocket. 'I'm going for lunch at the club. You like, you can tag along.'

'Got plans.'

His boss nodded absently, the offer already forgotten. They chatted for another few minutes, and then Richard made a show of looking at his watch. Grateful for the dismissal, Danny finished his scotch and saw himself out. He'd promised Karen a date, and he intended to make good.

The afternoon had turned out gorgeous, leaves glowing on the trees, sunlight warm on their shoulders. The Lincoln Park Zoo was mobbed, but neither of them minded. They joined the crowd, watching the sea lions circle endlessly; laughing at the flamingos' awkward poses; feeling a delighted shiver as a lion used its rough tongue to scrape chunks of meat from a bone the size of a canned ham. Danny sprang for cotton candy, and they sat on a bench and shared it.

When they were finished, he got up to throw the wadded plastic bag in the trash. On his way back he had one of those flashes when he saw her, really saw her. Not through the myopic eyes of habit and time, but as a real person, self-possessed and smiling. How had he gotten so lucky? Not only to get out, but to do it with a woman who knew his past yet was willing to bet on their future. He sat down, then spun and laid his head in her lap. She stroked his hair while the sky burned blue and the wind tossed autumn branches in kaleidoscope patterns.

'Happy.' He sighed. 'Very happy.'

She snorted. 'You better be. You want me to peel you a grape?'

He laughed and closed his eyes, listening to the sounds of rattling leaves and the joyful burble of Saturday people. Then something collided with their bench. Danny's instincts jerked his eyes open and had him bolt upright before he recognized it as a kid, a black boy maybe five years old. The kid paused for a moment and flashed them a dazzling smile, all dimples and white teeth, then rebounded off the bench in the opposite direction. He joined a group of children playing tag in front of the gibbons' cage, shouting as they raced the restless animals. Danny settled back to find Karen smiling down at him.

'What?'

'Nothing,' she said, in the tone that meant it wasn't nothing.

'Really, what?'

'You ever think about having one of those?'

'A little black boy?'

She laughed and bobbled his head with her knee. 'I'm serious.'

'Really?' He could hear the surprise in his own voice. 'A kid?'

She looked away, then back. 'No pressure.'

'No, I just . . .' In truth, he hadn't much thought about it. 'I don't know. It's scary.' He had a flash of Dad's pained expression as he stared around the visiting room of Cook County Correctional. That had been hard. But how much harder to endure the same bafflement and hurt on the face of a son? He'd long ago sworn never to have a kid so long as he lived the life.

But then, he didn't anymore. It was a fact that continued to surprise and please him, like discovering a wad of cash in the pocket of a coat he rarely wore. He'd been straight for

44

years, with a job, a home, and a relationship to prove it. Though he and Karen had never done the wedding thing, it was only because the ritual meant nothing to them. He didn't need a ring to be faithful. And they both brought in solid money – far more than he had been able to count on hustling.

Maybe in this new world he could be a father. Maybe such a thing was possible. If Danny Carter could have health insurance and mortgage payments, why not this?

'What would we name him?'

She laughed. 'You mean her.' And bent down to press her soft lips to his, under skies blowing wild as the hope in his heart.

7. A Good Score

It took Danny thirty minutes to fight his way down Clark, and another ten to find a parking place. The Cubs looked good, and the streets and sidewalks were thronged with fans hoping that maybe this year they wouldn't get their hearts broken. Danny was just hoping to finish his errands and get home before the sun set. It was Sunday, another beautiful day, and he had a date with an Elmore Leonard novel and the lounge chair on his fire escape.

He walked two blocks to a copy and shipping place. The air-conditioning inside felt stale. Two bucks in quarters and ten minutes worth of forms later, he was finally done with work. The girl who checked him out asked if he wanted anything else.

'Just a beer,' he said, and smiled.

She smiled back, a flirtatious look Danny didn't respond to. Just waved and strolled out, thinking of the easiest way to get home. He could probably cut over to Halsted and dodge some of the traffic.

Evan stood in front of him.

Danny dropped his bag. Chemicals pounded through his bloodstream, his nerves gauging fight or flight.

His old partner had a little smile on his lips like he was amused to have startled Danny. Like getting him off balance had been the point. People surged around them, wearing Cubs shirts and yelling to one another, but Danny hardly noticed.

'Hey.' Evan stepped forward, put an arm around his shoulders. 'Let's get a drink.'

Keep walking, a voice in Danny's head whispered. *Just go.* But he let himself be led into a dim corner bar with a neon skull-and-crossbones in the window. Evan dropped his arm once they were inside, and gestured to a corner table. By the time they reached it, Danny had his cool back. He signaled for the waitress and flipped what he hoped was an easy grin. 'Here for the game?'

Evan snorted. 'No.'

A pretty brunette with a friendly smile bounced over, and they both ordered, neither looking at the extensive chalkboard beer list. Danny waited till she was gone, then tried on a quizzical expression. 'So?'

'We didn't finish talking before. But now it's Sunday afternoon. So you won't have to get your panties bunched about work.'

Danny let the remark slide.

'You live up here now, huh?' Evan asked.

'Not far.'

'A house, a woman, a truck. All settled in, snug as shit.'

He nodded, thinking, A *truck?* Wondering if Evan had just made an assumption, why he hadn't said a car. The waitress appeared with two pints on a tray. Evan gave her a ten, told her to keep the change, and they clinked glasses with eyes locked.

'So that's what you get. Life as a civilian.'

'That's all I want.'

'Yeah? And what do I get?'

'For what?'

'For what.' Evan shook his head, smiling ruefully as he tapped a cigarette free. He lit the smoke with the Zippo, snapped it closed, set it neatly on top of the pack. Blew jets of smoke from his nostrils, eyes hard now. 'How long we known each other?'

'Since we were kids.'

'That's right. Just a couple of Irish kids in a blue-collar neighborhood, spics competing with blacks to see who could move in faster. We made it through that shit by sticking together.'

Danny decided to preempt the speech. 'You're pissed I walked out.'

Evan raised his eyebrows, not saying yes or no. His look said *street*. It said *danger*.

'Fuck you.' Showing strength was the first rule. 'You went crazy in there.'

'I hadn't shot him, that dude would have drilled you.'

'Bullshit,' Danny said. 'He'd have told me to freeze, called the cops. Anyway, we should have been out the back with the money before he even showed up. Nobody would have gotten hurt. Nobody would have gone to jail.'

'Always the man with the plan. How about this, Einstein?' Jabbing at him with the cigarette. 'You owe me. First I saved your ass, then I kept my mouth shut and went down alone. Twelve years the judge gave me and banged his little hammer, and you not even in the courtroom to see it. You know what I was doing while you were becoming a yuppie? Celling with a two-hundred-and-sixty-pound gangbanger named Isaiah. He knows I'm not affiliated, so he's eyeing me to decide if I'm a guppy or a shark. How would you sleep?'

Danny held his hands up for peace. 'I'm sorry. I didn't want it to work out that way.' He kept his game face up, but behind it, his mind hummed. Yesterday, he'd have bet his savings account that he'd never see his old partner again. Now it seemed like Evan might have other plans, and if so, Danny needed to find a way to mollify him quickly. And then get the guy out of his life for good. 'And I'm grateful you kept quiet.'

Evan leaned back, sighed, stabbed out the cigarette. 'Yeah, all right.'

They sipped their beer in silence. The memory of his own jail time came to Danny's mind. Summer camp compared with Stateville, but still plenty bad. The worst was the feeling, always, that danger rode hard on your back. Something as simple as holding a gaze too long – or not long enough – and bam, the shit storm started.

'I came out short seven years.' Evan seemed calmer, his voice level. 'Okay, bad beat. But I figure when I go home, I'll find my partner waiting with a new plan to make us money, that we'll get back to work.

'Only that's not what happens. Instead, my partner, he's nowhere to be found. I have to track him down. And when I do? He tells me he's legit. Then he buys me a beer and tells me good luck, 'cause he's got work tomorrow and can't be late.'

Danny kept his face calm. *Don't show any fear, and don't give anything away.*

'I say bullshit to that. From where I'm sitting, you got everything and I got nothing. You owe me.'

'What am I supposed to do? Dig out my tools and go back to work?'

Evan shrugged. 'Why not? The money is better as a team. And I been away too long. I need somebody who knows how to work. Someone I can trust.'

'I've been away as long as you have. If you need someone in the game, I'm not your guy.'

'I'm not talking knowing fences. I'm talking about spotting opportunities. Help me level us out.'

'No.' Danny spoke without any hesitation.

'No?'

'I'm not going back to work,' Danny said. 'Period. I'm not.'

49

'So I should just crawl back to my hole?'

'I don't mean any disrespect. But my life is different now, and I won't go back.'

'Then,' Evan leaned back, lighting another cigarette, 'we have a problem.'

Careful. Be very careful. He remembered Evan's temper all too well, how it could seize him, a white-hot fire that burned out his sense and self-control.

'I don't have any problem.' A play had been spinning in his brain since that night Evan had surprised him out with McCloskey. A little bit crazy, yeah, but still . . . maybe worth trying. 'In fact, I've got an idea.'

'Yeah?'

'But listen, you're going to have to relax and think it over. Don't just snap on me, all right, compadre?' He took a breath to steady himself. 'I can't come back. But I can help you earn.'

Evan leaned forward, his head cocked.

'I can give you a job.'

'You know a good score?'

'No, I mean a *job*. A civilian job.' As he spoke, he stared at Evan, trying to read a hint of a reaction. Hopefully he'd see it as a peace offering. Or maybe even a grift, and expect the money without the work. Danny couldn't let that happen, but he'd welcome the play. It would mean that they were at the negotiating table. Better than squaring off.

'A civilian job.' His face a mask, Evan held the cigarette to his lips, took a long pull. 'In construction.'

'Think about it. You know plenty to get started, and the pay is good.'

Evan shook his head, chuckling to himself. 'Unbelievable.'

'I'm making as much money as we ever did – more – and nobody can look at me sideways. This is a chance to start clean. It's a good offer.' Danny waited, but silence was the only reply. 'The best I can do.'

Silence. Evan wasn't biting. That was okay – Danny hadn't really expected him to, not immediately. But maybe he'd consider it, spot the opportunity to escape the shadow of prison. And if not . . . well, Danny didn't want to be sitting across the table from him if not. He stood up. 'Think about it. Let me know if you're interested.'

Evan crushed his cigarette.

'And thanks for the beer.' Despite the pounding of his heart, Danny made himself walk slow and steady, and didn't look back as he shouldered open the door and stepped into the afternoon.

8. Out the Window

'Smug, down-talking fucker.' Evan spat the words.

'Who is, baby?' Debbie Lackey – she hated 'Deb' and 'Deborah,' always 'Debbie,' like Debbie Harry – struck her best pout, flipping blonde hair back over one shoulder.

Evan looked annoyed as he glanced over, like he was surprised to see her there. 'The guy we're waiting for.' He turned back to stare out the driver's side window of the Mustang.

She wished he'd let her put on some music. They'd been sitting here half an hour, and he hadn't wanted to talk the whole time. She surveyed the street again, hoping for something to take her attention. It was pretty, lots of trees with bright October leaves, rows of graystone apartments fronted by expensive cars. The people who walked their dogs carried little plastic bags to pick up the poop. 'Your friend lives in a nice neighborhood.'

He nodded, still not looking at her.

'Lots of money. Remember I worked for the maid service? We did a lot of these places.'

'Stole a lot of watches and earrings.'

'Fuck you, Mr Armed Robbery.'

He snorted.

'How long are we going to sit here?'

'Until we're done,' he said. 'Not like you have anywhere to be, right? You quit your job.' He reached for his cigarettes, tapped the bottom, and pulled one out with his teeth, like a tough guy in the movies. Despite herself, it gave her a thrill.

'What were you doing again?'

'Massage therapy. I took a night course at the community center 'cause anything was better than waiting tables. I thought I'd work in one of those nice places, you know, with the candles and that Asian music and everything smelling good? But it turns out they all want experience. So I ended up at this joint on Twenty-fifth to work my way up. Only,' she laughed, remembering, 'these guys, I'd start on their backs, but when they rolled over, they'd be sporting wood. And that wasn't what I had planned to work my way up, you know?'

He laughed with his head thrown back, the way he used to. Nice to see. He'd become so much quieter than she remembered. Back in the early nineties, they'd had some good times. Tear-assing down Lakeshore with the radio up loud and his hand in her panties, the speedometer hitting 109 as he hit her spot. Or the time they cleaned out her liquor cabinet, starting with bourbon and tequila, and then when the good stuff ran out, moving to the party leftovers; coconut rum, vermouth, and finally shots of crème de menthe as the sunrise poured pink across the linoleum kitchen floor. Hell, some great times. She didn't mind starting them up again.

Down the block, a glass door shook, shivering the reflection of flaming trees, and then swung open. 'Morning, partner,' Evan said, stabbing out his cigarette without taking his eyes from the apartment. The same man they'd trailed the other day stepped out. Nice-looking guy in khakis and an open-collared oxford, turning to smile at the brunette that followed him out.

'What's her name?' Debbie looked over, but Evan ignored her. 'She's pretty.'

The woman leaned in to kiss the guy, rising up on her toes. She had her hands around his neck, and his rested on the small of her back. It looked like a good kiss, not the usual peck you saw couples giving.

'For people that've been fucking for years,' Evan mused, 'they sure get a kick out of each other.'

She thought of them in the zoo, the way they had lounged on a bench, the guy with his head in the woman's lap. Evan had stayed in the car, told her to follow them, to get as close as she could. But though she'd sat on the opposite bench, she hadn't learned much. They talked too soft, speaking just for the other. A world of two. 'I guess they're family.'

'Huh?' Evan turned to look at her.

'Family. In love.' She realized her voice sounded wistful, and quickly threw up her distant expression, the one she used on the guys at the bar. *You can look,* it said, *but that's all you get.* Evan, though, was staring at her like she'd said something deep. It was the first time he'd really looked at her all morning. Her cheeks went warm, and she felt stupid to have let her guard down, exposed herself that way. 'What?'

He shook his head. 'Nothing. Just – nothing.'

The guy had opened the door of a silver truck and tossed his bag on the passenger seat. He got in, and the woman stepped back with her hips cocked in a pose Debbie recognized from movie magazines. As the truck pulled away, the woman turned with a grin and walked back toward the apartment. Evan didn't start the Mustang, just watched the truck roll down the street.

'Aren't we going to follow him?'

Evan shook his head. 'Not anymore.'

'Why not?'

'Because,' he said, smiling at her, that thin smile that looked a little dangerous, the one that made her a little dizzy, 'I just thought of a way to get rich and even at the same time.'

9. Floating on Reflections

Overhead, the El rattled along the circular tracks that gave the Loop its name. A grim rain darkened the faces of crumbling parking decks as Danny stepped out of the Harold Washington Library. Green-tarnished gargoyles loomed eight stories above him, eerie personifications of the confusion he felt. Of the many thoughts jostling for his attention, one overwhelmed the others.

Coming here had been a stupid idea.

What on earth had motivated him to leave work early, drive downtown, pay the rapacious parking fees, and spend three hours researching prison? What would you call that? Shame? Guilt? Idiocy?

People always talked about the value of firsthand knowledge, and they were right. No book could convey the lonely terror of waking in an eight-foot cell, the way living so intimately with fear marked you. No amount of sunshine and fresh air ever truly wiped away the stain on your soul. Almost ten years since his last fall, but some mornings he still mistook the buzzing alarm clock for cell count, and he still spent midnight moments reconstructing himself after a dream casually obliterated his life. No doubt about it, firsthand knowledge was a bitch.

But there was a special awfulness to secondhand knowledge, too. Sharing a table with a bum dozing on a pillow of unopened books, Danny had read scholarly prose that set his demons howling. The information from the Bureau of Justice alone was staggering. America imprisoned more people than any other nation – even Russia, for chrissake –

with close to two million inmates. Many states spent more money on jails than schools. Amnesty International had actually condemned the American prison system.

And the devil was in the details. Seventy percent of inmates were illiterate, 200,000 mentally ill. If you were a black man, you were born with a one-in-four shot of serving time at some point, and you could count on serving longer. Insult to injury, in many places former felons lost certain constitutional rights; the result was that in some Southern states, as much as 30 percent of the entire African-American population had permanently lost the right to vote.

At least Evan's not black. Lucky him.

Danny turned his head upward, the rain soft on his face. He had a pretty good understanding of the machinery under his own hood, but he had no idea what had driven him here today. Was it guilt? Over what? Walking out, all those years ago? He replayed the look on Evan's face, that sense that something dark had been freed within him, the vicious kicks. No. He had no guilt for bailing out of that madness. He wished to Christ it hadn't happened, wished that he'd never seen the man's blood pooling on the floor, wished that he'd never heard the sounds a person made in that kind of pain. For that he felt guilt, no question. Simply for being there, being a part of it. But that wasn't what had brought him here today.

He leaned back against the wet brick. Taxis glided down State, floating on reflections of their taillights. Rain had driven the homeless out of the park next door, and they huddled together in doorways and under the El, smoking and staring. Across the street, Columbia students with backpacks and sandals sprinted through the rain, their laughter painfully young. Life went on.

There it was.

Life went on. Unless you found yourself in manacles one

bright morning, aboard a school bus that had grilles welded over the windows and a police escort. A bus that took you past people heading for work or breakfast or home, normal people for whom you had ceased to exist. Because more than anything else, prison was exile. Both first-and second-hand knowledge told him that. Prison was waiting, routine. All the while slowly succumbing to a world where violence was the only noteworthy break in the endless march of identical days.

They'd come from the same place, but the moment Evan had pulled the trigger in the pawnshop, their paths had irrevocably split. Thinking of that brought on the old mixed-up feeling Danny knew so well. All these years later, and he still couldn't say for certain if the owner would have shot him that night. He didn't think so – the guy was too practiced in the way he brought the gun out, the way he handled himself. And either way, it didn't make it okay to brutalize him, to beat the woman and try to kill her. But in his midnight hours, would he always wonder whether Evan had saved his life?

Probably. And maybe that was part of what had driven him here. But standing under darkening skies, he realized there was more to it than guilt.

There was also fear.

In all the times he'd imagined seeing Evan, he'd pictured the Evan from the pawnshop, the one whose temper seared and burned and left him all too ready to pull the trigger. The one who'd gone crazy, lost his head and his humanity. But for all of that, in his calm moments, a buddy. A partner. A childhood friend who had always had his back.

But that's not the way it worked. In all those fantasies, Danny had forgotten that time would have passed for both of them. He wasn't dealing with the same man. The real Evan had lived a maximum-security nightmare for seven endless years. Had come out of it twice as muscled and half as talkative. Had adapted to a world built to hide the most dangerous of men.

Danny turned up his collar and hurried across the rainy street.

What would that *do* to someone?

10. Better Than to Look Away

Danny recognized the boots. They were the same battered black work boots Evan had worn that night, seven years and a lifetime ago. Steel toes with a rigid sole that made far more noise than the jogging shoes Danny had preferred. But that wasn't what concerned him now. What concerned him was that he'd stepped into his apartment to find them propped on his kitchen table.

The retro clock on the wall seemed loud. Danny thought of gunfighters in the old West, the silence before the storm of bullets. He dropped his bag on a stool, tossed his keys on the counter. Kept his voice calm as he spoke – 'Make yourself at home.' His fingers tingled with adrenaline, but it was too late to back out now. It wasn't just dogs that could smell fear; criminals had a pretty good nose for it, too.

'What's with the Heineken in the fridge?' Evan leaned back in his chair, rocking it up on two legs, the picture of comfort. There were three empty green bottles on the table already, a fourth well on its way.

'Karen's.'

'Tastes like piss.'

Danny glanced around casually. If there were any other surprises planned, he wanted to know about them. The table sat in an alcove beneath the window, bright with afternoon sun. The rest of the kitchen didn't offer much cover, just a small counter and a pantry on the far side. The pantry was maybe large enough for a person, but the bifold doors would make for an awkward exit. How long had Evan been here? And how had he known Danny would be the first one home, and not Karen? 'Didn't seem to slow you down any.'

Evan shrugged. 'Been a while since I've been able to enjoy cold beer. I'm still catching up. Of course,' his eyes now hard, 'you've had plenty of time, haven't you?'

Something tightened in Danny's gut, that humid stirring through his entrails, like the wind preceding the subway. It was an old feeling, familiar, but not missed.

He turned away, went to the fridge. Grabbed a bottle for himself, thought of the cooler move, took another. Popped the caps and handed one to Evan as he sat down.

Evan finished the beer he'd been working on in one open-throated swallow. The black T-shirt he wore traced the lines of his muscles. The upper curves of a blue-black tattoo extended just past the collar. The design was ragged and messy. Ink from inside always was. Tricky to be precise with a straight pin and a ballpoint.

Danny played at being casual as he undid the top button of his oxford and rolled the cuffs, but his mind crackled and hummed. There was no good angle from which to see Evan breaking into his house. It ramped the tension between them, elevated it to action. The disrespect would have been intentional. Only one conclusion to draw.

Evan was stepping things up.

Which made cool all the more important. Cool was currency. Cool suggested a lack of fear, an equal footing. He raised the beer. 'Cheers.'

'Cheers.' They clinked bottles, looking into each other's eyes, neither acknowledging the tension. 'Just like old times, huh? Two friends bullshitting over a beer.' Evan's tone was jovial. 'You know what it reminds me of?'

Danny smelled a setup, chose to play along. 'What's that?'

'This con I knew in Stateville. Chico. Chico was a prison queer, shaved his chest and wore his jumpsuit half open. You remember the type? Suck your cock for two packs of smokes, or one pack of menthols. He belonged to Lupé, this big Norteño Mexican, but they had an understanding. Chico could work to keep himself in luxuries, long as he split the take.'

Evan paused, holding his beer by the neck, eyes still drilling into Danny. Didn't seem like he'd blinked yet. Danny met the gaze, knew better than to look away. The tension in his gut grew worse.

'I'd been in a couple months when Chico got a new cellie, some eighteen-year-old transfer. Word round the yard said it was love, that Chico'd been hitting his knees for this new boy with no smokes required. Truth be told, Lupé might have tolerated that – he wasn't a fag so much as a player – but Chico took it too far. Told Lupé they were through. He's a changed woman, and not working anymore.'

Evan paused to take a sip of beer. 'You know what? I'm coming around on this Heineken.'

Danny said nothing, glanced at the clock. Karen would be home soon. If he heard her key in the door, he wasn't going to have a choice but to raise the stakes himself. He'd been too concerned with her reaction to tell her about Evan's return. It wasn't the idea of getting caught that scared him. He just had no intention of letting the two of them be in the same room. Ever.

'Anyway, a couple days later, Chico and Boyfriend are in their cell splitting pruno when Lupé and his crew come for them. The pruno, that's what reminded me. You know the stuff? Prison liquor. You steal fruit from the mess, mash it up with ketchup, some water. Put it in a bag to ferment for a couple weeks. The color of the mold on top depends on the fruit you use; sometimes it's green, sometimes this sick orange. But if you skim that off, the liquid that's left will get you fucked up. Shit's worse than Mad Dog, though. It'll give you a headache make you wish you were dead.' He smiled.

61

'Nothing like the imported beer you've been drinking.'

Where was this going? Was he just flexing to show how hard he'd become? Hardly necessary – Evan looked like if you drove a truck into him, you'd just end up with a busted rig. There was a larger point, Danny knew. He just didn't see it yet.

'So Lupé's guys are serious gangbangers. By the way, you know what the bangers call a youth fall? Gladiator school. Nice, huh? Anyway, they get hold of our lovebirds, and right away they've got the gags in. Lupé's last into the cell. He makes sure that Chico is watching, and then he paroles Boyfriend. Leaves the shank sticking out of the man's throat.'

Danny couldn't taste the beer. He tried to keep his face a mask, to stay above it. The ticking clock made him think of time bombs, explosions straining to escape.

Evan leaned forward, corded forearms bunching. He smelled of beer and cigarettes. 'Then Lupé touches Chico's face real soft. Smiles at him, turns, and walks out.

'Chico senses what's coming, starts struggling. You can tell he wants to kill these guys, but he's just a prison queer. What he wants isn't important. After all, these three are gladiators. One gets him in a chokehold, and another lifts his foot up on the bunk, stretches the leg out straight. The bangers are laughing, two of them arguing who gets to do it, like Chico isn't even there. He's turning white and shit, but they don't pay him any attention. Finally the one on the bed holds Chico's leg taut, the joint locked. The third winds up, then stomps down, just *bam,* down, like snapping firewood, right on the knee. Chico howls, I mean, you can hear it through the gag. And no fucking wonder, because bone is sticking out the back of his prison blues. The bangers hoot, and slap each other on the back while Chico shrieks. Whole thing took maybe a minute. Guards find the pruno, the blade, Boyfriend's body, they choose to write it off as a lover's quarrel between the cellmates. Easier than actually looking into it. That's the mentality on the inside.'

Danny's mouth was dry, and the tension in his stomach had curdled into something sour. There wasn't a hint of emotion on Evan's face, none. Just the intense stare between them that he didn't dare break. He swallowed slowly.

'After that,' Evan spoke softly now, 'Chico didn't walk so good. But I'll tell you what.' He paused, and then the mask of his face cracked into a smile, thin-lipped and cruel. 'He never again forgot what he was. Or who he belonged to.'

Danny leaned the chair back, feet on the ground. His palms swamped up with sweat. He struggled for the remnants of his cool, and took a swallow of beer. It flowed warm and flat down his throat. 'Bad luck for Chico.'

Evan smiled broadly at that, but with none of the comradely warmth Danny remembered from their childhood. 'I thought about your offer.'

Here it comes.

'Fold it sideways and shove it up your ass.'

Danny shrugged, finished his beer.

'You owe me, Danny. But I've thought of a way to square us. And you're going to help, like it or not.'

11. Swept Up in Fire

The cigarette tasted sweet as a stolen kiss.

A funny expression, Evan thought, Ma's. She used to say it on good days, the ones when she'd sing, the ones when the bruises weren't too bad. He hadn't thought of her in a while, but now, strolling through Lincoln Park, watching families indulge in happy domestic bullshit, she came to mind. He couldn't say for sure, but he'd bet she'd not had too many kisses stolen.

After he'd jimmied the lock on Danny's window and let himself in, Evan had wandered from room to room. He wasn't searching for anything in particular. Just looking. He lingered over a photo of Karen smiling in a bikini, shielding her eyes from the sun of a lost afternoon. Took a shit in the master bathroom, thought about leaving it floating there, a little gift, but decided against it. Then he'd sat and waited with a smile growing inside. It felt good to be playing again.

And the game had gotten better once Danny arrived.

He took another drag, smoking the cigarette to the filter, feeling the melting resistance as the heat fused it. His favorite part, the cigarette yielding. He knocked off the cherry and flicked the butt into the grass. One of the Lincoln Park mothers, about his age, figure still tight and her hair expensive, glared at him. He winked, then laughed as she gathered her boy off the swing set and hustled him away.

Look out for the bad man, kid. Your mommy, she's still a nice piece of ass, and she's got instincts strong enough to tell her to move away. Funny how it worked. The more you had – a job, a house, a lover, a kid – the more you had to lose. Soccer Mom may not have spelled it out that way, might have chosen to push a truth like that out of her well-decorated world, but some elemental part of her understood.

Evan pulled the smokes from his shirt pocket and tapped out another one. The sun fell warm on his back and the top of his head, though the wind was cool. A perfect afternoon.

Danny had said no. Or tried to, anyway. In the end, he'd agreed to think about it. With the old Danny, the one he'd known, it would have been different. But now he was just an angle to be played, and he cowed the same as a prison queer or a soccer mom.

But then, he had so much. So very much to lose.

12. Liabilities

'Jesus.' Patrick turned, one hand still on the railing, to look Danny in the face. 'Are you serious?'

Karen had whipped up pasta for dinner, with spicy sauce and a bottle of red. She hated the criminal in Patrick, feared his impact on Danny, but Patrick the person, him she loved. So the three of them had sat at dinner, laughing and having a good time, all the while Danny raging behind a calm mask, desperately needing to talk to Patrick alone. 'Nevermore.'

'I can't believe he asked you to do that.'

'It wasn't so much asking,' Danny said, 'as telling.'

'Motherfu –'

'Keep your voice down.'

Patrick turned back to the sprawling night sky. After dinner Danny had led him out to their fire escape, ostensibly so that Patrick could smoke, but really for the privacy of it. The game had just let out, and Wrigley Field still blazed with light. The streets swarmed with fans shouting drunkenly for cabs.

'What are you going to do?'

'I don't know.' Danny shook his head. 'I really don't.' Was it only yesterday afternoon he'd sat at the kitchen table, knuckles clenched on the beer bottle, listening to Evan propose a plan to shatter his life? Hard to believe so little time had passed. He'd thought of nothing else since. Hardly slept, his mind spinning and grasping for a way out.

Your boss, Evan had said. *He's got a kid, yeah?*

Right then Danny had known what was coming, and fear climbed his spine one vertebra at a time.

66

To hear Evan talk, it was a simple thing, no big deal. Together they snatch Tommy, put him somewhere safe. Dick-twist Richard into paying as much as he could afford – not too much, Evan said, no point making it impossible – in trade for his son's life. Split the score and consider themselves finished, all accounts balanced.

'Jesus.' Patrick's face glowed as he dragged on his cigarette, eyes wide and dodgy. 'What did you tell him?'

'What do you think? Hell no. You know what his response was? "Think about it." He's sitting in my kitchen, boots on the table, telling me to think about it. He rocks back a little, so his shirt pulls up? And he's got a gun tucked in his belt.'

'He pulled a piece on you?'

'Just let me see it, like it was an accident. Then he asked when Karen would be home.'

Patrick blew a breath through his lips. 'So he's set on it.'

'The way he sees it, either we're partners or I'm disrespecting what I owe him.'

'You don't owe him shit.'

Danny shrugged. 'Not the way he sees it.' Which left Danny in a bad spot. The first times they'd met, there had been awkwardness and even a little fear, but also a faint and reserved fondness. They'd grown up together, suffered Sunday school together. Shared swiped menthols to impress fifth-grade girls in leather jackets and too much hair spray. Watched the sunrise from the top of a parking deck, twelve-year-old Evan afraid to go home, his eye blackened from stepping between his parents. They had history.

But when he'd walked in to find Evan at his kitchen table, fear was all he'd felt, a gnawing in his belly that grew as he listened. His friend had come out of Stateville changed. This man followed him. Spied on him. Broke into his house. And if he'd done all that, what was to stop him from doing worse? Danny shivered. 'I've got to find a way out of this.'

'Why's he need you at all?'

'I know Richard. I know his routines, I've been in the house. I even know his finances. Plus,' Danny said, 'figuring out how to do things, that's what I was good at.'

'Evan always was just muscle.'

Danny shook his head. 'He likes you to think so. He's got a temper, and he doesn't give a damn for anybody in his way, but he's . . .' He trailed off, searching for the right word. 'Cunning. Even so, yeah, he knows his odds are better with me planning it.'

Patrick nodded, lit a cigarette. 'You could always,' he paused, 'I mean, you could always do the job.'

Danny spun. 'You're kidding, right?'

'Well, just for discussion. It would be easy, no one gets hurt, and Evan is off your back.'

'You really don't get it, do you?'

'I know, you're out, I'm just saying –'

' 'Just this once,' right? Only bullshit, it doesn't work that way. Everybody always goes down on the last job. You know why? Because if they don't go down, they do another. Besides, we walked into a pawnshop at midnight, nobody even *in* the place, and still, somehow, we end up . . .' He paused, collected himself. Sighed. 'I don't want to go back to that world.'

Down on the street, a cab held his horn, the blare lasting five seconds, six, eight. Someone yelled back angrily. Overhead, indigo clouds moved against a dark sky. Patrick turned away from the railing, his boots rattling the metal grille of the fire escape. 'I'll talk to him for you.'

The words yanked Danny from his thoughts. 'What? No.' All he needed, Patrick getting wrapped up in this. He already had enough asses in need of covering, enough liabilities.

'Look, this still *is* my world. Let me help.'

'No way,' Danny said. 'I'm telling you, this isn't the Evan we grew up with.'

'Yeah, well, I'm all grown up too.'

'Listen.' Danny used his most rational voice. 'I know you're trying to help, and I appreciate it. But that's a bad play.'

Patrick stared back, like he was thinking of protesting further. Then he shrugged, turned, and flicked his cigarette off the balcony. 'Your call.'

Danny nodded, went to stand beside him.

'What are you going to do, then?'

'I have an idea, but I really don't like it.' Danny paused. 'You remember Sean Nolan?'

'Sure. I felt up his sister on the playground behind St Mary's. He chased me for a week. Would've kicked my ass, too. He's a cop now, still in the parish. Why?'

Danny just stared at the sky, let Patrick work it out. Funny, though the answer was perfectly obvious, it ran so counter to the lessons of Danny's old world that it took a minute.

'Jesus,' Patrick said, pronouncing it 'Jay-sus,' surprise revealing the edges of his father's accent. 'Going to the cops?'

'Just one cop. A guy we grew up with, from the neighborhood.'

Patrick whistled.

'Yeah. I'm not sure yet. Just thinking about it.'

'But –'

'What are you boys up to out here?' Karen stepped out smiling, carrying three beer bottles in one hand with practiced ease. She turned to close the door, and Danny shot Patrick a quick warning look. He hadn't told her about Evan's visit, convincing himself he hadn't wanted to scare her, knowing that was only part of the truth.

'Just watching the drunks,' he said.

'And the girls, right?' She smiled, handed a bottle to each of them. 'Speaking of which, Patrick, I have a friend you've got to meet. She's a nurse.'

Their eyes met, locked. Patrick started first, then Danny, the laughter bubbling up from within, loud, ceaseless peals of it, each fueling the other until it turned to sobbing for breath, their sides hurting as they fell into deck chairs.

Karen looked at them funny. 'What'd I say?'

It was enough to get them going all over again.

13. Better to Roar

The edge of the switchblade already glowed with a liquid shimmer, but he'd broken out the whetstone anyway. Patrick held the knife at thirty degrees and stroked it in a practiced motion. Once, twice, three times. And with each stroke, he remembered last night, and got angrier.

'He pulled a piece on you?'

'Just let me see it, like it was an accident. Then he asked when Karen would be home.'

Poor Danny had been trying to play it cool, but it hadn't been hard to spot the fury beneath his words. But there was something else there, too. A weird kind of helplessness it killed Patrick to see. He knew what it was; Danny was a civilian now.

And civilians were prey.

He'd raised a burr on one side of the knife, so he flipped it over and began work on the other edge.

After Karen had come out they'd had another couple beers, all three of them, the conversation on safe topics. Patrick had told them a story about this girl he'd met a couple years ago, a twenty-year-old chick who told him she lived with her daddy. They'd had a few drinks, one thing led to another, and then they were back at her house, ending up on the kitchen counter, of all places.

'You know, we're going at it, everything's good. And then I hear a door open. So I panic, grab for my clothes, thinking I better get out a window before her father comes at me with a shotgun, right?' Danny had laughed, and Karen had rolled her eyes. 'Only you know what she says?'

'What?'

'She says, "It's okay – daddy likes to watch."' He'd held the pause, dragged it out till he had them both on the edge of their seats, then gave it up. 'This whole time she'd been talking about her *sugar daddy*. Guy's a sixty-year-old broker likes to see his pet stripper with other men.'

That'd cracked them up, and from there the conversation had gone on like normal, stories and jokes. Danny had sat down in one of the chairs, and Karen had taken the arm and leaned back into him, looking perfectly happy, two halves of a greater whole. And Patrick, he'd had to watch the glow in Karen's eyes, the fear in Danny's, and pretend like nothing was going on. That had been bad enough.

But then it had gotten worse.

He was leaving, and they'd both walked him down to his bike, October winds knocking bare branches against one another, the clouds skidding dark overhead. He reached for his keys in his jacket pocket and realized he wasn't wearing it, that he'd left it upstairs. Danny volunteered to grab it, and left him and Karen alone.

'Listen, thanks again. The only time I get a meal isn't cooked in a restaurant is when you guys have me over.'

She laughed. 'Don't worry about it.' She'd wrapped her arms around herself against the cold, and smiled. One of those silences had fallen. Just one of those moments that happen between two people who are used to the presence of a third, and who don't really know what to say to each other alone. He'd brushed at a spot on the chrome of his bike, and she'd looked at the sky. And then, out of nowhere, she surprised him.

'Is Danny happy?'

'Huh?' He straightened, scrambling for his poker face. 'What do you mean?'

'I mean, I know he's *happy,* more or less.' She brushed her hair behind her ears. 'But sometimes I get the feeling he . . . I don't know, he misses the old life.'

'What makes you think that?'

'Nothing specific. He gets really distracted. Like he's thinking of something else. And I thought, you know, he might not tell me that, but maybe he said something to you.' She looked at him earnestly, like she really wanted to know.

'I can't – I mean, Danny's like my brother.'

'I know, I'm not asking you to –'

'Hold on.' He sighed. 'Look, I steal things. That's what I do, okay? And that's fine. Better than fine. And Danny, he used to do it, too. And he was really, really good at it, Karen. The times we worked together, they were the smoothest scores I ever had. And I trust him with my life. So I would love to see Danny come back to work.'

She nodded, her eyes narrowing a little bit.

'In fact, there's only one thing I'd rather see him do.' He paused. 'You know what?'

Karen shook her head.

'Not come back.' He watched his words sink in. 'He's happy, Karen. Happier than I've ever seen him. Maybe he misses the life now and then, for a second. But he belongs in the one you guys have. And he knows it.'

She'd smiled then, not the kind you flash on request, but the kind that boils up from somewhere deep inside. The kind you can't turn off. 'Thanks.' She'd given him a hug, and he'd taken it.

The whole time knowing what Danny was actually keeping from her. Knowing how much worse the truth was than her fears. And right then, he'd made up his mind.

He finished with the other side of the blade and tested the edge against his thumbnail. It took the barest pressure to cut a mark. He folded it, and slid it into his boot, then grabbed his sunglasses and walked out of what used to be the manager's office, where he'd set up his bedroom.

The service station had sat abandoned for three years before Danny gave him the idea. After all, what better place to park a tow truck? He could even store merchandise here if he had to. Not that he kept anything very long – you had to be pretty dumb to park the evidence in your front yard – but it never hurt to have cover available.

Besides, against all logic, women loved it. After he'd hosed the oil stains away, painted up the rooms and scrubbed out the shower, even your upscale types saw it as artistic. God bless the yuppies and their lofts.

His babies sat parked in the garage. He briefly considered the truck, then dismissed it. Good cover, but not enough style. Better to roar up on a bike. He traced one palm along the Triumph he'd rebuilt with his own hands, 750 cubic centimeters of gleaming engine and custom chrome fixed to the same body Marlon Brando rode in *The Wild One*. No point being bad if you didn't look good. He unlocked the roll door that fronted the garage and hauled it clattering upward.

He paused to kiss his fingers and tap the medallion hanging on his workbench. Danny's mother had given it to him, a zillion years earlier. Saint Christopher, half hunched, with a lumpy-looking baby Christ on his back. Patron saint of travelers, and a dude who helped his friends.

On one level, it bothered him to break his promise, but he didn't see much choice. Things were all messed up. Danny should have remembered that the only way to back down a guy like Evan was to take a stand yourself. That's the way it worked. Strength respected only strength. But Patrick could understand his position, see how he'd forgotten such a basic rule. The guy was a civilian now, and he had Karen to think about.

But that's what friends were for. The way he figured it, his oldest friend would be happier if Patrick took care of business.

So he would. Just like Saint Chris.

He straddled the bike, the leather soft between his thighs. The engine roared with power at the first turn of the key. He cracked his knuckles, put on his shades, and rocked off the stand. Leaving the helmet behind, he rolled out of the shop and turned south.

14. Between Worlds

Evan was out there. Somewhere.

Working on his car, the radio tuned to classic rock, a rag in his back pocket. Straining and sweating at his old weight bench. Or maybe sitting across the street with a pistol in his lap.

It meant that getting up and going to work was out of the question. Danny needed time to think. Besides, he didn't want to look Richard in the eye, not yet. So he'd called in, said he needed a day to take care of some personal business.

Then he sat and had a cup of coffee with his dead father.

It happened as he counted his options. The way he saw it, he had only four. He could refuse to help and risk Evan coming at him, tearing his life apart. He could bolt, leave his home and his job and the city he'd spent his whole life in. He could give Evan up to the cops, a violation of everything he'd grown up believing. Or he could help Evan and risk his relationship, his self-respect, even his freedom.

Dad appeared as he counted the last option, square jaw set in a disapproving grimace.

'I know,' Danny said. 'I know. I'm just thinking, okay?'

After the accident, Dad had started coming pretty regularly. Danny would wake up in Cook County Prison to find him perched on the edge of the bunk. Or riding shotgun as he went to meet Evan for a job. He'd stopped coming about the time Danny went straight, seven years back. But now, poof, there he was again, one arm propped on the back of the chair, his left hand tapping the table, the white ridge of the old circular-saw scar flexing. Danny rarely imagined him talking, but just like in life, his eyes spoke volumes.

'You know what I need, Pops?' Danny said. 'A joker.'

The trick to problem solving, he'd found, was to look at it like a deck of cards. At a glance, an implacable rectangle. But fan them out, start looking at the options, and you could usually find a way. Best of all was the wild card, the one that didn't figure into normal play. The joker was the solution people didn't think of, the one that gave you an edge.

Only problem was, no matter how much he shuffled and redealt, he kept coming up with nothing but minor variations of the same four tired options. He couldn't see a way that didn't risk everything he cared about. A way that didn't let his past poison his future.

His father stopped tapping, tilted his hand back to check his fingernails, his silence judgmental.

Danny glared. 'Ahh, what do you know? You're dead.'

He put his father out of his head and went back to shuffling. He was still at the table two hours later, when Karen wandered in. She wore a white baby-doll tee and panties, rubbed sleep from her eyes with one hand. 'You feeling okay?' she asked.

He nodded, told her he wanted to get a few things done around the house. She poured coffee and slid into a chair, her fingers cupped around the mug for warmth. 'Nice,' she yawned, 'seeing Patrick the other night.'

'Huh? Oh, yeah.'

She sipped her coffee, gave a loud sigh of pleasure. 'Hey, what were you guys laughing about?'

'Just that – well, Patrick thinks it's funny the way you try to set him up. He thinks you're trying to save him.'

She smiled. 'I guess I am.'

'He's okay, Kar. He's happy.'

'I know. I realize I can be kind of a bitch about him.

77

Stupid of me, but I sometimes hold it against him that he's still – you know. I don't care how he makes his money, it's just . . .'

'I know, babe.'

'Anyway, I was thinking about it last night, and I decided that was dumb. He's your friend, and that's that. I mean, I know you aren't going back.'

He kept his gaze level while heart and head warred. He wanted to tell her about Evan, about everything, just spill it. Take comfort in her arms, and talk it over together. Maybe she'd help him find his joker.

Or maybe she'd decide it was time to fold the hand. She'd made only one ultimatum in their whole relationship – if he took up the life again, she was gone for good.

'So,' she continued, 'I'm going to try to be adult, and not hold it against Patrick.'

He felt dirty but kept his tone light. 'I think he'd be happy if you'd just stop trying to set him up.'

'Okay. Though he really should meet Jenny.'

Despite everything – despite himself – he laughed.

She stood, walked to his side of the table, and slid onto his lap, one arm around his shoulders. Her face still bore faint red marks from the pillow, and the coffee barely covered her morning breath, but even so, she glowed. 'I love you, babe.'

His heart swelled in a way that made it hard to speak, and he kissed her instead, held her to him, soft and warm. When she climbed off his lap and padded away, he watched her go, her bare feet dirty, a faint sway to her hips.

He waited until he heard the shower, then went to the phone on the counter and dialed. Some decks didn't have a joker.

'Could I please speak to Sean Nolan?'

*

78

The diner was a storefront on West Belmont, tucked in among auto repair shops and warehouses. Across the street three flats bore upscale real estate logos in anticipation of the day when Wicker Park and Lakeview were finally and irrefutably full, though now there were more signs than tenants. Inside, fluorescent lights shone brightly off the fake wood paneling and cash register. A bald cook, not fat but Chicago-big, worked the grill.

Nolan sat halfway down the chipped counter, peering suspiciously at a laminated menu and twisting his wedding ring. He wore his brown suit too well to have a bulletproof vest beneath.

'Hello, Sean.'

'Danny.' The greeting was neutral, offering no clues. His eyes were watery and marked with crow's feet, but he looked good.

'Long time.'

'Ten years? Since you picked Marty Frisk up outta holding for that D-and-D.'

Danny shook his head. 'I saw you a couple of years ago, when you were still a regular cop.'

'Yeah?'

'You didn't see me. You were coming out of a 7-Eleven in the Loop.'

'Why didn't you say hello?'

Because he was too freshly clean. Because his new life hadn't taken hold. Because he was afraid Sean's gaze would cut him to ribbons, would confirm he was just a thief with an upscale address.

'I hollered. You must not've heard.'

The cop grunted. Danny slid onto the Naugahyde stool, turned his coffee cup upward to signal the cook. The smell of bacon sizzling on the grill tightened his stomach.

Was he crazy, sitting down with Nolan – *Detective* Nolan –

to solve a problem? All his street responses told him yes.

On the other hand, look where his street responses had gotten him.

The cook came over, coffeepot in one hand, spatula in the other. Danny asked for a BLT. Nolan ordered egg whites, skim milk, and wheat toast.

'I heard you got married.'

'Yeah,' Nolan said. 'Two kids, a boy and a girl.'

'Still in the neighborhood?'

'My folks moved to Beverly ten years ago, and Mary-Louise and I followed when we had Tracy. It's nice. No gangs, everybody shows up to cheer the St Patty's parade. Sundays I smoke a cigar and water my lawn. You want to see pictures, or you going to tell me why I'm sitting here?'

Danny sipped his coffee. It tasted sharp. 'You know I left the neighborhood, too.'

'So I hear.'

'I work in construction, as a project manager. I've got a place in Lakeview, second floor in a graystone. Nothing fancy, but it's mine, you know?'

Nolan nodded slightly, betraying nothing.

'It's nice to have made a place for myself. Something . . .' He hesitated, old habits making him nervous admitting anything. 'Legitimate.'

The cook set their order in front of them on white plastic plates, then snapped the grease off the spatula, set it down, and walked to the end of the counter. Nolan forked egg onto his toast, took a bite. His cool refusal to get involved irked Danny.

'I thought cops liked doughnuts.' Trying to engage the guy, not piss him off, his tone playful.

'I thought criminals stayed criminals.'

Danny laughed. 'I guess we're both wrong.'

Nolan gave him a slow, appraising look. 'Maybe.'

The coffee may not have been much to brag about, but the BLT was delicious. Danny took another bite before he spoke. 'Funny thing. When I started working construction, you know what I realized? Being a thief actually helped me out.'

'How's that?'

'Little ways. Knowing how to bargain, negotiate. Being able to plan. Mostly, though, to be good at either, you had to know when to take risks.'

'That's what you're doing here? Taking a risk?'

Danny nodded.

'Because I'm the police.' Pronouncing it '*poh*-lease.'

'Yeah.'

'So you're not clean.'

'Oh, I'm hundred-proof. Go to work, pay my taxes. I'm a civilian.'

Nolan shrugged. 'So why buy me breakfast? Just to tell me that?'

Danny's stomach felt sour. 'I've got a problem.'

The other man took another forkful of eggs, content to wait him out.

You came to dance, kid. 'Someone is harassing me. Following me around. My girlfriend, Karen, I think he's watching her, too. Friday, he broke into our apartment.'

That got the detective's attention. 'He steal anything?'

'No. He was waiting for me.'

Nolan's eyes narrowed. 'Waiting to do what?'

'To talk. To threaten us.'

'So this is somebody you know.'

Danny nodded.

'You file a report?'

'It's not that simple.'

'Why?'

'Because . . .' Danny took another swallow of bitter coffee. 'You know how much response an ex-felon gets when he yells for help?'

'Why do you think you'll get more here?'

It was a question Danny had been afraid to consider too closely. Nolan was three, four years older, and while they'd had mutual friends – no way to avoid it, growing up Irish in a South Side neighborhood that belonged to them less every day – they'd never been close. But even when Nolan had gone off to the academy, and the rest of his friends had started to speak of him with contempt, Danny had remained respectful. No point pissing the guy off, he'd thought then. No point attracting his attention.

It was a thin rationale to pin his hopes on, and he knew it. But it was Nolan or nobody. What was he going to do, call 911? He didn't have anything to tell them, not really, and he knew police procedure well enough to know he didn't want the attention. Karen knew about his past, sure, and Patrick, but as far as the rest of the world was concerned, Danny had always been in construction. He'd lied to get his first shot as a yard hand – plenty of people did, mostly Latins without papers – but he'd risen to a point where that kind of attention could hurt. How would Richard react to find he'd trusted the management of his business to a man with two felony counts?

And that was assuming things went *well*. He could suffer much worse than damage to his reputation. If Evan dimed him out on the pawnshop, he'd face charges. Lose his job, his freedom, maybe even Karen. Set himself back seven years – more, when you counted however long he spent in jail.

Which made this discussion even more delicate. Danny was counting on Nolan's discretion, a dicey prospect at best. The thought made his stomach burn acid. 'We don't owe each other anything, I know that. But I've been spotless for years. Worked my way up same as you, same as anybody. I didn't ask any favors doing it – I did it on my own, and I did it square.' He hesitated. 'I'm worried. For myself, for Karen, for . . .' He stopped himself. No need to mention Richard or Tommy.

Nolan set down his fork, looked over for the first time, his eyes searching Danny's face as if looking for clues. 'What aren't you telling me?'

The flush in his gut worsened. He broke off a piece of bacon, munched slowly. Didn't taste it. Point of no return. Once he crossed this line, he'd be giving up the last bit of honor among thieves. *Chips on the table, kid.*

'It's Evan McGann.'

Nolan was silent for a moment. He turned back to his plate, stabbed a forkful of eggs and passed them into his mouth, chewing vigorously. When he was done, he turned to look at Danny.

And burst out laughing.

'I'm not kidding, Sean.' Danny's knuckles went white on the edge of the counter. He felt like he might slide off the stool and right off the face of the planet.

'Oh, I believe you.' His face was red with hilarity, the freckles a scattering of dark buckshot. Danny stared in silence, the seconds passing, the pressure in his stomach mounting. The laughter finally wound down. Still merry, Nolan shoveled up the last of his eggs, speaking around a mouthful of them, flecks of egg spattering. 'Time to pay the piper, eh Carter?'

Danny's heart fell. Nolan wouldn't help him more than any other cop would. He'd crossed the line for nothing. 'Sean.' He kept his voice level and quiet. 'We're scared. Evan's not messing about.'

'I bet. Probably a little pissed about his last fall, yeah?

'Course, you wouldn't know anything about that. You weren't there, right?'

Danny forced himself to stare at the detective. 'I was always small-time. You know that. For chrissake, we grew up in the same neighborhood.'

'Bullshit.' Nolan's face went from the red of laughter to a more dangerous shade. 'Bullshit, Danny. Don't lay that on me.'

'You won't help?'

'Help you what? Your old partner is back in town, wants something from you? You're in construction, right? So what's he want?'

Danny said nothing.

'Yeah, I thought so. What, is he after some old score you spent instead of splitting? Or just pissed you bailed on him? You were in the pawnshop, weren't you?'

The answer would be inadmissible, but Danny didn't see any point in speaking.

'You crack me up, you really do. You're clean? Good for you. Most people have been their whole lives. You want special treatment because you mended your ways?'

'The same treatment would be nice.'

'A citizen would call in and have a squad car come by, get the whole story. You can't do that, can you?'

Danny shook his head.

'And that tells me all I need to know. Time to pay the fucking consequences. Overdue, if you ask me.'

'Sean –'

'It's "Detective."' Nolan stood, brushing crumbs from his pants. 'And Danny, word to the wise. Since you called me, I'm not going to make much of this. I got better things to do than dig in decade-old robberies. But I'm gonna watch you. If you make one move out of line, and I mean one tiny little step, I'm going to pack your Irish ass off to Stateville.

Where you belong.' He tossed the crumpled napkin to the counter. 'Thanks for breakfast.'

The bell tinkled as he walked out, leaving Danny alone at the counter, officially between worlds. He put his head in his hands and sighed. In that moment, if he'd been given the chance, he might have taken back his whole life.

15. White Stars

Finding the bastard was proving harder than he'd expected.

Patrick had started at Murphy's. A blue-collar institution, the neighborhood bar was a dim, narrow place nestled between gray tract houses. Thick dust coated an unlit Guinness sign in the window. A battered pool table sat in back.

Smilin' Jimmy had pulled pints for thirty years without cracking the permanent scowl that had earned him the nickname. Patrick said hello, ordered a shot and a beer. Jimmy knew everything happening in the neighborhood, but you couldn't ask him outright. There was an art to it. To get him talking at all you had to start with horses, so Patrick listened – for what had to be the hundredth time – to Jimmy's failsafe system for picking winners. He knew better than to question why the inventor of a fail-safe system still needed to tend bar.

After Jimmy wound down, Patrick asked him, keeping his tone casual, like he was just inquiring after a friend.

'Evan McGann?' The bartender glowered. 'Big guy, used to box? Yeah, he's been in.'

'I heard he got out of Stateville recently. Haven't seen him since. I'd love to catch up with him.'

'Sure he'll be around.'

'I might have some work for him,' Patrick lied. 'He say where he was living?'

'Nope.' The bartender wiped the wood with a dingy rag. His knuckles were thick knots.

'Mention if he was in the neighborhood, at least?'

Jimmy stopped wiping, looked up. His eyes had the cool distance of those of a man who'd spent his life breaking up fights between young criminals. 'He didn't say, and I don't ask.'

Patrick caught the hint. Murphy's was a neighborhood bar. You didn't ask somebody like Jimmy to air dirty laundry. It was a violation of neutrality.

He spent the rest of the afternoon cruising his personal map of Chicago. Not for tourists, this one – a ragtag of storerooms piled with liquor boxes, off-track betting parlors, delis reeking of sauerkraut, shabby ranches with crank-lab kitchens. If Evan planned to start operating again, he'd need to let people know he was back in town. It wasn't like the movies, where everybody worked in a vacuum. There was a community, and success depended in part on whether people recognized your bona fides.

The afternoon was a bust. For a man who said he wanted to get back in the game, Evan had been surprisingly quiet. Patrick went home thinking he might have to spend the next few days just hanging out at Murphy's, waiting for Evan to wander in.

The next morning, Monday, it hit him. Evan had been strapped that day in Danny's kitchen.

There were lots of ways to get a gun. The safest was to steal one from a civilian. That way you knew the piece was clean – the cops could still nail you with weapons charges, but you weren't going to have to answer for a murder somebody else committed. But that took legwork, and more patience than Evan possessed. Nor could Patrick see him tracking down one of the black kids who sold out of the trunk of a car.

Which meant he'd used a pawn.

He found it on the third try. AAA PAWNSHOP, the sign read. ELECTRONICS GOLD JEWELS BOUGHT SOLD!!! What it didn't say was that Rashid did a bustling and illegal trade in stolen handguns.

'Patrick, my friend!' Second generation, the man spoke perfect English, but affected awkward sentence structure in a kind of reverse pretension that baffled Patrick. 'But of course I have seen him. We did business only last week.'

'What kind of business?'

'Your friend had fine jewelry for me, earrings and a necklace.'

'And you gave him a fair price?'

'Of course, of course. As always.'

'Some of it in trade,' he said. 'Right?'

The man hesitated, said nothing.

Patrick took out his wallet, made a show of rifling through the bills. 'Did my friend happen to say where he was staying?'

Rashid smiled. 'I feel as though he did, but I do not remember where, exactly.'

From then on it was only haggling.

Rashid hadn't known an exact address, just that Evan rented a place on the south end of Pilsen. Cold winds blew grim clouds as Patrick cruised up and down the streets, past taquerias and discount shops with signs in Spanish. If luck was with him, he'd spot Evan's old Mustang. If not, he'd come back later and try again.

As it happened, luck one-upped him. The sports car sat with its hood open outside a run-down bungalow. Evan leaned over the grille, peering at the engine, a cigarette dangling from his lips. He was so engrossed that he didn't react until Patrick pulled up practically on top of him. Then he turned fast, a wrench clenched in one hand, the muscles in his shoulders and arms tightened to strike.

Patrick stared at him, a street look, his features giving

nothing away. He revved the engine to a throaty rumble to underline the moment. Evan took a rag from his pocket and wiped grease off his hands, then finished a last drag on his cigarette and flicked it into the street. 'Come inside.' He turned and walked up the cracked sidewalk.

The house was old, with a faint smell of mildew. Patrick cased the place on instinct. No pictures on the wall. The only furniture in the living room was a weight bench, the bar loaded with 250 pounds of cast iron. He followed Evan down a dingy hallway to the kitchen. A card table and folding chairs sat in one corner. Without waiting for an invitation, Patrick pulled out one of the chairs and sat down, his feet up on the table.

Evan chuckled, shook his head. 'It's been, what, eight years?' From a cabinet he took a half-empty bottle of Jameson's and two highball glasses. He spent a couple of moments rummaging in a drawer, his back to Patrick, and came up with a kitchen towel. He set the lot on the table, poured two doubles, and took a seat. 'What's on your mind?'

Adrenaline made Patrick's skeleton hum like crystal, and he savored it. 'I know what you're doing to Danny.'

'Is that right?' Evan asked. 'He send you?'

'I'm here for him.' No point splitting hairs.

Evan drained half his whiskey, set the glass down lightly. 'It's between Danny and me.'

'He's not in the game anymore.'

'So I keep hearing.'

Patrick took his feet off the table, sat up. He picked up his drink, using the opportunity to reposition the chair. He needed enough clearance from the table to move quickly. 'Why are you doing this? You guys were like brothers.'

'There's a debt.' Evan's voice was flat but firm. 'Danny pays it, we go back to being brothers.'

'Balls to your debt. Nobody cheated you. You fucked up.'

Evan smiled. 'That what you came to say?'

'No.' He leaned forward, his gaze hard. 'I came to ask you nicely. Leave Danny alone.'

Evan knocked back the rest of his whiskey. His T-shirt had grease on it, and there were yellow sweat stains at his armpits. 'Go fuck your hat.'

Patrick smiled, took a sip of the whiskey. So much for doing it nicely. Time to dance. When he set the glass down, he kept his hand moving, casual-like, to his lap. He could feel the switchblade poke against his calf. 'What happened to you inside, man? Just get too used to being a bitch?'

Evan's eyes narrowed and his shoulders tensed, like he was going to make a move. 'Patrick, you shoot your mouth off. Have since you were a little brat used to follow us around like the sun shone out of Danny's ass.' He refilled his glass and topped Patrick's off. 'Someday you're going to get slapped for it.'

Patrick slid his hand from his lap, careful not to dip his shoulder. This was the delicate part. He lifted his foot to meet his hand halfway, staring at Evan the whole time. He had to get the blade out without tipping Evan off. His fingers wormed into the soft leather of his boot. 'Doesn't it mean anything to you, all the jobs you guys pulled together?' Negotiations were over, but he had to keep him distracted.

Evan smiled. 'It meant more before he sent you to hard-case me.'

His index finger touched the butt of the knife, and he pinched it gently, sliding it out. The grip felt warm from his skin. He braced his feet, one a little ahead, ready to lunge from the chair. The trick would be to do it easy; fast, but not hurried. 'How's this for hard case? You back off Danny, or I'll come at you with everything I have.' He pictured the moves. Click the knife open, spring forward, clock Evan with a left – it would be clumsy, but it would sting – get the blade to his throat. Dig in enough to bring a little blood. Evan wasn't the only bad boy on the playground.

Evan smiled, laid one hand on the table atop the rag. 'Fuck you, Patrick.'

Now.

He leapt to his feet, the chair falling backward as he thumbed the stud. The knife opened smooth and clean in his right hand. Evan's eyes tracked him, but he hadn't stirred from his seat. Taken by surprise. Patrick drew back his left fist as he moved, feeling the blood surge through his body, feeling unstoppable, unbeatable –

The whiskey bottle exploded. Something sucker-punched him, white-hot in his chest. It didn't hurt, but it stopped him like he'd hit an invisible wall. He stared at the table, at the green bottle fragments and the shattered Jameson's shield. Evan's hand rested on the kitchen towel, which was smoking from a ragged hole, the edges burned powder black.

Oh. No.

Evan stood in slow motion, a hint of a smile on his face. His right hand blurred in a backhanded slap. The world burst into black-and-white stars as Patrick felt himself falling. His back smacked the linoleum, the wind springing from his lungs. It was the first thing that hurt.

The second was Evan stepping on his knife hand, crunching down on his ohgodjesus his fingers, his mother-fucking fingers!

Then a steel toe caught his temple, and darkness smothered him like a heavy wool blanket.

16. Mute and Far Away

It was after three in the morning, and the diner was nearly empty. Evan took a booth in the smoking section and scanned the place. Two cops hunched over coffee mugs at the counter. A table of twenty-something drunks told too-loud stories that all began with 'You'se guys,' like they were in a Scorsese movie. The Italians outnumbered the Irish in Bridgeport these days, but that was nothing to brag about. There was a Buddhist temple where he remembered a Catholic church. Half the signs were in Spanish. And Asians had taken over McGuane Park, trying to pose and play basketball like the brothers.

Once he had his stake, it'd be time to move on.

The waitress called him honey and touched his shoulder, her tits straining against the cheap uniform. He thought about kicking it back to her, asking when she got off, but it didn't seem worth the trouble. He ordered, then lit a smoke and took it deep.

So Danny had sent Patrick after him. Surprise move.

Typical, though, of the guy he'd become. A couple of years wearing a white collar, and Danny had forgotten what was important. The thought chafed at Evan, the idea that while he'd been doing his time, the smug fucker was busily erasing his past.

You could read the *Trib* through the burger the waitress finally plunked down. The soup looked like cream of corn-starch. It reminded him of prison food, and he imagined Danny waiting in line at the Stateville cafeteria for a plastic plate of mac and cheese with mashed potatoes, lukewarm milk to wash it down. He liked that image. Liked it quite a bit. A six-by-nine cell might be exactly what Danny needed.

Something to think about.

He ate without relish, keeping one eye on the cops at the counter. They talked quietly, making the most of their break, radiating that fuck-off attitude. He noticed the waitress touched their shoulders, too, cock-teasing for a tip. Everybody had a hustle.

Outside, the lights of the skyline burned above the Mustang, and as he dug for his keys he stared at the towers of money and influence. They were mute, and far away.

The cold air stung – it would be Halloween in a week or so – but he rode with the windows open anyway. A jumble of tract housing and bungalows spilled off either side of Loomis Street. Johnny Cash sang to him, telling him there was a man coming round taking names, telling him everybody wouldn't be treated all the same, and cruising alone through the neighborhood that used to be his, rolling under the concrete monstrosity of the Stevenson Expressway, heading for a river that flowed backward, he knew it was true.

Brandenburg was an industrial demolition firm with buildings on both sides of the street, maybe fifteen acres of storage and equipment. A dock wall ran along the river, oily water licking at the rusted faces of barges floating like rotting giants. The company had built its business on smashing things that were no longer useful and then disposing of the junk. What better place?

He glided into the parking lot in neutral, headlights off. Security was probably a couple of rent-a-cops playing gin rummy through the midnight shift, but no need to draw attention. He stopped in a pool of darkness and thumbed the trunk release button.

The black tarp shone like wet ink by the light of the

trunk. He grunted a little getting started – the angle was a bitch – but once he had it out, shouldering the load was easy. Twice a week he squatted several times Patrick's weight.

A funny place, Chicago. Something like nine million people, forty thousand violent crimes a year, more goddamn cars than you could count, but in the middle of the night, in the middle of the city, you could find quiet. All he could hear was the sound of his own breathing and the wet slap of the river. Evan stepped onto the dock running along the river's edge. The water glowed black a few feet below.

He bent down, lowering his burden to the concrete. A boot stuck out of the tarp like it was waving good-bye. Evan put one foot against the middle of the bundle and shoved. The plastic scraped to the edge, friction fighting him, then the weight overbalanced and it slipped off. Half a heartbeat of silence later he heard a splash like a dark fish jumping, and Patrick was gone.

Evan shook out a cigarette, lit it. The ripples spread out from below, semicircles drifting to kiss a barge forty yards upriver. He could almost see the silhouettes of teenage boys reclining on the mountain of trash it bore, stolen forty-ouncers in their hands and the skyline filling their eyes. What had happened to those kids, him and Marty and Seamus?

And Patrick. And Danny.

Tonight's work was done. Tomorrow he'd plan his next move. It baffled him that Danny had sent Patrick after him. Could he really be so fucking dense after everything Evan had done to make his point?

Apparently talk wasn't getting through.

He'd have to find a clearer way to communicate.

17. So Easily Stripped

Exhaust billowed white in the cold air, but no one sat inside the Mercedes.

Danny let the door to the White Hen swing shut behind him, and took a swig of coffee. An E500 sedan, V8, sticker probably sixty grand, and some asshole had dashed in to buy milk and left it running. He could have it downtown in ten minutes, find a shop through Patrick, and make two weeks' pay before lunch.

Danny shook his head, turned away, hopped in his truck. Richard expected him, and with midday traffic, he'd be hard-pressed to make the twenty-minute drive in forty.

He did allow himself a last glance as he pulled onto Diversey.

Work had been tough. He had to keep his routine up, pretend like nothing was going on – however this nightmare shook out, he couldn't afford raised eyebrows. The morning had been spent overseeing the final winterizing of the Pike Street loft complex. The foreman, McCloskey, had it well in hand. The infrastructure of the whole building was in place, and the open walls sealed off with plastic. Tools and materials had been stored, and by the end of the week, the site would be chained up. The unfinished loft complex and the construction trailer would remain untouched through winter's lonely haul, waiting, like the rest of the city, for spring to resurrect them.

As he turned onto Lakeshore, the wind lashed steel waves against the rocks, spray climbing tall as a man. It suited his mood. Nearly a week since he'd found Evan in his kitchen.

It wouldn't be long before he showed up demanding an answer. Nearly a week, and Danny still had no plan. All he'd managed to do was remind a detective he existed. That, and make Karen suspicious. He'd thought he was playing it close to his chest, but she knew him too well.

'Nightmares again, baby?' She'd touched the dark circles under his eyes and smiled tenderly at him in the bathroom mirror.

'Just busy,' he said, and put on his game face. She'd nodded, but he knew her mind was still chewing on it.

Not telling her was eating at him. It wasn't his way to hide things from her. Just the opposite. She came at things from different angles, fresh viewpoints, and together there hadn't been many problems they couldn't solve.

But the most dangerous one of the last seven years? That, he didn't dare share.

Wednesday, and the lawn crews had descended to service the wealthy. Day laborers called to one another in Spanish as they pushed mowers and raked leaves. A white guy with a clipboard sat in the heated cab of the pickup outside Richard's house. Late October, and Danny knew the workers must be getting nervous, all too aware that business would shut down for the winter. He had a flash of coming home in the afternoon to find his old man at the kitchen table, a cigarette smoldering untouched in an ashtray, and knowing that another construction company had screwed them; that this winter, like last, Dad would be getting up at four in the morning to help Kevin O'Bannon with the snowplow.

Richard answered the door in golf pants and a polo shirt, like he planned on hitting the back nine after lunch. 'What took so long?'

'Lakeshore was bumper-to-bumper.'

Richard nodded. 'Come in. Ignore this mess.' The way he said it, Danny wasn't sure if he was talking about the leaves on his lawn or the guys raking it. 'You bring those contracts?'

'Yeah.' He stepped in, shutting the front door behind him. Richard was already halfway down the hall, and Danny followed him into the kitchen. Skylights brought autumn sun flooding across granite countertops and stainless appliances. With two ovens, two sinks, and a massive chef's prep island in the center, the kitchen could service a restaurant, but he noticed the copper pans hanging over the chopping block had dust on them.

'You look everything over? I don't want to find out I got rogered again.'

The last time Richard had gotten rogered it had been because he'd ignored Danny's cost estimates, but Danny kept that to himself. 'They're clean.'

His boss nodded, sipping espresso as he flipped through the documents. 'How's Pike Street?' he asked, not looking up.

'McCloskey will have it locked down by the end of the week.'

'Good. And we've got him on contract for the spring?'

Danny started. 'Huh?'

'McCloskey. We've got him set for the spring?'

Danny remembered his conversation with the foreman in the trailer, how good it had felt to treat him like a man, to explain the situation instead of just lay down the law the way so many managers had laid it on his father. 'We're keeping McCloskey on over the winter, remember?'

Richard didn't look up from his papers. 'Yeah, I thought it over, ran some numbers, and it's not going to work.'

Had he heard right? 'What?'

'Jeff Teller has the other projects under control, and he

costs less. We'll dump McCloskey and his crew for the winter, pick 'em back up in spring.'

Danny's mind was racing. He'd promised that no one would lose his job. 'Teller's good, but not as good as McCloskey. And we could use help prepping next spring's bids.'

Richard shrugged, his mind only half in the conversation. 'I don't need a foreman to tell me how to throw a bid.'

Danny tried a different tack. 'You know, McCloskey's pretty connected. We let him go, we may not get him back.'

'The market's not going to be much better then. Besides, we can always find somebody else.'

There was no way around it. Danny said, 'I gave them my word that we had work for them.'

His boss's head snapped up, surprise on his face. 'You did what?'

'I told McCloskey the deal, why we had to shut Pike down for now, and I told him that there was work for him and his crew.'

'Why would you do that?' Richard squinted as if trying to see Danny more clearly.

'Don't you remember? We talked about it and agreed to keep them on.'

Richard shook his head. 'I never said anything like that. I might have said that it would be *nice* to keep them on, but that's all.'

Danny fought a sudden urge to break his boss's nose. 'We were sitting in the conference room. Reviewing budgets. You wanted to let them go, and I suggested we could keep them on half-time to get them through the winter. You agreed.'

Richard closed the contract and looked at him appraisingly. Danny met the stare unblinking. Finally his boss sighed. 'I know how you feel. But you know how rough things have been. Believe you me, nobody's been bleeding more than I have.' He took a sip of coffee and reopened the contracts, spinning the pen between his fingers.

Danny stood trying to think of something to say, his eyes ranging over the rich furnishings as if for the first time. A framed photo of Richard on his yacht, a silly captain's hat on his head. The Italian cappuccino machine. A laptop, casually placed half on, half off the counter.

With a scribble, Richard signed his name on the contracts and pushed them to Danny. 'Here. Make sure Pike Street is locked down tight. Don't want it turning into a homeless camp.'

Through the bay window, Danny could see two Mexicans in hunting vests and fingerless gloves bundling branches that had fallen in last week's storm. He wondered what he was doing on this side of the glass.

Later, heading south in his truck, Danny wasn't sure why he decided to skip the Michigan Avenue exit and continue south to I-55; why he got off at Archer; why he found himself driving through Bridgeport. But it might have had something to do with his boss standing in golf clothes, using a gold pen to cut blue collars.

It wasn't the first time he'd driven through the neighborhood since leaving, but in the past, he'd blitzed along, consciously not looking too hard to the left or right, avoiding the rawest of the old wounds. This time he went slowly and kept his eyes open, intent on yanking scabs.

Things had changed. Things had stayed the same.

Tan and orange bungalows still crowded sidewalks bordered by sagging chain link. The Gothic spires of half a dozen massive churches rose over faded tract housing. White Sox flags hung limp under hazy skies. Smokestacks and skyscrapers loomed at the edge of the horizon, blurring like fever dreams.

He pulled up at a red light as a group of Hispanic kids swaggered along the sidewalk. They wore long basketball jerseys and bright sneakers, hats cocked to mark gang allegiances. A fair-skinned kid with close-shorn hair eyed Danny's SUV, his lips opening in a threatening grin that revealed gold-capped teeth.

So there were still young lions in Bridgeport after all.

Danny stared back, putting all his street weight into it. It wasn't a look you earned in a North Shore private school like the one Richard's son attended. It required less gentle surroundings.

The kid held his gaze, slowing so that his crew moved past. For a few seconds they watched each other, a young predator and an old one, both bathed in the amber light of late afternoon. Then the kid smiled again, trying for scorn but not quite getting it, turned and pimp-strutted back to his friends. Danny watched him go.

Had he kept all of this from Karen to protect her?

Or because he was thinking of doing it?

Was that why he had come here, why his eyes had hungered for the class differences between himself and Richard? His new life, it couldn't be that thin, so easily stripped of veneer.

Was he just a thief with a better address?

The light changed. He turned the truck and steered north.

18. Safety

Salsa was hopping.

Leaning over the balcony, trying to take some weight off her feet – the heels were killing her – Karen had a prime view of the dance floor. The crowd was young, most of them midtwenties, the girls in skintight dresses with sparkles that ended only where flesh began, the men sweating through black linen shirts. Lasers cut rainbow swaths in the swirling cigarette smoke. It was a party bar, and people would stick till the lights came on, throwing down drinks with the accelerating pace of a dreamer who fears awakening.

She straightened, let her head fall back, rolling it from side to side to ease the muscles. The smoke had given her a headache, and she wanted to be rid of it before she went home. Danny had been withdrawn lately, private. Something was obviously bothering him, but he kept it to himself. Maybe if she slipped out early, showed up with a bottle of wine and a naughty expression, she could loosen him up.

She smiled at the thought, stepped away from the railing to weave through the upstairs. When she'd taken over managing the place, the first thing she'd done was convert the balcony to a VIP room. A certain breed of guy would eagerly drop three hundred bucks on a twenty-dollar bottle of Stoli to impress a date in a low-cut dress, and in one stroke she'd upped the bar's take 40 percent. Which made it her job to ensure that everyone upstairs felt like Very Important People. She moved through the crowd, chatting with regulars, touching men's biceps and complimenting women on their shoes. It was her routine, but something felt off tonight. She had a weird tingle in her neck. Some animal instinct, like she was being watched. Not gawked at – she was used to that. This was different. It felt like she was being studied.

Hunted.

The word popped into her mind of its own accord, and her skin went cold. She stopped and glanced around, eyes darting over men in Armani, women sipping Cosmos, an anorexic blonde checking her makeup in a compact. Nothing to raise alarms. She moved to the railing, looked down at the main floor, scanning the sweating mass below. A long-legged girl spun and swirled her skirt amid a triangle of men wearing expressions of pained lust. A couple leaned against the column by the bathroom, locked in a late-night kiss, his thigh riding between her knees. For an instant, a lighter flared, near the back wall. The glow revealed a hard face framed by brown curls. He stared directly at her. Not at the VIP area. At her.

Then he snapped the lighter shut and disappeared.

She squinted, trying to pick him out again. The light bouncing off the dance floor left her night blind, the rear wall a blur of inseparable shapes with way too many cigarettes to make his stand out. But someone had been there. She was sure of it.

Who was he? He had seemed, in that split second, strangely familiar. An old acquaintance? Her nervousness suggested not. Whoever he was, she felt sure they weren't friends.

'Karen!'

She jumped, spun around fast, heart pounding. Two of her regulars smiled down at her; Louis, a tall, elegant black man with his arm threaded around his partner Charles's waist. 'Join us for a drink?'

Adopting her best hostess smile, Karen turned from the

dance floor. If she wanted to get out early, she didn't have time to jump at shadows.

This was what job security looked like in the bar biz: ten past twelve on a weeknight, and still a line outside the door. The crowd was rowdy, already amped up on drink and eager to get in from the cold. She pushed through them, looking for Hector. Normally she walked to her car alone, but the stranger inside had made her nervous.

She found the bouncer at the head of the line, glowering down on a scrawny guy with a goatee, giving him the full impact of 250 pounds of tattooed muscle. 'You gonna wanna think about that again, hoss.'

'Hey, screw you, Cheech.' The man's face was red, though with booze or anger Karen couldn't tell. 'I told you, I just stepped out to make a call.'

'What's going on?' Karen asked, using her manager voice.

'This gentleman don't want to wait in line,' Hector said.

Up close now, Karen could see that Goatee's eyes were all pupil. Ecstasy, probably, maybe with a little meth to give it an edge. Normally she wouldn't care; half the crowd was hopped on something. But nobody messed with her staff. She shook her head. 'Get him out of here.'

The bouncer grinned. He clamped meaty hands on the man's shoulders, spun him around, and walked him protesting past the line. As he did, the crowd surged forward, a couple of similarly dressed guys, his friends maybe, pushing for the now unmanned door.

'Shit. Hector!'

The bouncer turned in time to see the men dash inside amid the thronging crowd. He growled and bounded back to the head of the line.

'Where's Rodney?' Karen asked.

'He wasn't feeling good, so I said I'd cover for him.'

Hector looked at her sheepishly. 'It was only for a couple hours, didn't think you'd mind.'

She grimaced. 'It's just I was going to ask you to walk me to my car.'

Hector pulled out his radio. 'Lemme get Kevin or Joe.'

They were both bartenders. The club was packed, everybody vying to get their last couple of rounds in. Pulling a bartender would slow things down, make everybody's life harder, and cut the take. All for a weird feeling. She felt silly all of a sudden.

'Forget it,' she said. 'I'll be okay.'

'You sure?'

She nodded, pulled out the pepper spray key ring Danny insisted she carry. 'Sure thing.'

He winked at her, turned back to the line of patrons.

Karen stepped out from behind the velvet rope and started down Ontario. Goose bumps massed on her exposed shoulders. Soon it would be time for jackets, gloves, layers. The unpleasant accoutrements of a Chicago winter.

The man from the bar haunted her. Who was he? Years of dealing with drunks had honed her instincts, and something about that guy had given her a bad feeling.

As if on cue, she heard footsteps behind her. A careful walk. The steps heavy and muffled. A man's stride. Had she been foolish not to pull one of the bartenders? She quickened her step and gripped the pepper spray more tightly. Part of her wanted to whirl around, but she was afraid of what she'd see. She could feel her heart, the thumping swift against her ribs. Should she run? The heels would slow her down; if someone was following her, the man from the bar, he'd catch her easily.

She turned onto Franklin. The Explorer was in an alley a block down. If she could get to it, she'd be safe.

The footsteps followed, closer than ever. She didn't think

she'd make it, not at this rate. Mouth dry, she spun, raising the pepper spray in her right hand, her left bracing against the building. A tall man walked toward her, face cloaked in shadow. Her hand shook. She opened her mouth to yell – this was a public street, there were people just down the block, surely someone would help her. The man took another step. Just as she was about to shout, the headlights from a passing car fell across him.

Deep wrinkles cut his forehead, and his eyes were sunken. His walk was careful, all right – geriatrically so. The gentleman had to be in his seventies. He stared far away, pulling a tan raincoat tighter as he passed.

She snorted, almost laughed, the tension draining away. Why had she gotten so jumpy because someone on the floor looked up at the VIP lounge? That was what made it a VIP lounge – it was where everyone wanted to be.

She shook her head and continued. The alley wasn't technically parking, but cops turned a blind eye for industry staff as long as no one complained. She could see a gleam off the truck's windshield, right where she'd left it. She started toward it, thinking of how to tell Danny the story, to convey her goofy fear. She decided that it would be in the details – the old guy, his wrinkles, that perv raincoat.

A shadow detached itself from the wall and reached for her.

She had time to gasp, to jerk the pepper spray up, knowing this time it was real. He was almost on her before her thumb found the button. She jammed it down to spit a stream of blinding poison.

Nothing happened.

He grabbed her arm, twisted it backward. Her shoulder and elbow blazed as she spun. A gloved hand stifled her scream with the taste of sour leather and cigarettes. She felt the keys yanked from numbing fingers.

'First,' his breath hot against her ear, 'you have to take the safety off.'

She could have cried at the thought of it, the way the button had to slide sideways before it could be pushed. It'd all just happened so fast. Horrible images flashed through her mind, thoughts of ending up a cautionary tale, used and abandoned in an alley, panties twisted around her ankles. She struggled against him, trying to tear free, but he was like machinery, his muscles pneumatic in their power.

'Relax, kitten.' He sounded amused. 'I'm not going to hurt you tonight. But you should be more careful. Chicago can be a dangerous place for a woman.'

Before she could process his words he pushed her, still holding one arm, as if they were dancing. When she reached the end of her steps he let go, and the momentum sent her sprawling to the ground. Gravel dug cruelly into her legs, and she yelped, not a proper scream, just surprise and pain. She was free. She raised her arms to ward off her attacker and drew in a breath to shriek.

And realized she was alone.

The guy, whoever he was, had walked away. At the mouth of the alley he stopped, his back to her. He had shoulders like a football player. He pulled something apart between his hands, and she heard the clatter of keys on the pavement.

Then he stepped out onto Franklin and was gone.

Karen wanted to cry, to sit in the dirt of the alley and bawl, to let out the scream that had been building in her. But she thought of the movies, how she hated it when the bimbo just lay there. Life had been safe and soft the last couple of years, but she'd grown up with two older brothers, neither unfamiliar with the wrong side of the law, and they'd taught her to take her licks.

Besides, she hadn't been hurt. Hadn't been raped. Hadn't

even been robbed. She didn't understand. But understanding, like crying, could wait.

One hand on the dirty metal of the Dumpster, she pulled herself up. Pain raked down the back of her thigh, but her legs held. There would be some bruises – what her brothers had delighted in calling raspberries – but nothing broken.

Correct that. One heel had snapped when she fell.

Somehow that made her laugh, actually laugh out loud, standing in the middle of the alley. The laughter was hard and high, and it didn't feel right; she could taste the curdle of panic in it.

Get it together, Karen. Don't go hysterical in the middle of the alley. Pick up your keys, run to the car, lock the doors, start the engine.

Then get hysterical.

She hobbled to the sidewalk and retrieved the keys. Down the street, she could see a group of a dozen partiers, the girls' thighs flashing, the men's laughter loud. They were less than a block down. They seemed half a world away.

The headlights on Lakeshore Drive blurring like those long-exposure photographs you saw on brochures.

The Explorer surging when she mashed the accelerator, substituting speed for control.

The soft green glow of the dashboard lights.

The snap of the radio dial as she turned it off.

An airbrushed sign for a nail salon on Belmont.

Trees flanking the sidewalks, the rustle of shadows cast by streetlights.

Then suddenly she was home, looking over her shoulder to park the truck, her blinker on as though everything were normal. She felt snapped back into her body. Like she'd been trailing behind it on a kite string. Their apartment was twenty yards away. She could see through the bay window to the living room, where a light burned, and it made her feel naked. Could anyone look in so easily? Did they walk around unaware of the eyes watching them? Had the man been watching her?

Was he still?

The thought tore through her like ten thousand volts of adrenaline. She whipped her head around, sure he stood beside the car.

There was nothing there.

Stupid, stupid girl.

She yanked the keys out of the ignition and threw the door open. Stepped out, forgot the broken heel, lost her balance, one knee slamming into the door frame, white-hot pain jamming up her leg. She kicked off the heels and stepped to the grass, limping as fast as she could. Front door. Light blue key. In, slam, lock. Stairwell door. Dark blue key. Up the stairs.

She made it halfway before the tears caught her. Fear and relief mingled and twisted into an emotion too raw to have a name of its own. Sobbing, she pulled herself the rest of the way up using the bannister, heard the door to their apartment swinging open, saw Danny framed against the darkness, a running silhouette. When he reached her, she threw her arms around him, the tears coming freely now, her fingers catching handfuls of his shirt, not so much hugging him as holding on.

They sat in the kitchen with all the lights on. The track lights, the one over the stove. The pantry door open and that light burning as well. She could feel the warmth of the tea through the cup, the warmth of the whiskey in her gut. Danny had his hands over hers, and it helped.

She'd told him about it, the words spilling all over the hallway, and he had guided her inside and listened as she told it again, not saying anything except that it was over now, it was okay, they were going to be okay. She'd let the tears come, and his T-shirt had a dark spot on one shoulder. She felt better for the crying. And for being home, with all three locks thrown.

'God, I just feel so . . .' She paused, looking for the right word, choosing the simplest. 'Stupid.'

'It wasn't your fault.'

'Parking in the alley, not having anyone walk me to the car . . .'

'Shhh . . .' He stroked her hands. 'You're sure you're okay? You don't want to go to the hospital?'

She shook her head. 'I'm fine. Just shaken up.' She tried a smile, knowing it looked thin. 'Really, I'm fine. Just ruined a skirt and a pair of heels when I fell. He didn't even take my purse.'

'What scared him off?'

'I don't know. I don't think anything. He just let me go.'

'Huh?' He looked up at her. 'What do you mean?'

'I tried to use the pepper spray you got me, but I forgot to take the safety off, and then he twisted my arm and took it away. So many thoughts were going through my head, you know, bad things, was he only after my purse, or was he going to rape me, was he some sort of psycho. But then he just kind of shoved me, and I slipped, and when I looked up, he was walking away.'

That memory burned brightest, the muscles of his shoulders cutting clean lines against the streetlight. She'd been certain she would see him advancing, his hands unfastening his belt. She shook her head, the two images, one real, one imagined, overlaid in her mind. Danny was staring at her, the weirdest expression on his face.

'What?' she asked.

'He just let you go?'

'Yeah. Well, first he said something.' She laughed

nervously. 'He told me that Chicago was dangerous for a woman.'

'He . . . what?'

She repeated herself, wondering what was going on in his head, why he looked so spooked. Danny sat quiet for a moment.

'Did you get a look at him?'

'Not really. I mean, I saw him in the club, but only barely, and it was dark in the alley. He was a bit taller than you. Really strong. Curly hair. He had gloves on.' She paused, remembering. 'They smelled like cigarettes.'

'Christ.' He stood up suddenly, hesitated, and then went to the counter for the bottle of scotch. Grabbed her glass and one for him. She could see that his mind was working, flying over something, but he focused on pouring, the amber liquid splashing up to the mark for doubles.

'What is it?'

'Huh?' He looked up, his expression startled. 'Oh, nothing, baby. I'm just so glad you're okay.'

'You sure that's all?'

'Yeah.' He set the bottle on the table, and sat down himself. For a moment, it seemed like a thought was playing in his mind, like he had something to tell her. But she could see the moment pass, and when he caught her staring at him, he smiled softly, concern and resolve in his eyes. 'I guess I'm just getting scared after the fact. You know, the way your mom used to get when she'd find out you'd done something stupid years ago. That's all.'

There was more, but she didn't care. Not right now. He pushed the drink toward her. 'Go ahead,' he said. 'It'll help you sleep.'

She picked up the glass, not really wanting it, but hating the thought of lying awake till dawn. The burn pushed away all other sensations, and that she did want. 'I think I'm going to take a shower.'

He nodded.

'Will you –' She paused, feeling self-conscious. 'Will you come sit with me? I don't want to be alone.'

'Of course.' His smile wrapped her up safe as a blanket in fall. 'And, baby – I promise. I'll never let anyone hurt you. Whatever I have to do to protect you, I will.' His voice firm.

Like he had made up his mind about something.

19. Exactly the Point

Evan tossed the butt out the window while he waited for the light to change. A kid in a fluorescent T-shirt stopped asking passersby if they had a moment for Greenpeace long enough to glare at him. Evan stared back, and the kid quickly looked away.

When red turned green he floored it, the Mustang roaring like it'd been kicked. He was finally out of the stretch of yuppie boutiques on Halsted, but on his way into Boystown, home to most of the city's fags and the corner where Danny wanted to meet. He powered past a drugstore, a liquor warehouse, and across Belmont before the traffic stopped again. On the sidewalk two stacked guys, one white, one black, walked with their hands in each other's back pocket. Funny to see. Inside it was different. Not like TV, or mostly not. Die-hard queers aside, in prison going gay was almost a way to pass the time. Another way the place humiliated you. Guys blowing each other just to break the monotony. Except you had to wonder, you spend long enough sucking off your cellie, at some point how different were you from the guys on the street here?

Evan had broken the nose of the first asshole who'd tried his luck, and stuck to jerking off.

Two blocks up, the car still creeping, he spotted Danny kicking back at a bus stop, his arms up on the bench's back. He had the newspaper in his lap, but wasn't reading it, keeping his eyes up and moving, scanning the traffic. Danny Carter, always too smart for his own good. He'd spotted Evan, but waited until the Mustang pulled in front of the bench before standing up slow and walking to the car. Evan leaned over to flip the lock. 'Hey, partner.'

Danny shot him a cold look as he climbed in. 'Drive, asshole. Take Lakeshore north.'

Evan chuckled, turned off Halsted onto a residential street, cut through an alley, and wound back toward the lake. Decided to ignore Danny's expression now that it looked like he might be doing the right thing. The guy had reached out to him, after all, calling Murphy's and leaving a message with the bartender. That made it his move. What would it be? Play the hard case, tell him if he ever laid a hand on Karen again, blah blah blah? It didn't seem his style, but as he kept being reminded, this wasn't the guy he'd grown up with.

They merged onto Lakeshore, the Mustang purring as it muscled past a CTA bus with an ad for some computer thing on the side. They were two miles up, Evan thinking about turning on the radio, when Danny spoke.

'Get off here.'

Evan squinted at him, decided to go along, and exited at Montrose. Danny gestured to the east, toward the lake, and Evan pulled into a parking lot. Maybe thirty cars, most of them pretty hot, Beemers and Benzes.

'Kill it. Let's take a walk.'

The lakefront was crowded with people biking and Rollerblading, a few jogging. A couple of old white dudes messed around on their sailboats in the marina, playing Jimmy Buffet, pretending they were in Margaritaville in June instead of Chicago a week before Halloween. In the summer the bike path was mobbed with chicks in bikinis, but now everybody wore a sweatshirt. Danny walked ahead, steering them past the marina, out to a point that jutted into the lake. It was a quiet spot, thin grass tapering to rocks at the water's edge. Danny stepped up on a boulder and stared out to the horizon like he was looking for answers. The air was still, the water calm.

Evan took out his smokes, tapped one free. Flicked the wheel on the silver Zippo, lit the cigarette, and held the flame a moment longer than necessary, looking at the lake through the flame, like he was setting it on fire. 'So we're here. Now what? You want to cuddle, watch the sunset?'

Danny didn't turn. 'Let's talk about the rules.'

'Rules?'

'The rules of the job.'

Look at that. Been trying to make a point to the man for two weeks, and he'd finally gotten through. Apparently Karen was the lever to move Danny's world. Worth remembering. 'So you're in.'

'Not much choice, right? I got your point.'

'Good.' He kept his tone light, with just a hint of steel in it.

'You want my help, though, there are three rules.'

'Yeah?' Just like Danny, to be talking rules instead of thinking about how much they stood to score. More worry than joy.

'First off, nobody gets hurt. Not a scratch, you hear? Especially not Tommy.'

'Who the fuck is Tommy?'

Danny sighed, glanced over his shoulder. 'Tommy's the boy, Evan. The one you want to kidnap. What, were you going to call his father and say, "I've got that kid that hangs out in your house"?'

Evan made quick fists to pop his knuckles, then forced a smile. As long as Danny played along, he'd handle him gently.

'Next,' Danny continued, his eyes once again on the rolling gray of the lake, 'is that you listen to me. You want my help? Fine. My way. No messing about on the job. All right?'

He nodded, thinking, *Now how you going to control that, Danny-boy?* But all he said was, 'The third?'

'The third rule is that this squares us. We do this, I never see you again. If I do, even once, I say to hell with the consequences and call the cops, and we go down together. You and I,' his tone still even, no anger in it, 'we're done.'

Evan kept his mouth shut. His hopes of brotherhood had died just before Patrick did. The guy with him now was only an angle to be played.

'All right.' Evan raised the smoke to his lips, stared at the horizon himself, wondering what Danny saw out there that was so damn fascinating.

'One more thing.'

The tone should have warned him, but he'd already dropped his guard. Danny swung around faster than Evan could get his arm up. The fist caught him square on the chin, snapping the cigarette, the world did that quick bounce-and-settle thing, and then, shit, his foot slipped on the wet grass. He fell, arms flailing. Hitting the ground smacked the wind out of him, and he felt the rage taking hold, all you had sometimes, the animal readiness to kill or be killed.

But Danny didn't press the attack. He stepped back to the boulder's edge, shaking out his hand. 'That's for Karen, motherfucker.'

Even before he'd gotten his breath back, Evan had his hand on the pistol tucked in his waistband. He started to draw. And then remembered where they were. Lincoln Park. Probably two hundred witnesses, and nowhere to hide.

Evan let go of the gun, took a breath. Now he knew why they'd come here. Propping himself up on an elbow, he laughed. He'd been outplayed. Old school, the way the Danny he used to know might have done it.

Forget it. This time.

Danny stepped forward, holding out one hand, and Evan took it to pull himself up.

'Let's go to work.' Danny's tone all business.

'Now?'

'Now.'

As they pulled into Evanston the gloomy humidity had finally given way to one of those noiseless October rains that soaked the hell out of everything. Rotting leaves tattooed the asphalt orange and brown. The bossman's house – Richard, it turned out his name was – looked cheery, porch lights glowing on either side of the carved oak door.

'Don't turn off the engine.' Danny stared out the window. Some of the confidence was gone from his voice, like seeing the actual house had taken something out of him.

'Why not?'

'We're not staying. This neighborhood pays for a security service to patrol, and we don't want them stopping by.'

Evan nodded. Rich cunts never failed. The more money they had, the higher the walls, the brighter the lights. Like hanging a target around their neck – just made it easier to spot a score. He rubbed at his chin. It was a little sore, but not likely to show a bruise. 'So what are we doing?'

'Looking at the house. Where do you want to go in?'

'Right now?' He was surprised, but game.

'Of course not.' Danny looked over at him. 'We don't even know who's inside.'

Evan pretended he'd been testing Danny. 'That's what I thought. So how about knocking on the front door sometime when we know the kid is alone? Grab him when he answers it?'

'Walk up with masks on? We look a little old for trick-or-treaters.' Danny sat silent for a moment, then said, 'We'll go in the back, break in.'

'House like this, there's got to be an alarm system.'

'There is, but Maria – Richard's maid – kept setting it off. They only use it at night now.'

Evan nodded. 'When?'

'Next week. We'll do it one day after school.'

'Do we need to worry about the maid?'

'I know when she comes.' Danny turned from the window. 'Let's go, before a friendly neighbor notices us.'

Evan put the car in drive and rolled forward, tires whisking on the pavement. He cracked the window to listen to the rain. 'Most alarms have a panic button, right?'

'Yeah.'

'How do we make sure the kid doesn't get to it first?'

'Or for that matter dial 911? I'll think about it.' Danny turned around to glance behind them.

'You do that. Meanwhile, I got a question for you.' Evan smiled.

'Yeah?'

'You hungry?'

It turned out to be beer they both wanted. Four or five bottles of Old Style apiece smoothed the rough edges between them to a tolerable level. They had the place to themselves, just a couple of Mexicans behind the counter paying them no mind. Evan finished the last bite of his second chili dog, crumpling the wax paper and dropping it on the counter.

'I love beer in the afternoon.' He smiled. 'Remember ditching school with Marty and the Jimmy brothers and smuggling beer into the soccer games?'

Danny smiled, too, it seemed like in spite of himself. 'The bleachers at St Mary's Academy. All those girls in shorts.'

'Yeah. And Marty down on the sidelines, offering sports massages.'

They both laughed, tipped their bottles back. Halfway through the swallow, though, Evan saw a little catch in Danny's face. Like he'd realized he shouldn't be enjoying himself. They sat in silence for a moment, Danny spinning his beer bottle on its base, his eyes far away.

'We'll need somewhere to stow him,' Evan said. 'The kid.'

Danny looked around, like he wanted to confirm nobody else was listening. Nervous as ever. 'Yeah.'

'Someplace quiet. Where even if something goes wrong' – that got Danny's attention – 'and he makes some noise, it won't trip us up.'

Danny nodded, didn't say anything.

Evan took another sip of beer. 'I'm thinking an even million.'

'Too much.'

'Bullshit. You see that house?'

'It's a five-bedroom, not the Playboy Mansion. Man doesn't have stacks of hundreds in a suitcase.'

'How many bedrooms you have growing up?'

'That's not the point.'

'Bullshit.' Evan put the bottle down hard, and Danny looked up at him. 'That's exactly the point. Don't you remember how it works? Guys like that, they make sure that the rest of us stay where we are. They hire us to work shitty jobs at minimum wage so we can rent one-bedroom tract houses with no windows. Tell us the world needs ditchdiggers, but bundle their kids off to private school. And they build jails for when we get upset about being on the shit side of that bargain. Fuck that. I'll play it my way. You used to, too, before you started pretending to be somebody else.'

Danny snorted. 'What, because I have a job I'm supposed to vote Republican? Fuck you, man. It doesn't work that way.'

'How does it work, then?'

'It doesn't work.' Danny leaned back. 'Your way. It doesn't work. You think putting window dressing on it makes it okay? You're a thief, Evan. Blame society, or the cops, or your father, that's all fine, but it doesn't change the fact that you're a criminal. And at the end of the day, criminals get caught.'

Evan felt the vein in his temple throb, the purr and rush of blood. He fought to keep his voice cool. 'My father was an asshole. This has nothing to do with him.'

They held the stare for a moment, then Danny put his hands up for peace. 'Yeah, all right.'

Evan leaned back, poured the rest of the beer down his throat. Lukewarm, it tasted like mop water.

'Listen, though,' Danny said. 'I'm right about the money. We ask for too much, he's going to call the cops.'

'So how much?'

'Two-fifty would be the safe play.'

'Half a mill,' Evan said.

Danny nodded reluctantly. 'Also, we need somebody else. To watch him.'

'Why not just tape him up and leave him be? Come in once a day to give him some water, let him take a leak.'

'Jesus, Evan. He's a little kid.'

'So? It's only a couple of days.'

Danny glared at him, a look that started the old smoldering, that made Evan want to reach across the table and smack the lips right off his face. 'I said nobody gets hurt. Leaving a twelve-year-old kid duct-taped in the dark counts, all right?'

'So you watch him.'

'I can't. I have to act like everything's normal. And you can't either, because the biggest risk is going to be when we take him. It's best that after that, he not be around either of us. Make it harder to describe anything useful to the cops once we let him go.'

'So who?'

'I don't know. Patrick, maybe.' Danny shook his head. 'I hate to bring him into this.'

Evan held his gaze level, gave nothing up. Danny wasn't the only one with a game face. He'd find out about Patrick sooner or later, but no point queering things now.

The man had a point, though. He didn't need to spend three days babysitting a brat. But they'd want someone they could control. Not anyone who might try to play them. *Boom.* There it was. 'I got it.'

'Who?'

'Girl of mine. I've known her awhile.'

'She'll be okay with this?'

Evan nodded. 'She's getting desperate. She'll do what she's told.'

'All right. I think I know a place.'

'Yeah? Quiet?'

Danny nodded. 'Let's check it this weekend. Sunday morning.'

'Why not now?'

'Because now I'm going home.' Danny stood and put on his jacket, soft black leather that looked new. 'Good night.'

Evan nodded to him, watched him walk out the door. Danny paused and looked both ways, like he was taking snapshots of the street, and then strode across the parking lot toward Belmont.

'Welcome back,' Evan said, his voice low.

20. Somewhere to Be

'This is Patrick. Give me one good reason to care that you called.'

Danny cursed. He'd tried three times already with no luck. If he knew Patrick, the man was right now curled up in a bed with too many pillows, plotting his escape from the girl sleeping next to him.

He leaned forward to hang up the phone and over-reached, scraping his bruised knuckles against the wall. The sudden sensation made him wince, and then smile. Popping Evan had felt good.

Not half so good as what he'd like to do to the guy, though.

Thursday night, when Karen had come in crying, Danny had been ready to beat Evan to death with a fucking baseball bat, damn the consequences. For her sake he'd kept his cool. Said soothing things. Put her to bed and crawled in beside her, stroking her hair until she fell asleep.

Then he'd turned to face the red glow of the alarm clock and imagined shooting his childhood friend in the face.

No, not imagined – planned. Figured out how to do it. Funny, all that time spent trying to find a loophole and he'd never really considered the most direct option, the one Evan would have come to first. But he considered it that night.

That night, a dark alley and a pistol with a grip-taped handle seemed like the answer.

But by morning he'd known better. The last time he'd held a gun he'd been thirteen, wilding with a rust-spotted piece Joey Biggs had snuck from under the sweaters in his dad's closet. They'd strutted the alleys popping at crows and beer cans and the occasional factory window. Kids' stuff a thousand miles from pointing at a human being and pulling the trigger. From watching Evan's head explode.

And in truth, it didn't matter. Because once he got past the anger and actually thought about things, killing Evan wasn't an out anyway. The moment the cops found his body, *Detective* Sean Nolan would look up from his desk and wonder who might want to be rid of Evan McGann. About five seconds later squad cars would be rolling up to their condo, and the rest would just be foreplay to the fucking Danny would take. No, killing Evan wasn't an out.

Nor could he go to the cops, confess everything, and take his chances. At this point, all they had on Evan was maybe a parole violation. A weapons charge if Danny got lucky. Whereas Evan could place Danny at the pawnshop, where a man had been shot and crippled, a woman beaten half to death. His new life would disappear like smoke.

If he did the job, he protected Karen. Hell, he protected Tommy and Richard, too, by controlling the situation, making sure no one got hurt. And at the end of it, he could go back to a regular life.

It was a lousy option, but it was the smart play.

A door opened down the hall, and he heard the hardwood squeak as Karen walked toward the kitchen. He'd been hoping to leave while she was in the shower. He scooped up his keys, turned as she walked in.

'You going?'

'Work.' The lie stung him. There had been too many lately, but what choice was there?

'It's Sunday. You're working too hard, baby.' She smiled at him, one hand going up to adjust a bra strap. Seven years they'd been together, but every time she did that, he lost his concentration. And odds-on she knew it.

He turned around, fumbled in the cabinet, wanting a moment to get his story straight. 'Yeah, you know. The winter and all.' He grabbed a glass from the second shelf, held it under the faucet.

'Danny,' her voice serious, 'what's wrong?'

'Huh?' He flashed a forced smile over his shoulder. 'What do you mean?'

'Something's bugging you. Something big.'

He'd read somewhere about mental patients that were basically catatonic because they'd suffered damage to the fragile connections between the brain's hemispheres. The result was that the two halves of their brain were essentially at war.

Lately he knew how that felt.

He wanted badly to tell her the truth, all of it, from Evan's reappearance in his – in their – lives right up until this morning. But the calculating half of him warned to keep his damn mouth shut and talk her down. The woman who'd sworn she would bolt if he so much as shoplifted – she was going to accept him going back to work? Even if he was doing it for her, for them? Best to play it smart. 'What do you mean, baby? Nothing's bugging me.'

She gave him a quizzical look. 'If you tell me what's wrong, maybe I can help.'

'Nothing's wrong.' He took a sip of water, set the glass down.

'Danny.' She did that bra strap thing again, and it drew his eyes to her body, clothed in one of his sweaters and a pair of black leggings.

'I . . .' He paused. 'I don't know what you mean.'

Something changed in her eyes, and the warmth vanished entirely. 'Okay.' She turned to open a drawer and started rummaging through it, her back to him.

'Karen.'

She ignored him.

'Karen, Christ, it's nothing. Just . . . just busy at work. The winter, all these things to handle before the snow, you know.' It sounded lame. He was normally a good liar – just not to her. Never to her.

She nodded, her back still turned. 'Sure.' She gave up digging through the drawer and slammed it shut. 'See you when you get back.' She put on a very thin smile and left, the sound of her shoes all business.

He turned to the sink and poured out his water. 'Shit.'

The girl with Evan looked familiar. Blond, pretty, though kind of a stripper vibe. Too much makeup, and the clothes – a ruffled skirt like a cheerleader and two T-shirts – a little out of date. He'd seen her somewhere.

'This is Danny Carter.' Evan nodded toward him, hands in his pockets. 'Danny-boy, Debbie.'

'Debbie?' he asked, looking up, wondering what thirty-year-old woman would choose that over Deborah or Deb.

'Like Debbie Harry,' she said, sounding friendly, though Danny couldn't help but be aware that she knew his last name and he didn't know hers. He gestured at the other side of the table. Debbie threw her purse in before sliding herself, flashing a little smile and a lot of cleavage. Evan dropped his keys on the table, his jacket on the booth seat. 'I'm gonna take a shit. Order me some eggs, they come by.'

Danny sighed and shook his head. Across the table, Debbie took one of the menus from the stand on the table, flipped it open, and started turning pages without paying much attention. He kept his eye on her, sizing her up. Unimpressed. Pretty face, but starting to get that worn look, like she'd spent a lot of time drinking cheap beer in smoky bars. Her blonde hair had darker roots. He'd definitely seen her somewhere.

'So.' She looked up, the menu framing her face. 'Evan tells me you're a thief.'

Danny leaned back, the Naugahyde seat cool through his shirt. 'I'm in construction.'

'Yeah? He said you were his partner.'

'Long time ago.'

'This must feel like déjà vu, huh?' She smiled at him, no hint of the game face he was used to in this kind of discussion. 'So is this like a one-time thing, like the movies?'

'Yes, it's a one-time thing. No, it's nothing like the movies.'

She nodded, looked back down at the menu. Flipped another page, then her face lit up like a little kid's. 'That's what I'm talking about. Chocolate chip pancakes with strawberries.'

He shook his head, took another sip of coffee. *This* was the woman Evan thought they should bring in on a federal job? Danny would have to call Patrick again. Much as he disliked involving him in this, they needed someone capable. Not some bimbo Evan happened to be fucking.

He realized Debbie was looking at him from across the table, and made an effort to smile.

'Lemme see your hand.' Her gum popped.

'What?'

'I'll read your palm.'

He shrugged, set the mug down and leaned forward. Her touch was cool. She held his hand lightly, turned it over, her fingers under his wrist. When she leaned in over the table he caught drugstore perfume, something candy-sweet.

'Hmmmm.' She peered closer. 'Interesting.'

He ignored the bait, kept silent.

'I see a couple of things.' She traced a line across his palm.

'Yeah?' He stifled a yawn.

She nodded. 'I see you think I'm a moron.'

He was surprised, the yawn turning to a smile. 'That's in my palm?'

'That's in your eyes.' She said it matter-of-factly, still looking at his hand. 'In your palm I can see that you're in management.'

'How?'

'You said you're in construction. While back, I dated an ironworker. His hands were like baseball mitts. Yours are soft.'

He laughed. 'What else?'

'You're not wearing a wedding ring. But you didn't check me out.' She brushed a lock of blonde hair behind her ear. 'Most guys do. So I bet you have a serious girlfriend, somebody you really love.'

He thought of Karen adjusting her bra strap that morning, how even in the middle of fighting with her, lying to her, it had sent a little shiver through him. 'Right again. What else does my palm tell you?'

'It tells me I should read a book on palm reading.' She released his hand, smiled up at him. They held the gaze for a long moment, and then he started laughing, a sincere laugh that started low in his gut. It felt good.

'What?' Evan stood at the edge of the table.

Debbie looked at Danny innocently and popped her gum. He laughed again.

'I think we'll get along fine.'

It was one of those days, the sky throbbing blue, fall light golden across the hood of the Explorer. This October had been shaping up colder than usual, today in the forties, but the sun was so bright it didn't feel bad, especially with Dylan on the radio, singing about helping her out of a jam but using a little too much force.

He turned right onto Randolph, the skyline swinging into his rearview mirror, the Sears Tower and the Hancock sharp-edged against the horizon. Behind him he could see Evan's Mustang, Debbie with her feet up on the dash. He wondered about her. She didn't seem like a hustler. Maybe a groupie, one of those smart women who like dangerous men. Regardless, he was glad to have her, if only to keep Evan away from Tommy. They might be partners again, but he wasn't about to lower his guard. Just do the job smart, get paid, go their separate ways.

The money. He hadn't even thought about it. Hell, he'd only decided to do the job to get clear of Evan. What was he going to do with Richard's money?

He thought of the lawn crew, of Richard smug in his designer house. Of Dad sitting at the kitchen table, a cigarette smoldering untouched in the ashtray.

Call the money a bonus. A karmic payout for everybody who'd ever screwed his old man. Stash it in a safe deposit box and always have an umbrella against gathering storms.

He forced his thoughts back to the road, watching loft complexes give way to industrial space. The El rattled a couple of blocks away. New residential construction crept ever outward, but it was still quiet here, few cars and nobody on the sidewalk.

When he turned on Pike Street, the loft complex sat snug ahead of him, five stories of structural steel swathed in dirty gray plastic. A chain-link fence circled the whole site. Danny parked in front of the gate and stepped out, digging in his jacket for a ring of keys on a clip chain. He popped the padlock and swung the gate open, gestured the Mustang through, then returned to the Explorer and drove into the rutted dirt of the yard.

Evan leaned on the car door and glanced around. He nodded. 'Not bad. They let you walk around with the keys?'

'It's my job. Come on.' He turned toward the trailer, O'DONNELL CONSTRUCTION neatly lettered on one side. It felt weird to walk the yard without his hard hat. Behind him, he heard the sound of a car door opening, Debbie getting out. He turned back, caught Evan's eye, and shook his head.

'Baby, wait in the car, okay?' Evan didn't make it sound like a question.

Danny pushed open the trailer door and stepped in, feeling it rock slightly. The inside was as he remembered it, only cleaner. The smell of old coffee scorched the air. A trickle of dusty sunlight came through the windows. He walked over and closed the blinds.

'Sure.' Evan looked around, moving to the couch, lifting one end and then dropping it with a thump, like he was gauging the weight. 'Seems private.'

'This area is still pretty industrial, not many homes yet. The owners got the land cheap, so they're rolling the dice on lofts.'

'Money in that?' Evan looking curious, like he might invest.

'No doubt. Used to be, people wanted to live in the suburbs. That's why Daley Senior put the housing projects in the city. Except now people are moving back, everybody wants to live downtown, ride the El to work. So everything changes. You know the Green?'

Evan nodded.

'Cabrini Green is one of the worst projects in the country. Something like ninety percent unemployment. So bad they have those chain-link walls on the hallways, so the cops can see inside from the street.' It had always made him a little sick, the people walking out their own front door to an exposed hall like a cage. Kids leaning against the wire with forties in their hands and anger in their eyes. 'But it's on great land. Close to the city, the trains. The only thing wrong with the area where the Green sits is the Green. So Daley Junior, he's been tearing down what his father built, one at a time. Technically they're building mixed-income housing, but what you got, there's a strip mall half a block away now with a Starbucks, the parking lot full of expensive cars. Lofts going for three hundred grand.' Danny sat at the table. 'You want to make money in Chicago, figure out where the poor people live and move them.'

Evan shrugged, his interest gone. 'Sucks to be poor.'

'Yeah.' Danny's eyes roamed the walls, the old instincts coming back, a strange rush with them. Was it excitement? Guilt? Hope? A bit of all of them. It set him on edge, like too many cups of coffee, his stomach jittery, wondering what he was doing here, knowing he had no choice.

'All right. We snatch the kid, get a blindfold on him, bring him here. Tie him to the couch.' Evan paused. 'What happens if a cop comes by, sees the cars?'

'Nothing, so long as we don't act stupid. They see cars in here all the time.' Danny scratched at his elbow. 'We make the call –'

'I make it.'

The words came too quickly, not the easy toss-out Danny would have expected. It set off an internal alarm. But Evan was right, it wasn't like Danny could call his own boss. 'You make the call. We ask for half a million. Tell him we'll call back in a couple of days to set up the meet. Debbie takes care of Tommy. How much does she know?'

'She knows she's babysitting. I told her she'd see twenty large on it. She doesn't know who the guy is.'

Danny nodded. 'I might need her help with something else, too.'

Evan shrugged. 'Whatever. She'll do what I tell her.' He moved to the couch, dropped down, put his feet up on the counter opposite. Leaned back with hands laced behind his head. 'You know what I like about this?'

'What?'

'Keeping the man's kid in his own trailer.' Evan's face split into a hard smile.

Later, back in his truck, the seat sun-warm against his back, Danny replayed that look. Saw how much the cruelty of the irony pleased Evan. It made Danny wonder, turning onto Halsted, made him question. Was he about to get back in over his head?

Enough. He'd been over this a million times. Given the choice between losing everything he cared about but standing on principle, or bending the rules in a way that didn't harm anyone, well, that wasn't any kind of choice at all.

Besides, he was starting to think they could pull it off. His problem would be solved, and Karen would never know a thing. And while he'd happily trade the money to get Evan out of his life, having a quarter million in a safe deposit box couldn't hurt. In fact, he was starting to entertain a strange sort of hope, an old excitement. The looming black clouds might turn out to be a summer storm, hard and fast, but gone without doing any real damage.

Before he'd left the trailer, Danny had cleaned up. He didn't want the kid to somehow accidentally see a piece of letterhead, an envelope, something that might help the police track them down. Though at half a million, Danny didn't see Richard going to the police. The guy was a blowhard and a bastard, but he loved his son. Why play games?

'It doesn't matter what kind of car it is,' he said, giving Evan his assignment. 'So long as it's decent-looking. The neighbors will notice a beater.'

'Sure. And afterward?'

'Park it in front of Cabrini Green with the keys in it. Give somebody a stroke of luck.'

Evan liked that.

'I'll bring masks and gloves.' Danny's mind churned, trying to think of all the angles. He'd talk to Debbie later. Stop by the store on the way home for some rope. Maybe a pair of nylons? Something that wouldn't chafe or scrape the kid up. There was something else, something important.

Oh yes. 'One more thing.'

'What?' Evan said, bored already. Always happier to be doing the job than thinking about it.

'Don't bring a gun.' Danny kept his voice level and his eyes hard, not trying to stare Evan down, just letting him know he was serious. 'Not a scratch, remember?'

Evan shrugged. 'Okay.'

Danny held the look for a minute, then nodded, went back to straightening up. 'Get the car tomorrow morning. You can pick me up at the same spot as last time, round one o'clock.'

'We going tomorrow?' Evan sounded surprised, turning to look up.

'What, you got somewhere to be?'

21. Trembled and Burned

When they were ten, they'd played a game called Pisser. It was a made-up game, but it lasted for almost two years, until Bobby Doyle missed his jump from the roof of a two-story CVS to the fire escape of the building next door and broke both wrists.

When Danny remembered the game, he always felt the way he did when he caught his own voice on an answering machine. It felt familiar, but a little off, too. Like someone else was telling a story that had happened to him.

The leader of the game was the Big Dick. It was a title they fought to earn, though mostly it meant that as they went about their lives, they kept their eyes open for the right kind of opportunity. Say, a new skyscraper going up in the Loop, the concrete and glass of the curtain wall only half finished, the dark silhouette of a tower crane looming sixty stories up.

Boom. Call a Challenge.

Meet at seven o'clock, the yard deserted except for the security guys drinking coffee in their trailer. Squeeze under the chain link on the far side, keeping low until you're in the building. The first floors would have actual staircases, what would become the fire steps. After that, plywood ramps. When those ran out, grab the A-frame of the crane, hoist yourself over the rail to the gridwork stairs, and start climbing.

At twenty stories, your calves burn.

At thirty-five stories, you've come farther than the outside wall. The wind hits.

At fifty stories, five hundred swimming feet of vertigo, people on the street are just dots. Cabs are those mini-Matchbox cars you can put a dozen in your pocket.

At sixty stories, you've run out of stories. The building drops away, structural steel blackened by welding marks. You're climbing the crane to the sky. Start counting steps. Ignore your legs Elvis-ing.

One hundred and eighty steps later, you've reached the operator's cab, the white box like the driver's seat of a semi. But it'll be locked, so go up twenty more, to the gangway on top of the mast.

Take panting breaths on the ceiling of the city, the sky indigo around you, the world spread out jeweled at your feet.

Now the Challenge, because that was just a warm-up.

Step onto the crane arm. The metal grid is maybe two feet wide, but it feels like a tightrope. Indian-walk one foot in front of the other, keeping low to fight the wind, nothing on either side, just a few inches of steel between you and a five-second trip to State Street. Hit so hard, they'd tell each other, your shins come out your shoulders. Hit so hard nobody can tell your head from your ass. Hit so hard your teeth bounce for blocks.

Step. Breathe. Step.

When you reach the end, take a bow. Then hustle back fast as you dare. If you're the first to ante up, congratulations. You're the new Big Dick. Pussy out, you're the Pisser, a little baby still whines for his mommy and wets the sheets. No hair on his nuts. No nuts at all.

It was vivid to Danny, like he could step back into that Challenge today if he wanted. The way his legs had trembled and burned. The way the air cut as he drew it in, far, far above the city-street smells of exhaust and garbage.

Once he took that first step, the fear would fade. His

mind would throw up interference, like radio static, that screened out everything but a calm inner monologue and his body's response to it. The first step wasn't the hard part.

No, the hard part came before he stepped into the void. The hard part was the waiting, his brain imagining all the things that could go wrong, all the things he couldn't control, all the ways that fate loomed beneath him, hungry, eager for him to slip.

The hard part was sitting in the passenger seat of the nice black Saab Evan had stolen – a sedan, probably a five-star safety rating, just the thing to drive your kid to private school – watching Evan light yet another cigarette. Watching the digital clock soundlessly change a four to a five. He caught his hands fiddling with the strap of the duffel bag, and made them stop. 'Go around again.'

Evan nodded, his cigarette bobbing up and down, the muscles in his neck rigid. He was feeling it, too. They stopped at a sign, then turned right, taking the block the other direction. On both sides of the car, wide lawns sprawled in front of five-bedroom houses nestled beneath towering shade trees. The streets had that oddly wide feeling of a neighborhood where every house had a garage, nothing like the crowded city parking he was used to.

'We saw the kid come home,' Evan said. 'What are we waiting for?'

'You got to put yourself in the mind of the boy, right?' Talking to relax. 'He gets home, drops his schoolbag, wonders what to do with himself. No brothers, and Dad won't be home till eight or nine. So the kid,' Danny wanting to avoid calling him Tommy, not wanting to think of him that personally, 'he's got the run of the house. What's he do?'

'Fuck should I know?' Evan said. 'Turn on the TV?'

'Exactly. That's where I want him. Watching TV. It'll

drown out noise, and I don't think there's an alarm console in that room.'

'So how long do we wait?' Evan seemed eager, almost anxious. Best to move.

'What's it been, twenty minutes? Now's probably good.' He unzipped the duffel for one final inventory. Everything was just as it had been the last dozen times he'd checked. Before closing the bag, he brushed the inner pocket. The plastic rectangle inside felt strangely reassuring.

Evan turned the corner, another right, Richard's house now in sight, a brick and shingle two-story with bay windows, architecturally a cross between a Swiss chalet and an English manor. The driveway was smooth blacktop that hummed beneath the tires as Evan turned in gently, letting the car coast up to the closed garage door. He threw it in park and rested his hands on the wheel. They'd both put on driving gloves in the McDonald's parking lot, and seeing Evan tap the Saab's wheel with his elegantly gloved hands, Danny had a flash of him as a chauffeur. Just put a jaunty cap on him. The image was funny, but he pushed it aside.

'Ready?' Evan's voice had a hint of excitement, a familiar note that Danny had almost forgotten. He used to have the same tone playing Pisser, just before diving off the Michigan Avenue drawbridge, or sprinting across Lakeshore at rush hour.

'One second.' Danny opened his cell phone and dialed. She answered on the second ring.

'Debbie. Give us five minutes.'

'Okay. Be careful.'

'Yeah.' Danny flipped the phone closed.

'What's that all about?'

'Let's go,' not answering Evan, grabbing the duffel bag and opening the car door. The October wind slapped at him as he left the heated car, the air high-thirties, way colder this year than most. Careful to keep his face pointed toward the house, he scanned the windows for any sign of life. Nothing.

He looked across the roof of the Saab at Evan, who also stood with his door open, and for a moment, they just held the gaze. Then Danny nodded, and closed his door.

Time to take that first step onto the ledge.

He turned and walked toward the near side of the house, around the garage, feeling Evan fall into step behind him. The adrenaline hit full force now, the rush of blood in his ears drowning out the fear, giving him the quiet he needed. They walked steadily around the garage, keeping up a front in case any neighbors happened to look out the window. *Nothing suspicious here, ma'am. Just checking the meter.* The side yard was neatly kept, the grass sparse from the shade of a maple that had to be sixty years old. The garage windows had gauzy curtains, but Danny could tell it was empty. Perfect. When they reached the back corner, he stopped and peered around.

Everything seemed quiet. The backyard was smaller than the front, with a line of evergreens marking the rear. A large deck jutted off the second story, and Danny had a sudden pang, remembering the company party last year, everybody on the deck, Richard playing Papa at the grill. Then he remembered that none of the yard staff had been invited. Besides, the man had asked everyone to bring their own beer. 'Come on. Keep low.'

Danny went first, fast now that they were out of sight of the neighbors, staying bent over so that hedges screened his movement from the house. He could hear Evan behind him, the crack of sticks as he stomped along. Thirty feet brought them under the wooden deck to a single door beside the air-conditioning unit, a big Trane that came up to

Danny's waist. He ducked to look at the lock. Evan came up and squatted beside the air conditioner.

When Danny had left his old life, he'd dumped all traces of it. Except his tools. For some reason, he hadn't been able to throw them away. In the movies, the bad guys always had a little leather pouch of lock picks, the kind locksmiths used, but he liked the ones he'd made. He kept them in the drawstring bag from a bottle of Crown Royal, hidden in a box of old junk in their basement. For the first time in seven years he unknotted the string.

He'd gotten rusty. The deadbolt held for almost two minutes.

'Jesus.' Evan's coffee and cigarette breath came hard over his shoulder. 'Took you long enough, Danny-boy.'

Danny gave him the finger, then turned the handle gently, praying the door didn't squeak. It was always the little things that got you caught.

It slid open with only a whisper from the hinges, revealing what Richard called his mudroom, a slim, chilly space with a washer and dryer, laundry piles on the floor. He could hear the sound of the television turned up loud in another room. Heart pounding and mouth dry, he stepped inside. Evan followed, closing the door behind them.

They stood in silence for a moment, Danny listening to the sounds of the house. Waiting for any semblance of alarm. When nothing came, he opened the duffel and took out two plain black domino masks, like the one Zorro wore. They limited peripheral vision, but tolerably. Danny had to stop himself from laughing when he saw Evan; his square jaw and evident muscles paired with the mask and jeans to give him the look of an underdressed pro wrestler. His partner adjusted the strap, nodded, and then took a step forward. Danny caught his arm and leaned in close to whisper. 'Wait.'

Evan looked at him quizzically, bounced on his toes, but didn't move. Ten seconds, twenty, thirty, Danny staring at his boss's dirty underwear, his palms sweaty. Evan gave him a *what the fuck?* look, his lips turned in a sneer, the waiting killing him. Danny shook his head, held a finger to his lips, hoping he hadn't made a mistake.

Then the phone rang, and he unclenched. Debbie had come through. They stood still and listened, two rings, the trudge of footsteps, three rings, four, and then from the kitchen, the sound of a sullen twelve-year-old voice.

'Hullo.' The word dragged out, offered grudgingly. There was a pause, then the voice again, only different, excited now. 'Really? I won?'

Danny nodded his head toward the door, and Evan moved forward, kicking at a pile of laundry in his way, sending jeans flying across the floor. A button on one pinged against the hot water heater, and Danny fought an urge to shush him. Goddamn it. He picked his way over to the open doorway to stand by Evan, digging the plastic rectangle out of the bag by feel before he set the duffel down. The molded grip fit his knuckles neatly. His thumb caressed the stud.

From the other room, Tommy's voice sounded like he'd just found out tomorrow was Christmas. 'Awesome! What? Sure!' They heard his footsteps running for the TV room.

Showtime.

Danny stepped into the hall, Evan close behind him. A surreal sort of déjà vu swept over him in a wave as he looked at the polished wood floor and familiar photos on the wall. He'd never expected to be in this house wearing the clothing of a thief. Or in any house ever again, for that matter.

Keeping close to the wall, he inched along the hallway. Through an open door ten feet down, the light of the TV flickered ice blue. He could barely hear Tommy's voice over throbbing hip-hop. Debbie would be telling him that they were about to show his name on the screen. Danny's heart was pounding, but he made himself step lightly, easily, the plastic rectangle loose in his hand. When he reached the door frame, he took a quiet breath and peeked around.

A VH-1 logo flashed across the flat-screen TV. Tommy stood silhouetted against it, the cordless phone pressed to one ear. He wore jeans and a rugby shirt, and bounced up and down, crackling with energy. The shell of preteen world weariness had fallen away, leaving a little boy excited about the prize he thought he'd won.

It was too much. The facts of what he was doing rattled through Danny like an El train. He was a thief – no, worse, a kidnapper – and innocents were at risk. Again.

He'd thought that by coming, he could control Evan, make sure that Tommy didn't get hurt. But now, standing here, he realized he couldn't go through with it. No way. If they left now, no one would be the wiser. The worst consequence would be Tommy's broken heart over a PlayStation that never arrived. Danny would find some other way of squaring up. He turned, intending to motion Evan back.

And found Evan pushing past him into the room, making no attempt to hide himself or be quiet.

Holding a gun in his hand.

22. Monsters Would Be Waiting

All his wavering vanished. Using his left hand on the door frame for leverage, Danny threw himself into the room, raising the rectangle of plastic he'd taken from the duffel bag. Tommy was already turning, the excitement on his face melting at the sight of Evan with a pistol. The phone dropped from his hand, and there was a frozen moment as it fell. Then it struck the wood floor with a loud clatter, and Danny lunged past Evan, thumbing the button on the stun gun and pressing it firmly to Tommy's shoulder.

There was an electric crackling sound, and the boy went rigid and then slumped. Danny caught him before his head hit the floor and set him down gently.

He turned, anger surging quick now. Evan stood casually six feet away, the gun at his hip, the arm moving loosely, like the revolver was tugging at it.

'I told you not to bring a gun.' Danny had to fight to keep from yelling.

'Yeah,' Evan's voice was slow, almost a drawl. 'I remember you saying that.'

Right then, if he'd a piece of his own, Danny couldn't have sworn he wouldn't have pulled it. He straightened, stepped away from Tommy. The stun gun was still in his hand, and that old anger throbbed through his veins. He stared at Evan, the part of his mind that calculated odds screaming at him to stop, to cool out, telling him that a thirty-dollar stun gun was no match for a thirty-eight-caliber pistol. Evan stared back, a hard smile on his face. Ready to play.

'Hello?' The tinny voice came from the floor, from the phone Tommy had dropped. 'Hello? Are you guys okay?'

Debbie's voice broke the spell. He blew air through his nose, turned away. Picked up the phone. 'Yeah.'

Her voice sounded thin, a little scared. 'I heard noises.'

'It's nothing.' He dropped back down to a crouch, checking Tommy's pulse. It was strong. He turned to look at Evan over his shoulder. 'Get the bag.' Danny peeled up Tommy's eyelids. The pupils looked a little dilated, but okay. To Debbie, he said, 'We're going to wrap up here. You're at a pay phone like I told you?'

'Uh-huh. A bodega on Western.'

'Good. Wipe down the phone and go ahead to the trailer. We'll meet you there.' He hung up.

There was a thump as the bag dropped down beside him. He could see Evan's battered boots just beyond. Danny reached for the duffel, unzipped it, not glancing up. 'The garage is at the end of the hall. Go open the door and pull the car in. Close it behind you.'

'He okay?'

'Yeah.'

There was a laugh. 'Electrocuting don't count as hurting him?'

Danny looked up. The gun was tucked in the front of Evan's pants. 'I needed a way to knock him unconscious without doing him any harm. This is the weakest stun gun on the market. But yeah, when I tried it, it hurt.'

Evan broke into a mocking smile. 'You tried it on yourself?'

'Before using it on a kid? Of course.' He reached in the duffel bag, took out another mask, the eyeholes on this one taped over. 'It hurts, but the pain doesn't last, and there's zero permanent damage. Which makes it a whole lot better than pistol-whipping him the way you planned to.'

'How long will he be out?'

'I don't know. A grown man probably wouldn't even lose consciousness. So call it fifteen minutes. You going to go get the car, or do you want to wait till he wakes up?' He turned back to the bag, pulling out Ace bandages and consciously ignoring Evan, who stood still for five seconds, ten, enough to prove his independence. Then he turned and went down the hall, his boots loud with every step.

Danny let his breath out.

Tommy gave a little moan, and one arm jerked slightly. It stabbed Danny's heart to see it. 'I'm sorry, kiddo.' He put one hand on the unconscious boy's cheek. The skin felt soft and warm, like he was just sleeping, and a bitter wave washed through Danny. 'I wish none of this was happening.'

Through the floor he felt the faint vibration of the garage door opening. Self-loathing would have to wait. He put the mask on Tommy's face. 'But you don't know this guy. Believe me, he'd be doing this with or without me. And as long as I'm here, you'll be safe.'

He didn't add that he only hoped that was true. Jesus Christ, bringing a gun. All those years in prison hadn't taught Evan anything. Not anything worth learning, at least.

Danny worked swiftly but gently, wrapping the boy in bandages. He was afraid tying his wrists would cut off circulation, so he just looped the fabric firmly around Tommy's whole chest, binding his arms to his sides in a wide cocoon. He repeated the process with the boy's legs. It wouldn't hold against serious effort, but it would serve their needs. Duct tape would have been more secure, but Danny couldn't do that to a twelve-year-old.

To Evan, maybe.

When he was done, he straightened, thumbed the safety and tucked the stun gun in his pocket. The phone was on

142

the ground, and he picked it up, walked to the kitchen and hung it up, swinging back through the mudroom to lock the deadbolt. When he returned to the TV room, he found Evan lifting the corner of a framed modern art print and peering behind it.

'You got to be kidding me.'

'What?' Evan asked.

'He's a contractor. Even if he has a safe, you think it's going to have bundles of hundreds?' Danny sighed. 'Grab his feet, I'll get the hands.'

Evan gave him a contemptuous look, bent down and came up with Tommy in a fireman's cradle. The kid probably didn't weigh much over ninety pounds, but still, the absolute effortlessness was impressive. Like he weighed nothing at all.

Danny stabbed the TV power, silencing a rap star tricking out his third Lamborghini with gold rims, and took one last look around. Everything seemed clean. 'Let's go.' He shouldered the bag and walked out.

The garage was orderly, no tools or lawn equipment, just a couple of bicycles and space for two cars. Evan had parked the stolen Saab dead in the middle, the trunk gaping open. The inside was lined with thin carpet, and the former owner's golf clubs took up half the space. They hadn't thought to check the trunk. Danny shoved the clubs to one side, frustration beginning to infect his cool. It was always the little things that got you caught. If he was going to get Tommy out of this, get himself out of it, he couldn't afford not to think of everything.

Evan bent over and laid Tommy in the trunk, more gently than Danny expected. 'Okay,' he said, brushing his hands off. 'We done?'

Danny nodded, started to shut the trunk lid, and stopped himself. They didn't have far to go, but still. 'One second.'

He turned and went back to the TV room. Half a dozen throw pillows of different colors and patterns rested on the couch. He grabbed three. Who really noticed their couch pillows? He walked back to the garage. The boy mumbled something and pulled unconsciously at his bindings.

'Shhh.' Danny ducked down and braced Tommy with pillows. He put one under his head, and the others on either side. Hardly the Ritz, but it would keep him from rolling into the golf clubs or the wheel well. Good enough. He closed the trunk. 'Let's roll.'

Evan smirked and shook his head, but reached for the car door. Danny caught the frame. 'I'm driving.'

For once Evan didn't argue.

'Greenleaf, Greenwood, Forest. These dumbfucks live in Chicago, but all their streets have tree names.' Evan's voice had a playful tone, the same as when they'd taunted each other playing Pisser all those years ago.

Richard's house was two blocks behind, and Danny wondered if they had closed the garage door. He knew they had; the worry was just part of the jangling of his nerves as he came down. Same with the urge to giggle, as though they were only shoplifting *Playboys* from a Loop liquor mart. He willed himself cool. They were away, but the job wasn't over yet. They had to get Tommy to the construction trailer. Then he could let himself relax.

A little.

Because nothing was over, he reminded himself, until Tommy was home. Until Danny could go back to his old life. Paperwork. Project management. Renting movies for couch-lounging Sunday afternoons after Karen slept off her night shifts.

That seemed about as real as a prison fantasy, a late-night conversation with a cellie about what you were going to do when you got out. The Italian beef with extra peppers, the redhead that seemed like she might wait. The promise that you'd never again do anything boneheaded enough to return you to jail. For a moment he imagined he were still in prison, that the last seven years had just been a particularly vivid dream.

Then he pulled his shit together. 'Yeah, well. Lots of trees.'

Evan grunted, looking out the window to shaded lawns fronting million-dollar homes. 'S'pose.'

'Okay. We head back to the trailer. Debbie meets us there. After we get Tommy inside, I'll make an appearance at the restaurant construction site. You take the car and get it stolen. Then –'

'Yeah, yeah, yeah.' Evan yawned. 'We been over this, man.'

'Then,' Danny continued, 'we meet up and make the call. We'll go over what you'll say beforehand, but it'll be short and simple. Then –'

'Then we get a pint and wait.'

Danny nodded, keeping to himself that he didn't plan to play buddies. The man wanted a drink, fine. He wasn't a freshman thief likely to start bragging on his fourth whiskey. But Danny was going home. He flipped the turn signal, his gloves against the wheel suggestive of the coming winter. They'd wind south to Lakeshore – there'd be traffic, but anonymity, too. The stop sign at the corner had a sticker that said RAPE pasted just below the STOP part. He checked his mirror as he slowed.

The sedan in his rearview had a blue siren on the dash. 'Shit.'

'What?'

'Security.'

'Shit.' Evan straightened in the seat.

The car was a recent-model Ford, the windows tinted just enough that all Danny could make out was the driver's silhouette. His heart banged against his ribs like an animal throwing itself at the bars of its cage. How long had the car been there? He'd been too distracted with his thoughts to know for sure.

A block or two, though.

He braked at the sign, a full stop. The bumper of the Ford crept up in the rearview. Danny touched the gas and turned, just another civilian going about his business in a nice car.

The blue light flashed on as he rounded the corner.

His sweating palms made the gloves sticky as he braked, gliding the car to a smooth stop. Put it in park but left the engine running. The Ford pulled up behind them, the light still going. Soundless, though. No siren.

'He alone?' Evan asked, not turning around.

The man stepped out of the car, a tall guy, thin, with a mustache. He wore a black uniform with a red patch on the chest. 'Yeah.'

Evan nodded. The revolver appeared in one hand. He opened the cylinder, spun it, and flipped it back in place. Then he rocked his head to either side, fast. Danny could hear his neck pop. Evan winked and transferred the pistol to his right hand as he reached for the door handle with his left.

This couldn't be happening. History couldn't be about to repeat itself, not while he just sat there and watched everything spin out of control.

It never was in control, Danny-boy.

You were just kidding yourself.

A thought gut-punched him: If the situation could be saved, it would be because he saved it. He flung open his door and stepped out before Evan could react.

The security guard jumped, one hand straying to his belt. His fingers cupped over something, it looked like pepper spray.

'Hi there.' Danny made himself smile, a resident talking to an employee. Out of the corner of his eye he could see that Evan had his door open an inch or two, but he hadn't gotten out. Danny took another step toward the guard, putting his body in Evan's line of fire.

'Sir.' The guard didn't smile, but his hands loosened on the pepper spray. He pointed to the trunk of the car. 'Can you step over here please?'

Every part of him tingled. The trunk of the car. Adrenaline tasted bitter in his mouth. He took one step, then another, thinking maybe he could sucker-punch the guard. He wouldn't let Evan do things his way, but that didn't mean he had to let a rent-a-cop bend and cuff him. Maintaining his smile through sheer force of will, he stepped over to face the man, hands at his sides, fingers dying to clench into fists.

'What's the problem, Officer?' Laying it on, like he didn't realize the guy wasn't police.

The man's expression didn't change as he pointed at the back of the car. 'That.'

Had Tommy somehow woken up and figured a way to open the trunk? Danny took another step, rounding the side of the car, his gaze following the man's finger, ready to jump the guy. Expecting to see the trunk partway open, Tommy's hands poking out. Certain that at any moment Evan would throw open his door and start shooting, the blasts loud enough to shatter the world.

On the right-hand side, the Saab's taillight was broken.

'Sir, that's very dangerous. You shouldn't drive with only one. I wanted to warn you before the police stopped you.'

Something inside Danny broke into manic laughter,

wet-cheeked and fearsome, like a little boy who turned on a light to realize the monster in the corner of his room was only a stack of clothes on the dresser.

And as he went through the motions with the pseudo cop, clucking and acting concerned, wondering aloud when it had happened, the whole time he was thinking how this sanctimonious jerk had almost gotten his head blown off. Thinking that if he hadn't moved just when he did, Evan would have come out shooting over a busted taillight.

Thinking that the problem with the relief the little boy in his bedroom felt was that at some point, he had to turn the lights back off.

And when he did, the monsters would be waiting.

23. Dead Leaves to Dance

The stolen Saab had been pure pussy to drive, more responsive and muscular than Evan expected. He'd taken a couple of long blocks around Cabrini as a victory lap, the accelerator to the floor so the crumbling world outside blurred: a chain-linked high school, a row of burned-out tract houses, a liquor store barricaded like a World War Two bunker. Half the buildings he passed were tagged with gang symbols, and at one point he'd sent a group of teenaged bangers jumping for the curb, their shouts after him making him laugh. Call it payback for the crews he'd had to deal with in Stateville. He wasn't racist or anything, but it was always the blacks in gangs, them and the Hispanics. He'd hated dumping the Saab in their turf, leaving it with the windows open and the keys inside. A shame to leave such a nice piece of machinery to perpetual losers.

Back in his own car, he munched on chips while he waited for Danny. He was parked in back of a gas station beside a wrecked Ford compact that looked like it had run into a semi, the front end crunched in, the windshield shattered, fragments of greenish safety glass scattered across the seat. The gun bit into his belly, and he took it out and tossed it on the passenger seat. Danny's face when he'd seen it had been almost as funny as those of the gangbangers diving for the curb. A beautiful moment, like watching a building collapse. Such surprise. Evan couldn't believe it – the guy had actually managed to convince himself that he was in charge, that everybody was going to follow orders like good little soldiers.

By the time this job was done, Evan had a hunch Danny's smug look of superiority would be nothing but a fading memory.

He'd finished his pack of cigarettes and been playing with the idea of going in for another, knowing he was smoking too much lately, not much caring, when Danny pulled in. Evan climbed out of the Mustang, the wind hitting with physical force, way too cold for this time of year. Soon as this job was over, he was taking his money and heading south. Find a place with bars that opened to the beach. Bikinis that would call him Daddy.

To the right of the gas station sat a freezer with bags of ice. Danny made a three-point turn to park his truck next to it, then climbed out the passenger side, using the truck to block off the phone. Such a Danny move, overthinking things – like anybody was going to spy on two guys talking in a parking lot. Especially in this weather.

The first words out of Danny's mouth were, 'Did you ditch the Saab?'

Evan decided to ignore him. 'What, you carry a change of clothes in the car?' Danny was back in faggoty khakis and a dress shirt, every bit the young professional.

'I went to a job site. Had to look the part.' Danny dug a hand into his pants pocket, came out with a couple of quarters, started tossing them hand to hand.

'Dorito?' Evan offered the bag.

Danny suddenly looked at him, hard. 'You went inside?'

'Checked it out. It's good. Clerk can't see us.'

Instead of being happy to hear it, Danny just clenched. 'The point was to stay out of sight.'

'I bought chips,' Evan said. 'I didn't rob the place.'

Danny shook his head. 'All right. You know what to say?'

'Yeah. I tell him I'm a friend of Danny Carter's, and that I've got his kid in my basement. What's the number?'

For a second he thought the guy was going to make an issue of it, and wondered how much longer he was going to have to deal with this shit. A couple of days at least, until things were solidly in motion. He might need Danny's knowledge of the boss man. Still, if Danny kept treating him like some punk pulling his first counter job, they were going to mix it up.

Danny handed him the quarters. 'The number's 847-866-0300. That's his mobile. He always answers it.'

He nodded, reaching for the phone. Danny caught his wrist.

'Wear your gloves.'

He snorted. 'Your asshole must be puckered so tight you need a shoehorn to take a shit.'

'Just put on the gloves.'

Evan shrugged, took them from his pocket and pulled them on. 'Happy?' Picked up the receiver and slotted the change, his energy up. Not as strong, as pure, as when they broke into the house, but still, that edge of power surging through him. He pitied the regular citizens that went their whole drab little lives without ever feeling this way.

'Richard O'Donnell.' A nasal voice, more than a little arrogant. Evan gave him a moment of silence, let the guy repeat his name, then said, 'We have your son.'

The man stuttered, asking, 'What?' and 'Who is this?' Evan cut him off.

'We have Tommy.' Shooting a wink at Danny. 'When I hang up, you can go home and see for yourself. But now you're going to want to listen quietly. You got me?'

There was only silence on the line.

'Good boy, Dick. Here's the story. To save your son's life, all you have to do is everything I say.' He paused, savoring the thrill of it, the fear in boss man's breathing. 'If you call the cops or do anything to make us nervous, Tommy dies.' He kept his eyes on Danny, predicting he'd wince. He did.

'How do I know he's all right?'

'No, Dick. We're not going to do that. I'm not going to send you a photo with him holding a newspaper. I'm not going to play a tape of his voice, I'm not going to threaten to cut off his fingers. I'll just kill him and disappear. Understand?'

The arrogance vanished. 'How much do you want?'

Evan stared at Danny, the guy keyed up, fingers clenched, eyes betraying his discomfort. *Just wait, Danny-boy. If you liked that, you're going to love this one.* A sheet of icy wind whipped through the parking lot, stirring dead leaves to dance. 'A million in cash.'

The look on Danny's face was everything he could have hoped for. He went white, then red; reached for the phone, stopped himself, and finally stood frozen with anger in his eyes. Evan smiled at him. 'You hear me, Dick?'

'I . . . I don't have that much.'

'Then your boy dies. Nice talking to you.' He winked at Danny again, loving this, able to twist the knife in both of them at once, the adrenaline kicking hard now. He could see Danny wanting to make it better, but just as helpless as the boss man.

Watching it felt good.

'Wait!' Richard's voice, a yell.

'If you don't have the money, this is a waste of my time.'

'I can get it. I mean I will get it.' He stuttered like a little kid trying to weasel his way out of a fight.

'I thought so. We'll call you again in a couple of days. Wait by the phone. And Dick? Remember that you're dealing with serious people. Doubt it for a minute and you'll spend the rest of your life wishing you hadn't.'

Evan hung up the phone, pleased with himself. A nice

note to end on. The guy was probably pissing himself right now, all the things he'd thought mattered to him stripped away. 'Not bad, eh? I could do this for a living.'

'You stupid fuck.' Danny's voice was strangled, his fists white-knuckled.

'What?' He smiled casually.

'We said half a million.'

'You said it, not me. Anyway, you should be thanking me – I just doubled our take.' *My take.*

Danny glowered at him, looking for all the world like somebody's dad. 'Half a million he could pull from his bank account,' he lectured. 'Cash in an IRA, sell some stock. But a million, it makes it more likely he goes to the cops –'

'Blah, blah, blah. Look, the guy was quick enough to say he could get it when he knew what was at stake. Besides, now he knows he's dealing with pros.'

'Evan –'

'You want to call him back?'

They stared at each other for a long moment, Danny still edgy, like he was thinking of making a play for it. Part of Evan would have welcomed that, but he knew the time wasn't right. He eased back on his stare, put a smile in his eyes. 'Relax. The hard part's over.'

No need to push Danny too far yet. He was still useful. If Danny disappeared, boss man might panic. Better to stay cool, finish the job, and get paid.

Then he and Danny could settle any final debts.

'Cheer up, partner. It's all downhill from here.' He almost chuckled saying it.

Danny shook his head. 'Sure,' he said, but he didn't sound convinced.

Evan watched Danny climb into his truck and shut the door. He could see the man checking him out in the rearview. Evan smiled and threw a two-fingered salute, the way Dad used to. Funny how the little things stuck. Danny ignored him, started the truck. Put it in drive, signaled, and gently pulled out. It made Evan sick. Even furious, the guy didn't have the *cojones* to squeal out of a parking lot.

Evan walked into the gas station and asked for Winstons. Soft pack. The Pakistani at the counter pulled them down without a second glance. Didn't even notice he'd been in forty minutes earlier, or if he did notice, didn't say anything about it. Evan imagined taking the gun off the Mustang's passenger seat, coming back in here, and having the guy empty the register. But instead he paid, snagged a pack of matches, and stepped outside.

He lit a cigarette as he walked to the car. The weather seemed to be getting gloomier, twilight falling though it was only five o'clock. Dark clouds reflected the city glow in shades of gray and green. As he climbed in the car, he had an idea. It took some digging around, but he found a pen under the passenger seat. He leaned against the dash to write, *847-866-0300. Dick.*

He smiled and tucked the matchbook in his pocket.

24. Slippage

The hamburgers at Top-Notch had been getting smaller over the years – no way that was half a pound of meat – but they were still good, juicy and dripping cheese, and when the waitress spotted the radios Sean Nolan and Anthony Matthews always left on the table, she'd write 'Police' on the ticket so the counterman rang it up half price. Which wasn't much consolation when Matthews's cell phone rang thirty seconds after their meal arrived. Nolan watched him roll his eyes and wipe the grease off his fingers before he answered.

'Hey. Lunch. Nolan. The Top-Notch. Yeah.' A pause. 'Where?' He began patting his pockets, and Sean pulled the pen from his own and slid it across the table. Matthews nodded as he wrote on the napkin. 'Okay. We'll be there shortly.' He laughed. 'No chance. See you in a bit.' He closed the phone and picked up his burger.

'What's up?'

'That was Willie. They just pulled a floater out of the river.'

'Where?'

'You know where the Stevenson and Archer cross?'

'Yeah.' Nolan chewed thoughtfully. 'A smokehound who went for a swim?' People could generally be counted on to die in stupid ways, but drugs always made it worse. He'd once handled a job where a nineteen-year-old BD, Black Disciple, had been found torched. At first he'd liked the rival Gangster Disciples for it. But the medical examiner said no, there weren't any indications of a struggle, and no premortem injury besides the fire. Turned out the genius had fallen asleep lighting his crack pipe, caught the mattress on fire, and was just too high to notice. Another criminal mastermind.

Detective Matthews shook his head. 'Not this time.'

'How do you know?'

'Because he's got a bullet hole in his chest.'

Nolan looked longingly at the rest of his cheeseburger. Most of the time he made himself eat well, and the occasional burger was a rare luxury. He sighed. 'Let's roll.'

A gust of wind tagged them as they stepped out, the kind Chicago was famous for, brutal, cold, and hard enough you could lean into it, let it hold your weight. They'd left the blue Ford in a no-parking zone, but cops knew cop cars, marked or not. Nolan fired up the engine, changing his radio frequency from the seventh to the ninth district in case any news came over while they were en route. 'He tell you where they were?'

'Just said east side of the river.'

The drive up to Bridgeport took twenty minutes, but finding the scene turned out to be easy. A dozen squad cars sat beneath the overpass, their lights painting the underside of the freeway in garish sweeps of color. Traffic racing above made the dim space hammer and thrum. One of the beat cops from the district, a tall guy with wind-burned ears and the barrel-chested look of a tactical vest under his uniform – Peter Bradley, that was his name – spotted them and came over with a grin.

'Hey, Detective. You slumming?'

'Yeah. You can go home now, Bradley – the real cops have arrived.'

The beat cop laughed, started to lead them toward the water. 'Detective Jackson is down here.'

'What's the story?'

'Couple of kids saw the body, called it in.'

'You take their story?'

'Cutting class, said they came down here to hang out. They're headed to the ninth now. Want me to have the sergeant save them?'

Nolan nodded. It wasn't likely they were involved, but they might have seen something useful. That was crucial these days. The running joke was that in the war on crime, the Felony Review Board was France. Way they saw it, you didn't have a witness, may as well surrender. Nothing like *CSI*, teams of researchers working round the clock to make the physical evidence. Unless you were dealing with a high-profile case, somebody white and North Side, it took upward of four months to get anything more complicated than a print back from the crime lab.

Amid the sea of blue-shirted beat cops, Detective Willie Jackson was easy to spot in green corduroy pants, a purple shirt, and a fedora with – no shit – a feather in the band. Before Nolan made detective, he used to wonder why they all wore hats. Once he got bumped up, he found that standing out made it clear to everybody who was in charge. It was a little thing that made a difference. Some of the guys, it tended to be the ones who wore big mustaches, they went so far as cowboy hats. He'd just gone with a brown leather golf cap. Made the point and kept his head warm.

Jackson stood with arms crossed, watching an evidence technician as she knelt beside the body. Nolan could smell it from here. Floaters were notorious. The scent lingered in your nostrils for hours, even after a shower.

'You guys bring me one of them burgers?' Jackson turned to them, nodded to Matthews, shook hands with Nolan.

'Shit, no,' Matthews said. 'You mess with a man's lunch, you're on your own.'

Nolan ignored them, moving over to get a better look at the body. He didn't know the evidence tech, a woman maybe thirty-five, neat brown hair, but she clearly took her work seriously. She had the dead man's arm laid out on the cold concrete as she painted his fingertips with black ink. The victim had washerwoman wrinkles on his hands, and she held each finger firmly to soak it with ink. It felt intimate.

When it came to bodies, Nolan had a method. He didn't like to start with the face. Better to begin with the impersonal parts, the limbs, the clothing. That way you could look without emotion. There was a trick to being able to screen your vision, see only a part of the whole.

The arms showed no tracks, no sign of junk abuse. A tattoo marked the inner forearm, the ace of spades. The skin had started to get the green-brown tinge of a body that had been in the water a couple of days, and was marked by typical postmortem trauma, the result of scraping against God knew what on the river bottom.

His gaze circled inward. Black jeans, boots. A T-shirt that might once have been white, now dingy with river water and blood. Gases had swollen the belly – that was what made it float. A ragged wound gaped in his chest. At least the rats hadn't been at it yet. Sometimes with a body out of the river, the only way to find a wound was to look where they'd eaten.

Finally, the facts straight in his mind, cataloged and filed, he looked at the man's face.

Matthews joined him, wrinkling his nose. 'I hate floaters.'

'He's pretty, huh?' Jackson said. 'Any takers that it's homicide?'

Matthews knelt down. 'He was shot somewhere else.'

'The lividity, yeah.' Jackson directed his voice toward the evidence tech. 'You able to pull clean prints?'

She laid the arm down gently before breaking her quiet communion with the dead. 'I won't know for sure until we try to find a match. It's tricky when a body's been in water.'

'How long you figure he floated?'

She shrugged. 'The skin hasn't started sloughing. A couple days? The medical examiner can say for sure.'

Jackson nodded, clapping his hands together and rubbing them for warmth. 'Man, I hate this weather. Not even Halloween and it's cold enough to snow.' His voice echoed and rebounded under the concrete of the overpass. 'Nolan, you're pretty quiet. What do you think?'

'Run the prints.' Nolan kept his voice low as he stared at the man's face. 'But that's Patrick Connelly.'

25. The Axle of the World

Evan had played him.

Knuckles white on the steering wheel, Danny remembered the previous afternoon in the construction trailer, the scorched smell of old coffee, Evan's feet propped up on the counter. Saying that he would make the call. Saying it too quickly. It had rung an alarm in Danny's head, but he'd let it go.

Dammit.

The guy had known then what he was going to do. Been planning it. Things had never been under control.

You got it, kid. Welcome back to the dance.

After the disastrous phone call, he'd found himself at loose ends. He wanted a place to think, and had set out for a bar in his neighborhood, but when he got there the idea of being so close to home felt sleazy, like bringing a mistress to the marriage bed. He'd gotten back in the truck, planning to head for another neighborhood, but ending up just driving, restlessly circling the city. He'd been doing it an hour now. Driving and talking to himself, punctuating his sentences with slaps to the wheel, going faster as the anger simmered in his belly.

No matter how careful he was, how much thought he put into it, Evan was a tidal wave, an earthquake, a tornado. A force of nature. Danny pressed down harder on the accelerator, feeling the buzz of pavement beneath his tires. You could rage at a whirlwind. You could pull your hair and scream logic and good sense. But in the end, if you stood in its path, you took your chances. Cars blurred as he hurtled toward the skyline, weaving between lanes. There was no reasoning with a force of nature, no relying on its judgment. He swung left around a Mercedes. He'd hitched himself to the cyclone, and there was no way back.

A horn screamed beside him, the Mercedes squealing in panic as he merged into its lane, his quarter panel nearly against the rounded hood. He yanked the steering wheel back, too hard, the tires screeching, and for a moment he thought he might lose it, end up on two wheels and then in a slow, stuttering roll, this whole drama brought to a sudden close, but his nerves cut in, and he eased the wheel back, turning gently, cars all around him honking. Back in his lane, he took deep breaths, ignoring the angry look and middle finger from the driver of the Mercedes. Tapped the brakes to test them, and when they felt solid, started to slow.

Too much, too fast.

He flipped his hazards and worked his way over. He didn't stop in the grandma lane, but edged all the way off the road, the tires humming and buzzing across the divots cut in the pavement as he stopped. He killed the engine and squeezed the steering wheel, the silence punctuated only by the rhythmic whir of cars blowing by.

His father sat in the passenger seat.

He looked the same, just the way he had when he'd visited Cook County Prison, the last time Danny saw him alive. His face weather-beaten and lined, but proud. Hard. The hands rough, the circular-saw scar white across the bridge of his thumb. A cigarette clenched in the corner of his mouth, firm and straight as the axle of the world. He stared at Danny, and that look came into his eyes, the measuring one. Appraising.

Judging.

Dad . . .

In his mind, he heard the squeal of tires. Imagined Dad pumping at the brakes, trying to regain control, a cigarette still between his lips.

Imagined the decision. The choice, and its consequences.

The slow motion squeal of tires. The shatter of glass and banshee wail as steel kissed concrete. The way the truck had jerked up on its front wheels, fast at first but then slowing, pausing, maybe holding for a terrible instant before toppling over. The strange silence – so quiet, so embarrassingly quiet – after the truck came to rest upside down.

Dad. I . . .

In his mind, he could see the disapproval in his father's eyes. Nine years dead, and still disapproving.

Danny shook his head. The skyline twinkled under velvet indigo skies. A semi passed in a rush of air that rocked the Explorer from side to side. Without the heater, the air grew swiftly colder.

Danny turned off the hazards, started the truck, and got back on the road.

The low thrum of blues bass rolled up his spine as he slotted a coin into the phone and punched the numbers.

'You've reached Danny and Karen, we're not in right now . . .'

Before, he'd thought he'd go home after the job. He'd imagined he might ease the pain of waiting by reminding himself of the life, and the woman, that his efforts were meant to protect. Instead he stood in a rib joint on Halsted, listening to the accusatory beep of his own answering machine.

'Hey, Karen. Just wanted to let you know that I'm going to be late tonight. You know, work –' There was a fumbling noise.

'Danny.' She sounded out of breath. He thought of her wrapped in a towel and running for the phone, and the ease with which he could picture it stung him. He adopted a haggard tone as he told her how work was keeping him late. How he was sorry about it. She was silent on the other end of the phone, and he could imagine her biting her lip.

'Danny –'

'I know. It's just a crazy week.'

She sighed. 'Okay.'

'I'll make it up to you, babe. I promise.'

She paused. 'How about tomorrow night? We haven't been out in a while. We could,' her voice rose provocatively, 'make it a date night.'

'Sure.' He paused. 'I mean, I'll try.'

She snorted on the other end of the phone. 'Okay. See you whenever, then.'

'Wait –' But she'd already hung up.

Lying to Karen to keep her safe. Rationalizing Richard's willingness to screw his workers as justification for ripping him off. Planning a kidnapping to protect the kid. He'd always dealt in shades of gray, but it was getting harder to spot the contrast.

Across the room, he saw a waitress set his order on the table, but he had another call to make. He slotted the coin, willing the guy to answer. Five rings, and then the familiar message, asking him for one good reason to care that he'd called.

Danny cursed, and waited for the beep. 'Patrick, it's Danny. I need your help. It's –' He paused, trying to collect his thoughts. How much could he leave on an answering machine? 'It's about that thing we talked about. Look, just call my mobile when you get this, would you? Day or night.' He started to say more, thought better of it, slammed it in the cradle.

Then he went back to his table and ate his half slab in silence, trying to think of ways to tame the whirlwind.

In the dream he stood in a warehouse under bloody spotlights. Karen held the hand of a little kid in a rugby shirt, different from Tommy but the same. They both stared over Danny's shoulder, slack-jawed in terror. He turned in agonizing slow motion, the movement taking years. Evan stood smiling, the gun raising as though of its own accord, like the pistol was moving his arm instead of the other way around. But instead of pointing at him, the gun fell on Karen and the boy. Before he'd seen the muzzle flare Danny had jerked awake, drenched in sweat, Karen a sheet-wrapped silhouette beside him, the digital clock reading 5:32.

He'd showered in a daze and tiptoed out, a ghost in his own life.

Now though, back in the Explorer, morning light bright and cold through his windshield, he felt better. Morning did that to him; he was a sucker for the promise of a fresh start. Evan might be a force of nature, but Danny knew his potential, could read the climate of his moods. As he turned into the Pike Street complex, some of his strange black hope even began to return. If this was to be a game, at least he knew the rules.

He slid the gate open – they'd left it unlocked so that Debbie could get out if she needed – and pulled the Explorer in, parking it next to a battered Ford Tempo, the back window covered in band stickers and duct tape holding the seats together. As he killed the engine, the only sound he could hear was the snapping plastic on the building.

He got out of the truck, a cup of coffee in each hand, and shut the door with his hip. As he walked toward the trailer, a motion in the window caught his eye, two fingers spreading a dark slit in the blinds.

The door opened and Debbie stepped out, her arms folded across her chest, shoulders huddled in against the cold. The look on her face when he handed her a cup of coffee was as close to glee as he'd seen in a long time.

'Bless you,' she said, holding it to her mouth to blow the steam off.

He nodded, glancing over her shoulder to make sure she'd closed the door behind her. 'How is he?'

'Fine. He was scared at first, but he calmed down. We're watching *Cheers* reruns. There's a marathon on WGN.'

'Jesus, you didn't take his mask off?'

'No. It's not like you need to see to watch *Cheers*, you know?' She met his stare. 'Weren't we past the part where you thought I was dumb?'

He laughed. 'Right. Sorry. He's okay?'

She nodded, and something in him unclenched. He'd agonized over a way to knock Tommy out without hurting him, trying to think of every movie device, fantasies of tranquilizer darts and chloroform, but in the end, the stun gun had been the best and safest he could come up with. Police across the country used it because it was not only effective, but also assured there wasn't any permanent damage. But still. 'I'd been worried.'

She cocked her head and looked at him, an unblinking, New Agey gaze that made him uncomfortable. Her hair was parted in the center today, and fell straight past her shoulders. There was something kind of hippyish about her now and then. 'You were, weren't you?'

He nodded.

'Huh.'

'What?'

'Well, I guess I thought you'd be, I don't know,' she said, 'more like Evan.'

The comment surprised him, and he stared back, trying

to read the meaning in her eyes. In a game like this, it could be tricky separating ally from enemy. He and Evan were partners, yeah; but if things went sour, they were competitors, too, and both of them knew it. He'd assumed she'd fall on Evan's side of the divide.

'Tommy's a tough little kid, though,' she said. 'I like him. By the third episode of *Cheers*, the one where Cliff tries to get his mom to marry this rich guy? Ever see it? Good one. Anyway, by then he'd opened up, and hasn't quit talking since. Told me about school, about his favorite band. Said his dad works all the time, doesn't know he's alive. He doesn't seem too scared.' She brushed hair from her face. 'But he said he saw a guy with a gun pointed at him. You didn't use a gun, did you?'

She seemed sincere, but he'd seen the sharpness of the mind operating behind the façade. Unsure of his footing, it seemed easiest just to tell the truth. 'I didn't.'

'Evan?'

He shrugged and watched her eyes.

She nodded, but all she said was, 'Can we talk in your car? I'm freezing my tits off.'

The inside was still warm, but he turned the key to get the heater running. She immediately leaned forward and flipped on the radio, scanning up and down the dial like she was searching for signals from space.

'I shouldn't stay out here long. I think Tommy needs to go to the Loop.'

'Huh?'

She giggled, told him how they'd worked out a system for the kid to go to the bathroom, how it was funny, even though he was twelve, he'd been ashamed to mention it at first because she was a woman. Held it till he was squirming.

'I told him to call it the Loop. That's what my mom used to say, "Honey, do you need to go to the Loop?" Don't know if he knows what it means, but he gets a kick out of saying it.'

He laughed at that, told her he'd swing by later with some groceries, microwave dinners. Asked if she needed anything, and she shook her head, still working the dial. He had this feeling there was something on her mind, but he didn't know how to get at it. After a few more minutes of conversation, he told her he should probably leave.

'Your construction job?'

'Yeah.'

'Can I ask you something?' She bit her lip. 'It's his kid, isn't it? Your boss?'

He went cold. 'How did you know?'

She turned back to the radio, hair swinging across to mask her face. 'It's okay. It doesn't matter.'

'Debbie.' His voice level. 'How did you know?'

'I guess I have a confession to make.' She paused, one hand on the dial, still not looking at him. 'I helped Evan. Before this, I mean.' She sighed. 'He asked me to follow you.'

It came to him in a flash. That was why, when they'd met, he'd been sure he'd seen her before. She'd been in the zoo that afternoon he'd gone with Karen. She'd sat on the opposite bench while they talked about having kids, planned a future diametrically opposed to what he was doing now.

'I didn't know you then,' she continued. 'And you know, he and I . . .'

He nodded. 'It's okay.'

'Really?' An expression of girlish relief lit up her face.

'Yeah. It doesn't matter now.' He smiled. 'Thanks for telling me.'

She smiled back at him, reached for the door handle. 'So I'll see you later?'

He nodded, and she hopped out and closed the door,

headed for the trailer. He rolled down his window. 'Hey.' He faltered, not sure how to say what he was thinking, not wanting to give her the wrong idea. Then, 'I like your car.'

'Yeah?'

'It reminds me of you.'

'I remind you of an eighty-three Tempo?'

He laughed. 'Just that at a glance, it might give people the wrong impression.'

She smiled, a friendly expression with no trace of game in it, and nodded.

Maybe he had more allies than he thought.

26. A Book in Reverse

There were things about being a detective that Sean Nolan loved. The almost entrepreneurial sense of being his own boss, working a case the way his instincts dictated. The look of gratitude he sometimes saw from people he treated with respect, people used to mistrusting the Poh-lice. Those fleeting instants when he knew, with a certainty that most citizens never felt, that by doing his job he made things better.

But then there were days he had to haul floaters out of his river only to find he'd known the victim. And moments when he stood with his holster unsnapped, one hand on the grip of his weapon, not sure what he was about to walk into, but knowing he would walk into it regardless.

A low-bellied gray sky threatened to open up on the old gas station at any moment. The blue Ford was parked behind them, beside where the gas pumps used to be. Matthews stood a few feet back and off to one side, keeping an eye on the street. It wasn't anywhere you'd expect someone to live, and Nolan would've assumed the address was bogus if he hadn't snuck around back to peer through a window at a tall wooden dresser and an unmade bed.

Yesterday, before they'd left what passed for a crime scene – the river had played hell with everything – they'd noticed that Patrick's back was a darker color than his front. When a victim's heart stopped beating, gravity pulled blood to whatever side was down. If Patrick had been shot on the riverbank and rolled in, there shouldn't have been a chance for the blood to settle so neatly. Which meant that he'd likely been shot somewhere else and dumped later.

It could have happened anywhere. But police work was about elimination. This defunct gas station apparently used to be Patrick's home. They might well find a pool of congealed blood inside. Or a killer trying to clean it up.

That was the thing – you had to be up for anything. 'Ready?' Nolan asked, feeling the edge of adrenaline. Matthews nodded, a hand on his own gun.

Nolan took out the ring of keys they'd pulled from Patrick's pocket. A sodden gray thing that might once have been a rabbit's foot dangled from them. Two keys looked about the right size, but the grooves on the first didn't fit the lock. Heart loud in his chest, Nolan slipped the second key in one notch at a time until he felt it seat. Then, gently, he eased the deadbolt back. He took a last look at Matthews to confirm the man was ready to move, drew his weapon in his right hand, and with the left pushed the door open wide. Before it had even finished opening he was in, gun pointing low. Matthews moved behind him, his back to the wall to cover the opposite corner.

Venetian blinds strangled the light. The room was an open space dominated by mismatched recliners facing a TV. A poster hung above it, Telly Savalas as Kojak. The air smelled faintly of popcorn and sweat socks. Nolan turned, still in a shooter's crouch. Canvas screens separated the back half of the room, where he'd seen the bed through the window, and there was a door on one wall. He nodded to Matthews, who crossed to the other side of the room, pistol up, as Nolan stepped quickly behind the partition. Clear. He spun back to the inner door. There was no lock. He yanked it open, staying low.

The room beyond was the remnants of the service station garage, and the only part of this place that looked right. The concrete floor was pitted and scarred. A low-loader tow truck sat in the center, a red toolbox beside it. The space was large, with corners he couldn't see from here. Time to step up.

'Police,' Nolan yelled, lunging into the open space with his gun leveled. 'Don't move!' His voice was a cop's best weapon, more effective than the pistol. Aggressive behavior cowed people. They'd freeze before they had a chance to think about it. Matthews came in behind him, moving well, the two of them fluid, Matthews yelling just as loudly. Nolan stooped to look under the truck, checking for feet. He sprinted to the side and spun around it, then leveled his pistol across the hood and nodded. Matthews darted to the opposite corner to clear his lines of fire.

But apart from their echoes, the garage was silent. There was nobody here. Nolan could sense it, like returning home after a vacation, the way a place just felt empty. They went through the motions on the rest, checking the remaining cover: inside the truck, the small shop bathroom at the rear, the closets, but they found no one. Nolan's nerves settled. He straightened and holstered his weapon. 'You want this one or the other?'

'I'll check the living room.' Matthews turned and walked back the way they'd come.

Nolan moved through the garage, careful not to touch anything. Tools lay strewn on the floor, a pile of tarps in one corner. There was a workbench with a Saint Christopher's medallion hanging on it. He guessed you could take the man out of the parish, but not the parish out of the man. A radio on the floor, what they used to call a ghetto blaster back before things got politically correct. The bathroom was tidy, the toilet and tile clean. The floor had plenty of stains, but most of them looked like oil.

There was no pool of blood to be found.

He cursed quietly. Murder cases had infinite variations,

but only two categories – those with witnesses and evidence, and those without. If you caught a break within forty-eight hours, then the first category had a good chance of being cleared. Unfortunately, this one was shaping up to be the latter. The body had been in the water about a week, invisible until the expanding gases in the belly brought it to the surface. That would have given a killer plenty of time to clean up his mess. The river also destroyed most physical evidence; about the best they could hope was that the medical examiner would pull a bullet they might be able to ballistics match. And with nothing at Patrick's place, their likeliest crime scene had turned up snake eyes.

He sighed and walked back into the living room.

'You knew this guy, right?' Matthews was poking around with the tip of a pencil, lifting a newspaper from the coffee table. Normally they would need a warrant for all of this, but in the case of a body, the residence was fair game.

'A little.' Nolan moved to the small refrigerator by the bed, put on a pair of gloves, and opened it: a couple of take-out containers and a six-pack of Harp. Nothing smelled too foul – it hadn't been abandoned long. 'We grew up in the same neighborhood.'

'He run with bad people?'

'Last I heard he was small-time, a car thief. He got busted a couple years ago in somebody else's Caddy.'

'He go down for it?'

'No.' Nolan turned in a slow circle. No sign of violence, no furniture knocked over, no broken glass. 'Owner turned out to be dealing heroin out of an apartment in Uptown, and the whole thing fell apart.'

Matthews nodded. 'So what now?'

'Interviews.' Murder cases were like reading a book in reverse. There was a personal drama that ended in a body. That was where the police came in. Without evidence, the thing to do was work backward, talking to family and friends, a boss if the victim had one. You were trying to figure out who saw him last, because that was the guy that dumped him in the river.

Matthews groaned. 'We don't find a witness, state's attorney's going to kick this back to us.'

'Yeah.'

'You ask me, the first squad on the scene should have thrown rocks at the body till it drifted back across the river. Let Area Four deal with it.'

Nolan laughed. There was an answering machine on the dresser. He went to look at it. The old-fashioned tape kind. The message indicator was blinking, and he pushed PLAY.

'Paaaaaatrick,' a woman's voice. 'Where are you, my bad boy? David's in Milwaukee, and I'm lonely.'

Nolan rolled his eyes at Matthews, walked over to check the bedside drawer. Condoms, a couple of motorcycle magazines. The woman went on for another minute, hung up without leaving a number. They'd have to pull the phone records and find out when she'd last seen him, work forward from there. Sounded like she was married – the husband could be a suspect.

After that were a couple of hangups, and then a male voice came on, blues thumping behind it. 'Patrick, it's Danny.' Nolan straightened, his fingers tingling. 'I need your help. It's – it's about that thing we talked about. Look, just call my mobile when you get this, would you? Day or night.' The machine beeped again.

The detectives looked at each other. Nolan pressed REWIND and then PLAY, and the voice came back, the captured blues riff repeating behind it. He listened carefully, trying to filter out the noise behind the voice, the distortion of the crummy answering machine. 'Huh.'

'What?' Matthews asked.

'I think I know that guy.'

'Yeah?'

He nodded. It made sense – if he remembered right, Danny and Patrick had been friends back in the old parish. Now Danny was running scared, with Evan out of prison and shaking him down. Maybe Danny decided he needed help. Maybe he thought back and remembered a name, a tough-enough character.

Maybe, just maybe, Danny Carter had hired Patrick to take Evan out.

It was thin. Way too thin for a warrant. But worth exploring.

'I think,' Nolan said, 'we need to have a chat with a guy I know, claims he's in construction.'

27. Shrapnel

The walk from the fenced parking lot into the back corridor, past the stale-cigarette reek of the break room, through the double doors that separated the blue-collar portions of the office from the posh bleached-wood-and-stainless-steel lobby the clients saw, and up the hall to his office with its modular desk and narrow window took maybe thirty seconds. A brief enough time, but this morning, Danny's first back in the office, it felt like an eternity.

He held his smile up like an ID, pointing it this way and that, nodding at Richard's assistant, muttering something noncommittal in response to a question he hadn't quite caught. His stomach felt buoyant, crowding upward into his chest.

Blue flecks dotted the gray carpet in his office. He'd never noticed that before.

Danny took his appointment book from his satchel, set it on top of a stack of architectural magazines and trade show invitations, and dropped into his high-backed chair, one of those office store jobs designed without sympathy for the human body. They were standard issue to everybody but Richard, who sat in a seven-hundred-dollar Herman Miller throne.

Good reason to kidnap his son, he thought to himself, then, immediately, *Stop it.*

After everything had gone down yesterday, he'd still had to make an appearance on the job sites, and it hadn't been easy. He'd felt a fraud, moving through the buzz of honest labor, giving directions like he deserved to be there. The whole time knowing that he was poison, the worm in the apple. But somehow, it had been easier than sitting in his own office. He used to take great pride in it, the idea that Danny Carter, from Bridgeport, was the senior project manager, an invaluable, trusted member of a team. He'd enjoyed worrying about the delicate budgets of half a dozen jobs, the work schedules of forty men. He used to know that he could put in an honest day, and that when he went home, he would have earned the life that awaited him there.

Now, all he could think about was a construction trailer, and Evan with a gun, and the teetering structure of lies that had become his life.

Stop. This will all be over soon. Tomorrow we make the second call, Thursday we get Tommy back to Richard, Friday everything goes back to the way it was.

He wasn't sure that was true, not 100 percent convinced, but it was what he had. So he picked up his pencil, opened his papers, and started working.

The morning dragged by in a morass of paperwork and blank periods when he found himself staring at the wall. He had an embarrassing moment at his lunch meeting, when a client had to repeat a question three times before he heard it. 'Jesus, Carter, where were you?' the man had asked, holding his gaze, then deciding to let it go, saying, 'Must be better weather than here. Can I come next time?'

That had burned. Not the client's smart-ass comment, but the idea that he couldn't hold it together. That with his skills and experience and goddamnit, brains, he was simply not pulling through. The anger at himself surged quick and hot enough to keep his nerves humming through the rest of lunch.

As he walked back into the office, he held onto that glowing ember, fanned it, urged it to scorch. Forget this nonsense of moping about. If he wanted to rebuild his life when this was over, he couldn't succumb. No more. He would throw himself into work. Hit the phone hard, check in on the bids they'd shipped last month. Get some things accomplished. And when the day was done, go home to Karen. Better pissed off than helpless.

Jeff Teller, one of their foremen, was walking a guy Danny didn't know through the lobby, giving him the grand tour. Danny nodded hello, and Teller stopped him, introduced the man as an electrician new to the team. 'He's going to be helping us this winter.'

'Hey, welcome.' They shook hands, the guy's grip firm.

'Danny,' Teller said, 'is one of our project managers. The one you hope is running your job.'

'Hey, Teller, we already have you on contract. You can stop kissing up now.' The trash talk coming easy, a rhythm he knew.

Teller laughed. 'Seriously. He's a good guy,' making the two words into one. 'One of the ones in management you can trust.' There was no trace of irony in his eyes, and Danny found himself touched, wondering how Dad would have felt to hear that.

'Danny.' Richard stood half in, half out of his office door. 'Could you join me?'

Danny's mouth went dry, the good feeling evaporating in an instant. What was going on? Could Evan have screwed up somehow, gotten caught? Could Richard know? Was there a roomful of cops waiting? Part of him wanted to turn and run, just bolt.

Stay cool. You're hitched to the whirlwind, and the only way to land safe is to keep your head. 'Sure. Let me just drop my things.'

His boss nodded and stepped back inside his office. No police officers boiled out to replace him. There must not be any in there; what kind of a cop would give him time to climb out the window? Though that didn't mean that

Richard didn't suspect something himself. Danny shook hands again with Teller and the new guy, then walked into his office, willing his pulse to calm. He dropped his bag in the chair, glanced around the room without knowing what he was looking for, then put on his work face.

Richard sat in his expensive chair, leaning forward to rest his forehead in his palms as he stared down at financial statements. The usually neat mahogany desk was crowded with paper, binders with the Merrill Lynch logo on them and a notebook covered in Richard's neat, feminine handwriting. Danny rapped on the wall with his knuckles, and his boss jumped a little, like he'd forgotten he'd asked anyone to join him. Then he gestured to a chair. 'Get the door, would you?'

That did nothing to quiet the alarms in Danny's mind. Richard rarely closed his door. It wasn't a hippie, open-concept kind of thing; he just liked the whole office to know when he was in a rage. Danny took a seat, keeping his face neutral as he studied his boss.

Richard looked like hell. Dark circles carved canyons under both eyes. Generally capable of a five o'clock shadow by ten in the morning, today he looked like he hadn't shaved at all, and the salt-and-pepper stubble made him look older, more frail. His tie was impeccably knotted, and gold dice secured French cuffs, but with his left hand he fiddled with a pen, spinning it nervously between his fingers.

His boss's evident distress sent a stab through Danny, but he quickly closed it off. Everything would be fine. It had to be.

Richard looked at him, rubbed his eyes, and then leaned back. He opened his mouth, stopped himself. Though he looked like a man with something important to ask, what came out was, 'How's the progress on the restaurant?'

'It's fine. They're running electrical this week.'

'They know they need extra breakers for the kitchen? Morris wanted every cook surface on its own.'

Danny nodded, waiting for the man to get to the point. They sat in silence for a moment, Richard gazing out the window at the convenience store across the street.

'And the wiring, they know to use the –'

'It's under control. What's on your mind?' He knew, of course, but didn't dare give any indication.

His boss turned back from the window and began shuffling papers around. 'Right. Well, I've just been going over the financials, and I wanted to see if yours were up to date.'

'As of last week.'

'Anything change since then?' Was that a note of hope in Richard's voice?

'No. Everything is pretty much on schedule.'

'We haven't gotten the advance from the Cumberland people, have we?'

Danny shot him a perplexed look. Work on Cumberland Plaza, a strip mall in Joliet, wouldn't begin until at least March. It was their big spring job, and would come with a healthy advance for materials and manpower – but not in October. 'No.'

Richard nodded, slumped back in his chair.

'Should I call them about it?' Danny asked.

'Yeah, why don't you do that.'

'Any reason I can give them? For wanting the money this early, I mean?'

Richard peered at his notebook, not looking at Danny. 'Tell them we can swing a twenty percent discount on materials.'

'How are we going to do that?' The question sprang from habit, the project manager side of him trying to protect Richard from the pitfalls he liked to dig in front of himself.

'I'll negotiate a ten percent on a preorder. And the rest we'll make up by running a tight project.'

'This bid was already tight. There's no pad in it.'

'Look, we'll figure it out when the time comes. Right now, we just need the money.'

'For what?' The moment the question left his mouth, he realized he knew the answer. The puzzle pieces had been in front of him all along, he just hadn't put them together. *Oh God.*

Richard looked up, his eyes watery. The normal type-A arrogance was nowhere to be seen. 'I . . . we have some things we need to cover.' He looked back down, his shoulders low. 'Just do it, okay?'

It was clearly a dismissal, and Danny rose slowly, feeling numb. A memory of dropping by Richard's house flooded through him. The den, with its modern art paintings and drug-dealer leather couch. The grim, defeated expression on Richard's face as he hurried to shut off the computer monitors. Telling Danny he'd been getting worked in the stock market. That shrapnel from the bursting tech bubble had cut him badly.

How much had he lost?

Enough, came the answer. *Enough that he can't pay the ransom himself.*

And as a small business owner, if you find yourself in a desperate situation, like, say, trying to find the money to pay the ransom on your son, where do you go?

He's going to burn the company.

The bottom fell from his stomach as he walked out. Richard didn't watch him leave, his attention buried in the company balance sheets, as though a solution might be written within them. But Danny knew the numbers as well as the old man. Better. He knew what Richard was discovering. The money was there, sure. But it was the support structure of the company. It covered rent, kept the lights on, bought materials. It paid salaries and health insurance. If you tugged it out, the whole structure collapsed – and everyone who'd thought their footing was safe was suddenly scrabbling at air.

Teller's earlier words rang in his ears: *'He's a good guy. One of the ones in management you can trust.'*

Oh God.

What had he done?

28. Rough Times

After thirty minutes in front of the mirror, Karen had decided to wear her hair back to show off her neck, and gone with lipstick two shades bloodier than normal. The dress was new, a soft, fitted black thing too thin for this time of year. She'd even strapped on a pair of heels. Never let it be said that she didn't know how to do date night.

Unfortunately, her date was nowhere to be found.

'Another?' The bartender gave her that flirty look reserved for women who'd been stood up.

She started to shake her head, remembered the phone call, the mysterious message that'd had her nerves jangling all afternoon. 'Why not.'

A server bumped her chair in passing, the rich smells of marinara and basil making her stomach growl. The hostess looked over, and Karen shook her head. The woman smiled sympathetically, girl to girl, and called out someone else's name for the table that was supposed to have been theirs forty-five minutes ago.

Out of professional habit, she watched the bartender make her drink. A little heavy on the vermouth and a lot heavy on the ice and the shaking. Bad enough to charge ten bucks for a martini; criminal to bruise it that badly. He set it between the votive candles that lined the black lacquer bar and gave her the look again. 'You waiting for someone?'

'Not for much longer,' she said, and turned away.

She'd come in from the gym that afternoon to find the answering machine flashing three. One call from a bar back saying she couldn't make it to work that night. A computerized voice from Walgreens, telling her a prescription was ready.

And sandwiched between them, that other message.

What had it meant? She hadn't recognized the voice, but the guy spoke like he knew all about them. She told herself it wasn't important, that it probably had to do with Danny's job. The icicle stab of fear she felt was probably just because she'd been anxious lately. That asshole in the alley had scared her more than she liked to admit. Normally she would have used Danny to help her get over it, let him serve as the mirror to reflect her own fear back until she could see it for what it was, until she'd dealt with it. But since that night, they'd hardly been in the same room. It was like he was running from her.

Ebb and flow, girl. Every relationship has trouble spots.

Sure. But if he didn't ebb-and-flow in here in the next five minutes, she was changing the locks.

She spotted him fighting his way through the crowd with two minutes to spare. He wore a black jacket over a soft gray oxford, and when he glanced at his watch, she could see him grimace and swear. Her heart caught a little bit, even after all the years.

He smiled at her, boyishly contrite. 'I'm sorry, Kar.'

'You'd have been sorrier in two minutes,' she said, standing and thumbs-upping the hostess, her voice mock angry. 'I look *good*.'

His laugh made her think that maybe date night would work out after all. As they walked to their table, he rested a hand on the small of her back. He didn't pull out her chair – she hated that – but waited to sit down until she had, and smiled at her again.

'So,' she said, 'they let you out of your cage.'

He nodded. 'Thank God.'

She folded the napkin in her lap and sipped her water. He

looked around the room as if taking it in. Their eyes met for a moment and then skidded away, like they were on an awkward first date.

'Good evening, folks.' The waiter stepped forward with an obsequious smile. He handed her a menu, then one to him, and set the wine list in the center. 'We have several specials this evening.'

They'd been coming here for years, and though Danny teased her for it, she always ordered the same thing. So instead of listening to the specials, she watched Danny fidget with his silverware. His shoulders were clenched. He nodded thoughtfully from time to time, but never in response to anything the waiter said. Truth be told, despite the sharp clothes, he looked wrecked, and her optimism about date night began to evaporate.

'You want another?' She gestured at the scotch he'd already drained.

'Guess I was thirsty.' His smile didn't quite fit.

'I'll catch his eye.'

He nodded absently, and turned back to the menu.

'Want to get an appetizer?' she asked.

'Sure. Whatever you want.' It would have sounded sweeter if he'd been looking at her.

'How about the shrimp?'

'Okay.'

'Danny.'

He looked up at her, dark craters under his eyes.

'You're allergic to shellfish.'

'Right.' He blew air through his mouth, not quite a laugh. 'Sorry. I'm not all here tonight.'

'Where are you?' When he didn't respond, she sighed. 'What's going on? And don't tell me work.'

He looked at her, then looked away. 'I don't know what to say.'

'You know,' she said, her voice sharp, 'a lot of women would start to get suspicious if their boyfriend was suddenly working late every night. Start wondering if "working" was a way of saying "sleeping with somebody else."'

That got his attention. He turned, his eyes firm on hers. 'Of course not.'

She felt ashamed. That had been a cheap shot. 'I know.'

He nodded, looked away again.

'Danny . . .' Her voice trailed off. Everybody had rough times. She wanted to believe that's all this was. But the signals he was giving off were all wrong. In the past they'd always worked through things together, but now he seemed to be pulling away. 'Is it me? Something I've done?'

'No,' he said quickly. 'It's not you.'

Somehow that was scarier. 'Then what?'

'Look.' He leaned forward, hesitated, like he was searching for the right words. 'Right now is just a crazy time. I have a lot of things going on, and it's starting to get to me. But this will all be over soon.'

'When?'

'By the end of the week. Things will be back to normal. I promise.'

It was the kind of answer she should have hoped for, but somehow, it wasn't comforting. She held up her glass and spun it idly, watching the wine swirl. She felt the grip of one of those weird moments when the physicality of the world – the noisy bar, the art photographs on the wall, the wine rolling red and glinting along the bowl of her glass – overwhelmed any sense of meaning. Left her feeling stranded. Without stopping to consider, she tossed the question like a grenade, hoping they wouldn't be wounded in the blast.

'Why did a detective call our house today?'

Silence. She looked up to find him staring.

185

'What?' he asked.

'A Detective Nolan. He left a number. It's on the machine. He said he had some things he wanted to ask you about.'

It was only an instant. But for a ragged fraction of a second, she saw clear through him. Past what he called his game face. Saw his mouth hanging open and his mind scrambling for a lie.

And then it was over, and his mask slid back into place. 'We've had some break-ins. Vandalism, some tools stolen. It's probably just kids, you know, but I have to go through the motions.'

She nodded. She didn't know what she'd seen, didn't know what it meant, but she knew she wasn't going to sit still for it. She'd always pitied women – people – who chose to blind themselves to what was right in front of them. Better to deal with things, even if they were painful. She looked at him again, took in his friendly expression and calculated look, and then she finished a last sip of wine and stood up.

'Good night, Danny.'

He blinked, stuttered her name. Asked her to wait.

She didn't.

29. A Thousand Needles

When he'd come by and said they were going to lunch, Debbie had said no. Tommy would be scared if she was gone for more than a couple of minutes. They stood in the construction yard, the skies gray and heavy, the motion of traffic barely visible through that orange slatted stuff they wove into chain-link fences. Evan had just looked at her, muscles and strong chin, soap-opera stubble, a tiny grin on his lips, and next thing she knew, they'd been up against the outside of the trailer, her jeans tangled at her knees, panties tugged to one side, the aluminum siding freezing when her breasts rocked against it. And as always, he'd gotten her off so hard her legs melted.

The girlfriends who tried to steer her away from the guys she liked had never understood that it was precisely the fact that they were bad that drew her to them.

Still, as the waitress plunked their burgers down on the Formica table, she fought a wave of guilt. 'We should hurry.'

He reached for the Tabasco and began to drench his fries in the stuff. 'Why?'

'You know.' She cut her hamburger in half, then in quarters. It didn't taste right otherwise.

He shrugged, seeming to lose interest in the conversation before it began. 'Proud Mary' played in the background, the volume way too soft. If you were going to do Ike and Tina, you had to be able to feel it. Otherwise, what was the point?

'So this is going to be a big score, huh?'

A waitress swayed by, a tired-looking bottle blonde with a

nice figure, and she watched his eyes follow her ass before he answered. 'Sure.'

'How much?'

'Enough.'

'For what?'

'Jesus, ease up, okay? I'm trying to eat.' His voice barely rose, like she wasn't worth getting annoyed at.

She shrugged, picked up a quarter of her burger. Overcooked but still yummy, and she ate quickly, glad to have a break from microwave dinners. When she finished she leaned back and tossed her napkin on the plate. He shook his head. 'You really are in a hurry, aren't you?'

She shrugged. '*The Rockford Files* are on at two.'

'So?'

'I told Tommy we'd watch it together.'

'What, are you playing at motherhood here? You want to adopt him?' He had a thin-lipped grin that she didn't like, that made him look like a school-yard bully. 'This is a job, Deborah.'

The name made her grit her teeth, and he knew it, so she stopped herself from correcting him. 'I know. That's why I want to get back.'

'So you can watch *The Rockford Files*?'

'No. Because Danny's plan –'

'Whoa. Danny's plan?'

'All I mean is, shouldn't we be there, just to make sure nothing goes wrong?'

'Jesus fucking Christ. You and he sound like the same broken record.' Evan pitched his voice girlishly high. 'Oh geez, I hope nothing goes wrong. Oh gosh. Things could go wrong.'

'Fuck you.'

'That's more like it.' He laughed, leaned forward to stub out his cigarette. 'Come on.'

'Where are we going?'

'To make a phone call.' He threw money on the table and got up, grabbing his leather jacket in one hand. She stood and followed him through the half-empty diner, the music now 'Papa Was a Rolling Stone,' still too low. They walked past the chrome-trimmed counter, the short-order cook behind it scraping at the grill, metal rasping on metal. Between the bathrooms, the phone hung on shabby brown paneling, the cheap kind that felt cozy only at 4:00 A.M., waiting for the caffeine to counter the alcohol enough that you could see yourself home. The restaurant was quiet here, just an old guy at the edge of the counter twenty feet away. Evan took a matchbook from his jacket pocket and opened it to a phone number.

'Who's Dick?' Debbie asked.

'Danny's boss.'

He fished for a quarter and stabbed it in while she processed that, it coming on her in a rush. 'Wait a second. You mean Tommy's –'

'Yeah.' He started punching numbers.

'You aren't going to call him from here, are you?'

'Why not? Something could go wrong?' Before she could reply he held up a finger for silence. 'Dick. You know who this is?' His voice into the receiver was slow and menacing.

Jesus.

She looked around, fighting rising panic. The old man at the counter seemed to be reading his newspaper. The hostess faced the other way, slumping across the register with her arms folded. It looked like they were clear.

Evan continued. 'That's right. You have the money?' He paused. 'Half the money, you get half your son. You want the top or the bottom?'

She hadn't wanted to hear this part. It brought it all home, changed it from babysitting a kid to something a million times more awful. Falling for bad boys was one thing. This was something else entirely.

'By tomorrow. We'll call later to tell you when and where.'

Putting on blinders and pretending it was an innocuous job was nonsense. She knew that, always had. But sometimes you went along to get along. Now, she was wondering how big a mistake that had been.

'And Dick, you know what happens if we even *suspect* you've called the police? We shoot your little boy in the head.'

Beside them, the door to the men's bathroom swung suddenly open. A chubby guy in a Bears jersey came out, not looking at Evan, his eyes on her for a second, just a second, but something weird in them, like he'd caught something he shouldn't have. Then he was past them, taking a jacket from a booth near the door.

She looked at Evan, his eyes narrow as he watched the fat guy at the register, the hostess asking if everything was all right, the man nodding, reaching in his wallet.

'Good. Wait by the phone, Dick.' Evan hung up, gesturing her closer. 'That guy heard.'

His tone scared her more than anything she could remember.

'No,' she said. Tried to smile. 'I don't think so.'

She could see him calculating, and suddenly realized that if she couldn't convince Evan, then that guy was going to get hurt. Or worse. She remembered Danny telling her about the gun Evan had brought when they took Tommy.

Then the right answer came natural as anything. She knew just what to say. 'Nah. He was too distracted.'

'By what?'

She smiled. 'My tits.'

He looked at her, steady for a moment, then breaking into a laugh. 'All right. Let's go.'

Relief boiled sweet through her, leaving her skin hot and hands tingling like a thousand needles. She'd done it. Part of her wanted to hoot for joy, but she had to stay calm. So she just started for the door, putting an extra sway in her hips to cover the trembling.

'Bye now,' the hostess singsonged as they stepped through the glass door. The air was fresh and sharp, the cold welcome. They walked around the restaurant to the parking lot in the back, by the Dumpster and the big air conditioner. The lot was bare, only a couple of other cars. The chubby guy walked ahead of them, toward an SUV parked beside the Mustang. She wondered if he'd ever know that she had saved his life. Did that karmic debt tie them in some way? She didn't exactly believe in reincarnation, but energy was energy, and you never knew.

'See?' Evan said, fishing in his jacket pocket for the car keys. 'I told you there was no reason to worry.'

She smiled over her shoulder at him. 'You're the man, baby.'

'Maybe I'll take you back to the trailer and fuck you up against the other side.'

Even after her earlier panic – or because of it – that sent a flush of heat through her, and as they reached the passenger side of the car she turned, her tongue flicking her lips, starting to lean back, ready to give him a kiss that would send lightning down his spine and back up the other side – only he kept going, pushed past her, and opened the driver's side of the SUV, the engine already running, the fat guy yelling as Evan leaned in and grabbed him by his shirt front and yanked him right out of the truck, slamming him up against the side of the Mustang like a rag doll, the guy grunting, his arms raised, Evan holding him with his left hand and using his right to punch the guy in the throat, not like the movies where men hit each other on the chins and their heads and hands snap back, no, Evan's fist continuing too far, and when it pulled back coming out bloody, the ring of keys still in his hand, two of them braced between knuckles dripping scarlet, and then winding up again, and again, three times, the guy not making a sound anymore, everything that fast, and Debbie still standing there, frozen in a vamp pose, her lips and her legs open, as Evan let the body drop to the cement, blood pouring from the neck.

He turned, his face a brutal mask. No longer the soap-opera bad boy of her imagination, but a wild-eyed beast kept too long in a cage. Then he thrust the bloody keys into her hand and ducked down to grab the man's feet.

'Open the trunk,' he said.

She took one look at the brass keys shining and wet in her palm, turned sideways, and booted her burger all over the pavement.

30. Gone

Half of Detroit burned down every year on the night before Halloween. Or it used to, back in high school, when Karen had lived downriver. In Wyandotte the pranks had been more on the level of blowing up mailboxes than torching warehouses, but she'd always hated Devil's Night anyway. Maybe because of her brothers; they'd always go out, prepared like commandos, dressed in black and packing duffel bags stuffed with eggs, toilet paper, M-80 firecrackers, spray paint, God knew what else. They always let her paint camouflage makeup from the drugstore on their faces, but when she would beg them to let her come along, David would laugh, and Brian would ruffle her hair and say that it was guy stuff. Then they'd leave on their adventures and she'd sit home stewing.

Now here she was, the day before Halloween. Thirty-two years old and still being excluded by the man in her life.

After storming out the night before, she'd come home, taken a bath, and gone to bed, waiting for the sound of the front door. Expecting Danny to come after her, ready to be honest about what was going on and put her worst fears to rest.

She was still awake at one o'clock, when he crept in and tiptoed past their bedroom to the kitchen. She heard the answering machine beep, and then the sound of the message. Then heard it twice more.

By the time he finally came to bed, she'd fallen into sweaty dreams of her brothers setting their condo on fire and laughing as she leaned out the window and begged them to stop.

When she woke up, Danny was gone.

She went to the gym and attacked the elliptical for an hour, then hit set after set of crunches, trying to use the fire in her muscles to burn away the suspicions that had grown since she'd heard the detective's call. She showered under blistering water, and treated herself to breakfast out. Sat in a booth and read the front page of the paper five times without absorbing a word.

Then she came home, replayed the answering machine message, and dialed the number, as she'd known she would since she woke up alone.

On TV, the cops sat at desks piled with papers. There were oscillating fans in steel cages, and the telephones were always old rotaries. Karen wondered if that was what it really looked like, and doubted it. They probably sat in cubicles like everybody else.

'Detective Nolan.' His voice sounded gruffer than on the machine.

'This is Karen Moss.' Her heart thumped against her ribs so loudly she was afraid he might hear. 'You called Danny and me yesterday.'

'Danny Carter?'

'Yes.'

'Is he there?'

'No. He's been busy lately, so I thought I'd see if I could help.'

'I'd really like to speak to him. Do you have another number?'

'Not really. He's in construction, you know, and he's away from his desk a lot.' He had a mobile, of course, but she didn't say that. She'd indulge her curiosity, but not to the extent of putting Danny in an awkward position.

'I see. What about when he gets home?'

'I'm not sure when that will be.'

There was a pause. 'Ms Moss, does Danny know you're calling?'

Her heart hammered louder. 'No.'

Another pause, then a sigh. 'You don't happen to know a guy named Patrick Connelly?'

Of course. This must be all about Patrick. Relief flooded through her, and she almost laughed at herself, at her foolish worries. Some part of her had actually started to imagine that Danny was the one in trouble, that Danny had done something irreparable.

'Sure, I know Patrick. Is something wrong?'

'Well . . .' He paused, one beat that stretched to two, and then three, and she felt spiders of dread crawling back up her arms. 'I'm sorry to have to tell you. He's dead.'

Her fingers went cold, and she felt like she was going to drop the phone. 'That can't be. He was just here for dinner.'

'He was?' Nolan sounded surprised. 'When?'

'I don't know. A week and a half?' What had happened? Some accident on his bike, maybe? She knew he didn't wear a helmet half the time. Unbidden, an image rose in her mind, Patrick splayed and broken across the hood of a car.

'So he was a friend of yours?' Nolan asked.

'Of ours, yes. Will you tell me what happened?'

There was another pause. 'He was killed last week. Maybe Monday or Tuesday.'

'Killed?' She tried to think of another way Nolan might have meant the word. 'Do you mean – what do you mean?'

'He was shot.' He paused. 'I know that's hard to hear. But I think it might be good for us to talk in person.'

Her mind felt numb, woolly. Patrick murdered.

'Ms Moss?'

'Sorry. Now?'

'You live up near Wrigley, right? I can be there in an hour or so.'

'No.' The word came out fast, unplanned. She didn't want the detective in their home. 'I'll meet you somewhere.'

'Where?'

She gave him directions to a restaurant on Belmont, and promised to meet him in an hour. When she hung up the phone, the quiet stung her ears. Thoughts came quick and chaotic. Who would shoot Patrick? He was just a boy, more mischief in him than evil. She knew he stole cars, that he robbed people, but still, she more easily pictured him in a tree house than in a coffin.

Then the next thought. Danny. This would tear his heart out.

She wandered into the bathroom, took off her clothes and started the shower, thinking it would give her a place to cry. While it heated, she sat on the bed, staring out the window at the brick wall three feet away, thinking about the detective and feeling dread tighten her stomach. Detective Sean Nolan. She tried to put a face to the name, imagined a young Pacino, eager, a cop on the make. Why had she agreed to meet him? It felt like meeting a plague bearer. He lived in a world she and Danny had left behind; what if the traces that lingered on him infected the life they had built for themselves?

And *she* had called *him*. There was cruel irony there. Some part of her had been afraid that maybe, just possibly, Danny had involved himself in that old life again. But it turned out she was the one who had opened the door to let it in.

Get a grip, Karen. Patrick would be dead either way.

In the end, she spent forty minutes going from the bed to the couch, the couch to the kitchen, pacing and anxious, before finally turning off the water in the shower, putting her clothes back on, and walking out to meet the detective.

Ann Sather was a Chicago institution, a cavernous Swedish restaurant filled with the smell of coffee and echoing with noisy conversation. She would have known Nolan even if he hadn't described himself. It wasn't the buzz-cut hair, the silver tiepin, or the brown leather golfer's cap. It was an air of confidence, like he'd been tested in ways most people would never face, and felt good about the way he'd scored. She recognized it easily. Danny had the same thing.

'I'm Karen Moss.'

'Sean Nolan.' His eyes were a watery blue, at once kind and hard. 'Thanks for coming.'

She let the hostess guide them to a table, wondering what she was doing here. They sat in awkward silence as the waitress weaved between the tables to take their drink order. Karen asked for an orange juice she didn't want. He ordered decaf and a cinnamon roll. She laughed, the pitch nervous.

'What?' he asked.

'Not exactly what Serpico would've ordered.'

'Pacino never had to fill out offense reports or try to remember the abbreviation codes for the vehicle database, either.' He smiled. 'But I see why you and Danny get along.'

'What do you mean?'

'Just that he's a smart-ass, too.'

He said it lightly, smiling, and it disarmed her enough that it took a minute to catch the obvious. 'Wait. You know Danny?'

He nodded. 'A little. We grew up in the same neighborhood.'

She groaned. 'Of course. I should have guessed.'

'What?'

'"Sean Nolan." It's as Irish as "Danny Carter."'

He laughed. 'Guilty. I still think of the South Side more in terms of parishes than neighborhoods.'

He gave and took shit casually, in a bantering way that made her comfortable. It must be crucial in his business, the ability to win people's trust. She realized that she was starting to like him, and the thought brought her up short. She didn't want to like him. She didn't want to know him. Detectives had no place in their life.

'So.' She leaned back and crossed her arms. 'What can I help you with?'

He sensed the change in her tone and met it, his voice becoming more official. 'Well, first, again, I want to say that I'm sorry about Patrick.'

'What happened?'

'We're not sure yet. There's not much I can tell you at this point, except that we're working hard on it.'

'Not much you *can* tell me or much you *will* tell me?'

'Both.' He said it matter-of-factly, without malice.

The waitress arrived and plunked their drinks in front of them. His coffee slopped over the rim and spread a thin brown stain on the paper placemat.

'Where did you find him?' Karen asked, a catch in her voice.

He hesitated. 'His body was in the river.'

She looked away, the world going smeary in front of her eyes. Shot and dumped in the river. 'Did you know him, too?'

'Yeah.' He looked away. 'A little.'

'I'm sorry.'

Nolan nodded brusquely. 'When was the last time you saw him?'

'At dinner. I think it was the Saturday before last.'

'He came to your house?'

'Yes.'

'So you were close.'

'Yes. Well, really, Danny was. Patrick was practically a brother to him.'

A look flickered across the detective's face, like she'd said something important, and it put her on her guard. Why would Danny's relationship with Patrick matter?

'Did Patrick ever talk about his business?'

She opened her mouth, then closed it, not sure how to answer. It was a complicated sort of simple question. Did they know that their friend was a car thief, a bar fighter, a hijacker of trucks? If so, well then, what kind of people were they? It was part of the reason that no matter how much she liked him, even loved him, she always felt uncomfortable around Patrick. Danny assumed it was because she was afraid of him backsliding, but it was more than that. She was afraid being close to Patrick meant that nothing fundamental had changed.

The detective seemed to read her mind. 'Karen, I know that Patrick wasn't an altar boy, and I'm sure you do, too. I'm not trying to bust him – or you – for anything. I'm just trying to find out who might have killed him.'

'We knew what he did.' She paused. 'That he stole things. But he never really talked about it.'

'Not to Danny either?'

She shrugged. 'I doubt it. They were old friends, but Danny's in construction. I can't see Patrick talking about what he did.' Neither her voice nor her conscience quivered. Calling the detective to find out what was going on was one thing. Inviting him to search their closets for skeletons was another.

Nolan smiled, his lips thin. 'How's construction working out for him?'

'Fine.' She kept her tone cool. 'Busy.'

'I'll bet. Harder work,' he paused, locked eyes, 'than his old life, huh?'

The sudden transition scared her. He was after something. 'What do you mean?'

'Just that he wasn't always in construction. Did you know that? That he wasn't always in construction?'

She fought back the urge to throw her orange juice on this cop who had appeared from nowhere to mess with their lives. Instead, she made herself smile sweetly. 'I know everything I need to know about Danny, Mr Nolan. And I don't think there's anything else I can do for you.' She reached for her bag on the seat beside her.

He nodded. 'Sure, sure. So you know he came to see me last week, then?'

'I . . . he told me that he had been talking to you about some vandalism, something at one of the construction sites.'

He shook his head slightly, his eyes never leaving hers. 'Danny called me last Monday, asked me to meet him for breakfast.' The friendly Irishman look had been replaced by an analytical stare. 'I hadn't seen the guy in years. Not since I was a beat cop.'

Last Monday. The day Danny had inexplicably taken off from work. She caught her hands shredding a napkin under the table, a nervous habit from when she was nine.

'But he says it's urgent, so I meet him at this diner on West Belmont. When he gets there, he hems and haws for a while, then finally says he has a problem.' He hesitated, looked at her. 'He didn't tell you any of this?'

She felt off balance, like she needed air, or a drink of water. But she kept her expression neutral. 'Any of what? I don't tell Danny about every breakfast I have.'

He smiled slightly, just a flicker, like throwing a salute. Then his hard expression resettled. 'He told me that Evan McGann had come to see him.'

The room warped. Her knuckles went white on her purse straps. Something laughed from her dark place, the one that reveled in car accidents and natural disasters. It laughed, and its laugh told her that she had been right, that the suspicion she hadn't let herself acknowledge was 100 percent dead-on. She saw a flash of a woman's face, bruised eggplant purple. 'That's not possible. He's in jail.'

'Not anymore. Walked from Stateville about a month ago.'

The booth fell out from beneath her. 'But – he was sentenced to twelve years.'

'Welcome to the American criminal justice system.' He stabbed a piece of cinnamon roll, the cloying smell making her stomach roil. 'After Danny came to me, I checked with McGann's parole officer. The PO said that after the guy was released, he disappeared. Never called in, not once. Do you know what that means?'

She shook her head.

'It means that he has no intention of trying to get clean. It means he's staying a criminal. But that's not the interesting part. The part that gets me is that the first thing he did,' his eyes drilled into hers, 'was get in touch with his old partner.'

The air in the café seemed sticky. Her pulse was pounding, and she felt a reckless disconnection from things, like an alcohol buzz. Danny had seen Evan, and he hadn't told her about it. His old partner, the guy he'd grown up with, robbed people with, the one who had shot a man and beaten a woman half to death. And Danny had smiled, and told her it was a busy season in construction.

Oh God.

'There's more,' Nolan continued. 'Yesterday we searched Patrick's house. There was a message from Danny on the answering machine. A message about a job.' The detective leaned back.

'I don't – I . . .' She stared at him, feeling the room contract around her. Her thoughts piled up like a car crash in the movies, each tearing and cutting and wrenching at the one before, and she knew that when it all ended, when silence fell at last, nothing would ever be the same.

'Karen?' The detective's voice was level and calm, his eyes lasers on hers. 'What's Danny up to?'

She stared at him, wondering the same thing, the last weeks coming into focus. The late nights. Danny's distraction, feeble excuses, and inability to discuss anything. Last night's promise that it would all be over soon. That suggested a task, a goal. A specific job to complete. All the things the detective wanted to hear, wanted to know. The detective with his South Side patter and easy smile hiding the knife he used to shred their world.

Fuck him.

'I'm sorry.' She slid out of the booth, her purse trailing behind. 'I don't know what you're talking about. And I can't help you.'

The move startled him, and she used the momentum to escape, let it block out his voice, his last question, the one that in the movies would have stopped her in her tracks, but in real life she didn't even hear. She stepped past the hostess and out to the open air and noise of Belmont. The sunlight startled her. A cab honked as it went by, but she shook her head and began walking.

In the whole of her years with Danny, she'd made only one unretractable promise. It was after going to court for him, listening to a nasal prosecutor in a brown suit explain that in the photographs the jury was examining, the bloody boot marks on the body indicated where the victim had been kicked *after* he'd been shot. She'd only met Evan once before then, but she knew how much he had meant to Danny, and she watched him, wanting to see some remorse, some regret. It wouldn't undo what he had done, but it would put it on a level she might understand. But Evan had looked perfectly at ease, his calm unruffled.

It had made her want to vomit.

She'd sat like a statue, teeth clenched, through the whole trial. Then she'd come home and made her one and only ultimatum to Danny.

If he ever backslid, ever fell back into the life, she was out of there.

Gone.

31. Whatever Followed the Truth

Even having been here before and lacking the time now to appreciate it, even with a federal crime on his conscience and a detective on his trail, even with his girlfriend furious and his life upside down, Danny couldn't help but find Union Station's Great Hall breathtaking. Pillars lined the mammoth room, gracefully vaulting upward to support Beaux Arts alcoves and balconies. Eighty feet above, the domed glass ceiling cut the twilight sky into neat blue-gray geometries. The room had the echoing quiet of a church. The benches dotting the floor even looked like pews, though instead of a gathering of the faithful, the benches held a congregation of the unwanted, men and women with a pallor of dirt that couldn't be washed away by a thousand showers, whose hacking coughs and newspaper shuffles bounced incongruously around the airy space.

Danny walked down the marble steps, conscious of the bored watchfulness of the homeless. The Great Hall was out of the question for his purposes. He nodded briefly at a staring old man with a scraggly beard. The guy didn't acknowledge him, just swiveled his head to trace Danny's path across the floor. Hallways led in several directions, and he went left at random, following a gentle ramp into a more modern section, all fluorescent lighting and corporate plants.

As he wandered, he found himself thinking about last night. Dinner with Karen. He'd rarely seen her so mad, the anger simmering just beneath the surface. She obviously knew something was going on. When she'd asked if it was her fault, something she'd done, he'd almost told her everything. Almost spilled the whole foul mess out to steam on the table between them. But the quiet voice inside had whispered, *Steady on.* Told him that he was nearly safe. That this would all be over in a few more days, and then he could devote all his energy to making it right with her.

He'd spent his whole life listening to that little voice. Listening to it had saved his butt plenty of times. But he was starting to wonder if it was the best source of relationship advice.

Not to mention that in a few days I'll have bankrupted my boss and cost forty men their livelihoods, all in commission of a felony that could land me in a backwoods super-max prison.

The thought put him in mind of Nolan, of the phone message that had shaken Karen up. Shit, shaken him up, more than he'd dared show.

'Danny, this is Detective Nolan. We need to talk. Some things have come up I want to ask you about. Call me. ASAP.'

What did that mean, things had come up? What things? His first thought was that Richard had panicked and gone to the police. But he couldn't figure a way that made sense. After all, Richard shouldn't have been able to connect the crime to Danny. And if he somehow could, then Nolan wouldn't be calling his house – he'd be waiting outside it with two squad cars as backup.

Danny took an escalator up one level to the ground floor and found himself between a newsstand and a McDonald's. Glassy-eyed commuters milled in all directions. Definitely a no-go. He stepped off the up escalator, turned, and hopped on the down. Glass doors ran across the opposite wall, with signs pointing to Metra trains, Amtrak trains, more food and convenience stores blocked by throngs of people. It was five o'clock, rush hour, a good bit earlier than they would be working. But that was the point. Better to scope it out at its worst. If he could find the right spot under these circumstances, then he'd have confidence for tomorrow.

Even if Nolan's call didn't have anything to do with Evan, with what they were doing, he wasn't sure he wanted to call the detective back. He didn't need another factor confusing things. It was complicated enough trying to stay a step ahead of Evan and ensure that everybody got through this disaster unscarred.

Except Richard and every honest man that works for him. Every man just like Dad.

In the movies, ransom exchanges always went down in a parking deck, or out in the country somewhere. Two cars parked thirty yards apart, pleas to see the hostage, brusque orders to show the money. But he'd seen the way Evan acted in a private space. He'd pulled a gun on a startled twelve-year-old – how could he be trusted to keep cool faced with a murderously angry father holding a million in cash?

Hence Danny's current errand. He needed a place that was public enough that even Evan couldn't shoot anybody, yet private enough they could do the exchange. And it had to offer enough escape routes that they wouldn't accidentally find themselves gridlocked on the Dan Ryan next to Richard and Tommy. They needed street exits, multiple levels, cabs, trains, and lots of people. The best place to hide a needle was in a needlestack.

All of which added up to Union Station.

It took him another hour of wandering and watching. At first he liked a quiet hallway off the beaten path, but a sudden crowd debarking a train blew that one. Finally, he came on a dull antechamber at the top of a stopped escalator. An abandoned gift shop flanked one side. The other connected to an adjacent office building. In the twenty minutes he waited, only one person came through, a harried-looking guy in a blue suit, who rushed from the office building, letting the door slam behind him. By ten tomorrow, the office would be cleared out – the odds of anyone coming through weren't nil, but they were acceptably slim, and wildly preferable to anywhere that might give Evan the privacy to go kill-crazy.

The only problem he could think of was how to conceal their identities. He didn't dare leave the exchange to Evan, and of course he couldn't walk up to Richard himself. But then, you could hardly wander around Union Station in a mask, could you?

The answer hit him like a slap, and despite everything, he found himself grinning. *Sure you could.*

One day a year.

After all, tomorrow was Halloween.

Danny picked up his truck from the parking deck at the Sears Tower – speaking of robbery, twenty dollars for a couple of hours – and headed west. His day was nearly over. A final stop at the office to keep up appearances and drop off the updated work schedules from the job site he'd visited earlier, and then it was time to go home.

What he would do when he got there was a bigger question.

The way Karen had stormed out on him last night, leaving him sitting alone at the table – she didn't act that way normally. It had made part of him smile – what a woman, like an old-time movie star – but still, it was a problem. She'd had an intuition that something was wrong before Nolan called; now she was clearly sure of it. Worse, even if the call had nothing to do with the kidnapping, it had inadvertently pointed her in the right direction. She must be wondering if he had gone back to his old ways.

If he had backslid.

And she'd be right.

Danny almost heard the voice out loud. He looked over to the passenger seat where his father sat, a cigarette smoldering. As a kid, Danny had always tried to convince him to quit, saying it would kill him. He'd been wrong about that. About so many things.

'It's only two more days,' he told his father. 'Then I go back to the truth.'

His father stared at him, his face craggy and hard as stone, his eyes judging. Danny didn't need to imagine him talking. He knew what the words would be.

'I know,' he said aloud. 'I know. Gold statues with clay feet. Can't build truth on lies, right?'

Still. With a little care, couldn't he get through the next day without Karen ever finding out? Once the job was done, Evan would be out of their life. He'd have protected Karen and Tommy both. Things could go back to normal.

'Tell the truth. Do the right thing. Be a man. It was always so easy for you to say.' But even as silence swallowed his words, Danny knew them for a lie. Nothing in his father's life had been easy. An eighth-grade education and no skills in anything but construction. A twice-mortgaged tract house with a wife and child inside. There had been no blinders on his eyes, no visions of financial ease or early retirement. But every morning he'd gotten up, squared his shoulders, and done what was needed. His life had been a monument to doing things anyway.

Danny turned left, heading for the office, past hot dog joints and pawnshops with signs that glowed against the dying sky. For what had to be the ten thousandth time, he asked himself the question.

What if he went home and told her the truth?

Would she understand?

Would she leave?

There was no way of knowing, not really. As much as she

loved him, he knew her terror of that old world was strong. Maybe stronger. Telling her could go either way.

Only suckers played even money. Even money meant you won as often as you lost. With stakes this high, the smart play was to lie low.

In the passenger seat of his imagination, his father snorted with disgust and looked away.

And suddenly Danny realized that the question wasn't what she would do if he told her. It was whether he could live with himself if he didn't. Whether he wanted to be the kind of person who could live with that.

Was he content to be just a thief with a better address?

'Okay,' he said. 'You win. I'm going to drop these papers off, and then I'm going to drive home and bet everything that matters on your principles. Happy?'

His father was as silent in death as he had been in life. But as Danny pulled into the firm's parking lot, he felt something in him loosen, like his chest had been wrapped with bands of steel that suddenly gave. He took a deep breath that filled him to the soles of his shoes.

Screw the smart play. He'd tell her the truth.

Danny stepped out of the car, grabbed his bag, and started for the back door. Overhead, the sky glowed an imperial violet, the city light stretching to bounce off the clouds. Dry leaves crunched under his shoes, and the air smelled clean, crisp with autumn and its promise of winter. Five minutes here, and he'd be on his way home, toward whatever followed the truth.

'Danny?'

The voice from behind him was female and scared, and the moment he heard it he knew something was terribly wrong.

32. What Was Left

He'd been thinking of Karen, and so some part of him was surprised, when he spun around, to see Debbie. She looked lousy, her back slumped, eyes raw, cheeks a slapped red. There was little trace of the rock diva pose she usually affected. His first instinct was primal, a male urge to comfort a female, to put his coat around her cold shoulders and make everything okay.

His second was to wonder what she was doing in the parking lot of the man whose kidnapped child she was supposed to be babysitting.

'Debbie.' He glanced in both directions. No one in sight, but there were still a dozen cars in the lot. Including, he noticed, her beat-to-crap Tempo. Why hadn't he spotted that coming in? 'What are you doing here?'

'We need to talk.' Her voice came out with a hint of sniffle.

Was she losing her nerve? Just what he needed, something else to shake the fragile structure he was holding together with will and prayer. 'You shouldn't be here.' His voice came out harsh, and she shrank back a half step.

'I know. I'm sorry. I just, I need to talk to you.'

He shook his head. 'I'll come by the site in the morning, we can talk then.' He took her arm and steered her toward the Tempo. He had to get her out of here before somebody came out the back door and saw them together. Even her car was a problem – it was a small company, people noticed things, and half the car's back window was covered with punk band stickers, not exactly par for the construction business. She let him hustle her along, but kept talking.

'No, look, it's important. Danny, I'm serious. It's important!' She yanked her arm out of his. 'It's Evan.'

His stomach dropped, and he felt the bands on his chest cinching back up. He looked at her, and saw how wide her eyes were. This wasn't her touchy-feely side freaking out. Something was actually wrong.

'Okay.' He looked around again. 'Only not here. Okay?'

She nodded, and he gestured to her car as he started for his own. 'Follow me.'

They got out of the parking lot without anyone spotting them, and part of him relaxed, until he looked in his rearview mirror and saw the intent expression on Debbie's face, her lips pressed thin and pale. *It's Evan*, she'd said. What could that mean? Nothing good had ever followed those words, and there wasn't much reason to hope this time would be different.

He drove half a mile to the Sunshine Plaza, a strip mall boasting a Jewel-Osco, a tanning salon, one nail place with signs in English and another with signs in Spanish. The parking lot was only half full, but he steered past empty aisles, turned left at the side of the building, and pulled around back. The mall's Caribbean-fantasy façade was replaced by gritty reality: generators and air conditioners, graffitied brick walls, rows of delivery bays. He backed in beside a Dumpster as she pulled up. Sour milk and old exhaust filled his nostrils when he stepped out of the truck.

'Okay. What is it?'

She looked at him, looked away. 'You have a cigarette?'

'I don't smoke.'

She nodded. 'I quit a couple of years now.'

He waited.

'I'm sorry for jumping you like that. I was trying to find you, and I remembered that we'd followed you there, and the only other place I could think of was your house. But I thought that would be a bad idea. I figured you wouldn't want your girlfriend to see you talking to me.' Her voice sounded sad, like it was a line she had too much experience delivering.

He nodded, trying to keep his voice reassuring. 'Just don't do it again, okay? I know it seems like a little thing, but –'

'– It's the little things that get you caught.' She smiled. 'Evan told me you used to say that all the time.' Her face suddenly darkened at the name.

'What is it?'

She looked away from him, staring out toward the road, watching traffic pass. 'I didn't know he was going to do it. I should have known, I guess, but I didn't. Really.'

'Do what?' Silence. 'Debbie, do what?'

She looked back at him, her eyes shot through with red, tears rolling down her cheeks. 'I didn't know Evan was going to kill him.'

He felt the ground roll, and reached out a hand to lean against the SUV. Kill him? What did that mean? Kill who?

'We were out to lunch, I didn't want to go, but he convinced me that Tommy would be okay. When we finished eating, he said he had a call to make. He got out a matchbook with a number on it, and I tried to stop him from calling, but it was too late, he was already talking to Richard.' Her words came fast, piling on one another, her eyes wide like a child's. 'He said if he didn't get the money he was going to shoot Tommy in the head, and just then some guy walked out of the bathroom, and I don't know if he heard or not, but Evan followed him to the parking lot, and, and . . .' Her voice choked in a sob, and she turned away, then bent over, her hands knit across her stomach.

A bead of sweat ran down his side. Overhead, he could

hear the faint buzzing of a plane. Evan had killed someone.

Oh, sweet Jesus.

'Debbie.' He waited for her to straighten up, to take a breath. 'Where is Evan now?'

'He put the guy in the trunk of his car and made me follow him to O'Hare long-term parking. He said he'd deal with the body later.' She shivered. 'Then we went back to the trailer, and I told him I needed to get out for a couple of hours. That I had to shower.'

'Good. You go home now.' He pitched his voice level and even, as if talking to a teenager. 'Forget any of this ever happened.'

'What do you mean?' She looked at him, confused.

'Walk away. Be done with it.'

She shook her head. 'I can't.'

'What do you mean?' She couldn't still have a fire burning for Evan, not after this. Danny had pegged her as a groupie, a smart woman who liked bad men, but it couldn't run this deep. 'You've got to get clear.'

She looked away. 'I'd cut off a finger for a cigarette right now.'

He stepped forward, grabbed her by the shoulders. She tried to squirm away, but he held fast. 'I can't,' she whispered.

He stared at her, mute.

'Think about it,' she said. 'If I bail, what's Evan going to do? *I saw him kill someone.*'

Her eyes were red and tired of the whole world. The punk-rock princess was gone, and what was left was a scared little girl. But she was right. Evan might go after her. Or he might panic and kill Tommy.

He nodded, let go of her shoulders. 'Okay.' He stepped back, reached in his pocket for his keys. She winced when she saw them, but he didn't have time to ask why. He turned and walked toward the truck. 'Go home,' he said over his shoulder.

'What are you going to do?'

He stopped, the car door open, and turned to look at her. 'I'm going to end this.' Then he climbed in, started the engine, and gunned it. The tires squealed as they bit, rocketing the car forward. The speed felt right, clean and pure as anger. He looked in the rearview when he reached the street, and saw that she was still standing there, staring after him, though at this distance he couldn't tell if her expression was hopeful or despairing. Then he turned onto the street and she was gone.

Evan had killed someone.

What had happened to Evan? What had he become? He'd always been reckless and too hard. But this took things to a new level. Maybe it was prison. Maybe it was desperation. Something had turned Evan into the kind of man who could decide a stranger needed to die and then kill him.

Jesus.

And the call! Why had he made the call from the diner? Why make it at all? To impress Debbie, to show his independence? Why call Richard for that?

Wait a minute. More important than why was how. In order to make the call, he would have needed the phone number. Danny thought back, trying to replay Debbie's fractured monologue. She'd said something about him taking out a matchbook with the number on it.

Which meant that after the first call two days ago, Evan had taken the trouble not only to remember the number, but to write it down. Not exactly brain surgery. But also not the kind of thing Evan did. Unless he'd already been planning, even then, to act without Danny. The thought sent a chill down his spine, immediately followed by a flush of furious heat.

Maybe it shouldn't have surprised him. But it did.

In front of him, traffic slowed, a sea of brake lights. Everyday people trying to get home. At this rate it would take him twenty minutes to make ten blocks.

He swerved over to the shoulder, ignoring the honking, and jammed his foot to the accelerator, half on, half off the road. Cars blurred by. Farther down the shoulder became parking, so he turned into a diner, slowed enough to engage the four-wheel drive, and then rolled right over the grassy embankment separating it from the southbound street. It was a quiet road that took him six blocks before dead-ending in one of the small parks that dotted Chicago. He didn't even slow down, just took the curb at speed, the wheels jamming into it before catching, jerking him forward till the seat belt bit. Two black teenagers sharing a cigarette on top of the playground equipment spun to watch him, their mouths open, but it didn't matter, because on the other side of the park lay Pike Street, just down from the site.

He was running on anger, never the smart play, but right now, he didn't care. All the lethal thoughts he'd entertained the other night were bubbling to the surface. He covered the last two blocks and pulled up to the construction fence. The gate was closed but unlatched, and he nudged it with the front of the truck and drove right through. He was out of the car before the engine had even fully stopped.

Evan sat on the cinder-block steps of the trailer, a cigarette in one hand. He rose, his shoulders back, and flicked the half-finished smoke to one side. 'Hey, partner.'

Danny didn't speak, just let the momentum carry him the four paces to the steps, his eyes on Evan's, his arm snapping back into a swing that caught Evan off guard, Evan's hands coming up too slowly to keep Danny from connecting with his jaw, a hearty, dead-on smack that left Danny's hand throbbing with shards of pain. Evan fell, caught himself against the side of the trailer, and came up in a lunge, his fists quick, forcing Danny back. He blocked one, stepped away from a second, but a brutal right caught him in the temple, the world leaping and resettling, and then it was on, the two of them scrabbling and fighting like kids from the old neighborhood. Danny managed to bring a knee up into Evan's gut but took two quick jabs to his side in the process, both men breathing hard, gritting teeth, murder in their eyes. It was all coming out in Danny now, every stress of the last month, every setback and failure and lie and calculation he'd sworn he'd never make again, and it burned hot as gasoline. He landed a cross that spun Evan's face and bloodied his nose, but in the process overreached and left himself open. He saw the mistake too late, Evan's fist coming round in a hurtling uppercut, all the strength of his body behind it, and then suns exploded behind Danny's eyes as the force of the punch lifted him off the ground. He fell back, the gravel rushing to meet him, slapping his back. A steel-toed boot slammed into his kidney, and he jerked to his side, at once gasping for air and gagging viciously.

Evan stepped away, breath coming hard, blood trickling from his nostrils. For a moment they eyed each other, glares hard, and then Evan gave a little laugh. 'So the dumb cooze found you, huh?' He wiped the blood from his face with the back of his right hand in a childish gesture. 'Thought she might. I figured that whole thing about a shower was bullshit.'

Danny took air in long gulps, willing the pain to die. It took more strength than he expected to stay propped up on one elbow. He kept an eye on Evan, watching his boots, trying to prepare for another attack. 'She was scared.'

'Yeah, well, I'm not going back to Stateville over some fat-ass citizen.'

Danny reached deep, trying to picture a calm place, an

underground lake, cavernous and cool and dark, where the pain was far away. When he had it, he pushed himself up to his knees, and then his feet. Evan backed away, on his guard.

'It was a stupid move.'

'Why?' Evan sneered. 'Because it wasn't part of your plan? I got news for you, Danny-boy. I don't fit into your plans.'

Danny nodded, his vision grainy, his head sore. 'I'm learning that.'

The remark seemed to please Evan, like it had been a compliment. Like he hadn't understood the real message. 'About time.' He lowered his fists, then reached into his jacket to fumble for his cigarettes.

'Evan. This changes things.' He straightened his back, feeling the vertebrae pop, each of them a sharp twinge. 'We need to rethink.'

'Nothing,' Evan paused, lit a smoke, blew a thin stream of gray, 'changes.'

'We're talking murder. The police are going to be looking for you.'

Evan shrugged. 'So what? Tomorrow we'll have a million bucks.'

Could he really be so cold about it?

You know the answer to that one, kid. You learned it the hard way. Don't ever forget it again.

Still. 'I know you don't like to think about it this way, but hear me out. The smart play is for you to leave tonight. You killed this guy in a parking lot, right? You know how much evidence you probably left? Fingerprints, footprints, tire tracks, his blood, your blood. This isn't a pawnshop we're knocking over, man. You stick around, they will find you. And if we're sitting on the kid at the same time, we'll both go down. Maybe for good.'

Evan stared at him, a sneer on his face. 'Ahh, Danny.' He took a long draw on the cigarette, shook his head. 'Come with me.' He turned and started to walk toward the trailer.

Danny didn't move. 'What for?'

Evan had a hand on the door. He stopped and turned around with exaggerated patience. 'I want to show you something.'

Every nerve in Danny's body tingled. Something in Evan's easy manner scared the hell out of him. It could be a trap. Evan didn't need his help any longer. He didn't think the guy would just shoot him casually, but he could hardly be sure.

He pictured Karen. If something went wrong now, she'd never know the truth.

Evan held the door wider and smiled. 'After you.'

On the other hand, it could be nothing. If he wanted to get out of this, to see Karen again, to try and find a happy solution, he didn't have much choice. His bruised face throbbing with every beat of his heart, Danny stepped into the trailer, his ears straining for warnings.

The television lit the interior in flickering shades of blue and white. Cardboard packages from microwave dinners littered the counters. The air smelled dank. Tommy moved on the couch, struggling to sit up. His hands and feet had been duct taped to the arms of the couch. There was a strip of tape over his mouth, and another across his eyes. What skin was visible shone pale white and freckled.

'You taped him?' Danny couldn't keep the disgust from his voice.

Evan just smiled as he walked over to the couch.

Then he pulled the gun from his belt and pressed the muzzle against Tommy's forehead.

It happened so fast Danny couldn't believe it. One minute no gun; the next, gun. The kid's struggles ended immediately, replaced by a soft whimpering like a kicked puppy.

Horror and adrenaline coursed through Danny. His fists clenched, and he could hear the roar of his heart. He took a half step forward, and then caught himself as Evan cocked the hammer back.

'Now you see. Now you're starting to get it. All that crap you were spinning out there? You were right about one thing.' Evan smiled at him, a mocking look. The cold light from the television carved his features from granite. 'This isn't a pawnshop.'

'Wait –'

'No. Enough talk.' Tommy whimpered as Evan pushed into him with the gun. 'It's time you understood something, amigo. You walked out on me once. It won't happen again. Not without consequences.' Evan pushed the gun harder, the kid burrowing into the cushions to get away. Danny could see sweat marks on the fabric.

Then, holding a cocked pistol to a twelve-year-old's forehead, Evan winked.

Everything had gone wrong.

And there was nothing Danny could do about it.

33. Monsters

Everything hurt.

It had been a lot of years since his last fight, and he'd forgotten the layers of aches that followed a serious scrap, the symphonic balance of pain: a dull soreness across his body, a wobbly necked pounding in his head, a blood-warm throbbing at his swelling left eye, a sandpaper raggedness on his knuckles. None of it was overwhelming, but it all put him in mind of his age. When he'd been eighteen, man, you could hit him with a locomotive and he'd just bounce. But bodies in their thirties weren't built for street fighting.

Worse than any of the physical pain, though, was the image seared in his mind. The gun appearing in Evan's hand like magic, the slow-motion effect of him leaning forward to press it against Tommy's forehead. The boy's little whimper, a sound he knew would forever haunt his dark moments. The feeling of being utterly trapped, knowing the right thing, wanting the right thing, and doing the wrong.

After Evan had made his point, seen the horror, the capitulation on Danny's face, he'd lowered the gun. Tommy had fallen back on the sofa, panic breaths whistling furiously through his nostrils. Danny had considered jumping Evan then, but the guy kept the gun out. Never explicitly threatening, more like it just happened to be in his hand.

'Don't look so worried,' Evan had said, as he led the way outside. 'Everything's under control. I'll get Debbie back here to babysit. Tomorrow we call Dick, tell him where to meet us. Before the kids are done trick-or-treating, we'll have a million in cash, and this will all be over.'

Danny had nodded, not believing, knowing now that it would never be over, that he'd finally woken into his recurring nightmare. And even so, trying to control the damage. An engineer on the *Hindenburg*. 'I've got the meet location picked.'

'Where?'

'Union Station.' He'd told Evan the logic, leaving out the hope that doing it in public would keep him calm.

Evan had shrugged, scratched his neck with the barrel of the gun. 'Whatever. That'll work.' Then he'd dismissed Danny with a wave of his cigarette.

Now, back on his own block, Danny stepped out of the truck and closed the door quietly. The air had grown chillier, with a breeze that blew through his shirt to cut at the skin beneath. His street radiated the easy calm of a place where monsters only came out on Halloween. He shouldered his bag and started down the sidewalk, trying not to see Tommy's face in every shadow.

As he passed the weathered steps of his neighbor's porch, a high-pitched shriek burst from the graystone. The scream gave way to an evil-genius laugh, and a strobe flashed on in the bay window, where a medical skeleton loomed amid drugstore cobwebs. After a moment the recorded sound track shut off, but harsh white light kept splashing up every few seconds. Danny stood in front of the window, watching as the beam flared, died, flared, died. In the periods of darkness, the streetlights were enough to turn the window into a dark mirror, and within it he could see himself reflected. A normal-looking guy with a few scrapes on his face and the beginnings of a shiner under one eye. Other than the bruises, not the kind of face that earned a second look.

A month ago, he would have said the skeleton was the scarier monster. Now, he wasn't so sure.

How had this happened? How had it gotten so far? He'd

done everything he could along the way, tried to think through every step, and still, here he was. Somehow, playing it smart just wasn't enough.

The light was on in their window. Karen was home. He winced to think of his lies, of the betrayal and confusion she must be feeling.

There was still one thing he could try and make right. He straightened his shoulders and walked away from the play monsters.

The outside of their own condo was minimally decorated, just some desiccated cornstalks the downstairs neighbor trotted out every year, the husks picked clean by the squirrels. The mailbox was full, and he opened it and took everything out, then shook his head and stuffed it all back in. No point pretending it was life as usual. He unlocked the stairwell door and took the steps quietly, trying to collect his thoughts. How to tell her?

Despite Karen's intuition that something was up, this was way beyond what she would be imagining. The key would be to do it slowly. To tell her they needed to talk. Sit down at the kitchen table. Start small, let her see the way the thing had built up, the net that had been woven around him. Get to the kidnapping last, after she'd had time to grasp everything else. She was whip-smart, and a realist; if he could make her see the reasons behind his decisions, she might understand.

He stood in front of the apartment door, took a deep breath, slid his key into the lock. What he was doing was right. He felt good about finally coming clean. Even dared to hope things might work out. *Here goes.*

For a split second after opening the door he wondered if he'd somehow gone one flight of stairs too far and opened the door to the wrong condo. Things looked different. It took his tired mind a second to figure out why.

Two suitcases and a half dozen moving boxes stood by the door.

'Hello, Danny.' She straightened from the cabinet she'd been packing. 'You're just in time to say good-bye.'

34. In Our House

She'd practiced the phrasing, had run through it in her head, somehow knowing that he'd show up before she was done. Wanting him to? She couldn't say. So when she heard the door open, she rose and said her line, calm as you please. No choked-back sobs, no trace of the crying fits prompted each time she opened a new cabinet, packed a coat he'd given her, weighed whether to take her books now or return for them later. She stood and said her line and only then looked at him. His face was a mess, a bruise purpling beneath one eye, scrapes across his cheek like he'd been jumped. He looked at her, and then at the boxes, and then he sagged, his shoulders slumping like something vital inside him had snapped.

Despite everything, she had to fight the urge to go to him, to hold him close and smell his skin and tell him that they would work it out, that everything was all right. But everything wasn't all right, and instead they eyed each other like gunfighters.

When he finally spoke, it was in a thin, hoarse voice. 'I didn't know we had gotten this far.'

She looked away, undid her hair band to free her sweaty ponytail, then gathered it back neatly. She had planned to be furious at him, had every right to be, but it wasn't coming. All afternoon her emotions had blown back and forth, and exhaustion was setting in. 'You've been lying to me.'

He looked at her, looked away. 'Yeah.' He stepped into

the apartment, closing the door behind him and weaving his way through the boxes to drop on the couch. He shook his head, snorted. 'It's funny.'

'What is?'

'Just – I was right now coming to tell the truth.'

She shook her head, squatted back down in front of the cabinet to stack a photo album in the box beside her. 'It's too late. I already know the truth.'

'You do?'

He sounded shocked, and that pleased her. She dusted off her hands, walked over. There was a box in the chair opposite him, and she moved it to the floor before sitting down. His eyes followed her, but she couldn't be sure what she saw in them.

'You're back to it, aren't you?' She faltered, the words hard to frame. 'You're a criminal again.'

He looked away, hesitated. 'I don't know how to answer that.'

His evasion got the anger flowing. She slapped him, her hand just flying out to smack his cheek before either of them knew what had happened. 'Don't *lie* to me.' She wanted to slap him again, to hurt him. To heap all the uncertainty and doubt she'd been feeling back on him. 'It's a simple question.'

His eyes blazed. 'No,' he snarled, 'it's not.'

'I know the truth.' Her voice had that shrill tone she hated in women in the movies, but she couldn't help herself. 'I met Nolan today.'

'What?'

'Your old buddy Nolan. The detective. I wanted to know what was going on, and you wouldn't talk to me, so I called him.'

'And what did my old buddy tell you?'

'He told me Evan McGann was out of prison. That . . .' She paused, forced herself to say it. 'That you and he were partners again.'

'He told you what?' He leaned forward, surprise on his face.

'He said that you had come to see him about Evan.'

'That's true. Did he tell you why?'

She thought about it, realized he hadn't. Of course, she had stormed away before the detective had a chance to finish.

He laughed, a bitter, mirthless sound. 'No, he wouldn't. Better to stir you up, see if you knew anything. If you could contribute to his case.'

Now that she thought about it, there was something odd about what Nolan had said, something that didn't add up. Why would Danny have told a cop about Evan? At the time, it had seemed to make sense, but she'd been stunned by everything, in a hurry to escape, and she hadn't thought to clarify. 'So why did you go see him?'

He leaned forward and put his hand on hers. The touch was so comfortably familiar that more than anything she wanted to curl her fingers up around his. She didn't.

'There's a lot I have to tell you, and none of it is good.'

The earnestness in his expression siphoned off some of her anger. 'Is it the truth?'

'Yes.'

She took a deep breath. 'Tell me.'

He gave her a smile like a lily beaten down in the rain. 'About three weeks ago, Evan came to see me. He was out on parole, and wanted to go back to work.'

Even though she'd known it, the words stung. It was like Danny telling her he'd been visited by the tooth fairy – or the boogeyman. 'Why didn't you tell me?'

'I don't know. I wish I had. I was scared to even bring the

idea of Evan back into our lives. I guess I thought . . .' He sighed, absently touched his bruised eye, then winced and pulled his hand back. 'I thought I could get rid of him.'

'But you couldn't.' It wasn't a question.

He shook his head. 'When I told him I wasn't interested, he started pressuring. Showing up on the street, threatening us. I didn't know it, but he was also following me. And then one day I came home and found him sitting in the kitchen.'

Her head went light, and she yanked her hand from under his. 'He was here? In our house?'

Danny stared back. 'Yes.'

She had a flash of Evan at the defense table, all those years ago, calm and peaceful while the prosecutor described the hideous things he'd done. He'd been here. Had touched their things, sat on their couch. Maybe laid in their bed. Her skin crawled. 'Why didn't you call the police?'

'That's when I went to Nolan.'

'I mean the *regular* police.'

He sighed. 'Because . . . you know why. I'm an ex-con. And I was in the pawnshop. They'd have started digging through all of that. At least with Nolan, I thought maybe he'd understand, help out. But I couldn't tell him everything either.'

She looked at him appraisingly. 'You couldn't tell him why Evan was in our house?'

He shook his head.

'Why not?' She stopped as it began to click. 'You couldn't tell him because Evan wanted you to do something illegal.' She tapped her fingers on the table. 'And you were thinking of doing it.'

He nodded, his expression neutral.

'Danny, what did he want you to do?'

He paused, looked away, and then back. 'He wanted me to help kidnap Richard's son.'

She laughed. The idea was so absurd, so beyond the pale. Danny was in construction. They had a regular life. They were talking about having children, for God's sake. The whole thing was preposterous.

Except Danny just sat and looked at her.

Her laughter faded awkwardly. She stared at him, willing him to say something, to nudge her, to tell her it was a joke. But he didn't. He just watched her, the bruise on his face swelling. 'You mean . . .' She squinted. 'You didn't.' He said nothing. 'Oh my God.' Her voice came out a whisper. She rose, jerked away from him. 'Oh my God!' The room was spinning and she felt desperately ill. 'You did it. You helped him.'

'Karen.' He stood, took a half step toward her, stopped when she moved farther away. 'It's not what it seems.'

'Did you do it?' She clutched her hands to her mouth. 'Please tell me you didn't do it.'

He sighed. 'I can't.'

She stared at him in horror. 'Why? Why would you do that?' She felt hysteria beckoning, her voice coming out almost a shriek, the feel of it cutting her throat.

'I had no choice.' He was on his feet now, hands out and his eyes wide. 'You have to understand –'

'Understand what?' Her words came fast, trying to keep him from telling any more terrible truths. She couldn't hear more of them, couldn't stand it. 'You're going to get caught.'

'Listen –' His voice growing heated.

'I can't. I don't want to.' How could there be any explanation? 'Oh God, and that poor little boy. What did you do to that poor little boy?'

'Goddamn it –'

'You're a monster.' The words slipped out, and the moment they did she wanted to grab them, to shove them back in her mouth, but it was too late.

'You're not listening to me!' He turned, his hand balled in a fist, and lashed out at the mirror beside the couch. Their reflections shattered into a thousand fragments.

It was the most irrational, violent thing she'd seen him do in the eight years she'd loved him, and it stunned her into total silence.

He turned back to her, nostrils flaring. 'I did it because I had to. Because I thought I could pull it off without anyone getting hurt. I did it because it was the only way I could see to make him leave us alone. But that's all bullshit.' He paused, sighed. 'It's all true, but it's not the reason I did it.'

His hand was bleeding badly, the knuckles vibrant red. Ruby drops of blood fell to the hardwood floor. They were strangely pretty.

'The truth is, I did it because he threatened you.'

The words jerked her gaze from the puddle on the floor. 'What?'

'Last week.'

And suddenly it came clear, all of the horror lurking behind the façade of the last few weeks. The strands of web that led to the spider. 'The guy in the alley.' She knew before he nodded. That had been Evan, sending a message. Telling Danny that he knew how to get to him. She remembered how spooked Danny had seemed, but how resolute, too. How he'd promised to do anything to protect her.

She stared at him. His mirror-smashing fury had drained away, and he looked like a soldier after a long campaign. His eyes were pleading, but not hopeful. She murdered half a dozen thoughts before they reached her lips. Finally, she pointed to his hand. 'You're bleeding.'

He looked down. 'Oh.'

She stepped forward, took his hand gently in hers. The cut was in the meaty part beneath his little finger. There was a chunk of glass stuck there, and she used her nails, catching a reflection of herself in the mirror as she pulled it from his skin. Thick blood oozed. She looked around for a rag or a cloth, and seeing nothing, pulled off her shirt to wrap his hand. He gasped as the fabric touched the gash. 'Come on.'

She led him up the hall to the bathroom. Spinning the faucet to cold, she held his hand under the water, the blood streaming thin and pink to spatter against the porcelain. 'Keep it there.' She went to the kitchen pantry, found gauze and Neosporin. Back in the bathroom she used a paper towel to pat the wound dry. Clean now, it didn't look so bad. Jagged, but not too deep. The lips of it already quivered red, so she moved fast, squeezing the ointment, placing the rectangle of gauze and then deftly affixing it, wrapping the white tape in a stripe across his palm. She didn't meet his eyes, just worked on his hand, and throughout he stood silent and let her. It was calming, something she could handle. Just a cut, a perfectly normal cut. It was life-sized.

But eventually the bandage was in place, and she couldn't distract herself from everything larger.

'Danny.' She held his hand by the fingers, her gaze darting around the room. 'What are we going to do?'

He put his other hand on her cheek. It was so familiar, so safe, that she both feared and wanted to fall into it. She met his eyes, saw herself mirrored in them. She saw him weighing words, and realized she was praying he found the right ones. Whatever they were.

'I don't know.' He paused. 'But,' his hand caressing her cheek, 'I'd like your help figuring it out.'

For a long moment she stared at him, tried to think dispassionately. She wanted to make proclamations, to hear him swear that there would be no more lies. She wanted him to feel what she'd been going through, and promise that he would never turn away from her again. But none of the phrases she auditioned sounded right. Maybe there was nothing to say.

In the end, she just put her arms around him and laid her head on the hollow of his chest. They stood together under the bright bathroom lights, holding on to keep from being swept away.

For a moment, it worked.

And then she realized something terrible.

35. Choices

Despite the impossible mess that had become his life, despite the soreness of his aching body and the steady throb of his cut hand, as Karen put her head on his chest Danny felt strangely safe. Spent, both physically and emotionally, but safe nonetheless, as though the confession had created some sort of karmic loophole, a time away from reality. He knew none of their problems had been solved. But he was so tired. Everything could wait, at least a little while. He just wanted to lose himself in their warmth.

Then she pulled away from him. 'Baby?'

'Yeah?'

'What about Patrick?' She bit her lip. 'Did he know about Evan threatening us?'

He'd been honest with Patrick, but not with her. That would cut. But he'd had enough of lies. 'Yes.' He stepped away and leaned against the counter, his good hand holding the lip of the sink. 'I told him when he came over for dinner.' She stared back at him with an intensity that scared him. 'I'm sorry,' he said. 'I needed to talk to someone, and it should have been you.'

She shook her head. 'It's not that. It's –' Her voice broke.

Fear ice-picked him. 'What?'

'Patrick . . .' She paused. Took a deep breath, very deliberately, then stepped closer, her eyes locked on his like she was trying to beam him something from inside herself. 'He was murdered.'

'What?' He couldn't have heard her right.

'He was shot. That's why Nolan called.'

No.

Oh Christ, no.

The room seemed to pitch, the ceiling looming. A giant fist gripped his heart. Not Patrick. The ten-year-old boy who'd replaced the holy water with Sprite. The joker who always had a story. The friend who'd been part of every stage of his life.

The closest thing he had to a brother.

Spots danced in front of his eyes, and he squeezed the counter. He willed his lungs to breathe, to suck oxygen in, but the air felt thick. He let himself slide down the face of the cabinet to squat on the floor. 'What happened?'

Karen's voice was raw. 'Nolan wouldn't tell me very much.' She sat across from him, her legs folded, and took his hands in hers.

'What did he tell you?'

'Just that Patrick was shot last week.'

His throat filled with bile. Last week. His friend had been dead for days, and Danny hadn't known it. Then a far worse idea occurred. 'When?'

Karen hesitated. 'They think Monday or Tuesday.'

Right after Danny had told him about Evan. Patrick had promised to stay out of it, but Danny knew with bitter certainty that this was one promise his friend had broken. 'Evan killed him.'

Karen stared at him, her lips trembling, and nodded.

Blackness swam at the edges of his vision, and his chest felt tight. He scrambled to his feet and stormed out of the bathroom, habit carrying him toward the front door before he realized he had nowhere to go. He wanted to smash something. To smash everything. He spun in the living room and kicked one of her moving boxes, sending a pile of loose photos flying, each image spinning in flashes of color and memory as it fluttered to the floor.

Patrick was dead.

Because of him.

'It's not your fault,' Karen said from behind him, her words so eerily aligned with his thoughts that he wondered if he'd spoken aloud. 'It's not. If you want to blame some-one –'

'I do,' he said. 'I do want to blame someone. I want to blame Evan.' He looked at the mess of photos around him, then sighed and dropped on the couch. 'But it's not that simple.'

'Why not?'

'Because none of this would have happened if I'd just . . .' He trailed off. *If you'd just what? Not told Patrick? Not walked out seven years ago? Not swiped that first* Playboy *in '81? How far back do you want to go with this? Because your catalog of errors is many things, but short ain't one of them.*

'I fucked everything up, baby.' He felt bone weary. The world had hollowed him out. 'I'm sorry.'

'It's okay.' She sat beside him and stroked his hair. Her voice was soft and unhesitating. 'We'll find a way.'

He wanted a quiet, dark place to cry. To mourn his brother.

But more than that he wanted to find Evan, pin him to the ground, and beat him to death. Punch and kick until his legs failed and his knuckles broke.

Hold on to that. Anger is a gift.

One deep breath, and then another. There would be time to mourn Patrick later. The question was how many other regrets he'd be carrying at that point. Painful as it was, he couldn't think about Patrick right now.

Instead, he had to think about the man who killed him.

'Evan is still out there.' He could feel her muscles clench at the mention of his name. It didn't matter. 'I've got to go after him.'

'You?' She jerked away. 'No. We'll call the police.'

'They can't help us.'

'If we tell them about Patrick –'

He shook his head. 'It's past that.'

'Is this some macho thing?' She stared at him. 'I don't want to lose you over something from the movies.'

'It's not that. It's Tommy. Richard's son. Evan will kill him at the first siren.'

'So why does that mean you have to stop him? Why don't we just get out of here, get away?'

'You'd do that?'

She hesitated, looked around their living room, and then nodded slowly.

He leaned in and kissed her soft lips, let himself dream it for a moment. Just hop in the car and go, take what money they had and start over. Somewhere without winter winds and bleak history. Somewhere they could be different people.

It was a beautiful dream, but that was all it was.

'Evan would kill the boy just to spite me. And maybe Richard, too. And even if he wouldn't,' he paused, 'I think I've done enough running in the last seven years.'

'Then what?' She stared at him. 'Pretend you're John Wayne?'

He sighed, closed his eyes. 'I don't know.' Unbidden, an image of Patrick rose up in front of him. That day at the pub, not a month earlier, when he'd watched in the mirror as Patrick came in, flirted with the girls in the corner booth. How he'd thrown his head back and howled with laughter when Danny shot him in the mirror. Danny rubbed at his eyes, wanting to smear the image. '"Running just breeds faster problems."' He opened his eyes. 'Dad used to say that.'

She was silent. He knew her mind was working, trying to

find them a way out, an option where they walked away unscathed. A smart play.

'Did I ever tell you how my dad died?'

She softened. 'Of course. In a car accident.'

He nodded. 'His brakes went out. He drove an old Ford pickup with big tool chests in the back.' He smiled. 'My friend Seamus and I used to take the tools out of the compartments and climb inside, pretend we were smuggling ourselves in the *Millennium Falcon*. We'd fight over who got to be Han and who had to be Luke. That was twenty years ago, and Dad was still driving it when he died. The money was never there for a new one, so he just rode it into the ground, even as the salt ate holes in the underbelly and the rust crept up the doors.' He sighed. 'You know the last time I saw him, I was in prison?'

She nodded, her face creased.

'He came to see me. He looked so out of place. He'd worked his ass off since he was a teenager. Work was part of being a man to him. Criminals, people who would steal instead of earn, they were beneath his contempt. He hated that I was there, hated what I'd become. But I was his son, so he came to see me.' He shook his head. 'We talked about baseball.'

'I'm sure he knew that you loved him.'

He blew air through his mouth, stared at the ceiling. 'That was December. A couple weeks later he was driving that ancient piece of junk down the Eisenhower. It was snowing, and the roads were very slippery. Sunday morning, but he was on his way to a job anyway. His brakes failed.'

Karen moved behind him, put her arms around his neck, her chest warm against his back. 'Baby, you've told me all this. You don't have to relive it now.'

He shook his head. 'What I didn't tell you was that the cop who'd responded to the accident call came to the funeral. That really touched me.' Danny remembered him perfectly. A football player's build, cop mustache, and bone-cracking handshake, but a voice that was almost a whisper. 'I went over to thank him, and he told me something that I've never been able to forget.'

Karen tightened her grip on him, but it felt like he'd gone numb.

'He was a beat cop, and he'd seen a lot of accidents. After a while, he said, you learned to read them. A story written in skid marks and broken glass and points of impact. They were mostly the same, he said. People asleep at the wheel, or drunk, or careless. But Dad's had been different.'

'How?' Karen said, her cheek against his.

'It was the tire marks, the cop said, that gave it away.' Danny sighed, remembering the 'of course' feeling. The way the scene had flashed in his imagination, clear in every detail. Dad at the wheel, talk radio playing low, a cigarette in his mouth. The patched seats radiating cold. Suddenly, the sense that something wasn't quite right. His father pumping the brakes, feeling them go soft. Staring out at the snowy morning, at the lines of cars crowding him.

'Dad swerved into the concrete barrier on purpose.'

'Suicide?' Her voice was incredulous.

Danny shook his head. 'His brakes were gone. The roads were icy, and there were a lot of cars. He could have tried to move to the right, off the road, hoped that everyone would get out of his way. But if it didn't work, he might have crashed into another car. Maybe a family.'

He turned to look at her. 'So instead of risking other people, he jerked the wheel to the left. They were widening the road, and there was a concrete construction barrier on that side. The cop said he was going fifty or sixty miles an hour. Dad didn't have a chance, and he knew it.'

Karen held his gaze, but her eyes were wet.

'I've been living with that for years. I had to be escorted to my father's funeral by marshals. I thought that was bad enough. But worse was that three months later, when they let me out of prison, I went right back to my old life. Oh, I pretended to go straight. I got a new apartment, a job tending bar, but I knew I was bullshitting myself. It wasn't two months before Evan and I ripped off the manager as he deposited the night's take, and then it was back to old habits. It wasn't until the pawnshop that I even started trying to do what I should have done all along. What my dad did without hesitation.'

The memory burned. For a guy who thought he brought intelligence to the table, he'd made a mess of a lot of things. When Evan had come back into his life, they'd sat in a hot dog joint and argued about the reasons, Evan claiming that it was economics, that the system put the gun in his hand. That they were in a fight to the death with the odds stacked against them. In a world where men like his father worked seven days a week just to survive while men like Richard had everything handed to them, he couldn't deny that there was some truth to the argument. But it was too simple to be complete. Because the fact was that there had been moments when two choices had opened up before him, and he'd made the wrong one. Made it knowing it for what it was.

'No more.' As he said the words, looking into Karen's eyes, he realized that he meant it. No more fear of consequences. No more convenient wrong choices.

No more smart plays.

And suddenly he knew what to do.

36. That Old Tightrope Feeling

Through the broad front windows, menacing clouds mottled a chill blue sky. The morning sunlight was pewter, stark and lacking warmth. Halloween had always seemed like the first day of winter to Danny, and this year that felt particularly true.

'I'm at the coffee shop.' He heard a faint echo half a heartbeat behind each word. They kept making cell phones smaller instead of making them work. 'I'm going to wait a few minutes to be sure. Then I'll head over.'

'Let me come. I can make the call from anywhere,' Karen said.

'No.'

'Danny –'

'We've been over this.' He said it gently.

'I could help. We're in this together.' She sounded frustrated.

'I know.' He leaned on his elbows to glance out the front window. Traffic seemed normal in both directions, no signs of heightened police presence. He didn't expect any, but they'd agreed there was no point taking chances. 'But if you're with me, Debbie might spook. This has to go perfectly. Please.'

She sighed. 'All right.' He could hear stress beneath her calm.

'We're going to get through. It'll be fine.'

'Just be careful, okay?'

'I promise. You have the number?'

She read Nolan's cell phone number back to him.

'Good. Stay by the phone. I'll call you as soon as I'm done. And listen –' He paused. 'I'm sorry you have to deal with this.'

'Just come home to me.' She hung up.

He took a sip from his coffee and glanced around, more from nerves than necessity. Oversize canvasses painted like comic books hung on the brick walls, and the counter guy had piercings in his eyebrows and those weird metal rings stretching his ears into hoops. The coffeehouse was in the vanguard of gentrification, one of a handful of new businesses trying to capitalize on the building boom in the area. It was a little premature. Ukrainian grandmothers and Latino day laborers still dramatically outnumbered hipsters willing to drop five bucks on a cappuccino. But it fit Danny's needs perfectly – quiet and empty, with big glass windows opening onto the street. If he craned his neck to the right, he could see the Pike Street construction yard where Debbie watched over Tommy.

The idea had come to him last night. It was a dangerous move, sure, but at least it was a move. Proactive instead of reactive. The idea had popped into his head, and he'd straightened suddenly and said, 'Tommy.'

'The boy?' Karen had looked confused.

'He's the key to all of this. If we take him away, then Evan has nothing.'

She'd stared at him. 'He still has a gun.'

'That's true.' He'd met her gaze. 'But at least it's not pointed at anybody innocent.'

They'd turned the plan over between the two of them, trying to plug holes. After a while they'd gone to bed and made love for the first time in weeks. It had started soft and sweet, but pretty soon they were going at it with a rawness that hadn't been part of their sex for a long time. Afterward, she'd left her thigh flung across his body and fallen asleep with him still inside her. He lay there like that and stared at the ceiling, turning the plan over in his head.

It was simple enough. Snatch Tommy when Evan wasn't around. Talk Debbie into hiding out for a little while. Once the boy was safe, Karen would call Nolan from a pay phone and tell him enough about the murder in the diner parking lot to get his attention. Then she'd tell him that the man who committed it would be coming to the Pike Street site later that day. If all went well, Nolan would stake it out and pick Evan up. The guy would have parole violations and probably a weapons charge, more than enough to hold him while the murder charges got sorted out.

What would happen then was a little dicier. But at least Evan wouldn't be able to hurt anyone again.

He stood up, lacing his fingers and stretching them above his head, feeling his body pop and crack. The counter guy didn't look up from his novel as Danny stepped outside. Rush hour was largely over, and traffic moved fluidly, battered vans and downscale cars, the occasional cab. He unlocked his truck and hopped in, feeling the chill of the seat through his light jacket.

After turning onto Pike Street, he drove past the construction site, scanning for danger. The slats in the fence made it difficult to see inside, but everything looked normal. He went up a block, came back, and circled again. A couple of cars were parked on the other side of the street, a few pickups, a hot-rod Camaro with tinted windows, but there was no sign of Evan's Mustang. Perfect. The worst would soon be over.

He pulled up to the gate and stepped out. The wind tugged at his clothes, cold and with a hint of chocolate from the candy factory a mile away. He kept his motions calm and even, inconspicuous. Everything looked right – the trailer was shuttered and dark, the door closed. Debbie's Tempo sat beside it. Thank God. Evan had called her back in to babysit Tommy and not stayed himself. Danny felt sure that once he explained the plan, she'd come over to his side. She was scared, and would likely jump at any opportunity to get out.

The chain clanked as he unlocked it and let it dangle against the fence. He pushed the gate open, adrenaline pounding. He got in the truck, pulled into the yard, and made a quick three-point turn to back the Explorer up to the trailer door.

If luck was really with them, Evan wouldn't mention the kidnapping once he was in custody – after all, it was a federal charge and would add time to his sentence. Danny suspected the guy wouldn't care. Evan would tell the cops everything just to lash out at him. But by then Tommy would be safely back with his dad, and Danny would know the name and location of the only eyewitness to the murder in the parking lot. That would give him some leverage – the state's attorney might be willing to drop weak charges against him in trade for an assured case against Evan. Provided that the boy was safe and Debbie co-operated.

And if not?

Then he was going to jail.

Danny took a deep breath and popped the rear door release. Showtime. Leaving the engine running, he hopped out and started for the trailer, expecting the door to open at any moment. Debbie must have heard him drive up, but he saw no sign of her – the blinds didn't part, the door didn't move. Was she still panicky from yesterday?

He took the cinder-block steps in a stride, opened the door, and stepped in. The lights were off and the windows were shuttered. After the bright morning sun, the trailer was dim as a cave. A thick smell of burned coffee and rotting garbage filled the air. If Debbie was there, she was sitting in the dark.

He almost called her name, stopped himself. She clearly wasn't there; no point in Tommy overhearing anything now. Where could she be? The plan relied on her help. Did he dare wait? Time was precious – Evan could show up at any moment.

Suddenly, he realized that Tommy hadn't made a sound. Not when he'd thrown the door open, and not since.

He remembered the little moan Tommy had given as the pistol pressed his forehead, the way Evan had smiled and winked. His imagination furnished a terrible vision of Tommy silent and still, duct tape binding his arms and legs, dark brown blood surrounding a hole like a third eye in his forehead. Danny lunged toward the couch, but his eyes hadn't yet adjusted to the darkness, and he slammed his knee into the cabinet. Stars lit up his vision. Cursing, he leaned forward, his fingers fumbling in the shadows.

He felt fabric, cushions. His hands patted the sofa wildly, covering it in broad sweeps. Nothing.

Panic seizing him, he scrambled to his feet and reached for the light switch. The glare spilled across the tacky sofa. The fabric looked garish, stained and sunken. Scraps of duct tape dangled from the arms and legs of the couch, their ends ragged. The torn cover from a box of microwave quesadillas lay precisely in the center of the couch.

With shaking fingers, Danny reached for it. On the flip side, a note had been scrawled in black ink: *Partner – Change of plans. Sorry.*

He blinked, stared at the note, back at the sofa.

Tommy was gone.

Danny backed away, bumped into the cabinet, knocking the note free. It flipped as it fell to the floor, the bright colors of the package design giving way to the dark of the cardboard, bright, dark, bright, dark.

He had to get out of there. Regroup, figure something out.

What? What can you possibly do now?

Evan had somehow anticipated him. It seemed like every time he made the slightest progress, something conspired to take it back. He felt that old tightrope feeling, like a lean in any direction could be fatal. Without Debbie, without Tommy, Danny had nothing.

He shook his head, ordered himself to move. Time had been tight before. Now it was absolutely desperate. Somehow, he had to think of a way to turn things around before Evan got in touch with Richard. Every second counted. He bent, took the note, folded it, and tossed it in the trash. Pulled the duct tape off the couch and threw it in as well. The trailer needed a thorough cleaning and wipe-down, but he couldn't afford to do it now. He turned off the light, reached for the door handle, and stepped out into the glaring sunlight.

His truck was where he'd left it, but now a blue sedan blocked it in. At the rear stood a man he didn't recognize, a black guy in a fedora and a hawk-eyed expression.

'Danny Carter. Just the man I've been looking for.' Sean Nolan stepped out from beside the car, a hand casually resting on his gun hip. 'Remember when I said I'd be watching you, asshole?' He smiled. 'Turn around and put your hands on your head. You're coming with me.'

37. Unmarked

The Camaro reeked. What was it with Mexicans and their fucking air fresheners? Evan had fallen for the car the moment he saw it, with its stripper's curves and tinted windows. He'd jimmied the door, broken the ignition, stripped the wires, and had it purring in a minute. But though he'd thrown the cardboard Christmas tree out the window, the smell had seeped into the fabric. His cigarettes were smoking sour, and Debbie was alternating dead silence with talking too much.

'I'm going to go open the trunk, let some air in.' She reached for the handle.

'Sit back.'

She turned to glower at him, that naggy glare all women had. 'He's going to suffocate.'

'He'll be fine.' He kept his tone level but firm. Sometimes, he swore to God, it was like talking to a dog.

'I don't see why we had to move anyway. It was nicer in the trailer.'

He stabbed out his cigarette, ignoring her. He'd parked up the block from the construction site, and had a clear view in all directions. A row of run-down apartments sat on the right-hand side, and in the hour they'd been parked, he'd seen only one person leave, a tired-looking black woman wide as she was tall. The Camaro pointed away from the fenced entrance to the loft complex, but he had the mirrors angled to cover it. He could feel the tension winding in him, like thick cables cranking a notch at a time. Prison had taught him to use that. The long, slow menace of years stretched you thinner and thinner, forced you to learn to sit still, to turn the growing tension into strength. The tighter the cable wound, the greater the force when you let it snap. By tonight he'd be a millionaire, and Danny would be left to clean up the mess.

As though thinking his name had conjured him up, the silver Explorer slid into Evan's rearview mirror. He could see Danny at the wheel, and though he couldn't make out an expression at this distance, he imagined pursed lips and a wrinkled brow, like an old lady.

'Man doesn't have a clue.' The Explorer loomed steadily larger, running maybe five below the speed limit. Danny checking things out, but not wanting to get noticed. 'Fifty says he drives right by us.'

Debbie looked over, puzzled, and then the truck passed them and continued to the end of the block.

'Hey,' she said, 'wasn't that Danny? It looked like his truck.'

The left blinker came on, and the SUV vanished around the corner.

He turned to her and smiled, enjoying her confusion. 'You owe me fifty bucks.'

She tried to smile back, but he could see the flicker of fear in her eyes. It'd been there since yesterday in the parking lot. And it had gotten more pronounced this morning, when he'd made her blow him to pass the time. As her head had bobbed up and down in his lap, he'd been able to tell that she wished she were anywhere else, and that had added a little spice.

Funny thing was, if she hadn't snuck around on him, hadn't gone running to Danny, he would have given her the money. Now she was just one more thing Danny could deal with.

He waited, watching the mirror. Like clockwork, the

Explorer came back around and stopped in front of the gate. Danny got out, opened the gate, then drove the truck through, making an elaborate turn to back the ass-end up to the trailer. Always overthinking.

'What's he doing?' Debbie was turned around in her seat to watch as Danny got out of the truck and walked into the trailer.

'Making his play.'

She looked back, and he could see her figuring it out. 'We didn't move Tommy because you were afraid of the police. We moved him to get away from Danny.'

He nodded, not looking at her, staring toward the trailer instead. He could imagine it, Danny stepping into that dark space, looking around. He'd be getting that tingling nerve sense in his fingers and feet, catching the first hints that something was wrong.

Can you feel it, Danny? All of your betrayals are coming round again.

The weird thing was, some part of this stabbed him, made him wonder what he was doing. The man in that dark trailer had once been his brother.

Once, but long ago.

'Who's that?'

Her voice pulled him from his head. In the rearview mirror, a light blue Ford was pulling into the open gate. There were two men inside, both wearing hats. The car moved into the construction site like it owned the place. Detectives in an unmarked.

The tension in him wound further. Danny must have gone to the police. It wouldn't change anything, but it made his blood burn.

'Evan, what's going on?' Her voice went up to an irritating whine. 'Are those cops?'

With the gate wide open, he could see most of the way to

the trailer. The blue car had parked right in front of Danny's, blocking him in. The doors winged open, and the detectives got out, both of them with hands high up on their sides. They moved with professional ease, each checking a different direction, trusting each other. A black guy in a bright orange shirt and an old-time hat stood on the side of the car closest to them, squinting in their direction.

'Oh God, he's gonna see us,' Debbie squeaked. 'We've got to go.' She reached for his arm, shook it. 'Come on.'

He didn't let the cable inside him snap. Just slip a couple of notches. An open-handed smack sent her tumbling toward the dash. He moved fast enough she didn't even gasp. Just came back up with both hands at her cheek and the look of a scared little girl.

'Be quiet,' he said, locking the car doors with a flick of the switch and then turning back to the construction site. The door was open, and he could see Danny standing in the frame. The cops were both turned toward him now, their hands resting on their guns, neither drawn. Evan wished he could hear what was being said.

And then Danny raised his hands, turned around, and laced them behind his head. The white detective took the cuffs from his belt and locked Danny's hands behind his back.

Danny hadn't gone to the police at all. Somehow, they'd come after him.

Debbie had started whimpering, but kept it quiet enough that he ignored her.

The detective guided Danny into the back of the car, then closed the door and stood talking to the other cop. He gestured to the trailer, and the black one shook his head. Evan's eyes narrowed. There might be enough inside to piece together what had happened. He hadn't counted on cops, and his heart raced as one of them climbed the cinder-block steps. But the guy only shut the door, then got into Danny's truck and followed the blue Ford out. Maybe they didn't have a warrant. Both cars stopped just outside the gate, and the white cop got out to close it.

Would you fucking look at that. Sean Nolan, from the parish. Small fucking world.

Nolan latched the chain, then took a long look up and down the street. There was no way they could be seen, not with the tinted windows and glaring morning sun, but Evan thought the detective's eyes paused on the Camaro. He moved a hand to the ignition, ready to roll, but Nolan got back in his car. They pulled out, turned right, then left, and were gone.

What the fuck had just happened?

Evan twisted around to face the windshield, ignoring Debbie's accusing stare as she wriggled as far against the door as she could. Somehow the police had found Danny. It couldn't be an accident. He must have given himself away somehow.

Danny could've told him three reasons it had happened, probably have had them alphabetically. But at the end of the day, who cared why? The fact was that Danny was on his way to the police station, and when they got there, the police were going to start leaning on him. Hard.

Which made it cover-your-ass time.

The cops couldn't have known about the kidnapping. He'd seen street fights where sixteen squad cars rolled up in minutes. No way they'd send just two detectives for this. So it all came down to what Danny did next. What he told them.

And that made his next move clear. He smiled, popped his head from side to side, and started the car. 'Buckle up, honey pie.'

'Where are you taking me?' Her voice was cold, and the contempt in it amused him.

He turned to her. A bright red mark burned on her cheek. He smiled. 'We're going to get ourselves a little insurance.'

38. In His Wake

Square and six feet on a side, the holding cell looked like a janitor's closet. The smell of industrial cleansers couldn't quite overwhelm a lingering odor of diarrhea, the product of years of junkies. The walls were concrete, chipped and worn, with rebar showing through in spots. Graffiti was scratched into every surface – the walls, the floor, the heavy wooden bench, the rail where they cuffed down violent suspects. On TV, people were usually put in lockup with other prisoners, but that was nonsense. After all, he wasn't being charged with anything yet. They'd been careful to make that clear.

'What's this about?' Danny had asked Nolan in the car, wondering how much they knew.

The detective's eyes had flicked up to the rearview mirror. 'You're a hard man to get hold of.'

'I've been busy.'

'So Karen told me. To track you down, we've had to visit all the construction sites your company is working on. Lucky we bumped into you, huh?' The detective winked at him. 'But you know, you really should return phone calls from the police. You know who doesn't?'

Danny had stared back, seeing the line coming.

'People with something to hide. You got something to hide, Danny?'

He'd shaken his head and looked out the window, telling himself to take advantage of this time, to use it to plan his next move. He was smart, he'd think of something.

But that had been four, maybe five precious hours ago.

In that time they'd driven him to the Area One station on Fifty-first, processed him, taken his watch, wallet, keys, and shoelaces. They'd put him in an elevator, taken it up one flight, and steered him through surprisingly corporate-looking halls to this holding cell. Unlocked the solid wood door, removed the cuffs, told him to take it easy, and then left him to pace tiny circles and think.

And despite all that time, he hadn't come up with a plan worth a goddam.

Okay. Methodical. What do you know?

It was a short list. He knew that the exchange would happen sometime today. He knew that the police could hold him for something like forty-eight hours without charging him. Which meant he knew time was not his friend.

The list of things he didn't know was more daunting. He had no idea where Evan had stashed the boy. No idea what his time line was. No idea where he would set the meet – though now it surely wouldn't be Union Station. He didn't even know where Evan lived, or what his phone number was.

Somehow everything had ended up backward and upside down. Evan was free and holding all the cards, while Danny was in jail and helpless. Frustration rattled through him, and he dropped on the bench, head in hands. How had this all happened? Just a few weeks ago he'd been lying on a different bench with his head in Karen's lap. That day at the zoo, a million years ago, sunlight filtering through the trees. They had talked about having children, and he'd let himself wonder if such a thing was possible.

It seemed absurd that his entire life could be ripped away so quickly.

The bare wooden bench felt oddly comfortable, and he had the urge to lie down and close his eyes. Give it all up. Quit this unwinnable fight. What would be the harm at this point? Evan would go through with the exchange and vanish, and that would be that.

After all of this, you're going to lie to yourself? You know that if you don't stop this, Tommy and Richard are dead.

He shot upright. Was that true?

He thought of Patrick on a lonely morgue slab. Imagined the poor citizen in the parking lot, murdered for bad timing.

Evan had killed twice in the month he'd been out of prison. Why stop now, especially when with a few more squeezes of the trigger he could assure that no one came after him?

Bile burned his throat. Danny got to his feet, walked to the door, raised one fist, planning to bang on it and demand his release. Caught himself. If he played this wrong, he'd spend the next two days sitting here, while Evan finished the job and disposed of the evidence. It wouldn't matter if the cops found out about the kidnapping – he'd have the blood of two more innocents on his hands regardless.

He had to be careful. If Nolan had anything on him, he'd trot it out soon enough. Otherwise, this was a fishing expedition. If that was the case, he might be able to talk his way out of here in time to prevent more violence.

He turned and began pacing again, counting his steps and trying to focus.

Thirty minutes passed before he felt a tingling on the back of his neck, a subconscious warning. He scanned the room, the walls, the door. There. The peephole was dark. Someone was looking in at him. He turned, his hands at his sides.

'I'd like to make a phone call, please.' He used his citizen voice.

There was a moment of silence, and then the scrape of a bolt being drawn, and the door opened. Nolan stepped into the door frame, his posture calm. The other detective stood beside him. He'd taken off his fedora.

'Calling your lawyer?'

'Calling my girlfriend.' He smiled, shrugged. 'Karen was expecting me home. Don't want her to worry.'

Nolan smiled, playing the game. 'Sure. Detective Matthews, would you take Mr Carter to make his phone call?'

Matthews nodded, and put one hand on Danny's arm, his grip firm but civil.

'And when he's done, could you bring him into Interview One?' Nolan made it sound like he was asking Danny in for coffee.

The detective guided him out of the bank of holding cells and down the hall, keeping the grip on his arm. For a moment, Danny imagined throwing him off, making a break for it, but rejected the idea immediately. That was panic, and that he couldn't afford.

Matthews sat him down at an officer's desk, a black fabric half-cubicle. He cuffed Danny to the chair, gestured to the phone, and stepped across the aisle to chat with a guy in a suit.

He dialed carefully, trying to collect his thoughts. One call to Karen to let her know what had happened. The phone rang. Then he had to convince Nolan that he didn't know anything useful, and do it fast. The phone rang. If they didn't have anything on the kidnapping, it would just be about Patrick. The phone rang.

Where was Karen? She had said she'd wait by the telephone.

The machine clicked on, his own voice playing back at him. He felt his pulse quicken. Had she panicked? That wasn't her style, but he was supposed to have called hours ago. She might have come looking for him, wanting to help.

The machine beeped, and he spoke loudly. 'Karen? Karen, pick up.' There was a crackle and a click as the machine cut off. 'Thank God. Karen, listen –'

'Partner.'

Evan.

Danny's stomach fell, and he gripped the phone with white knuckles.

'I'm sorry,' Evan continued, 'Karen can't come to the phone. She's tied up, if you know what I mean.'

Danny's heart beat against his chest like a wild animal trying to free itself from a snare. 'I'm warning you –'

'Shut up, you arrogant prick.' The playful tone dropped from his voice. 'She's okay. But you just be very careful what you say to our friends, huh?'

It all fell together. Somehow Evan must have known that he'd been brought in for questioning. This was his way of making sure Danny didn't bring down the police. He forced himself to breathe. 'I understand.'

'Good boy. Gotta go.'

And then the phone went dead.

Oh God. The unthinkable had somehow gotten worse. He didn't buy Evan's deal for a second. There was no way he'd let Karen go, not now. He'd almost certainly kill Tommy and Richard, and they were far less dangerous to him. If Danny couldn't stop him, Evan would leave three bodies in his wake.

One of them hers.

Detective Matthews stepped over and looked at Danny inquisitively. 'Bad news?'

For a moment, Danny thought of confessing everything, telling him the whole story and enlisting the cops' aid. But then he remembered the easy speed with which Evan had put his pistol against Tommy's forehead. The risk was too great. The police would only make things worse.

He was the only hope Karen and the others had.

Danny looked up, let his breath out. Made himself smile. 'Nah. You know women.' He hung up the phone, hoping the detective didn't notice his finger shaking. 'You guys ready for me?'

39. The Demons of Long Ago

The two-way glass between them dimmed Danny's features, but even so, he looked pretty calm to Nolan. Danny sat at the table, cuffs off, glancing around the room with just the right blend of interest and discomfort. Acting the citizen.

'How do you want to do this?' Matthews asked.

'I'll start alone.' Nolan straightened his tie, fingers feeling as clumsy as usual. Every morning Mary-Louise tied him a perfect half-Windsor – it was part of her morning ritual, a domestic incantation to bring him home safe – but by day's end, the knot had usually degenerated into a lumpy half-hitch.

'You know, the dude seems awfully cool. You sure he's dirty?' Matthews asked.

Nolan smiled. 'Your experience, how's somebody done nothing wrong react when you put the cuffs on?'

'They start telling me I don't need them.'

'Exactly.' Nolan made a final tug at his tie. 'Danny, he just turned around and stuck out his wrists.' He shot his cuffs, stepped out of the observation room, and opened the door to the interview room.

Danny glanced up at him with a bland smile, but Nolan kept his own expression neutral as he took measured steps to the table. He stood for a moment sizing Danny up, letting the silence draw out a few seconds longer than was comfortable. Finally he pulled out a chair.

'So,' he said, 'I'm obligated to remind you that you can have counsel here if you like.'

'Do I need it?'

Nolan shrugged. 'I just want to ask you a few questions.'

'This is about Patrick?' Danny's voice caught slightly, and the sadness that flickered across his face seemed real enough.

'Mostly.'

'I can't believe what happened. We're still shocked. If there's anything I can do to help, I'd be glad to.'

The mask was back up, Nolan noticed. 'Let's start with you telling me how you knew him.'

'We grew up together.' Danny continued, talking about Bridgeport and Back of the Yards, their mutual old neighborhood. How they'd been friends in grade school, and how when Patrick's parents died, he'd come to live with Danny. A very Irish, very old-school story, and one Nolan mostly already knew.

Still, Nolan let him talk, prompting here and there with questions to keep it flowing. Timing was crucial. He spent more than an hour establishing the basics, just letting Danny get used to talking. He asked about their friendship, about Danny's past. Every time he spoke about Patrick's death, he saw that same flash of sadness. Once, Nolan had thought that Danny might have had to dig deep to come up with someone still in the life, someone he could pay to get rid of Evan. But that obviously hadn't been the case.

'You guys have been friends all along, right? So you knew what he did.' Nolan made it a statement, holding his gaze on Danny's.

'Sure.' Danny didn't flinch. 'In general terms.'

'And you felt okay being friends with a felon? I mean,' he paused, readying the barb, 'this guy was a real piece of shit.'

A vein in Danny's forehead throbbed, but he kept his tone pleasant. 'He was a good guy, Sean.'

'Yeah?' He paused, changed tacks, trying to keep Danny off-kilter. 'Hey, who gave you the shiner? Looks nasty.'

'This?' Danny touched his cheek, where the skin was purpling. 'Dumbest thing. I was working in the basement. Walked right into the cold water shut-off valve.'

'That scratch up your hands, too?'

Danny smiled. 'Guess I should wear gloves when I work, huh?'

Nolan didn't return the smile. 'I was wondering if maybe it had to do with that thing you came to see me about.'

'Evan?' Danny shook his head. 'Haven't heard from him in a couple of weeks.'

Fifteen years as a cop gave you an eye for reactions. Danny was a good liar, Nolan could see that, but he was lying just the same. 'Just went away, huh?'

'I guess he realized I wasn't much of a target for a shake-down.' He shrugged. 'I don't know, maybe he got tired of the weather. Either way, I haven't heard from him.'

Nolan nodded slowly. It was a good play. Any admitted contact with Evan would give Nolan something to hammer away at. He knew Danny was lying, knew that Evan was still in his life, that they were up to something. He'd been able to see it on Karen's face, and in Danny's actions. But knowing wasn't the same as hard evidence.

Unfortunately, evidence was in short supply. Unless circumstances changed, the only way he was going to get somewhere was if Danny slipped. He had to keep the pressure up, keep him off guard. With a smile on his face, he attacked.

'So who killed Patrick?'

The sudden change of topic seemed to throw Danny. His hands fidgeted on the table. 'I don't know.'

'I think you do.' Sean stood up and leaned into the table, his hands on it, using the height advantage to bring more power to his gaze. Danny looked up at him. 'I think you did it.'

'Huh?' His tone stunned.

'I think you hired him to get rid of Evan, and Evan took him down. Which means, basically, you killed him.'

Danny paused like he was fighting for composure, and Nolan knew he'd hit on something. Time to run his bluff.

'We've got you on tape, asking Patrick to call you about a job. Sounding desperate. This is a couple days after Patrick's supposed to have finished Evan off, and you're getting worried.'

'What tape?' Danny injected just a hint of scorn into the question, but Nolan knew he was upset.

'Come on, Danny, admit it. You were scared. You needed help. You paid your childhood friend to take care of it for you. But Patrick got killed, and that's why you've been running from us.'

'I don't know what you're talking about.'

'Remember,' Nolan said, trying a different direction, 'Evan is still out there. And I'm sure he figured out who sent Patrick after him. You're going to need protection.' He could see that something was churning in Danny's mind, could almost watch him calculating. 'We can make a deal here, Danny. You'll have to face some charges, but you can put Evan away for murder. Be able to stop looking over your shoulder.'

Danny stared at him.

'Help us out and this can all be over.'

He'd made his play, and knew he'd hit a nerve. Nolan kept his eyes hard, his body language aggressive, wanting Danny to feel the pressure of his presence. To feel leaned on. The two men locked glares, Nolan willing him to speak. *Give me something, asshole.* Just a tiny crack, anything, and he would hammer away till Danny shattered. All night, if that's what it took.

Then Danny smiled. 'Detective,' he said, his voice calm, 'I don't know what you're talking about.'

Forty minutes later, Nolan was still smoldering. Back in the observation room, that smug expression of Danny's hung in the shadowed air in front of him. On the other side of the glass, Detective Jackson was talking to the man, getting the same stonewall answers. Danny had made his decision. He was hiding behind a pretense of normalcy.

And the part that burned was that no matter the fact that Nolan knew, just *knew* that the guy was dirty, all he had to connect the two was a phone call that wasn't nearly as incriminating as he'd tried to make it sound. In fact, on the surface, the call was completely innocuous.

The door opened, and Matthews stepped in to join him. He was silent for a moment, then nodded toward the glass. 'Willie taking a run at him?'

'I sent him to ask the same questions, see if anything changes.'

'Any luck?'

Nolan shook his head. 'He's sticking to it.'

'Maybe he's got nothing to stick to.'

Nolan looked over at Matthews, then back through the glass. He could see his own reflection in it, very faint in the darkness. He paused, then spoke softly. 'You ever know anybody in the Program?'

'AA?' Matthews hesitated. 'Yeah. My daddy was in it.'

Nolan nodded. 'Mine, too. He stick with it?'

'For a while. Till the Zenith plant moved to Mexico. He went on a three-day bender. Ended up cutting a man in a bar fight. Went on the run, never came back.' The detective's eyes seemed distant, like he was grappling with the demons of long ago. Then he shook his head, looked over. 'How 'bout yours?'

'He stuck with it. Did his twelve, went to commitments twice a week.' Nolan paused. 'It worked for him. But you know the whole basis of the thing? You pledge not to drink today. That's all. Tomorrow, you get up and do it again. You're never really cured.'

'So?'

'It's all about avoiding temptation. The thing about recovering alcoholics, you put a glass in front of them, sooner or later they drink it.' Nolan nodded through the glass. 'Danny's the same way.'

'You think someone put a job in front of him.'

'And he took it. Yeah.'

Matthews nodded, shrugged. 'Okay. So what you want to do?'

Nolan shrugged. 'Let him go.'

'We can keep him here, sweat him. Wake him in the middle of the night and go through it again. He might slip.'

'He might not. And if he doesn't, we'd end up dealing with the state's attorney before we could pick him up again.' He straightened, checked his watch. Almost five. 'When Willie's done, turn him loose.'

'You're going to let him walk clean?' Matthews sounded incredulous.

'Hell no.' Nolan reached for the door handle. 'I'm going to let him go and see where he leads me.'

40. A Thousand Curses

The scream he'd been strangling for hours was starting to scrabble and tear at his insides. But Danny kept his citizen face up, trying to strike a pose of annoyed politeness as the old cop fumbled in a manila envelope.

'One wallet, leather. One pair shoelaces. One ring of keys.'

He noticed that his toe was tapping impatiently and made himself stop. Almost out. But then, frying pans and fires. Somewhere beyond this police station, Evan held all the threads of Danny's life clenched in a callused fist.

'And one cell phone. Sign here, please.'

He snatched the pen and scribbled his name on the clipboard. 'Where's my car?'

'Sir?' The officer blinked at him.

'My car. One of the detectives drove it here.'

'Let me check on that.' The man reached for the phone with the alacrity of drying cement.

Danny swallowed the scream, bent down to lace his shoes. He tried to avoid looking at the watch as he fastened it, but couldn't help himself. Jesus. Five thirty. In a day when every second counted, he'd just lost seven hours.

Karen spent that time with Evan.

The thought made his hands quiver, a pale anger rising in him, the scream almost escaping, making him want to shake the white-haired cop till his eyeballs rattled.

Instead, he took a breath and adjusted the plastic smile on his face.

The cop hung up the phone. 'Sir, I believe you'll find your car in the visitor's lot in front of the station.'

Danny turned away before the man finished. Everything in him wanted to run, but he forced himself to take measured steps, to move swiftly but not recklessly. He skipped the elevator in favor of a flight of steps he took in four leaps. In the lobby, a fit black beat cop stood behind the desk, patiently explaining something to a finger-pointing Latina. The evening's crop of homeless and lost filled the benches, staring with wary eyes. Danny hurried past, opened the door, and stepped into the evening air. Traffic on the Dan Ryan buzzed white noise. As soon as he was out of sight, he broke into a run, sprinting past broken-down pickups and old Caddys. In his mind, the slaps of his feet were the ticking of a clock, *tick-TOCK, tick-TOCK*. He found his truck and had it in gear almost before the engine finished cranking. Roaring out of the parking lot, he swerved across two lanes and jumped on the highway.

The whole time he'd been at the station, his mind had been racing, trying to think of a way to track Evan down. The man didn't have a cell phone, had carefully kept his address from Danny. The last time he'd needed to get in touch with him, he'd called Murphy's and left a message with the bartender. Evan wasn't likely to return his call this time.

Which left only one route that Danny could think of. Slaloming through traffic with his left hand, he flipped open his mobile phone with his right. He pulled up the menu, then the call register, and selected CALLS DIALED.

There it was, dated just three days earlier. Felt like years. He punched DIAL and whispered a silent prayer as he counted rings. The line went to static as he shot under a bridge, swerving to the left shoulder to dodge a long line of traffic. A chorus of honking counterpointed the third ring. 'Come on, Debbie. Pick up the phone.'

Her voice truncated the fifth ring. 'Hello?' She sounded tense, high-strung with panic.

'Listen, I don't have much time. I need you to pay attention. Evan has lost it. He went to my house and kidnapped my girlfriend.'

There was a pause. 'I know.'

'What?' His ears seemed to ring. He couldn't process what she had said.

'He . . . he made me help him. He hit me, told me he'd kill me, that he'd –' She broke off in a choked sob.

The image played out in his mind, Evan caressing the gun, Debbie wanting to do the right thing, but too scared, too weak to defy him.

'It's okay.' He spoke soothingly. 'I understand. I'm coming. Where are you?'

'The bathroom. I needed to pee, and . . . he just tied her up. He didn't hurt her any.'

'Debbie, *what* bathroom? Where are you?' The highway ahead was a parking lot, and he exited to surface streets, scanning for patrol cars as he jumped the light.

She took a deep breath. When she spoke, her voice was an accusation. 'You said you'd take care of everything.'

The words cut. He remembered the parking lot the day before. Telling her to go home, telling her he'd end this. Saying it with a certainty, a bravado, which today seemed faint as dawn stars. 'I tried.' He paused. 'Yesterday was different.'

There was a long pause. 'Danny, I'm scared.'

He sighed. 'I know.' Stoplight after stoplight was mercifully green. 'Me, too. It's okay. Just tell me where you are.'

'No.' Her voice was at once faint and resolute. 'I can't. If you show up, Evan will kill me.'

His stomach seemed to shrink. Somehow he'd never

considered that she might not help him – that she might decide Evan was the safer bet.

'Debbie, I know you're scared.' LaSalle was oddly quiet, and he gunned the truck, the blocks disappearing under his tires as he tried to be reasonable enough for both of them. 'And I know that you're hoping things will just turn out all right. That you can ride them out. But you can't. If you don't help me, Evan will kill Karen, and probably Tommy and his dad, too.'

'You don't know that.'

'Yeah, I do.' He sighed. 'I used to think I could make this go away by playing along, just like you. But it only keeps getting worse. Sooner or later you have to realize it won't stop. Unless we stop it.'

There was a moment of silence, and he let it hold, afraid to push too hard for fear of shutting her down. Five seconds stretched into ten, ten into fifteen. He could imagine her thinking about it, weighing his words. He fought the urge to tell her to open her fucking eyes, to remind her of the diner parking lot and the dead man in a trunk at the airport parking lot. Then, in the background of the phone, he heard a sudden banging sound and a muffled voice. 'What the fuck's taking so long, Deborah?'

'I'll be right out.' She sounded shrill as glass. There was a pause like she was waiting to hear Evan walk away. When she came back on, she was barely whispering. 'I've got to go.'

'Wait!' He yelled. 'Debbie, please.' Terrified that he might lose her now that he was so close. 'Tell me where you are.'

There was a sniffle, and he pictured her, sitting fully dressed on the toilet of some thin-walled bathroom, the scariest monster she'd ever known stalking outside the door. Her mascara stained and running, a bruise from wherever he'd hit her. The picture killed him. Then he remembered that she was the safest of the people at risk.

'Please.' He whispered the word. 'For Tommy.'

He heard a shuddering intake of breath. He waited for her answer, ready to spin the car in any direction. Wherever they were, he'd have the element of surprise. It would put him back in control. All he needed to know was where to go.

'I'm sorry,' she said.

And then hung up the phone.

He held it to his ear for stupefied seconds. She'd abandoned him. The only one who could tell him where Karen was. The only one who could save Tommy's life. She'd hung up the phone.

God*damn* her.

A honking horn yanked him back to reality, and he spun into a gas station, barely avoiding the front end of a Volvo. He jerked the car into park and looked at the phone. Calling back was a risk to her. It might make Evan nervous, might make him question her loyalty.

Fuck that.

He hit *redial*, held the phone to his ear.

One ring. Then, 'Hi, this is Debbie. Leave your digits and I'll hit you back.'

She'd turned off her phone.

He was out of options.

He almost threw the mobile through the window. Stopped himself. Dropped the phone on the seat and his head in his hands. For what seemed like long moments he just sat there. Then he put the car in drive and continued up Clark.

By breaking every rule of the road, he'd made amazing time, but it was hard to get excited about the prospect of arriving home. He had no idea where Evan was, no idea how to stop him. All he had was an empty house, a ticking clock, and a head full of useless plans.

He double-parked in front of the apartment and got out. Things were unnervingly normal. Halloween decorations blinked and flashed. Down the block, a couple laughed as they struggled to hoist a pony keg up their front steps.

He took the steps two at a time. Evan had said that he hadn't hurt her, but there was no way to be sure. No way except to step in and pray not to find her bleeding out on the hardwood floor. The door to their apartment was slightly ajar. He put a hand against it, feeling the touch of the wood, wondering if this was going to be one of those permanent moments. If after this, his life would be divided into the time before he stepped into the apartment and the time after.

He pushed the door open.

The place was a shambles, and it took him a moment to realize that much of it was the mess from the night before. Boxes sat with clothes stacked beside them, and loose pictures were strewn across the floor.

But there were other things wrong. The lamp by the couch was knocked over. The glass top of the coffee table was cracked in spiderwebs.

He stepped in and walked down the hall. The bedroom was empty. So was the spare. There was a broken water glass on the kitchen floor. The back door stood wide open. On the counter was a tuft of brown hair, stained dark at one end, as though it had been ripped out.

But there was no body.

Rage and relief surged through him. Relief at not finding her dead; seething, sun-blind rage at her violation. The animal part of him rose up, made the blood ring in his ears, his vision blur. He forced himself to breathe, one hand gripping the counter as he gulped oxygen. There wasn't time for this. He had to be able to think. Had to get the anger under control. Had to harness it, to make it a tool he could use.

A weapon.

He closed his eyes and forced himself to count, banishing visions of Evan holding a gun to Karen's temple. He couldn't waste time or energy. He needed his faculties at 100 percent. With every breath he pictured his chest filling with cool blue air, and with each exhale forced it all clear, till his lungs were down to their dregs.

Think.

He walked out of the kitchen, down the hall to the bedroom. The bedspreads were tangled from last night, when they'd made love and then dropped off to sleep. Her pillow still had a crinkled indentation. He dropped to the edge of the bed and held his head in his hands.

Think!

He didn't know where Evan lived.

He didn't know where Evan was.

He knew the meet would be tonight, but not when. Evan would probably wait for dark, but twilight already bruised the sky outside their bedroom windows.

Debbie wouldn't help him.

Patrick was dead. Murdered.

Karen was a hostage.

He stood up, kicked the bed frame savagely, the pain ringing up his leg. He was going in circles. He couldn't afford to keep following the same arguments.

He had to remove himself. Think of it in purely strategic terms.

See the whole situation.

See not just the problem, but the constraints that defined it. Not just the attack, but the weaknesses it was intended to capitalize on. Like those black-and-white drawings of faces and candlesticks, where the negative space was a different picture from the positive.

Ignore the faces. See the negative space.

And then it hit him.

There was another person who knew where the meet would take place.

41. The Easiest Thing in the World

Danny put the car in park and killed the engine. As his headlights faded, darkness rushed in to fill the void. Outside the passenger window, the house looked as he remembered, red brick with an elaborately shingled roof that peaked like a cathedral. But now he felt like the house was somehow watching. Judging. The rest of the neighborhood blazed with light, silhouetting groups of kids running from porch to porch with winter jackets over Halloween costumes. Richard's home hunched silent and dark.

The last time Danny had been here, he'd crossed the line from citizen to criminal. The last time, he'd picked a lock and crept in the back door as a thief. Now he had to walk up to the front door and confess.

The prospect made his palms sweat. Not because there would be no going back — he'd already crossed the point of no return — but because he had to face Richard, look him in the eyes, and admit to being the architect of his sorrow. Admit to taking the most important thing in the man's life.

And then, somehow, convince him he was here to help.

The dashboard clock read seven. No time to waste. His mind was cloaked in static as he stepped out of the car and started across the lawn. The laughter of the trick-or-treaters seemed haunted, foreign, part of a world he didn't belong in. A reminder of his sins. On the way over, he'd tried to plan what he would say to Richard, to anticipate the man's response. But now, as his sneakers carved canyons in the dew-wet grass, everything vanished.

He stepped onto the porch and rang the doorbell. The

windows on either side of the door showed blackness. He prayed he wasn't too late, that he hadn't missed Richard. He rang the doorbell again. Nothing.

Danny cupped his hands and put his forehead to the glass. Faint ambient light silvered the edges of furniture, gleamed off the hardwood, but there were no lamps on, not in the foyer or in the hall beyond. He felt a burning sickness. If Richard was gone, this whole drama was over. He leaned on the doorbell, holding it down, eyes intent on the inside. The chime rang *Ding-dong-Ding-dong-Ding-dong-Ding-dong.*

He had almost given up hope when he saw a flash of motion down the hall, as though someone had leaned out of the darkened kitchen to check the door. Releasing the bell, he yelled, 'Richard!' He banged on the door, shouting his boss's name again and again, conscious of the stares from a group of children, the wary look from the father escorting them. He didn't care. He'd bang until neighborhood security took him away.

Finally the shape moved down the hallway. Danny stepped back, hands at his sides, his heart roaring. The door swung open. Richard's eyes were sunken, and a three-day growth of beard shadowed his cheeks. 'Now isn't a good time.' He started to shut the door, but Danny moved faster, snaking a hand in to catch the edge.

'I need to talk to you.'

'Later.' Richard pushed against the door.

'I know why you can't talk.' He kept his gaze level, meeting his boss's eyes. 'I know where you're going. Trust me. We need to talk first.'

The pressure against the door eased, Richard staring back at him. Finally, he glanced at his watch, cursed, and opened the door. 'One minute.' He stepped back into the hallway.

Danny stepped inside, shutting the door behind him.

He stood opposite his boss. The man looked like a wreck, and sour guilt corkscrewed in Danny's stomach.

'What did you mean,' Richard said slowly, 'when you said you knew where I was going?'

Danny swallowed, the spit going down hard. 'I know about Tommy.' The words dropped like stones. 'I know he's been kidnapped.'

Richard gaped at him. 'How do you know that?'

Danny took a breath, forced himself to meet Richard's eyes. 'Because I helped do it.'

Total silence fell humming across the room. Time slowed, and Danny found himself noticing incredible detail in things. The individual hairs of Richard's beard. The grain of the hardwood. The clammy trail of a bead of sweat sliding down his side.

And then Richard lunged, his arms up, his pupils wide. He swung wildly, fists flailing, an angry growl coming from his mouth. Danny held his hands at his sides, taking the hits, letting Richard drive him back. 'Stop!'

His boss ignored him, throwing an awkward punch that set Danny's bruised ribs singing.

'I'm here to help,' he said. His foot caught on the edge of a throw rug, and he staggered against the wall. Richard stepped forward and wrapped his hands around Danny's throat.

His mind raced. He could stomp the heel of his foot down on Richard's arch. He could punch him in the throat and drop him, gasping. He could lean forward and drive his knee into the man's groin. Breaking an amateur choke was the easiest thing in the world.

But he held still and let his boss squeeze, the pressure on his throat growing. The pain was surprising, blunt and ragged, and he fought to suck air down his windpipe. Automatically, his hands clenched into fists, but he made himself loosen them. Richard leaned close, his face right in Danny's, the man's breath sour with coffee and anger. Fairy dots danced in Danny's vision, the darkness of the hallway throbbing with his pulse. He kept his eyes on Richard's, trying to put it all into them, the pain and regret and fear, willing Richard to let go, let him help, knowing that Richard had an animal right to do what he was doing.

Finally, summoning all his strength, he managed to whisper, 'Tommy.' For an instant, nothing happened, and then the grip slackened slightly. He spoke again, the words sandpaper on the inside of his throat. 'I can help you save him.'

Richard leaned forward, his nose almost touching Danny's. Then he gave a last squeeze, grunted with frustration and anger, and let go. Danny dropped to his knees, gasping for air. The hardwood swam. He fought for balance, every pump of his heart sending his head spinning. Richard stalked back and forth, his steps loud.

When he had his breath back, Danny rose, keeping his hands at his sides.

'Where's my son?' Richard's eyes glinted in the darkness of the hall.

Danny shook his head. 'I don't know.'

'Is he all right?'

'Yes.' He paused, forced himself to speak the truth. 'At least, he was yesterday.'

Richard's hands balled into shaking fists. 'What do you mean?'

Danny swallowed. An electrical storm raged across the inside of his throat. 'We don't have a lot of time. But there are some things you should know.' In broad strokes, he told Richard about his past, about Evan, how Evan had come looking for him. His boss stared at him, his mouth open.

'You kidnapped my son because this man asked you to?'

'I had no choice. He threatened Karen, jumped her in an alley last week.' He paused, made himself meet Richard's glare. 'Evan is impulsive, rash. That's what makes him dangerous. I knew he'd do it either way. If I didn't help, he would have hurt Karen. And I thought that if I were involved, I could protect Tommy.'

His boss glared, turned away, then back. 'So why are you here now?'

'Because if you deliver the money alone, Evan is going to kill you and Tommy both.'

'How do you know that?'

'He's killed two people since he got out. One of them was my best friend.' He saw the flicker in Richard's eyes. Danny was reaching him. 'The other was a guy who over-heard his call to you. This is his big score. He won't take any chances.'

Richard turned away, hid his head in his hands. Danny heard a sound like a sob, quickly choked off.

'I'm here to help.' Danny stepped forward. 'I know that sounds crazy, but it's true.'

Richard looked up at him, anger in his eyes. 'You've lied to me for years.'

'Yes.' There was no point in softening it.

'Why should I trust you now?'

'It isn't just Tommy. He —' His voice broke. 'He has Karen, too.'

Richard snorted. 'That's why you're really here. Not for me, not for Tommy.'

Was that true? Would he be taking these risks if Karen's life wasn't also at stake?

He hoped so. Sometimes that was all you had.

'No. I'm here to set things right.' He gambled, put a hand on Richard's shoulder. 'I'm here to get your boy back.'

His boss stared at him, a complex mix of emotions in his

eyes. Pain, rage, and hatred. But Danny thought he also saw something else. Maybe hope.

'Evan called you today,' Danny said, hoping to draw him out.

Richard nodded slowly. 'An hour ago. I only know his voice.' His eyes narrowed. 'It's nice to have a name to hate now.'

'When is the meeting?'

'You don't know?'

Danny shook his head. 'Evan took your son and disappeared last night.'

Richard stared at him, the calculations clear on his face. Danny knew this was the moment of truth – either Richard would trust him, let him help, or else it was over. The seconds ticked long and slow.

'Nine o'clock. At the Pike Street construction site.'

Inwardly, Danny groaned. Of course. The irony had appealed to Evan so much, the idea of using Richard's own space to hide his son. How much better, how much crueler, to have the meet there? He should have guessed.

'What are you supposed to do?'

'Drive in, park my car facing out, and leave it running.' The words started to come more easily. 'Walk into the building with the money in a duffel bag. He said he'd take the money and my car, and leave Tommy with me.'

Danny shook his head, one hand massaging his sore neck. 'He'll check the money, and then he'll shoot you.'

'We should call the police.'

Danny turned fast. 'No.'

'You said he's going to kill me, kill Tommy. What else am I supposed to do?'

'Believe me, Richard, you bring the police, Tommy and Karen die. Evan will be watching. You'd save your life, but it will cost your son's.'

'What if it was a specialist, or a SWAT team, something like that?'

Danny snorted. 'It doesn't work that way. You call now, you'll get squad cars, maybe a couple of detectives. They'll be noisy and they'll be slow. As for deploying SWAT teams, well, that only happens on TV.'

Richard looked like he wanted to argue, then sighed. He leaned against the wall, let himself slide down to sit on his heels. 'All of this only happens on TV.'

Danny felt for the guy. Like his own, Richard's whole life had been ripped away. In some ways, it had been worse for Danny because he had watched it happening, had to suffer every moment of it. But at least it had left him in a world he understood. Richard was lost.

But understanding this world didn't change basic facts. Evan held the position of strength. If they were going to stop him, they needed an edge.

'You don't,' Danny asked, 'happen to own a gun?'

'With a kid? No way.'

Danny nodded, tired. It was the first time in his life he'd wanted the answer to that question to be yes. 'Okay.' He sat down against the wall beside Richard. In the silence, he could hear the faint ticking of the antique grandfather clock in the living room.

'Why is this happening?' Richard's voice was faint.

Danny took a long moment to collect his words. He knew the answer. He'd known, on some gut level, since childhood. It had defined the way he'd grown up, the choices he'd made. Even after he'd gotten out of the life, the consciousness of it had haunted him. It was the true reason behind his monthly nightmares, the reason he always looked over his shoulder.

'Because you have something. Your life is blessed. Nothing is out of reach. People like Evan and me, we grew up differently.' He paused, shrugged. 'It's not complicated. It's happening because you have something and others don't. And that's all the reason some people need.'

'People like you.' Richard's voice was flat.

Danny sighed. 'Once.' He thought of Karen, that day at the zoo. His head in her lap as he watched her smile dance against wild blue sky. They'd talked about having children, and he remembered the rush of sweet possibility he'd felt. 'Now, all I want is to earn what I've got.'

There was a long pause, and then Richard turned to him. 'What's going to happen?'

I don't know. I honestly don't know.

But what he said was, 'We're going to get your son back.'

'How?'

How indeed? Richard was a civilian, certainly willing to fight for his son, but of limited use in a scrap. Danny had been in a dozen serious scuffles by ten, but he still didn't like his chances against Evan. The man was a prison-hardened killer. He'd learned to fight in the Golden Gloves and honed his lethal edge with a maximum-security sentence. He was strong, fast, ruthless, and armed. Plus, he was expecting them.

Wait.

Not quite.

'You know what?' Danny turned to look at his boss, a hint of a smile on his lips. 'We've got one advantage.'

'What's that?'

'He doesn't know I'm coming.'

It took a moment, but Richard managed a smile back.

42. A Treacherous Place

Richard was upstairs changing when Danny saw the duffel bag. Black with a dull silver zipper and padded handles, it looked like any other gym bag.

But Danny knew different.

He hefted it, surprised at the weight. Thirty pounds, maybe more. The zipper pulled smoothly over thick teeth, a quality item like everything else in Richard's world. Danny eased it down slow, not to tease himself, but out of respect to a certain deadness he felt toward the bag and its contents. Once, this would have fired his heart and set his mind racing. Once, he would have been planning how to escape with it, envisioning the things he could do.

Now, as he stared down at the neatly bundled currency, all those Jacksons, Grants, and Franklins staring up at him, he felt only a vague nausea. Paper. Stacks and stacks of green paper. After all the discussion, after all the philosophy, that was what this came down to. These were the answer to Richard's question. These were the lives of the people they loved, the futures of the people they worked with, the prime movers of darkness. Fate had borrowed the scales from Justice, set blood on one side and these dirty slips of paper on the other, and judged them even.

He thought of Karen's brown sugar smell, the wet sparkle in her eyes when she laughed, the soft curve of her back. Acid soured his stomach. He zipped the bag and stepped away from its gloomy gravity.

Richard's footsteps sounded down the stairs. He'd done

as Danny asked, changed into loose, dark clothing: jeans and an old sweatshirt.

'You have any black tennis shoes?' Danny asked, gesturing at the white Nikes, their reflective swoosh bright even in the dim light.

Richard shook his head. 'Just these.'

'All right.'

The doorbell rang, kids yelling, 'Trick-or-treat!' They ignored it, their gaze locked. The bell rang again, and then the kids moved on to the next house, a parade of normalcy.

'Should we bring a weapon?' The question sounded bizarre coming from Richard.

A knife block stood in the center of the kitchen island, and Danny slid an eight-inch chef's out, feeling the weight. German steel, well balanced and heavy. Perfect for chopping. He tried to imagine slipping it into Evan, blood spilling over his hands like soup.

He put the knife back in the block. 'It will just get in the way.'

For a moment Richard looked like he was going to argue, but finally shrugged. 'What time is it?'

Danny looked at him. 'Time.'

The garage looked the same, and Danny swallowed a wave of guilt as he remembered Evan carrying Tommy's limp body in his arms. Richard heaved the money bag in the back of the Range Rover and climbed into the driver's seat. Danny joined him, feeling the first tingles of fear knit his stomach.

Easy, he told himself. Stretch it out. They had forty minutes yet – no point arriving adrenaline-sick and shaky.

The neighborhood streets were bright with the warm glow of porches and the sweeping arcs of flashlights. Children ran from house to house, their cotton capes and rubber monster masks providing a surreal background. Danny clenched and unclenched his fists, popping his knuckles.

'You want to go over it again?'

'I'll drop you off a couple of blocks away.' Richard spoke mechanically. 'Then find somewhere to park and wait. I show up at nine, and do everything Evan says. You sneak in and find Tommy and Karen.'

Danny nodded. 'When you're talking to him, remember not to say anything about Karen. We don't want him to have any idea I'm there.'

'Right. You free them, tell them to get out. I try to stall Evan until you can jump him from behind.'

'There you go.' It was so flimsy it could hardly be called a plan. There were a dozen things that could go wrong. But in a situation with no time, no advantages, and no foreknowledge of the setup, it offered a chance to get the innocents out. Catching Evan was secondary to that. Everything was secondary to that.

Besides, Danny reasoned, Evan would be on unfamiliar ground. A construction site at night was a treacherous place. Danny had spent the last seven years on them. He could stride a twelve-inch beam without hesitation, could visualize the blueprints for each level, and knew every piece of cover. That might give them the edge they needed.

'It's funny.' Richard's face glowed pale in oncoming headlights. 'My son would never expect me to do this.'

'What?'

'Rescue him.' Richard sighed. 'I've been a lousy father. When I grew up, my dad was always gone. Working, building this company for me to inherit. He was proud of that, that it would one day be for me. Only, in the process, he forgot to actually be a father. I swore that I'd be different, that I'd be there. But I've been as bad as he was.'

The confession surprised Danny. Richard had always kept up a gruff front, never revealing this kind of emotion. Had he maintained the same face around his son? Debbie had said Tommy told her his father didn't know he was alive.

'My father worked hard, too,' Danny said, his voice quiet. 'I used to hate him for it.'

'He was gone a lot?'

'Yeah, but that wasn't it.' He remembered the way Dad would leave the house in the morning, his posture upright, almost military despite his dusty clothes and lunch box. 'I hated that we were poor. I hated eating potatoes and fried mush to stretch the grocery budget, hated that we had to listen to Sox games from the parking lot because we couldn't afford tickets. I'd see these kids on the El, North Side kids, with trendy clothes and headphones, money to spare, and I'd hate that I didn't have what they did.' He started cracking his knuckles one at a time. 'One day I stole the Walkman out of a kid's schoolbag. Suddenly I had something I wanted, just because I had the balls to take it. I was proud of that. Kept it under my pillow.'

'Let me guess. Your father found it.'

Danny nodded. 'He was stern, strict, and I thought he'd beat me blue. Instead, he sat me down and tried to explain why it was wrong. Said that you had to earn things. That a man was measured by the way he acted, not what he had.' He shook his head. 'As he's talking, I'm thinking about how Joey Morgan's older brother makes two grand a week stealing cars, and gets to spend most of his time in the bar. Compared to that, my dad seemed like a fool, busting his hump every day and never having anything to show for it . . .' He trailed off. 'It took fifteen years to begin to understand what the old man really meant. And by then, he was dead.'

They rode in silence. The skyline loomed larger, a bright harvest moon hanging above it. They'd left Lakeshore for surface streets five minutes ago. Just a few more blocks. The roads here were quiet, with few cars and no pedestrians. The same things that had made the construction site a good place to keep Tommy made it a good place for Evan to plan the meet. A couple of gunshots would go unobserved.

That brought back the sliver of fear, the old tingle in Danny's fingers and wrists. No fighting it this time. He thought of Karen and Tommy, bound and scared. All of the last weeks came down to the next half hour.

More than that. All of his life.

'Over there. By that park.'

Richard nodded, steering the Range Rover to the playground. Shallow ruts marked where Danny had driven across it yesterday. The loft was two short blocks from here. On foot, he could wend through dark alleys and approach unseen. It would do.

Danny reached for the door handle, then stopped and looked over at Richard. The glow from the dashboard carved his face from the darkness. He looked ready, resolute, but a deep sadness had inscribed itself on his features. Richard had discovered what really mattered to him just in time to lose it. Danny winced, fought the urge to look away as he spoke. 'I'm sorry, Richard,' he said softly. 'I'm so sorry to have dragged you and Tommy into this.'

Richard glanced at him. 'There's no forgiving you.'

Danny nodded. 'I understand.'

'But I know you had no choice.' Richard's eyes were weary. 'That helps.'

But you did have a choice, the voice inside Danny whispered. *In the beginning. You could have gone to the cops and taken your chances. Even if they'd tried to charge you for the pawnshop, at least you wouldn't have fucked up any other lives.*

You had a choice and you made the wrong one.

Never again. He gripped the handle, took a deep breath, exhaled loudly. Then he opened the door, slid to the ground, and closed it behind him. The city's hum filled his ears. Not waiting for Richard to pull away, Danny sprinted for the shade of the alley, keeping low. He didn't stop running until he had his back against the cold brick of a building. He glanced in both directions, then loped off to the west, dodging from shadow to shadow.

It was time to clean up his mess. No matter the cost.

43. An Actual Situation

Considering the thing cost twice a detective's salary, the Range Rover seemed awfully impractical. A gas guzzler, a bitch to park, and, oh yes, incredibly easy to tail.

Sean Nolan had hung back through most of the drive, staying football lengths behind Danny and Richard as they tooled down Lakeshore. The riskiest part had been in Evanston, at the man's house. When Danny had started banging on the door, Nolan felt sure he'd turn around, spot him parked two doors down. But he didn't, just kept pounding until the man let him in. While Danny was inside the house, Nolan had radioed in the address. Dispatch told him it belonged to a Richard O'Donnell. The same name was on the signs at the construction sites. Whatever was going on, Danny's boss was involved.

Nolan didn't have it figured yet, not quite, but he could feel it coming together. Enough time as a detective, you started to tap into something. Like using the Force. A part of you just started to sense something about to go down.

He thought about calling Matthews or Jackson, asking them to saddle up and join him. Detectives rolled solo all the time, but a smart man never walked into an actual situation without someone watching his back.

Thing was, they'd be in Area One, probably Englewood, where the bangers ran. For some reason, the bad guys loved holidays; even around Christmas, there was always a huge spike in crime – domestic violence, armed robbery, suicide. And Halloween brought the crazies out in force. If he called for backup, he'd be pulling cops away from what was sure to be a bad scene.

Not yet. He'd give it a little while, see what shaped up.

Ahead of him, the Range Rover abruptly stopped beside a small park. There'd been no warning, and he swung over hastily, pulling the sedan into the empty parking lot of an ironworks. What were they doing? Some sort of a meet? If so, Danny was losing his touch. The Rover wasn't what you'd call inconspicuous in this neighborhood.

Then, as Nolan squinted at the truck, the passenger door opened and a figure in black jumped out. The man started sprinting the moment his feet hit the ground, cutting across the park and heading for an alley just beyond it. The Rover pulled away from the curb.

Danny had been on the passenger side.

Now Nolan had two targets. He could easily ride Danny down. But it would mean blowing his cover, and ending whatever was going on. The net result would be no different than it had been this afternoon. He needed to lie low until he figured out what was going on. With a soft curse, Nolan put the car in drive and followed the Rover, keeping a hundred yards back. If he had to, he'd ride this tail all the way to hell.

44. Blacker Than Night

Cold air sawed in and out of his lungs as Danny hauled himself up the electrical conduit behind the abandoned Quik-E-Mart. His sneakers clung to the brick, and once he had a good grip on the roof, it was just a matter of getting a knee up. He paused for breath, then crabbed his way to the edge of the building.

Despite the moon, the night was dark, the scattered pools of sodium light doing little to alleviate the gloom. Danny glanced at his watch. Quarter till nine. Call it seven or eight minutes of recon before he had to move. He unfastened the watch and slid it into his pocket, where it couldn't reflect a stray beam of light and give him away. The roof gravel poked into his chest as he lay down to stare across the street.

The Pike Street building rose five stories, each less finished than the last, until the top floor girders poked upward like broken bones. A streetlight on the opposite corner backlit the skeletal structure, marking the concrete shaft that enclosed the fire stairs. October wind made the sheeting on the face snap and pop. On one hand, that was a stroke of luck; it echoed loudly, and would cover his approach. But it also meant he couldn't see inside at all. The only part he could make out was the top floor, which had no plastic to screen it. Danny started there, scanning carefully. His eyes probed shadows, traced girders. Any detail could be the difference between life and death – and not only his own. Mentally, he overlaid the blueprints. The struts, the framing, everything exactly as it should be.

Wait.

There, by the upper entrance to the stairwell. Something caught his eye, a dark shape not geometric enough to belong. Then it moved, and he saw that it was two somethings.

Tommy and Karen.

It made sense. Tie them up out of the way, somewhere they couldn't escape. Steel bands tightened around Danny's chest. He couldn't see Evan on top of the building. He could have been hiding, lying flat, but Danny doubted it. More likely he was on a lower floor. After all, he only expected Richard, and wouldn't be spooked.

The door to the construction trailer was open, and the wind banged it against the siding in a lonely clatter. Could he be inside? It would have been Danny's choice. The trailer offered privacy and an easy escape. But somehow he doubted Evan would use it. Not a bold enough gesture.

Then he saw a flash of light on the third floor, a quick flare of yellow that lasted two or three seconds. A lighter. Evan had fired up a cigarette and given away his position.

Danny could have laughed, except it was bad news. The plan had been to free Tommy and Karen while Richard distracted Evan. But to reach them, Danny would have to sneak up the stairs, right past Evan, who would be keyed up, at the top of his game. Plus there was Debbie to think of. He had no idea where she would fall in this equation, so he had to assume she was the enemy.

Frustration surged through him. Couldn't he catch one goddamn break? Was that so unreasonable? Just a little help? He rolled over, the stones sharp against his spine. The sky above was a wash of starless midnight blue, the moon heavy and ominous. They were screwed.

Unless . . .

He flipped back over to stare at the building. It was a long shot. He was thirty-two, not sixteen. And even at sixteen it would have been a ballsy move.

Still.

Whatever the cost.

Danny wormed his way back to the alley side of the roof, swung his legs over, and dropped to the ground. With his back to the brick, he slid along the wall. From the mouth of the alley, he surveyed the building again, marking the place where Evan had stood – with any luck, he'd be watching the gate to the south, not the street to the east. Danny slid the watch from his pocket. Five till.

What the hell.

Staying low, he walked across the street, forcing himself not to run. Darting motion might catch Evan's eyes, but a black shape stepping slowly between darknesses should be able to sneak past. The cracking of the plastic grew louder, but not loud enough to drown out the rushing blood in his ears. Thirty-nine steps took him to the edge of the fence, the old Hitchcock flick flashing in his mind. Fear sparked random thoughts. He pushed it away, pushed everything away, and eased himself along the fence, eyes on the jagged building with its gray skin. No sign of any motion. Reaching the far fence corner, he straightened, then bent to touch his toes, stretching his leg muscles. Tightening up could be fatal.

As his fingers gripped the chain-link fence, he allowed himself one final memory. A golden afternoon last summer, not a cloud darkening the horizon. Karen laughing and shrieking as he dragged her into the cold water of Lake Michigan.

I'm coming, baby. Whatever the cost.

The chain link bowed inward as his black sneaker bit, hands reaching for the crossbar, the metal cold in the night air, and then he hauled one leg up and over, careful not to kick the fence, and dropped to the dark ground within. He landed soundlessly and jogged toward the northeast edge of the structure, eyes on the rough dirt.

At each corner of the building, thick steel ran from buried concrete foundations all the way up to the top of the building. Up close, the H-shaped girder seemed blacker than night. He ran his hand over it, feeling the rough spots of welds, the bolt marks and torch holes. Crossbeams branched out at every floor, twelve feet between them. Sixty feet up, the metal ended in dim skies.

This can be done. You've seen this done.

Except that the guys he'd seen do it were twenty-year-old ironworkers with muscles like a romance novelist's fantasy. And mostly they did it to get down.

All of a sudden, he was twelve again, playing Pisser. The same palm sweat and stomach stitches, the same mad desire to back out. Like that moment before the first hill on a roller-coaster, when you wonder if you couldn't just jump out and take the maintenance ladder.

Grimacing, he planted his feet on the inside of the H-beam, his heel against the ground and toes to the steel. Then he grabbed the outside of the girder, arched his back to increase the tension, and started to climb.

He made it head high. Then he leaned in too far and lost his balance. His feet flailed wildly, and he slid down the steel, fingers burning. He landed hard, shocks jolting through his knees, and fought the urge to curse.

This is crazy.

The building swayed when he looked up, and his stomach flipped. The top floor seemed an impossible dream.

Whatever the cost.

He took a deep breath, planted his feet, and started again. *Push with the sole of the feet. Grip with the fingers. The posture is key – use your waist as a pivot, and only your waist. Don't let any other part bend, or your feet will slip. The traction is good. The steel is rough as sandpaper. Don't listen to your body's fear. Let your mind drive the flesh. Move your hand.*

Pull.

Now a foot. Push.

Again.

Again.

Again.

The first floor fell away, but he didn't notice. He forced everything else out of his mind, the world narrowing to his hands and feet and the steel. Slide. Pull. Again. In the darkness, he could see patterns in the metal, clown faces and leering spirits. The girder shielded him from a gust of wind that set the tarps snapping in a lunatic dance. Sweat ran slick from his armpit. The muscles of his stomach burned. Slide. Pull. Again.

The second floor.

The third. *Don't look down.*

At the fourth, he looked down. His throat shut, and his heart and stomach tugged in different directions. The world wavered, and for a terrible half second he was overwhelmed by an urge to let go. To jump, and fall spinning to the ground. The true meaning of vertigo – not the fear of falling, but the hunger for it. His muscles trembled. He could picture the ground rushing up, the comfort of oblivion. A warm and quiet place.

He sucked in his lower lip and bit until he tasted blood.

The pain clarified. Reestablished focus. He stared at the beam as though it held all the mysteries of life. Slowly, fingers tingling and arms shaking, he forced his right hand to move. Pushed with both feet. A tiny bit at a time. *There is no up. There is no down. There is no Evan. There is no you. There is only this.*

Again.

Again.

Again. Whatever the cost.

And then his hand bumped into something. A crossbeam.

He'd reached the top floor. He edged his legs up twice more, until his arms were almost horizontal. Guts roiling, he slid his right hand off the girder and onto the beam. The instant the tension released, his legs swung free, kicking out over fifty feet of nothing. He felt a hot flush of panic in his bowels as he dangled by one hand. His shoulder screamed and his sweaty fingers slowly began to slip.

He flung his other arm up, fumbling for the horizontal strut. His right hand began to lose its grip, the ragged steel cutting into his fingers. For a moment he hung there, left hand on the way up while right fought not to come down. Some removed part of himself wondered which would happen first. Then his left banged against the metal, fingers locking on. With a last surge of strength he hauled himself up onto his belly and rolled his legs off the edge. He lay panting on his side, fingers stiff and brittle, arms on fire, chest heaving.

He'd made it.

Then he heard Evan's voice.

45. Shadows in Dim Light

'Stop there.' Evan's voice was commanding.

Danny's limbs shook and burned, but he made himself keep moving. Legs wobbling and head spinning, he forced himself to his feet, scanning for Evan. The top floor lacked a roof, though vertical girders ascended to mark its future location. City light bouncing off the clouds gave the space a soft silver glow. Near the stairwell, he could see the bound figures of Tommy and Karen. Wherever Evan was, his profile should have been clear against the bright sky, but Danny saw nothing.

'Under the light there. Lift your jacket and turn around.' Evan's voice again, still loud. But also muffled. Then it clicked. Evan wasn't shouting at him. He was on the lower floor, yelling instructions. Richard must have arrived while Danny was focusing on the climb.

Moving as quickly as he dared, Danny stepped to the edge of the building and looked down. A tingle shivered his calves as he peered cautiously over the edge. The Range Rover sat inside the gate, exhaust steaming white from the tailpipe. Ten feet from it, Richard stood illuminated by a streetlight, one hand holding the duffel bag, the other pulling up his jacket as he spun around.

Danny cursed silently. The climb had taken longer than he'd thought. He'd hoped to rest for a few minutes and let his muscles recover, but now he had to move. He jogged to where Tommy and Karen knelt, their arms stretched up and tied over the stairwell railing. They struggled as he approached.

'Shhhh.' He put one finger to his lips, the other hand digging for the mini-Swiss Army knife on his key ring. He pulled the duct tape off Karen's mouth and cut the bindings on her hands. She threw her arms around him, body shaking, tears running down her face.

It was the best he'd felt in he couldn't remember how long. But there wasn't time. He extricated himself, locking eyes and smiling at her. Then he turned to the boy.

'Tommy, I'm with your father. We're going to get you out of here. But you have to be quiet. Understand?'

The boy's eyes were huge in the moonlight. He nodded quickly, and Danny cut his bindings.

Below them, the yell sounded again. 'Good boy, Dick.' Evan amused, firmly in control. 'Come on up.'

When the building was finished, there would be escape stairs at each end, but right now, only the central set beside the empty elevator shaft was in place. No telling for sure where Evan was. But Danny had seen his lighter flare on the third floor, near the stairs. Was there a different way he could get the others down? He glanced around frantically. Karen spent three mornings a week at the gym, and might be able to return the way he'd come up; heading down would be easier, just a matter of controlling the slide. But Tommy? *A rope, or a cable, some way of lowering him* . . . But the site had been cleared for winter, and he knew there was nothing to find.

'Okay,' he whispered, 'here's the plan. We're going down these stairs. Be as quiet as you can. I'll go a little bit ahead. Karen, you take Tommy all the way down.' He tried to put in his eyes all the things he couldn't say in front of the boy. 'Get in Richard's truck and get out of here.'

'What are you going to do?'

'I have to get off on the third floor.'

'Why?'

He kept his gaze steady. 'To help Richard.'

She shook her head, alarm in her eyes. 'That's crazy.'

'It's the only way. It'll be two on one, and Evan doesn't know I'm coming.'

'No.'

'Karen.' He smiled at her, made a tiny motion toward Tommy with his eyes. She had to understand. 'Please.'

Her lips trembled, and she looked away. Slowly, she nodded. He leaned in and kissed her. Her lips were cold but her tongue was warm and sweet. *One for the road.*

And in that moment, he realized that he didn't expect to get out of this.

Did it matter?

Breaking the kiss, he put a hand to her cheek, cupping her face. A bedroom tenderness they'd shared a thousand times.

Did it matter? Not as much as getting them free. As cleaning up his mess. If his life was the cost, so be it.

'I've got to go.' He stood. 'Count to thirty and then follow me.'

Danny stepped into the stairwell. He wanted to look back but didn't dare. The cinder-block walls cast the shaft into inky darkness broken by patchy light from the open doorway of each floor. The concrete stairs had no railing, and he hugged the wall, moving carefully, feeling out each step with his feet. His breath seemed loud. Two flights separated each story, and he'd reached the doorway to the fourth floor when he heard the faint scraping of Karen and Tommy above. He took another flight and paused on the intermediate landing, listening, the angle not letting him see much of the third floor.

'I brought the money.' Richard's voice, not too far. To the left? The echo made it impossible to say.

'Show me.' Evan sounded calm. Good news. If he suspected Richard wasn't alone, Evan would be keyed up and at his most dangerous; hopefully, facing a man he didn't consider a threat, he'd lower his guard. Danny eased down the steps, mouth open to improve his hearing. He slid along the wall until he stood beside the open stairwell doorway, his back to the cinder block. From outside, he heard a zipper pulled. Richard opening the bag. Gambling that Evan's attention would be on the money, he leaned in just enough to see.

Twenty feet away, Richard stood facing him, holding the bag open. Evan had his back turned, the gun in his hand. The two were outlined against the glowing plastic. Half-walls and piles of building materials lived as shadows in dim light.

It was as good an opportunity as he could hope for.

Praying that Richard wouldn't give him away with a glance, Danny flowed around the corner. His soft-soled shoes moved soundlessly across the floor. The ruffling tarps underscored his motions in a macabre symphony. He couldn't be more than twenty feet from Evan. So close to ending this.

Then he saw Debbie.

She stood a dozen feet away, her back to a girder, a nervous cigarette dancing in her hand. Her hair was messy, and in the faint light, the dark circles on her cheekbones made her look like a corpse. The prom queen from a zombie movie.

Her eyes were fixed on him.

Her mouth came open, and he tensed. If she made a sound, it was over. There was no way he could make it to Evan. A cough from her would mean death.

'Go ahead, check the bills. It's all there,' Richard said.

Danny stared at her, trying to put everything into his eyes. All of the wrong choices that had led them both here. Begging her, across twenty feet of darkened nightmare, not to make a final mistake. Not to kid herself that this wasn't the real thing.

She looked back at him, then over at Evan. It could only have been a second or two their eyes had been locked, but it felt like a lifetime. Like a staring contest as a little kid. A beam angels could have walked across.

Finally, Debbie moved. She raised the cigarette to her lips. Took a drag that made her features glow orange.

And very deliberately turned to stare out the plastic sheeting.

Danny let himself breathe. To anyone else, just turning away would hardly seem heroic. But he knew something about wrong choices, and how hard it could be to make the right. He could've kissed her.

He looked back at Evan and Richard. His old partner had pulled out a wad of bills and was holding them up in the gray light. No more than fifteen feet away.

Danny began to move again, gentle as a spring breeze. But not directly to Evan. Four steps out of his way took him to a waist-high pile of neatly stacked lumber. Most of the two-by-fours were twelve feet, construction length, but a few scraps rested on top. His hand closed on a piece about the length of a baseball bat. Not daring to take his eyes off Evan, he lifted it slowly, the wood dry and cool against his sweating palm. A splinter popped, and Danny tensed to dive, but Evan didn't react.

Danny raised the two-by-four and took another careful step. A few more. Just a few more and he'd be in striking distance.

Evan held the money under his nose and breathed it in. 'Ahh, Dick. I could kiss you.'

'Where's my son?' Richard spoke with surprising force.

'Yeah.' Evan popped his head to either side. 'About that. Change of plans.'

Fear sang in Danny's blood. He took a hurried step, then another. So close.

Then Evan raised his right arm, the same balletic grace and speed as before, the snub-nose pointing straight at Richard's head.

'Dad!' A ragged cry of fear sounded behind them all.

Still six or eight feet away, Danny flung himself forward, the board humming through the air. Evan whirled, the gun tracking with him, his eyes white and wide and suddenly close. He planted one foot and brought his left arm up in a reflexive block. The off-balance lunge had cost Danny power, and Evan's leather jacket absorbed most of the hit. He stepped forward, tucking a shoulder, and suddenly Danny found himself flipping over Evan's back, his own velocity used against him. He had an upside-down fun-house view of Tommy sprinting from the stairwell, Karen an arm's length behind, her mouth open, and then his spine hit the floor and the breath burst from him in a gasping rush. Lightning flashed behind his eyes. The board clattered from his grip.

'Danny Carter.' Evan put his boot on Danny's throat, the pistol up to cover the others. 'I was kind of hoping I'd see you again, partner.'

46. Marker

'Get in here, kitten.' Evan swiveled the gun to Karen. She hesitated, her face a mask of hatred and fear, and then she walked over to stand beside Richard and Tommy.

From the ground, Danny saw Evan smile, and felt a quick push to his throat. His head burst in a kaleidoscope of colors, and then the boot was gone. He heard Evan retreating. Danny rolled on his side, coughing. Through tear-bleary eyes, he could see Karen take a half step toward him, and he quickly shook his head at her. She froze.

'Deborah, that was a really excellent job of keeping watch.' Evan glared over his shoulder at her. 'You doze off, or were you just hoping he'd take you away from all this?'

'I was looking outside.' Her voice sounded stronger than Danny expected, like she'd been preparing herself. 'Watching for cars.'

Evan grunted. 'Come on, Danny. Get up.' His old partner had moved back a dozen feet to stand next to Debbie, at the entrance of a half-built room. The gun held the four of them in a narrow killing arc.

Danny struggled to his feet, every part of his body screaming. His eyes darted for some advantage, a play that could save them. The third floor was half constructed, the exterior walls not enclosed, but open stud walls divided the interior. A few sections, like the one Evan and Debbie stood near, had even been Sheetrocked. To the left, toward the exterior, were four-foot bundles of bricks meant for the 'exposed' walls of future apartments. Behind them and to the right was all open space.

'Do me a favor, would you, buddy?' Evan gestured to the duffel bag with the barrel of the gun. 'Bring that bad boy over here.'

There was no reason for Evan to keep them alive once he had the money. But it wasn't like he couldn't just shoot them and pick it up himself. Better to spin it out a little longer, give the guy time to gloat, while Danny stayed ready. He took a slow step toward the bag, playing up a limp. Let Evan think he could barely stand.

His senses hummed with hyper-real perception. He could make out the leathery texture of his shoes, could smell the piney sawdust of the lumber, and above it, the sweet drugstore perfume Debbie wore. The weight of the duffel bag pulled him to one side as he walked toward Evan, hoping for a tiny lapse of attention. At this point, any chance was worth taking.

'Slowly now.' Evan kept the black eye of the pistol fixed on Danny as he moved, the barrel unwavering. Debbie stood beside him, her lower lip caught in her teeth. 'Set it down.'

He did, wondering if he could make the few feet between them, knowing he couldn't.

'Good boy.' Evan gestured toward the others, and Danny backpedaled slowly to join them. A building under construction would normally offer any variety of makeshift weapons, hammers and saws and nail guns, but here everything had been neatly tucked away for the winter. The bricks were bound with steel bands. The two-by-four he'd dropped lay at Evan's feet. He stepped beside Karen, laying one hand in the small of her back. He wanted to take her in his arms, but knew that if a chance came he couldn't risk being tangled up.

Evan stepped forward, bent down, and hoisted the thirty-pound bag like it was tissue. The gun never moved.

'Right.' He smiled, only half his face visible in the gloom. 'I know this is the part where I'm supposed to say something cold, but words were always more your side of the action, Danny. So let's just leave it at good-bye, huh?'

His thumb rocked up to cock the pistol.

Danny could feel the ragged working of his lungs, the twinges of pain in his chest. Stared at the gun. Wondered if this was it, the end of everything he cared about. Failure in a flash of light. He watched Evan's finger move on the trigger, gentle and firm, his hand strong.

And then he saw another hand.

Debbie threw herself at Evan, scrabbling at his right arm, shoving it upward, the two of them locked like statues in the liquid play of shadows, a frozen image burned in Danny's brain, and then orange fire spat at the ceiling and the world accelerated, too many things happening at once.

Danny used the hand on Karen's waist to shove her into Richard and Tommy, their arms and legs tangling in a clumsy fall behind the bundle of bricks.

Evan's left hand shot up to Debbie's throat.

And from the stairwell, someone yelled, 'Freeze!'

Whirling, Danny saw Sean Nolan charging out of the darkness of the stairway, his gun up and leveled at Evan.

For the first time in his life, Danny could have wept for joy at the sight of a cop. Then he turned back to Evan and saw him already moving. His pistol swinging over with that gunfighter speed as he flung Debbie toward the detective and sprang back. Debbie flying forward, her legs scrambling to keep up, her body between Evan and Nolan.

Two gun blasts split the world. And in the burned-out light of the muzzle flashes, Debbie's chest exploded.

Her arms spread like an angel beseeching grace.

Her lips framed a moan.

And then she fell.

Danny wasn't sure if he yelled or not. He stood in place, watching as her body hit the ground. As the blood began to darken the floor. Remembering another body on another floor. Another shooting he hadn't been able to prevent. Another victim he hadn't been able to protect.

So many years, and yet here he was again.

And then, from a position behind the lumber pile, Nolan was firing. The blasts broke Danny's reverie. He whirled to see Evan lunge into the next room, bag in one hand and pistol in the other. Chunks of Sheetrock blew out where the cop's bullets followed him. Danny took a last look at Debbie, wanting to run to her, knowing it was too late, that it would be a pointless gesture. Maybe a suicidal one, with Evan somewhere in the darkness.

Gritting his teeth, he forced his eyes away from her body.

The others crouched behind the bricks. Karen was frantically gesturing him over. Nolan had settled behind the lumber pile in a target shooter's stance, his attention entirely on the room where Evan had disappeared.

Behind and to the near side of the detective, the stairwell was clear.

There might not be a better moment. Danny darted over to the bricks. Richard gripped Tommy in a bear hug, the boy's arms wrapped around his waist. Karen crouched beside them, her pupils wide.

'Can you run?'

She nodded. He grabbed Richard's shoulder.

'The stairwell. Let's go.' Without waiting for a reply, he leapt to his feet, sprinting forward. If Evan fired, he wanted to be the target. His feet slapped the ground. A gun blast exploded from somewhere, shatteringly loud. Behind him, he could hear the fumbling sounds of the others. Nolan glanced at him and cursed, started to swing the gun over and thought better of it, turning back to cover them. He fired twice, the flashes painting his face in garish colors, and then Danny reached the open stairwell door and stopped to help the others through. Karen came first, light on her feet, dragging Tommy behind her. Richard took up the rear, vanishing into the darkness. As Danny spun to follow, another blast roared. A patch of cinder block exploded right where he'd been standing, chips and dust showering down, and then he was in the shaft, the others already running down the stairs. Karen turned to see that he had made it, and he gestured her on. 'Go!'

The four of them hurtled down the dark steps, Karen and Tommy a flight ahead, holding hands. More gunfire exploded above. He and Richard ran together, taking stairs four at a time.

As they stepped on the landing just above the first floor, he heard three shots in rapid succession, followed by Nolan's scream.

Danny froze. Richard stopped beside him, his look quizzical and eager. Only silence from above. His heart pumped panic, his lungs sucked fear.

Ahead of them, the stairs were clear. No way Evan could catch them. The Rover was unlocked and running. They could be out the door and safe in seconds.

Upstairs, Nolan was alone. Wounded. And facing the monster Danny had helped create.

'Come on.' Richard shook with impatience.

When Debbie had fallen, Danny had felt for a second like he was back in the pawnshop. Evan gone kill-crazy and a body on the floor. The last time he'd chosen to walk out. Now here he was again, faced with the same options.

Who said fate lacked a sense of poetry?

Danny grimaced. No more wrong choices. 'Get them out of here.'

For an instant they locked eyes in the twilight gloom, two

men pushed to the naked edge of reason. Something passed between them. Something like understanding. Then Richard nodded, turned, and dashed down the steps. The last Danny saw of him was his bright Nikes as he raced out of the stairwell.

Danny stood alone in the darkness, his body jittery with adrenaline. On the roof, he'd realized that he didn't expect to make it out alive. He'd sworn a silent promise that if saving the others meant sacrificing himself, it was a deal he could accept.

Time to settle that marker. For Patrick. For Debbie.

For himself.

He took a breath and started back up the stairs.

47. A Line of Blood

A strange calm had descended. His heart still pounded, but now he felt a mastery over it, a lightness. He moved upward as silently as speed would allow, taking the steps in long strides, his eyes fixed on the open doorway. Sean had been hit, that much he knew. But how badly?

Reaching the landing, he pressed his back against the wall. He wanted to wait, to figure out exactly where they were, but knew that could be fatal for Nolan.

Breathing softly, he peered around the edge of the door.

The detective wasn't by the woodpile, and it took a moment to spot him. When Danny did, he found himself torn between standing rigid in fear and running out like a fool.

Nolan knelt at the building's edge, some fifty feet away. Blood stained the upper part of his torso black. Evan stood in front of him, pistol pressed against Sean's forehead. The duffel bag lay on the floor a half dozen paces away.

Without pausing to consider, Danny stepped out, keeping low but moving fast, sure at any moment he would see a plume of orange, watch Nolan's lifeless body fly backward.

Fifteen feet took him to the lumber. Good cover, but not much else. The once neat stack had toppled and spilled sideways. The shorter pieces were hopelessly entangled with the larger, and there was no way to extract one without making noise. Danny still had the knife on his key chain, but it was a laughable match for Evan's pistol. Which tool would he use, the can opener or the folding scissors?

Besides, sneaking that close to Evan seemed impossible. The space was too open.

On the building's edge Sean knelt with his head bowed, apparently paying no attention to whatever Evan was asking. The stain on his chest continued to grow, and a small pool of blood had formed under his knees. Staring helplessly, Danny noticed a trail of black running from the pool. Evan must have dragged the detective to the lip. Enjoying the theater. Unconsciously, Danny's eyes followed the trail. There was a silver shape lying where it began, some twenty feet away.

A gun. Nolan must have dropped it when he got hit.

Danny snuck another look at Evan. He still couldn't make out any words, but something told him the shot was coming soon.

Retrieving the gun meant leaving cover, crossing into an open area. If Evan heard him, it was over for both of them.

Moving lightly, he crept out from behind the lumber. His heart sounded in his ears, *thum-thUMP, thum-thUMP*. He kept his weight on the balls of his feet as he walked the long tightrope across the room. His body tingled all over, the soreness of his muscles forgotten. The night air felt cool but very distant. Ten more steps. He tried to bring to mind everything he knew about guns. Beyond undoing the safety, it wasn't much. He lifted a foot, leaned in, set it down gently. Every move precise. Careful. Not once giving in to the voice that yelled inside him. The whole weight of his life, and of Nolan's, depended on doing this perfectly. Five more steps. Evan's voice drifted through the air. The words sounded slow motion, dragged out like a tape loop. Weird, alien murmurs. He wondered if the others were away, if they'd made it to safety. He could feel each nerve in his feet, each current of air on his skin.

And then he was bending to scoop up the gun. It felt

heavy in his hand, heavier than he'd expected. Hot and vaguely oily. He fought a mad urge to come up blasting away like in some seventies cop show. He had to get closer.

He walked on tiptoe, his arm rigid ahead of him. Locked on Evan like a compass pointing north. Each terrible step brought him nearer. He became aware of his breathing, how shallowly he was drawing air into his lungs. The weight of the gun kept his muscle tensed. How much time had passed? Probably only seconds. Felt longer. Felt like eternities had flowed beneath his feet. He thought of Debbie, eternally reaching for grace. The veins in his throat throbbed. He could taste sweat on his upper lip. Every careful step brought him closer. He wanted to cock the gun, but was afraid the noise would give him away. He thought it would fire anyway. Wasn't cocking just to make it faster, smoother? He thought of Patrick, his laughter silenced with a bullet, body dumped in the river like trash. Danny ached from the beatings of the last days. The agonizing pace made him feel every movement. On the edge of the drop, Nolan said something, his voice dismissive. Evan laughed, a deep, cold laugh. The sound of a man who knew he'd won. Then he popped his head to either side and leaned forward, the pistol touching Nolan's forehead.

A dozen feet away, Danny stared down the length of his arm, his childhood friend square in the sights. He closed one eye and pointed the pistol at Evan's chest, dead center of his beating heart. Concentrated so hard that everything lost focus. So that Karen and Tommy and Debbie and Patrick all disappeared. So that Evan became only a pattern of colors. Then he squeezed the trigger.

The click echoed loud in the open space.

Evan whirled, instinct driving him back from the detective, bringing his arm over, aiming without hesitation. Danny stood frozen, impotent in the face of death, and waited for the impact. Some part of him wondered if you heard the shot before you felt it.

Then Evan laughed. 'All those times you told me not to play with guns, you should have been learning how they worked.'

On TV, the cops slid the top part of the gun back before firing. He tried it. But when he pulled the trigger again, another click rang out.

'It's empty.' Evan smiled, his pistol never leaving Danny's chest. 'Dirty Harry over here didn't see me sneak around. All I had to do was wait till I heard him pop the clip to reload.'

Danny let his arm drop, the gun falling loose to clatter on the ground beside the duffel bag. He was too far from Evan to charge, and there was no cover for forty feet in any direction.

He was out of moves.

'Funny.' Evan smiled. 'We got ourselves a reunion tonight. All the boys from the neighborhood.'

'Except Patrick.' His voice came out weary, too tired for rage.

'Can't make an omelet, you know?' Evan shrugged. 'But it's still quite a picture. We got the whole range. The criminal. The cop. And whatever it is you are, Danny.'

'I'm . . .' He paused like he was hesitating, then took a step forward. 'I'm just a regular guy.' If he could get close enough, he might be able to make a lunge.

Evan smiled again. 'You're starting to piss me off. Stop trying to win. Don't you get it? You scored last time. Now it's my turn.'

Danny froze, his arms out. 'Easy.'

'Easy my ass.' With his left hand, Evan dug in an inner pocket, came out with cigarettes. Shook the pack until one popped up, took it in his lips, lit it with his silver Zippo. His gun hand never wavered. 'You know what? Since we're here, let's settle something. Which are you, Danny-boy?'

'Which am I?'

'I know you like to believe you're an innocent civilian, but it's getting a little thin, don't you think? Fighting, breaking-and-entering, jacking a car, kidnapping, plus you just tried to shoot a man in the back. That's a hell of a week. Tell the truth.' He blew a puff of smoke. 'Felt good, didn't it?'

No point in lying. 'Yes.'

Evan smiled, took a step back, and turned to Nolan. 'You hear that, Sean? Got your cuffs handy?'

Nolan's voice was calm, almost clipped. 'Shut it, convict.'

Evan's smile twisted into a snarl. His fist lashed out, pistol-whipping the detective across the face. Nolan's head snapped sideways, but he didn't make a sound. A line of blood cut across his cheek.

'A little *respect,* motherfucker.'

Danny's mind felt sluggish, tired. An overdose of adrenaline had turned his limbs to concrete. He considered his options, dealing them out in front of him. Not a winning hand in the bunch.

'Hey,' Evan said, his voice suddenly light as he turned back to Danny. 'Wanted to ask you. How'd you get up to the roof, man?'

'I climbed.'

'No shit?'

'No shit.'

'Now that sounds like fun. I bet you felt more alive than you had the last ten years.'

Danny shrugged, looked down. An idea occurred to him. A slim chance, but the only one he saw.

'Come on, admit it, man. It's just like the game. You remember? Pisser?' Evan smiled, an old comradely grin.

'I remember.'

'You miss it, don't you?'

'Sometimes.' Danny spoke slowly, cocking his left hip out. Putting all the weight on it. *Last call.* 'Sometimes I do. But you know what, Evan? Mostly, I'm tired of it. I don't want to play anymore.'

Evan stared at him like he was reading something in his soul, the smile slowly fading. He was silent for a moment. When he spoke, his voice came out soft. 'Don't you get it? The game never ends.'

And despite everything, for an instant, Danny saw through the man in front of him, the hardened killer, the engineer of his undoing. In his place stood a twelve-year-old boy with freckles and curly hair and a taunting smile that seemed to float in the air. Floated above the thousand humiliations of poverty, above the bruises from his father, above the whole stinking unbalanced system that would lead him here. A smile that floated because it had to.

And then Evan shook his head. 'Ah well. Time to go.' He raised the pistol to point at Danny's head. 'It'll be quick, amigo. For old times' sake.'

The slapping of his heart seemed to bend the ribs of his chest. Danny's mouth went dry, his tongue a slab of meat. The round eye of the gun stared at him, eager to offer that fatal wink.

'Wait.' He stared past the pistol, to Evan. His fingers tingled. 'One last favor?'

Evan cocked his head. 'Your credit isn't much good here, Danny-boy.'

'For old times' sake.'

'What?'

'Do him first.' Danny gestured at Nolan with his head, careful to keep his hands out.

Evan narrowed his eyes. 'Why?'

Danny stared back, blinked. 'Because ... it's like the game. It'll be easier once I see it done.'

Evan looked at him for a long moment. His eyes grew colder, and darker. 'Never would have believed it.' His voice dripped contempt. 'You're a coward.'

Danny looked away, looked back.

Evan stared at him, then slowly shrugged. 'All right. For old times' sake.' He took two steps toward the snapping plastic, and turned to Nolan. 'Good night, Sean.' He raised the gun like a piece of clockwork, bringing it to Nolan's forehead.

Danny jerked downward, his right hand finding the strap of the duffel bag and hoisting it up. Keeping his momentum going, he hurled himself forward, his left leg planted as a pivot, arm flinging out and up from the weight, putting every last cell of screaming muscle into it.

The thirty-pound duffel bag took Evan dead in the chest. He staggered backward, arms flailing, fire blasting from the gun. His back hit the sheeting, and for one terrible moment it held.

Then his weight ripped it from the ceiling and Evan McGann fell out into the city night.

The silence that followed was broken only by the wind-whipped crack of the loose tarp and the sound of Danny's beating heart. His legs went rubbery, and he dropped to his knees. After all of the pain and exhaustion, he wanted more than anything to collapse and sleep.

More than almost anything.

With trembling arms, he crawled over to the open ledge and looked down.

Evan lay splayed across a stack of metal girders three stories below. The top and bottom half of him seemed somehow wrong, like an action figure twisted too far. One arm curled around the duffel bag. The seam had split on impact, and a handful of bills spilled out to swirl in the October wind, the money blowing like dreams, tangling in the dirty weeds and sullen mud. Beside him, he heard Nolan speaking into his radio, calling for backup. Sirens sounded immediately, beat cars only blocks away.

Danny rocked back to his knees, shut his eyes, and let the darkness come.

48. The Final Tally

'You don't have to do this.' Karen's voice was flat.

Danny looked over at her, rigid behind the steering wheel. Her face was strained, but at least it wasn't slack. Sometimes he'd find her staring out the window or standing in the kitchen folding and refolding a dish towel, her eyes a thousand miles away. Gone so deep that even speaking wouldn't break the trance. Those times he would slide an arm around her waist to remind her she was safe, and watch her come back slowly, blinking like she was swimming up from the bottom of some enormous sea.

Her wounds would heal in time, he knew. But he also knew they'd leave scars. Wounds always did.

'I do have to. I . . .' Danny almost said 'owe it to him,' caught himself. 'I need to finish it. What's that word you like,' he asked, 'the Men-Are-from-Wherever word?'

She smiled. 'Closure.'

'Closure. That's what I need.'

She didn't nod, but she didn't disagree, either. Just flipped on the blinker and eased into the turn lane. Threadbare snowflakes drifted halfheartedly past the windshield. A voice on the radio said they should expect a couple of inches. Warned them Valentine's Day was only a week away, and told them nothing said love like Russell Stover chocolates. He snapped it off.

Was he doing this for closure? Seemed like part of the equation, certainly. The opportunity to put everything to bed, to face the last of the consequences. Clear the slate and focus on the future. But it felt like there was more to it.

He stared out the window and wondered what he would say. The tangled web of brotherhood and betrayal was too complicated to be undone, or even encapsulated, by mere words. Words weren't big enough.

The Blue Line El rattled past, filled with everyday people, and he wondered if their histories seemed as complicated to them; wondered how many saw their past as a confluence of uncontrollable events shaping their present. Did any of them?

Did they all?

He reached over and put a hand on Karen's belly, feeling the warmth and life beneath her thin sweater. She put a hand over his, smiling with the newfound bloom, the one she'd had since Christmas, when three separate tests turned blue.

The new Cook County Hospital squatted a mile west of the Loop. Though possessed of all the poetry of an office park, it had shouldered its predecessor's 150-year legacy of offering medical care to even the poorest of patients. Karen waited for traffic to ease, and then turned into the driveway, the Explorer's tires humming softly on the blacktop. She parked just short of the covered walkway and turned to face him. In the way she brushed a lock of hair behind her ear he recognized a prepared speech.

'I can't come with you.' The words tumbled out. 'I'm sorry, but I can't.'

He shook his head. 'I know. I'll handle this part alone.'

She glanced out the window, and then back again. Danny wanted to scoop her up and carry her back to their apartment, to wrap her in quilts and love and tell her she would never have to face another monster. Instead he kissed her, breathed her in, reveling in her. Every time they touched he felt blessed. Different, better, than before. No more living on borrowed time.

He stepped out, pulling his jacket around him. A family walked into the hospital, the automatic entrance swishing open. To the east, he could see the skyline against gray clouds. He reached for the car door, started to slam it.

'Danny!'

He turned. 'What?'

'Promise me . . .' She hesitated, like she wasn't sure what to say. 'Promise you'll come back to me.'

He stared at her, feeling like his heart might soar out of his chest. 'I'll do you one better. I'll never leave again.' He reached across the empty seat, and she seized his hand.

'You better not.' Her eyes had the old playful sparkle in them. 'Or I'll find a hunky Lamaze teacher to run away with.'

He laughed, and leaned in to kiss her again, and again.

He got directions at the information desk. The comfortable lobby quickly gave way to antiseptic corridors. Fluorescents shone bright and hollow off linoleum floors. He took the elevator up. A uniformed cop lounged in a chair outside the door.

'I'm Danny Carter. Detective Nolan cleared me to visit today.'

The cop matched his driver's license to a list on a clipboard, and asked him to sign in. 'You want me to come in with you?'

Danny shook his head. 'Thanks.'

'Suit yourself.' The cop gestured to the door, then flopped back into his chair.

The room looked like any of a million other hospital rooms, clean, sterile, and cold. A whiff of ammonia lingered in the air. The television was tuned to a Hispanic network, soccer players racing up and down some warm field. A wheelchair sat in one corner.

Evan looked up from the bed as he walked in. His stare grew hard. 'What the fuck do you want?'

'I'm not sure.' Danny closed the door behind him.

In the months since Halloween, Evan had aged ten years. His bulk looked out of place in the adjustable bed, but forced rest had cost him that coiled edge of fitness. Several days of stubble darkened his chin.

'Sure you are. You want to gloat.' Evan flipped off the TV, planted his hands on either side, and dragged himself to a sitting position. He pulled the sheet aside and pointed at his useless legs. 'Take a look. This what you came to see?'

Danny shook his head, spun a chair around, and sat down beside Evan. 'Nope.'

'What, you want to play cards?' His voice rang with bitterness. 'You candy-striping now?'

'Maybe I thought I owed something to you.' Danny kept his eyes level on Evan's, forcing himself not to reveal the storm of emotions within him. Half of him saw a broken monster, a predator ironically rendered prey. The other half saw a tough little bastard of a kid with a floating smile.

Evan snorted, looked at his hands. 'That don't even begin to touch on what you owe me.'

'That's where you're wrong.'

'I saved your life in the pawnshop. I did seven years for you.'

Danny shook his head. 'Maybe you saved my life. I don't think so. But the years, those are all on you. And so is Patrick. And Debbie.'

'Oh, fuck that,' Evan said. 'They were in the life. They knew the risks.'

'J. A. Pinianski wasn't.'

'Who?'

'The man you killed outside the diner. He was a civilian.'

Danny leaned forward. 'Never so much as a shoplifting arrest.'

Evan shrugged. 'You want me to get all teary? Besides,' his voice fell and he glared at Danny, 'the high school kid they assigned me as a lawyer, he says they found the body. Problem is, only Debbie and I knew where I stowed fat boy. So she told you about our ride out to O'Hare, and you Judased me. Right?'

The night rose before Danny with Kodak clarity. The cold wind whipping the sheeting. The throbbing of every limb, and the deeper ache within him. He'd felt a hand on his shoulder, opened his eyes to see Nolan. The detective dropped glinting handcuffs in his lap. Danny had looked up at him, and Sean had nodded, just barely, and Danny had fixed the cuffs on his own wrists.

The next days had been a blur of holding cells and interview rooms. An assistant state's attorney, a small man in a trim brown suit, pacing back and forth. Detectives questioning him again and again. Richard's lawyer talking to cops in the hallway, all of them casting furtive looks his way.

Danny kept it simple. Told the cops he could help close another case. Their eyes had lit up when he mentioned it was the murder of a civilian outside a diner on Ashland. He told them he knew where the body was, along with the physical evidence that made it open and shut. On every other subject he kept his mouth shut and let the cops and the bureaucrats fight it out.

He'd given himself five-to-two that he'd end up doing time, maybe serious time. But he didn't count on the wild cards.

The first was Sean Nolan. Danny still didn't know exactly what story Sean had told. Whether he'd acknowledged Danny had saved his life, or admitted that Danny had come to him earlier for help. All he knew was what Detective Matthews told him: From a hospital bed, Sean had fought for him. Hard.

The second was Richard O'Donnell. He'd refused to testify against Danny. Refused to identify him as having been part of the kidnapping. Sent his lawyer down to make sure the message was clear.

He'd also fired Danny cold, but that didn't worry him much.

In the end, the assistant state's attorney was left with a choice. Prosecute Danny on a weak case and maybe lose. Add to that an unclosed murder file on Pinianski. Two black marks that wouldn't look good on his record, or do much to help his boss's reelection bid.

Or they could make a deal.

By the end of the week, Danny was a free man. Detective Matthews told him he was the luckiest bastard on earth, and then drove him home.

'I told them what happened,' Danny said. 'But you Judased yourself.'

Evan glowered. 'Yeah, I figured you would. The smart play, right?'

'Just the truth.'

'So Danny Carter wins again.' He shook his head. 'That what you came to say?'

'No.' Danny stood up and walked to the window. In the snow, the parking deck was just a hazy shape, like a dream of ghosts, or a memory of his past. 'I guess I came to say I'm sorry.' He sighed.

'I'm sorry for the way things worked out for you. For us. I think back to those days, the way we ran crazy, like nothing had consequences, and I wish I could turn back the clock.' For the rest of his life, he'd carry a load, a guilt that wouldn't fade. You didn't have to do terrible things to have guilt. Not preventing terrible things from happening would work, too. And sometimes, guilt and pain were just waiting for you, the obvious destination at the end of a road you never meant to choose, but hadn't fought hard enough to leave.

A psychiatrist would tell him it wasn't his fault, and he'd be right. But he'd be wrong, too.

'You got a funny way of showing that,' Evan said, 'sending me back to prison.'

Danny shook his head. 'You don't get it, man. I'm sorry for not changing things before it was too late. I feel sorry for the boy from the neighborhood, the kid who used to be my best friend. But the man you became?' He turned to face Evan in the bed. 'Prison is where you belong.'

Evan stared at him, his glare heavy with the weight of years. When he spoke, his voice was flat. 'Get the fuck out.'

That old tension filled the air. Once, it would have put Danny on his guard, had him looking for exits. Now, it only made him sad. He nodded. Picked up the chair and moved it back to the wall. Took one last look at his old friend and recent enemy, then walked away.

'You should have killed me.' There was no threat in Evan's voice, only a muted sound that might have been pain. 'I wish you had.'

Danny paused, his hand on the doorknob. 'I know.' He opened his mouth, closed it. 'So do I.' Then he stepped out of the room.

Nolan was waiting in the lobby. A gray canvas sling held his right arm in place. His vest had stopped two of the bullets, but the third had shattered his collarbone. 'Figured I'd catch you here. You get what you wanted?'

'I'm not even sure what that was.'

Nolan looked at him, nodded. 'Just good-bye, maybe.'

'Maybe.' He shrugged. 'How's the arm?'

'Sore as shit. Keeps me awake. Catholic or not, I don't heal soon, Mary-Louise is going to divorce me for a good night's sleep.'

Danny laughed, feeling warm toward the guy, but also nervous. A silence fell, neither sure what to say. They had the shared awkwardness of men who had loaned each other money but lost track of the final tally. Was there a debt? Who owed?

Some accounts were too complicated for mathematics. Danny spoke first. 'Thanks.' He let the word hang a moment, his eyes on Sean's, then gestured toward the elevators. 'For putting me on the list, I mean.'

'Sure.'

Another moment passed, Danny tracking the progress of an old couple, had to be in their eighties, the woman smiling coquettishly as she leaned on the man in a slow shuffle step. Something about it moved him. 'Listen, I should get going.' He zipped his jacket. 'Hope the arm feels better.'

Nolan nodded, stepped aside.

Through the front glass of the hospital he could see the Explorer parked, a splash of color in a swirl of white. Squinting against the brightness, he moved toward the door.

'Danny.'

Nolan stood in cop pose, his chest cocked and expression stern. If his hand wasn't in a sling, Danny had the distinct impression it would be on his gun. Then the detective smiled. 'Be good.'

Danny snorted. Raised two fingers and tossed a salute. Then he turned and walked out.

After the stifling hospital corridors, cold air was sweet relief. He hiked to the car, opened the door to find Karen singing along with an eighties song on the radio. She grinned at him. 'You get your closure?'

'Almost. Just one more thing to do.'

Against the dark granite, the collected snow seemed bright as a dream of the world. Danny paused in front of it, his breath tight in his chest, and Karen squeezed his hand.

'I'm okay,' he said.

She gave him a smile laced with sadness, then stepped forward to brush off the headstone.

A simple cross. Gray. Danny had never had to pick a headstone before. As he'd browsed the catalog, the undertaker nodding solemnly beside him, he'd found himself baffled. How did you sum up a life? What words tied all the ragged strands in a knot?

In the end, he'd gone with just 'Patrick Connelly' and 'Friend.'

Karen finished dusting the marker and stepped back, her boots crunching the frozen grass. She took off one glove and wormed a warm hand into his, and together they stood, looking at the cross and counting the costs. The snow muffled the world.

Finally, he reached in his jacket pocket and took out the necklace. Most of the stuff in Patrick's place they'd given to charity, the rest consigned to the trash bin. He'd kept a handful of photographs, his friend's old motorcycle jacket, and this. A black cord bearing a small silver charm of a hunched man with a staff, a glowing baby on his back. The words PROTECT US lettered on the bottom.

'What is it?' Karen leaned closer.

'A Saint Christopher's medallion,' he said. He stepped forward and draped it over the cross. The metal clinked quietly against the stone. 'Patron saint of travelers.'

She smiled wanly. 'He'd like that.'

He nodded.

A few moments passed, and then she shivered. 'I'm getting cold. Mind if I wait in the truck?'

'Not at all.' He smiled, his eyes flicking to her belly. She wasn't showing yet, but they'd already decided on names. Circumstances made it simple. Patrick for a boy, of course; for a girl, Debbie. Like Debbie Harry. 'Want me to come?'

She shook her head, moving away. 'Take your time.'

He nodded, and squatted to straighten the medallion. The headstone was cold, the ground underfoot hard as steel. Unbidden, his imagination traveled the six feet between him and his brother. To the sepulchral darkness beneath. Nothing but the quiet echo of snowflakes and all the time in the world.

He didn't realize he was crying until he felt a tear turn to ice on his cheek.

Eventually he stood, his hands thrust in his pockets. He wanted to say something, but couldn't think what it would be. An apology? A farewell? A promise?

Patrick wouldn't have wanted any of them.

Finally he just kissed his fingers and touched the necklace. 'Safe travels.'

As he walked away, a gust of wind caught the medallion and set it rocking against the stone. The quiet, rhythmic clatter sounded a little like laughter.

The snow fell in earnest now, fat laundry detergent flakes. The path through the cemetery was covered an inch deep. He walked steadily, his breath steaming. Everything that had been there when he'd come in – the faded skyline, the dingy town houses, the tired winter grass – had disappeared beneath a clean coat of white. Seeing it, he felt the weight on his heart easing. He knew it would never truly leave him. But maybe the weight in our hearts is all that holds us to earth.

In the parking lot he saw the truck running, thick exhaust

spilling out the back. Karen sat inside, and when he caught her eye, he could see her smiling across the distance.

He put his hands in his pockets and let her draw him home.